BRUNDANNON'S DAUGHTER

Through the Realms of the Woodwose
Book One

Corinna Newton Downes

Typeset by Jonathan Downes,
Cover and Layout by SPiderKaT for CFZ Communications
Using Microsoft Word 2000, Microsoft , Publisher 2000, Adobe Photoshop CS.

First published in Great Britain by Fortean Fiction

CFZ Publishing Group
Myrtle Cottage
Woolsery
Bideford
North Devon
EX39 5QR

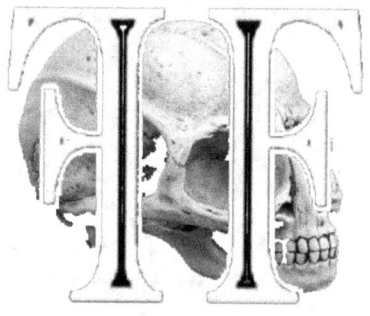

ISBN: 978-1-909488-33-5

BRUNDANNON'S DAUGHTER; THROUGH THE REALMS OF THE WOODWOSE

BOOK ONE

BY

CORINNA NEWTON DOWNES

DEDICATED TO

'BIGGLES' (2008 - 2010)

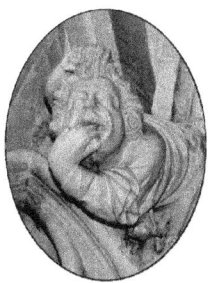

"... a strange madness came upon him. He crept away and fled to the woods, unwilling that any should see his going. Into the forest he went, glad to lie hidden beneath the ash trees. He watched the wild creatures grazing on the pasture of the glades. Sometimes he would follow them, sometimes pass them in his course. He made use of the roots of plants and of grasses, of fruit from trees and of the blackberries in the thicket. He became a Man of the Woods, as if dedicated to the woods. So for a whole summer he stayed hidden in the woods, discovered by none, forgetful of himself and of his own, lurking like a wild thing."

Geoffrey of Monmouth, *Life of Merlin* (ca 1150)

I

The spider was busily wrapping up her prey just as the first drops of rain began to fall from the heavy grey clouds above. In the distance, the first rumble of thunder echoed across the valley and she began to spin the cocoon around her victim faster as the wind picked up its speed, her web beginning to vibrate in its wake. She was hungry, but her appetite would have to wait out the storm. She finished her task and scuttled up her web to shelter in the leaves to avoid the downpour that would follow on the heels of the wind, satisfied that she had safely incarcerated another meal within a tight parcel of sticky gossamer threads.

She need not have bothered.

Minutes later a hand swept away her delicate work as a figure lolloped through the thicket. A streak of lightning illuminated the ground, revealing the shape of a human, bent over with fright from the sounds of the storm. In the brief seconds of brightness afforded by the lightning to anything or anyone that may be watching, it could be seen that the figure was that of a man, covered in a thin down of hair; his head covered in matted black tangled knots, and his eyes wild with a madness not known.

His home was in the woods that climbed the valley to the tor above. The impending storm had taken him by surprise whilst he had been outside his dark sanctuary, eagerly picking the dark plump fruits that hung in plenty from the entwining branches weaving in and out of the thickets edging the wood. The dark red juice stained his fingers, and his tongue took on a purple tinge as he licked his lips for any traces of the sticky liquid that had escaped his hungry mouth. Whilst at his ravenous toil, he had failed to notice the dark clouds floating their way broodily towards him. However, the scent on a sudden gust of wind warned him of the rains to follow, and he continued to pluck the berries in earnest, taking no notice of the punishing scratches meted out from their protective branches. He also knew that it would soon be dusk and that he would have to leave his foraging until the sun rose again the next day, but his stomach was urging him to continue supplying it with the sweet fruits of autumn for as long as possible. However, it was the distant rumble of thunder that had finally urged him back into the bowels of the wood.

Thunder petrified him – it made him howl with fear as he loped through the trees, and he shook his head to try to rid himself of the monster that roared within it for his madness gave him the belief that *such* a hideous thing was coming after him. By the time the lightning illuminated the sky and ground he was well under cover. But he could still see the brief flash of light overhead and the outline of the trees' branches against the darkening sky, and he screamed in terror at his perceived thought of the great beast that would soon crash through the trees, and tear him limb from limb, before it devoured him hungrily.

He ran as swiftly as his body would take him, which was not very fast. His right leg dragged slightly behind him – it had never been the same since he twisted it many moons before when he lost his footing on the hillside and slid down between the trees before coming to rest awkwardly at the bottom. And those who may have known him before he became this man of the woods would tell you that he had been here through the waxing and waning of many moons.

Perhaps once he had known how many years he had been living wild in the woods, but time and disinterest had long ago wiped this knowledge from his thoughts. He knew only a few things now: where to find food and water, and the route to his home in the woods no matter from which direction he approached. He had also learned from bitter experience to keep away from the green pastures in the valley and beyond.

The crash of thunder crackled directly overhead as he threw himself into the hollowed out bole of the aged oak tree that was his home. He scrabbled on his hands and feet to the farthest corner of his sanctum and curled his knees up to his chin, wrapping his arms tightly around them. He began to rock slowly backwards and forwards as the storm raged in the world outside. His eyes showed a madness that should not belong to man as they stared into the darkness. It was not a savage madness, but a pitiful one, and there was terror within those eyes as they picked out every shadow and turned it into a daemon.

II

Berowen!" echoed the frustrated cry through the upper rooms. "Berowen!" The frantic cry increased in volume as its agitated owner neared the hall.

The hound laying prostrate by the fire half-opened his eyes at the sound of the lady of the house voicing her frantic calls. It shook its head, yawned, and pulled itself into a sitting position beside its master, before resting its head on his knee.

Aelwulf shook his head and groaned under his breath as his long-suffering wife entered into his presence. He stood up and turned to face her.

"Have you seen that child?" she asked him. "She has disappeared again and we are supposed to be working on her gown."

"Do not fuss so, wife," replied Aelwulf calmly. "I am sure she cannot be far."

"Husband, neither near nor far is where she should be. She *should* be in her chamber. Aelwulf, our only daughter has always been your favourite and that is the problem. You have let her get away with her wayward behaviour for too long. See where it has brought us. We are to leave in three days – THREE days," she continued, waving her arms in despair as she spoke. "How is Morgen to finish her needlework in time, if Berowen insists on making herself invisible all the while?"

Ethwen bustled off in the direction of the kitchen muttering under her breath as to how impossible the situation was and how, as a result, ruin would befall them all because of her youngest child's selfishness.

Upon her leaving, Aelwulf slumped back into his seat and sighed. He patted the wiry head of the hound that returned to its previous position and laid its head once again on his master's knee. Aelwulf loved his wife dearly, but she had become a veritable scold since it had been arranged that Berowen would enter into a union with Brack. For her to accuse him of favouring his daughter above all of his offspring was not entirely untrue, however. Although he loved each child as much as he did the other, he had to admit that Berowen held a different place in his weary heart, for not only was she his only daughter, she also possessed the essence of himself within her. She reminded him of his own wayward youth – more so than any of his three sons did – when he used to run amok around this very hall. He half-smiled to himself and for a brief moment his eyes gleamed, but they soon dulled again when he thought of Berowen's impending fate.

Although the union would reinforce the existing alliance between two of the oldest families in the kingdom, a deep unhappiness stifled him. His daughter would be entering into a marriage that she did not desire. When she had been informed of the agreement, she had borne it with grace, and Aelwulf had been proud of her countenance although he knew that her heart must have trembled with foreboding.

It had been during the last weeks of spring that year that Aelwulf had met with Brack's father, Modig. And he could remember the day that Berowen had been given the news as if it were yesterday. He closed his eyes and, not for the first time since it had taken place, he re-lived that event again in his mind.

∞

Berowen had been standing by the fire in the hall singing to her brothers as they huddled around near the warmth. One of her great loves was to sing the tales of wandering minstrels that she had learned from Iuwine, a minstrel himself of great renown who spent his days travelling from settlement to settlement entertaining the inhabitants, and earning a meagre living from a coin here and there that would be thrown at his feet. If he was lucky enough to place himself near a pie stand, he may even receive a hot morsel for his efforts, hence he had found such a spot to be the most satisfying during those years on the road. No accord was ever spoken between the pie-seller; it had always been a silent trade-off for his music and tales being able to lure would-be customers to close proximity of the stall, to have their nostrils teased and tempted with the delicious aromas that wafted from the pies on view.

However, this payment of welcome sustenance also depended upon how skilful the resident curdogges were at stealing these morsel trade-offs, especially if these tasty offerings had been left too close to the edge of the pie stand.

In the evenings, he would visit the inn or feast hall, and with luck would receive a free jug of ale for his entertainment. If the proprietor of such an establishment was pleased with the night's custom, thus possessing a cheerful frame of mind, Iuwine would even sometimes be able to bed down for the night; clearly the much preferred choice when the evenings turned chilly.

As with most settlements, rumours were rife in Berowen's home. She had heard that Iuwine was once a minstrel at the court of a great King from over the vast waters. But, as this tale had been told many times, and because she had begun to notice slight changes in the 'facts', she was more than convinced that it was most likely to be merely an old tall-tale passed down from the lips of the tittle-tattlers of the small settlement that sat within the bailey walls of her home.

It was one of Iuwine's short tales that she sang that night, while the light from the candles in the wall sconces threw down a warming glow upon the happy group. Berowen stood with her back to the huge oak door as she strummed her lute in accompaniment to her singing. She was completely oblivious to the fact that her father had entered the hall and was standing in the shadows, watching the contented scene and listening to his daughter's able, yet not perfect, singing voice.

Eneas had noticed his father's presence first. He had jumped to his feet and bowed to Aelwulf, this sudden action prompting the other two brothers to investigate their sibling's movement, and soon to do likewise. All three left the cosiness of the fire to greet Aelwulf on his return from his travels.

However, Berowen was so involved in her playing and singing that she had her eyes closed as the song flowed freely from her lips. When she opened them and turned her head from side to side, she found herself slightly bemused at the sudden disappearance of her brothers, but upon hearing her father's voice in the background, she ceased her playing immediately.

She turned just at the moment that Aelwulf waved the others away and she wondered what news he had to share with her that did not require the presence of the others. She became slightly anxious.

"Welcome home, father," she greeted. "Your presence around the fire has been greatly missed these past weeks."

"My thanks, daughter," he replied as he approached her.

She put her lute down on the seat, embraced her father warmly, and kissed his right cheek.

"I trust that your journey was untroubled and that your business was successful in its outcome?" Berowen continued, as calmly as she could considering that she was now very unnerved by the troubled look upon her father's face. It seemed almost like an expression of guilt, but she could not think why he should possess such a feeling.

"The journey was long but uneventful, Wynnie," he replied using his private pet name for his youngest child. "As for my business, it was completed to the satisfaction of all parties concerned at the time."

"It pleases me to hear thus," Berowen responded, although slightly confused by his last three words. "I fear though that you have something to tell me, father."

She then stood with her hands clasped together in front of her. She looked down at the floor briefly and silently took a deep breath in readiness for whatever information or news was about to be broken to her. As she looked up, Aelwulf ran his hand down her left cheek tenderly before taking her hands in his and briefly holding them tightly before releasing them again.

"Berowen, my dear child," he began. He had rehearsed this meeting so many times to himself on his return journey, but he had not realised just how difficult it would be to tell her in person.

"I am your father and as such, and as head of this household and its noble name, I have to take it upon myself to do things that may not meet with the wishes of others. Some of these matters may not even be to my own desire, but they have to be considered nevertheless."

"I know father, and I understand that whatever you have done, or will do in the future, is for the good of our name and of our family."

"You possess such a wise head for such a young woman, daughter," he continued.

Mustering her courage she demanded of her father what it was that he needed to share with her. "Father, you are clearly in great distress about something of which you have to inform me. Pray just tell me and release yourself from this obvious torment."

He felt somewhat relieved that his daughter possessed such a trait as to wish to receive news delivered with such frankness rather than have it delivered hesitantly.

"You are the only daughter of this household, Berowen ....," he began softly, but he didn't really have to carry on, for it was at the deliverance of those few words that she realised exactly what was to come.

"You have found me a husband," she said flatly, trying desperately not to show her distress at this news. He did not have to reply for she saw the truth in his eyes. "Do I know him?"

"I believe you may have met him once, many years ago when you were younger, but you probably do not remember him as your mind would have been on much less onerous tasks than thinking about future husbands," he replied. "His name is Brack, eldest son of Modig of Grimfell in the Wellonaw Marshes. As you are aware, daughter, this is the home of the family who share a special allegiance with us in these dark times, but one that will be tighter with your union with Brack."

Still maintaining her composure she enquired, "I am aware of the importance of this alliance, father, but I have no memory of such a name. Is he much older than me?"

"He is in his 30th year. His first wife died last year."

"And do you judge him to be an honourable man, father?"

"You should not take my previous words about my tasks as head of this household so plainly Berowen. Yes, I have had to make decisions that I perhaps did not wish to, and there is no doubt that I will do so many times in years to come. This does not mean that I would willingly and blindly let my only daughter enter into marriage with someone with whom I did not have satisfactory feelings about."

Aelwulf took her hands into his again. "My duties as your father are of the utmost importance Berowen. Brack is likeable enough and from what I have seen of him whilst in his company, he holds himself in a most honourable manner. Berowen, my dearest child, the night that your mother brought you forth into this world was one of the most joyful occasions of my life. But the happiness was tinged with sadness for I knew then that this day would come, and this thought has been a heavy burden upon my heart ever since. During these last seventeen years, I have watched you grow into a young woman with a spirit in her heart that is a delight to behold."

Berowen noticed a tear in the corner of her father's eye and breathed deeply so as not to weep herself. She knew her father was troubled by his burdensome decision, and although she was desperately unhappy, she knew that his actions were born from the right reasons.

She released her hands from his, and put her arms around his shoulders and hugged him. "I understand father, and accept my chosen path with hope in my heart that this union will tighten the pact between the two families."

Berowen saw her mother approach from the side of the hall.

"You have told her, Aelwulf?" she asked as she neared the fire.

"He has told me, mother," replied Berowen instead.

"Good," responded Ethwen. "I hope you realise how important you have become in the survival of this family. It is of the utmost importance that Grimfell and the house of Aelwulf remain in allegiance with each other."

Releasing himself from Berowen's embrace, Aelwulf turned to face his wife and tersely said, "Enough Ethwen. The child is well aware of her duties and there is no need to dwell upon the point. Let her be to take to her chamber. I am sure she would welcome some solitude at this time."

"Hmph," grunted Ethwen under her breath. "So be it. Go, Berowen, to your room if you wish. Tomorrow we must begin arrangements for the making of your marriage gown."

Aelwulf had winced at his wife's thoughtless delivery of her remark, but Berowen had seemingly either not heard her mother or had chosen to ignore it, and had picked up her lute and retired to her bower in silence.

III

Dawn broke over the dark wood and its early rays flickered through the boughs. The man slowly opened his eyes and rubbed them roughly for they prickled with the lack of sleep that he had endured the night before, and the lids were reluctant to remain open. They urged him to allow them to close for more rest, and he could quite easily have obeyed their persistent unwillingness to open. The storm had passed sometime during the early hours of the morning and he had managed to quieten the voices in his head, just long enough to allow him some small slumber, but it was not enough. Added to this, his belly growled with anger at not having received enough food in the impending gloom of dusk the day before when the storm interrupted his fruit-gathering efforts.

During his short escape from consciousness, he had involuntarily moved his body on to its side, still with his knees tucked into his chest and he was still in this position when he awoke. Dragging himself out of his hole beneath the mighty oak tree's roots, he stretched himself as much as his stiffened body would allow. His right leg ached from having to run the evening before and with a pained expression he rubbed it to try to soothe the dull throbbing that spread from his ankle to just above his knee. Gingerly he put weight upon it and winced at the effort, but he would have to ignore such minor niggles if he was to satisfy his hunger and thirst.

The storm had left freshness in the air and his doom-ridden hallucinations of the night before seemed far away in the depths of his mind; for now at least.

His den, in the woods known locally as the Writhing Wood, was located near a small stream that ran from the hills, and it was these refreshing waters that he visited first. Easing himself down on to his knees and trying to ignore the pain from his throbbing limb, he cupped his hands into the clear liquid and raised it to his lips. The busy babbling of the stream as it rambled down the hill, coursing around and splashing the stones and rocks in its way, were soothing to his mind.

All around him the leaves were shedding drops of rain that had trickled and splashed their way down from the tops of the trees, their final destination being the drier ground below that had been sheltered by the giant arms of the boughs above. The ever-thirsty earth sucked them up and the roots of the trees took advantage of the small offerings. There was a chill in the air; the kind of chill that comes with that season's mornings, and the leaves were already turning golden brown in the dappled sunlight that streamed through the boughs. The birds of the wood were already feasting on the bountiful crop of various different berries that were dropping from over-laden boughs. They knew. And he knew. It would be a harsh, winter this year.

Soon it would be time for the creatures of the dark wood to move on to their wintering grounds. Once the trees had shed their last dead leaves, they would offer much less protection from the outside world. Although the knotted and gnarled boughs twisted together around the wood's perimeter to form an impenetrable barrier to keep out any wandering traveller, or opportunistic hunter looking for the boar or deer that shared the wood's safety, many of the dark wood's inhabitants preferred to winter in the forest across the moors. It was there that the trees never shed their leaves and offered shelter from storms of rain or snow. It was to there that they always shared the coldest months with the children and beasts of the forest. It was dark and dank in that place, but the shelter it afforded was one that enticed their annual migration across the open moorland.

Once a year a slow procession of creatures would climb the hill to the tor and descend the other side to the moorland that stretched before them. Upon the return of the spring months, the same procession would return by the same path to their home in the dark wood. The man would soon need to begin his journey to the other place. And it was a path he hesitated to tread, for it meant a long walk across the unwelcoming moorland with its bogs, boulders, and encroaching mists. It would mean passing the crossroads and that place brought fear to his very soul – if in fact he had one. If you were to ask some, they would deny straightaway that he possessed such a thing. If you asked others, they would question whether a soul could behold such darkness within itself and that if he did have one then it must have been marred long ago.

Until the time came to move on, though, there would still be enough time to take advantage of the fruits that were abundant in the hedgerows, and - his thirst quenched - this is what the man set out to do next.

IV

It was Ethwen returning to the hall who awoke Aelwulf from his musings. "She is nowhere to be found. I have had people looking for her high and low."

Aelwulf had seen Berowen earlier that afternoon when she had arrived at the ring armed with her sword, bow and quiver with the usual expectant look in her eye at the thought of some weapon practise. He had known that she should not be there and that her mother and the seamstress were waiting for her. As much as he had not wanted to chastise her in front of the others, he knew that he had to send her to her chamber. He had assumed that she had returned to her room and whilst not surprised that she apparently had not, he was now greatly concerned that she may have wandered off outside the confines of the bailey walls. If she had, then he would indeed have to chastise her twice in one day, for it was not safe for anyone to be wandering alone on the grasslands.

Aelwulf had had no misgivings of teaching his daughter the skill of combat, as she had proven to be a most eager student; as adept as all three of her brothers, and could certainly be as good as any of the men he was coaching now if she continued to progress as keenly as she had so far. But he knew that his daughter had other more important tasks that day, and indeed for the next few days. There was much to be achieved, and the entire fortress was busy in preparation for the departure. Aelwulf, Eneas and Amleth would be escorting Berowen and Ethwen over the hills to the Grimfell in the west. It would be a long and arduous journey.

Gar would be remaining behind with his wife and three young children. Now in his twenty-sixth year Gar had grown into a formidable young man, a brave warrior who would give up his life rather than let Brundannon fall. Gar dearly wished that he could see his little sister wed but knew that it was left to him to watch over his ancestral home.

"Eneas has gone out of the walls to see if she has taken it upon herself to try to escape her obligations," continued Ethwen.

"I am sure that she would not do that, good wife," answered Aelwulf. "She does not possess that character, as I am sure you are only too well aware. And even if she did, she has had plenty of opportunities to leave Brundannon in the months since she learned of her future. No. She is not far, I am sure of it."

V

The sound of the stag bellowing in the early morning mist greeted the man as he emerged from the quiet of the dark wood and stood in the shadows of the thickets that wrapped their gnarled arms around the perimeter. Further down in the valley he could see the great beast standing in its magnificent defiance at any that would challenge its autonomy over the does that grazed behind it. As it lifted its head to utter its warning again, he could see the breath rise from its mouth and dissipate in the air.

Slightly to the right approached another male, roaring his challenge, and the man eased himself down to sit and watch the unfolding battle that would surely ensue. As the two sidestepped towards each other, they lowered their heads and massive antlers to the ground. He had seen these fights year upon year and sometimes was astounded at the courage of some of the smaller stags that decided to try their luck. These encounters were usually nothing more than a threat from the dominant male – he would bellow at them, before approaching them and standing at his full height to display his bony headwear to good advantage. This was usually enough to halt any further thoughts from the younger males.

On this occasion though, he knew it would be different. They were a well-matched pair and the man knew the fight would be a serious one. As the two adversaries approached each other the defending stag attempted to intimidate his antagonist once more by letting out a loud roar, but upon this being ignored, he lowered his head again and charged. At the same moment, the newcomer rushed forward and the two pairs of antlers locked together with a crash that resounded up to the man's vantage point, along with a loud grunt from each animal.

The defender, being on higher ground, had the advantage and the challenger had to use every inch of muscle to push himself forwards to good effect. But push himself he did, and the man was impressed at his strength. For a fleeting moment, it looked as if this newcomer would win the day, but suddenly the defending champion forced his antlers into a deeper lock, and with a concerted effort pushed his way into his opponent until the other lost his footing slightly and had to step backwards. This was the winning move from the defender and the attacker released himself from the lock and turned to flee. The winner chased after him for a while before returning to guard his herd. He let out a victorious roar and stood with head held high, and peace returned once again to the valley – for the while at least until another possible usurper took up the challenge.

Standing awkwardly to his feet, the man knew now that he would be leaving in a few weeks time – this annual spectacle always marked the time for preparation to move on and many more such fights would be witnessed along the way. It was also a time for the occasional lucky find of meat provided by the fatality of an old or young beast from wounds suffered from such a battle. But once this yearly event was over it would also bring with it more need for caution. The deer's antlers were much prized by craftsmen, and it was during November that the grasslands, woodlands and pastures would become a regular haunt for those who gathered the fallen structures for their craft. And it was then that it would not be wise to be found wandering outside the protective branches of the Writhing Wood.

As this last deliberation crossed his mind, his eyes started to glare with madness again and he began to grunt deeply to himself. His whole body began to twitch and he started to tear at his hair in some desperate attempt to rid himself of these thoughts. His hands clawed at his arms and he unconsciously ripped out tufts of fine hair. He didn't feel himself doing it and he felt no pain. He began to sob and wail, and his spittle clung to his beard in cloudy clumps on its coarse and wiry hair.

A triangle of geese flew across the valley, their noisy cries of 'rronk rronk' breaking the silence of the morning. The man started to jump up and down, and began to imitate their cries. His voice became louder and louder until his throat became dry and sore. Suddenly he dropped to the ground and lay still for a few minutes, the rise and fall of his chest slowing down gradually until it became normal again.

His lids closed over his mad-ridden eyes and sleep took him into her arms.

There was a rustle from the bushes and a tiny wrinkle-faced creature tiptoed towards him. She was not much bigger than the pelt of the hare in which she was adorned; the skin of its forelegs were stitched crudely around her arms and that of its hind legs likewise around her own legs – the forepaws could be used as gloves and hind paws as shoes in the cold weather. The unlucky beast's head acted as a hood, and was loosely hanging down the creature's back. She was one of the faerie folk of the dark wood, and had come to take the clumps of hair recently ripped from his skin. She quietly and carefully removed them from the loosening grip of his fingers before running off back into the thickets from whence she had emerged.

VI

Berowen sat absent-mindedly dangling her toes into the cool river, her fingers busily, and without thought, braiding and un-braiding her waist-length hair as she gazed into the river's clear waters. Overhead the blue expanse of sky was uninterrupted by clouds. The only thing to be seen in its vastness was a buzzard as it hung lazily on the thermals above Brundannon, occasionally beating its huge wings slowly to gain height. An occasional cool breeze rustled the tall bull rushes at the river's bank as the autumn sun beat down. Behind her in the fortress, she could hear the faint clank of the anvil, the occasional bark of a dog, and the odd whinny of a horse.

She felt as if her life of happiness was to end forever. She was to become the wife of someone she did not know, and the thought terrified her. Apart from the minor details of his general stature, over these last months she had not learned much more about Brack, other than the extremely worrying fact that he had two young children by his first wife. This piece of detail, although told her many weeks ago, had recently become a burden upon her thoughts. She did not know how they would react to her, and was scared at the thought of it.

For her part, Berowen liked children and often played with her eldest brother's two little sons - Halig and Scur - and daughter – Eadlin. Halig and Scur were twins in their sixth year, and looked so alike that even their parents, Gar and his wife Aidith, could be fooled briefly at times. The only way of telling them apart if you did not know them well, would be the brown blemish upon Scur's bottom. When they were babies and it came to bathing time, it was a subject of great mirth when it was related that this mark on his left buttock never failed to confuse Aidith, Berowen or her mother into thinking it was a stubborn stain left by an inefficient clean and they would try to scrub it off. No matter how many times they had been fooled, they always seemed to fall into the same trap the next time. The poor child must have suffered much chafing from the scrubbing and may explain the wailing that would emanate loudly from his protesting lungs in accompaniment to this cleaning routine.

Eadlin was eight and a pretty child with hair as black as a raven, and as full of tight curls as the clasping tendrils of ivy that wrap their way tenaciously over anything that comes across their path.

All three children would rush through the corridors and across the great hall in their never-ending games of chasing each other and the sound of their happy giggling and raucous laughter rang through the whole keep. Berowen would oft join in with their noisy playing, and hoodman's blind was a great favourite, although not quite as rough as it could be when played by older contestants. She had acquired many a bruise or scratch when playing this game with her brothers not so many years ago.

Trying to cheer herself up she began humming to herself as she kicked her toes in the water, watching the ripples spread out in ever-increasing circles. She knew her mother would scold her when she returned as she had been supposed to be helping her in the wedding preparations. Morgen, the seamstress, would also be less than pleased with her. Berowen knew as well that she would incur her father's wrath for wandering so far from the safety of the walls. But Berowen did not want to partake in such things as her betrothal preparations. She did not want to be reminded that she would soon be leaving her home to become the wife of a man she did not know. She wanted to be with her father as he overlooked the daily practice of the soldiers of the garrison, and some of the young boys who were learning how to wield the sword and use the bow. She had been allowed to join in ever since she was strong enough to lift a sword and pull the bowstring.

It was a tradition amongst her people that women were given as much training in the bow, blade and spear as the men. It is, after all, mostly the women who are left behind to defend the old and young while the men are away at battle.

As she sat quietly humming to herself, she recalled the moment when she picked up a sword for the first time. It was but a light sword, made for children with which to practice, but it was still rather long for her tiny frame; so long that she had to take the hilt firmly with both hands. How her brothers and father had laughed as she had swung it. The force of her swinging it was so great that it had pulled her little body around completely, causing her to lose her footing and tumble to the ground on to her bottom. Although winded, it had not put her off, and she had immediately gotten to her feet and tried again, and again. Eventually her father had taken the sword from her hand and she can remember to this day how he tousled her hair and said, "I think, my young warrior, that you should perhaps try a small bow first until your body grows a bit more and catches up with your desire for the sword."

Alas, though, on this particular day her father had chastised Berowen when she arrived at the ring that afternoon to join the practice, armed with her sword, bow and quiver. He had embarrassed her in front of the men and sent her away, much to their amusement. She turned on her heel furious with Aelwulf. What she would not have known, though, was that if she had looked back, she would have seen Aelwulf's sympathetic look at delivering such a disappointing order.

Thus, Berowen had escaped to the river.

As her thoughts drifted, she looked up and gazed towards the horizon. At that moment, something in the distance caught her eye, she could not quite make out what it was, but it looked like a figure riding in the direction of the village. She slowly got to her feet and raised one hand to her eyes, shielding them from the glare of the sun, which was now beginning to set, squinting in an effort to make out whom it could be. It was not often that strangers were seen wandering the land in such dangerous, unpredictable times and she became intrigued instantly by the lone figure as it slowly made its way towards the river.

"If father finds out you are out of Brundannon he will tan your hide." Berowen recognised Eneas' voice and swung round.

"Oh brother you made my heart jump, do not creep up so silently," she scolded him.

"You were lucky it was me who was creeping," he replied. "And besides I was making enough noise to wake the dead. What are you looking at so intently?"

As she turned her head back to the horizon, Berowen pointed towards the direction of where she had watched the approaching stranger. "There, look, who could it be do you think?"

Eneas followed the direction of her pointing finger. There was nothing there but the waving grasses. Berowen turned back to her brother with a quizzical look on her face. "There was someone coming, really there was. A dark figure on horseback. Slowly riding this way. Where could he have gone?"

"I think we should get back to Brundannon. Now!" urged Eneas, grabbing his sister's arm with one hand, and drawing his sword with the other. "Come, quickly."

"Oh Eneas, you worry too much.   One rider cannot do that much harm against our two swords," she laughed.

"Behind one lone rider could be a hundred more," Eneas protested. "Do as you are bid sister."

He earnestly pulled her arm and urged her on. It was as much as Berowen could do to make a grab for her shoes as her brother tugged at her arm. They began running back towards the stronghold, Eneas continuously checking their immediate vicinity, his sword poised ready for any attack. When they reached the approach to the north gate Eneas pushed his sister onwards. He turned round to make one last check and then, slowly walking backwards, his sword glinting in the setting sun, entered the safety of Brundannon. At the giant gateway, Berowen stood, her eyes searching the way they had come from the river. Then she saw the horse wading across a little further downstream from where she had been.

"There, Eneas, look – there," she whispered to her brother as he came alongside her. "He has forded further downstream, do you see him now?" she pointed.

"Yes, I see." Shouting to the men on the ramparts Eneas ordered them to fetch his father and brothers from the great hall. "A stranger comes amongst us."

By the time the stranger had ridden to the foot of the causeway Aelwulf, Gar and Amleth were standing beside Eneas and Berowen, swords drawn. Aelwulf glanced at his daughter, "Berowen, go to your mother."

"But..." began Berowen.

"Now," growled Aelwulf and he tapped her on her behind with the flat side of his sword. Berowen looked into his face, realised that this was not the time to cross her father, sighed, and walked off up the steps towards the great hall.

The men watched the rider slowly approach, and when within hailing distance Aelwulf called out, "Stranger, state your name and purpose." The rider reined his horse to a halt. "I am Thurstan, youngest son of Bertwald from the north, and nephew of King Caedmon of the northern kingdom. My horse is in need of rest and my stomach is in need of food. I was looking for a soft place to sleep for the night. I have heard that Brundannon welcomes those in need of shelter, but if I am not welcome I shall ride on."

"You are welcome, nephew of King Caedmon. We are indeed honoured to welcome such a visitor," invited Aelwulf. Berowen's brothers, Gar, Amleth and Eneas, stood aside to let the stranger pass.

At the steps of the great hall, Berowen had stopped at the huge oak door. She turned just in time to watch the rider enter through the north gate. She watched as he dismounted and patted his huge chestnut mare, and she watched as her father and brothers sheathed their swords and the five men walk through the village towards the keep. The stranger was tall and slim and he walked with a long slow steady gait as he led his horse along the path between the wooden houses. Villagers stopped and looked as they walked past. The five men were deep in conversation as they approached the steps. Aelwulf beckoned to one of the guards to take the stranger's horse to the stables. As it was led away, its owner patted its rump affectionately.

Berowen opened the great oak door and disappeared inside. She knew her mother would be angry with her and braced herself for the sharpness of Ethwen's tongue. She did not have to wait long.

"Berowen!" Taking in a deep breath Berowen walked quickly across the hall to the stairs that led to the chambers above. Her mother was calling her from the top of the flight, standing with her hands on her hips. This was a pose that Berowen knew meant trouble was afoot.

"Where have you been?' her mother scolded. "You are supposed to be helping Morgen and me with your betrothal gown. Do you know what trouble you have caused me in trying to find you? Many daylight hours have been wasted on your selfishness."

"I am sorry mother, I am here now," was the soft reply. "I did not realise the sun had fallen in the west so much, mother, until just now. Truly I am sorry."

Footsteps behind her caused Berowen to turn her head and upon doing so she saw Eneas rush passed her on his way up the stairs to inform their mother of the unexpected guest. As he did so, he threw a quick wink in her direction and she smiled. She could always rely on him to raise her spirits. She would miss him dearly when they parted.

She saw the expression on her mother's face change from one of anger to one of resigned desperation at the thought of the extra platter at dinner that night. Berowen heard the heavy sigh as Ethwen descended the stairs to inform the kitchens of the extra mouth to feed, but as she did so she threw her daughter a scolding glare and patted her behind with much more vehemence than Berowen was expecting.

"To your chamber daughter. I will join you soon."

As Ethwen reached the foot of the stairs Aelwulf, her two eldest brothers and the visitor entered the hall. Before she disappeared into the kitchens to carry out her allotted task, Ethwen looked towards the stranger, curtsied and said with no hint of anger or unwelcome in her voice, "You are welcome to take supper with us sir, and to rest before you resume your journey."

"Thank you my lady," Thurstan responded quietly, bowing his head in return.

VII

The man opened his eyes suddenly and he caught his breath at the shock of finding himself lying on his back staring up at the cloudy sky. The last thing he remembered was the fight between the stags, and he could not quite understand how he had allowed himself to fall asleep in such an open and unprotected place. Hauling himself to his feet, he quickly retreated into the shadows of the trees.

His arms started to smart, and he wondered whether he had been bitten by a swarm of tiny insects while he had been asleep, such was his memory lapse about what had taken place earlier. His lips were parched and his mouth was dry, and his stomach was again grumbling for food. He hesitantly moved back out into the daylight and searched out the berry-laden branches, eagerly plucking the fruits and thrusting them into his mouth, his eyes constantly searching the area around him for any danger that may be lurking.

He sensed something was not as it should be, but what he could not quite fathom. He felt as if something was watching him, but could neither hear nor see anything untoward. His appetite sated and his thirst satisfied enough to ease the dryness in his throat, he made his way back towards his home in the oak tree.

As he passed the patch of ground where he had been asleep, he caught the glimpse of something out of his eye. It moved too quickly for him to form a proper picture in his mind, but in those fleeting seconds it was in his sight he thought he could make out a hare hopping through the undergrowth. It seemed to his eyes that a scut was quite visible in those few moments before it disappeared into the dense maze of roots that curled above the ground.

The man grunted to himself and shuffled through the ever-increasing carpet of golden leaves beneath his feet.

VIII

For pity's sake, stop squirming girl," Morgen pleaded with frustration in her voice, as Berowen wriggled in the gown.

Ethwen and Morgen stood back and admired their handiwork. The gown fitted perfectly on Berowen's frame.

Morgen's young assistant sat in the shadows of the room fidgeting. She was a thin young girl of eleven and the daughter of the stablemaster. It had been decided that she – Beatha - would learn the skills of the seamstress as Morgen had no issue to continue her craft after she died. Although a promising student, Beatha still possessed the lack of interest and patience as most eleven-year-olds do, so she found herself immensely bored at the events occurring around her. She knew that she would be busy in the days to come helping Morgen to stitch on all the tiny pearls, and yearned to go home and sit with her mother and father rather than be sitting where she was. She yawned a bit too loudly, for the sound caused Morgen to throw her a stony glance. "Why is yer mouth gapin' girl?" she hissed.

At the sight of her daughter standing in the gown, Ethwen's heart melted and all the anger and frustration that she had felt during the past few hours dissipated in a second. There was still much to be done – the sewing of all the seed pearls around the neckline, cuffs and hem would take many more hours of stitching, but she was overcome with the transformation before her. As Berowen stood there in front of them, with the dying rays of the sun streaming through the small window, her cheeks still flushed from the cooling autumn air outside, Berowen looked beautiful. The light caught the faint tint of russet in her hair as it tumbled down her back in never-ending waves, and glinted off the circlet that crowned her head.

There was a light tap on the door and upon Berowen's wish that whoever had instigated the request to enter her chamber could so do, the door opened slightly and Berowen's sister-in-law, Aidith, peeked her head around with a cheerful smile upon her face.

"Dear sister, you look wonderful," she gasped. "The gown is nearly finished I see. What a perfect bride you shall make. I only wish I could be there to see you make your betrothal."

Aidith walked towards her sister-in-law and embraced her fondly. She knew very well what Berowen was feeling, as she had been joined with Gar in an arranged marriage also. "I am sure you will be able to love Brack one day, my sister, as I learned to adore your brother. As long as he is kind and gentle, your heart will learn to love him."

"I know not,' Berowen replied. "But I hope that what you speak is true."

"Mother, I am again truly sorry for causing you such vexation earlier," she said looking towards Ethwen.

"Bah," retorted Ethwen. "I forgot myself child. I have been so busy with the preparations that I neglected to think how you must have been feeling at such a time as this. Aidith reminded me of my own fears when I wed your father. But what she says will be. I am sure of it."

Ethwen hugged her daughter as tightly as she dared for fear of damaging the gown. Suddenly she pulled away and exclaimed, "On my honour! This will not do, we have a guest downstairs, and I completely forgot."

Berowen forced a smile, "Indeed mother. And surely it is time we fed his empty stomach for he looked halve-starved."

"Indeed. You are quite correct," Ethwen agreed, reddening with embarrassment for having forgotten.

Aidith began to giggle. "He will think the house of Aelwulf at Brundannon quite rude. After all, he is the nephew of a King. Alas, one that I have never heard of, but a King nevertheless. Father must be sorely vexed."

Her daughter-in-law's giggling was infectious and Ethwen began to see the funny side of their long absence.

"Come child, out of that gown before you do something dreadful to it," she laughed. "Knowing you, you will catch a sleeve in a candle and singe it. Then it will be Morgen here who will suffer from choler, and we will never hear the last of it!"

Aidith and Ethwen left the room in such a rush that they nearly fell over each other, but they were so involved in their joint mirth that they just laughed even louder. Morgen tutted under her breath, and assisted Berowen's inelegant efforts to remove the gown.

Poor Morgen. She was a sour old woman and possessed not an inkling of humour about her. She was an excellent seamstress, but it was nigh on impossible to make her smile.

Morgen was very old and had been born in the small settlement of workers within the bailey walls. Her mother had been a seamstress before her and had taught her the skill, and her father had been one of the guards of the motte. Alas both parents died when she was a young girl, leaving her an orphan with no siblings, so she turned her hand to stitching as a means of earning a living and, although she had never taken a husband, it was said that she had many a young suitor who had been drawn to her beauty. To look at her now, with her wizened face framed with wisps of thin grey strands of hair that escaped from her wimple, and her shrunken frame as it shuffled from one place to the other, it was hard to believe that she could have been so beautiful to have received a steady stream of prospective marriage opportunities.

She hardly ever spoke whilst going about her stitchery and you could oft times find yourself sitting with her for hours with not one word spoken at all. She would continually be tutting under her breath to herself as her fingers worked the cloth and on the odd occasion, she would shake or nod her head as if having a private conversation with herself in her head.

However, Morgen was a perfectionist and if she was not happy with a piece of intricate embroidery she would rip it out and start again, even if that meant destroying delicate work that had taken her days to create.

Morgen snapped at Beatha to help her carry the gown back to her house outside in the bailey. "Don't you be thinkin' you be gettin' any sleep tonight my girl," she said harshly. "There be lots of thread to be used whilst the candles burn this evenin'." Berowen saw Beatha's shoulders slump and heard the slight sniff from the corner where the poor child was sitting. "Don't you be snivelling you silly child. When there is work needin' to be done, there's no use puttin' it off till the morrow. Come. On the way we will tell your mother and father that you won't be 'ome tonight," Morgen barked.

"But I ain't 'ad no supper yet," whined Beatha as she carefully took the material in her arms.

Morgen tutted again. "If your fingers work 'ard enough there may be broth for you. So stop whining like a whelpin' pup and move yerself." They both left the chamber with as much haste as possible considering they carried such a delicate and important item.

Berowen felt such pity for poor Beatha.

Once out of the gown, Berowen had shivered in the chilly evening atmosphere of her chamber and had quickly dressed herself back into her ordinary tunics and secured the girdle around her hips. She then replaced her veil and left her chamber to join the others at table.

Berowen descended the stairs just as her family and guest were seating themselves around the long table in the hall. As she did every night, Berowen took up the jug of mead and commenced pouring it into the goblets, on this occasion the guest's being the first she attended, to be followed by that of her father.

"We shall have an extra sword with us on our journey," announced Aelwulf to his daughter as she poured the mead into his goblet. "Lord Thurstan is travelling in the same direction as us and has decided to rest his horse an extra day in order that he can accompany our group."

"That is good father. I am sure the Lord Thurstan will be most welcome on our journey," Berowen replied as she looked across at the visitor and, throwing him a small smile, she continued on her way around the table.

IX

Mog had waited until the man-beast had arisen from his sleep before she had left him. She had placed the hair inside the tiny pouch that hung from her waist and had sat cross-legged amongst the brambles whilst he slumbered. She was pleased with her find that day and sang happily to herself. There was still much for her to do before she and the rest of her clan could leave to go to the forest, but as one of the guardians of the wood, she could not leave until she knew this man-beast was safe.

So there Mog sat; her large pointed ears twitching endlessly for any sound of threat. Her wrinkled features with dark eyes, long hooked nose, and wide smiling mouth may well have put fear into any normal human that saw her, but in her world her features were nothing but normal, for she was a faerie and this is how they looked. They were not malicious by nature, but if any human wandered into the wood to do harm to the creatures within its shelter, they would enjoy tormenting them from their hiding places until the trespasser ran from the wood in terror of what might be abusing them.

No doubt when these humans returned to their wooden structures, they would spin yarns of wild dangerous creatures that attacked them to within an inch of their life, but Mog and her kind had not a care. Those tall creatures that trespassed upon the confines of their home were not welcome – they never had been and they never would be.

So why did Mog care for the man as he lay asleep? Because this was a man shunned by his own kind long ago and was one who had sought sanctuary in the shadows of the trees. The faerie folk knew him as the 'wildman of the wood' and they watched over him in his madness.

He did them no harm and in turn they harmed not him, in fact he was probably not even aware of their presence close to him, for they usually kept themselves to themselves and were normally only about their business during the hours of the sun's rest. There were times that they would venture out during the daylight hours but this was only usually if there was lots of work to be seen to. At this time of the year this was just so.

They would wander their boundaries foraging for food or anything that they found of interest or could use. Their light came from lanterns carved from hollowed-out wood and filled with a solid block of honeycomb foraged from the beehives that could be found within the Writhing Wood. The oozing block of honey attracted swarms of fireflies that feasted on the sweetness, their glowing bodies affording a boost to the faeries' eyesight in the dark. And so they would creep through the roots followed by a never-ending escort of moths that were attracted by the soft light. The faerie folk did not rely on these little beetles too much for they could see in the dark well enough, and it was just as well, for the beetles could be fickle little creatures and sometimes refused to be taken advantage of in such a way.

When the wildman had awoken, Mog had pulled over the head of the hare skin and had bounded off to finish her tasks for that late afternoon.

X

The last two days of her life at Brundannon would be spent busily preparing for a banquet and packing for the journey ahead and saying goodbye to those with whom she had grown up throughout the confines of the bailey walls.

The first of the last two evenings would see a banquet in honour of Berowen and all the settlement would attend.

There had been music, dancing, singing and much merriment in celebration of her forthcoming nuptials; the children of the settlement had rushed around the hall playing hide and seek, and Halig, Scur and Eadlin had had so much fun putting their secret hiding places to good use against those of the others. So much time did it take on one occasion that when Halig had eventually been found, he was curled up fast asleep and had to be coaxed into joining in the fun again.

Although it was the last thing that she wanted to do, Berowen had eventually been persuaded to fetch her lute and sing. The chatter in the room quietened and everyone sat in silence as she filled the room with sagas of heroics, loves lost, and loves won. After she had played five songs, she noticed that most of the children were now either sitting dozily on the laps of their mothers or fathers, or yawning as they sat leaning against pillars, or chair legs. She even noticed several who had somehow managed to climb on to the long table unseen and had curled themselves into tight balls where they had fallen fast asleep. Scur had managed to secure himself the enviable position of lying asleep wrapped up in a tangle of legs and fur as he hugged Pax and Ro, her father's two faithful hounds that were fast asleep under their master's seat. Upon seeing these innocent young faces with the imminent condition of sleep soon to take them into the land of dreams, if indeed they had not gone already, Berowen decided to end the evening with a lullaby. It did not take long for those young ones who were half-awake to close their eyes and drift off. Even a few of the mothers seemed to droop their weary heads, and nod off as they rocked their children on their laps to sleep.

The next morning had been the start of a difficult day overseeing the packing for the long road ahead. Berowen had been determined to take as much of her personal belongings as she could with her to her new home, and would not let even the smallest item become overlooked.

The day passed quickly and the supper that night would be the last time that Berowen would eat with her family around the long table. There had been great effort to make it a happy affair, but the occasion had been tinged with a sadness that was unavoidable and impossible to hide. Berowen could not eat much and played with the mutton on her platter. She could hear chatter around her, but was too wrapped up in her own thoughts and fears to hear most of what was said. Occasionally she would feel Eneas gently nudge her foot under the table when she neglected to answer a question from one of the others present. It would bring her back into the present in a daze, and she would have to ask for the question to be repeated. But even then her brain could not collect itself together enough to make a coherent answer, and she would usually just nod in agreement or make as little a statement as possible in reply.

She found herself in the predicament of wishing to be on her own and fall asleep as quickly as possible so as to get the inevitable in motion, but also not wishing to fall asleep so that she could make the fateful morning of her leaving somehow longer to arrive.

Although having been invited, Thurstan had not been present; he had deemed it not fitting to attend such a private occasion and had elected to eat with the guards instead. He had bid the family a good evening and had left them to their last evening together.

Halig, Scur and Eadlin would all be still fast asleep when the party would leave in the morning, so it was decided that Berowen would take them up to their cots that night so that she could say her farewells. Although they knew their aunt was leaving, in their young minds they did not really understand the full significance of what this meant. They may not see her again for many months or even years. There was also the possibility that they may never meet again, but this did not enter their childish thoughts, only that she would be gone for a while.

They had kissed their parents goodnight, and then their grandparents and uncles before Eadlin locked her fingers round Berowen's left hand and Halig and Scur wrapped their tiny hands around two of Berowen's fingers of her right hand and, chattering gaily, went with her upstairs to their chamber.

"It is time for you to lay down your sweet heads dear children," Berowen stated as they entered into the children's chamber. "Come Halig and Scur, let me aid you."

She helped the boys into their night attire whilst Eadlin sat on the side of her cot chattering ten to the dozen about this and that, but nothing in particular. She swang her legs over the side as she spoke and her arms waved around in grand gesticulations to prove her point, whatever that may be.

Once the boys were tucked up underneath their blankets Berowen bent over Halig and kissed him on his cheek. He swung his arms around her neck and gave her a big sloppy kiss back. "My love to you Halig and may your dreams be sweet tonight."

Then it was the turn of Scur, who copied his brother by raising his arms even before Berowen had managed to bend down towards him. He gave her a kiss on her cheek and giggled when she did the same to him.

"Dear sweet Scur," she said. "You have always had the faerie about you young lad, but I hope it serves you well in the years to come. Goodnight young fellow and may your dreams take you to exciting places."

Then it was time to settle Eadlin into her cot. Berowen helped her out of her tunics and into her bed attire, before brushing the curls that shone in the candlelight. She held open the blankets while Eadlin jumped into her cot, still chattering gaily. Once she had laid her head upon her pillow, Berowen bent down, hugged her and kissed her cheek. Eadlin responded likewise, but unlike her brothers, she held on to her aunt for longer and seemed reluctant to let her go. She also ceased her chattering. "May you sing to us aunt?" she eventually whispered. "I fear we shall not hear your voice for a long time."

Eadlin released her aunt and Berowen sat up, choking back the tears that threatened to pour down her cheeks at any moment.

Berowen began to hum a tune softly and then sang the children's favourite lullaby. As she did so, she stood and walked over to the boys as they lay in their cots. She watched as they slowly closed their eyes and she reached out and gently stroked their hair. When she was confident that they were asleep, she returned to Eadlin who was still awake upon her pillow, but whose lids were getting heavier and slower to open again upon each blink. Berowen moved to the tiny window and blew out the candle, the flame of which was wafting in the faint breeze that found its way through the tiny cracks around the window. By the time she had returned to Eadlin, the girl was fast asleep.

"Goodnight and fare thee well sweet Eadlin," she whispered as she gently stroked the child's cheek. "May you tread your life with happiness and may your path be crossed with luck." Saying goodbye to her niece was so much harder for she knew – like her father had known since her own birth – that Eadlin would almost certainly have to experience exactly what she herself was going through now, as had Eadlin's own mother and grandmother before her. She could but hope that this dear sweet little girl would grow into a strong woman who would face all adversity to come with braveness and fortitude.

Creeping over to Halig and Scur where they lay sleeping, looking as innocent as newborn babes, she again whispered: "Goodnight and fare thee well my sweet little boys. Be good and grow strong. Continue to run these halls and fill them with laughter, but learn your lessons well. When it is time to put away your toys, tread these halls with honour for they are your ancestral home. Long may you live in peace."

As Berowen pulled the door behind her, she turned for one last time and blew each child a kiss on the night air. Then the tears came and she retreated to the solitude of her own chamber before eventually returning to the family in the hall.

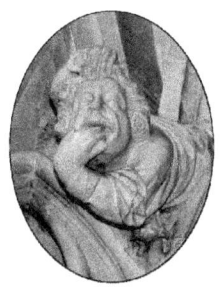

XI

In the early hours of the next morning, before the sun had risen from the east, Berowen said goodbye to Gar and Aidith. It was an emotional moment for all three, and the tears ran freely as Berowen hugged and kissed each of them farewell.

Ethwen came to urge her daughter to finish her goodbyes. She seemed out of sorts at this time of the morning and Berowen hoped it was just the early hour that was disagreeable to her. Ethwen looked drawn, pale and very frail in the ghostly light from the braziers' flames and it concerned her daughter greatly. The journey ahead would be arduous for the most seasoned traveller, but for a woman who did not make it a normal daily activity to go riding, it would surely be unbearable.

One more goodbye, hug and kiss to her brother and sister-in-law and Berowen turned and followed her mother to where the party had gathered. Eneas helped her mother and sister into their saddles and mounted his own horse that was standing patiently behind that of his father. Aelwulf turned in his saddle when his son mounted and checked down the line of travellers behind him before kicking his horse gently into a walk.

And so, as dawn came upon Brundannon, the small party descended the causeway from the keep through to the settlement below. People waved and cheered their best wishes as Berowen rode by. Even Morgen was there, and as Berowen rode passed her, she moved forward and pressed a bunch of heather into Berowen's hand, before patting the back of it and stepping backwards once more. Berowen was slightly shocked at this act of unexpected thoughtfulness and could but stare briefly at Morgen with her mouth open, before her horse took her further down towards the gate.

Berowen managed to smile for as long as the short journey took to reach the north gate. Once through the great arch her smile evaporated and she stared blankly ahead. The party rode in single file through the gate, to where Thurstan had been waiting for them, and joining them he followed the procession as they turned west towards the great hills. Two guards rode at the head of the file, two brought up the rear. They were flanked by five more on each side. Inside this protective barrier, the wedding party consisted of Aelwulf, Amleth and Eneas riding at the front, followed by Ethwen and Berowen. The four packhorses came next, being led by the two elected soldiers for that day. Thurstan followed at the back, some distance ahead of the guards at the back of the procession. .

Mercifully, clouds obscured the sun for most of the day, which made the journey slightly more bearable for the travellers; although the season of the great harvest, the sun could still shed uncomfortable heat down upon those who were out of shelter. Aelwulf was unhappy about travelling in the open and wished to reach the foothills by nightfall so they did not stop to rest or take water; they drank as they rode. Several times Berowen had to ride to her mother and gently tap her on the shoulder to wake her up. Ethwen was really far too frail to make this journey, but she was determined to see her only daughter wed.

Thurstan occasionally rode ahead of the party then stopped until the line passed him before settling back in his position behind the packhorses. Berowen thought he seemed preoccupied, as if he was expecting something. They could see for miles around while crossing the flat plains, but she discerned that he was searching into the distance at all times.

At the end of the day, just as the sun was disappearing on the horizon in an orange haze, they came upon rockier ground. The hills loomed upwards ahead of them. Tomorrow they would have to climb to the top. Berowen had never been this far from home before and she had mixed feelings about ascending these dark hills; she knew not what was beyond them, but had heard tales of dark forests, winding rivers and waterfalls, and of faeries, dragons, and even wildmen.

A suitable place for camp was agreed, and the party dismounted. The packhorses were unloaded and led away with the other mounts to be tethered for the night. Ethwen was exhausted after a day in the saddle, and it was left to Berowen to help her mother find a comfortable bed for the night.

Looking back over the way they had come, Berowen searched for the reassuring shape of Brundannon, but could see nothing in the dimming light. Wrapping her arms around her slight frame, she looked up into the darkening sky where the velvet cloak of night above her began to twinkle with hundreds of bright stars. A faint breeze wafted against her skirt and fine wisps of loose hair fluttered against her forehead. She knew not when, or indeed if, she would ever see her homelands again.

XII

Above, in the nearly naked treetops, there fluttered, squawked, and bickered fifty or more rooks. Their black shapes stood out against the blue sky of the late afternoon as they argued between each other, creating such a cacophony that the man stopped drinking from the stream to look upwards. They were always noisy, but upon this morning they seemed more agitated than usual. Suddenly, as one, they all took flight, creating a thick black coat across the sky. Something had spooked them, and upon their panic, the hair down the back of his neck stood on end.

Mog had been asleep beneath the moss-covered rocks that nestled on the other side of the babbling waters further upstream. The sudden flight above awoke her from her slumber, and she leapt to her feet shaking the dew from her hair. Peg was already awake and looking skyward. They looked at each other and babbled furiously before turning on their heels and running through the wood towards the valley where the stag had recently defended his herd, and where Mog had sat with the wildman whilst he slept.

When they reached the perimeter, they both stared across the green valley below. A great thunderous sound reached their keen ears and the earth beneath their tiny feet began to vibrate. In the near distance, they saw a group of twenty great beasts galloping across the valley. As the group approached the wood, Mog and Peg could see great red-haired men sitting upon the large beasts' backs. They had never seen men that size before, nor with such red hair and beards. They scratched their heads and looked at each other in puzzlement.

The deer in the valley scattered as the riders sped through the herd, obviously with some malevolent duty to perform, and even the great stag seemed hesitant to challenge them. He merely tossed his great head in agitation, and then stood still, waiting for the threat to leave.

At that moment, Mog and Peg heard something crashing through the undergrowth behind them and they darted under the cover of the brambles. The man had reached his vantage spot at last, just in time to see the riders disappear over the brow of the hill, but it was long enough for him to see their great size and the fearsome look of the horses on which they sat.

He grunted to himself and then scratched *his* head. To his left he noticed a few of the last berries had ripened and set about picking them busily, completely unaware that on either side of him, within a footstep away, hid Mog and Peg.

Mog babbled something to Peg, but their speech was so quiet that the man did not hear it above the sound of the breeze. Mog became impatient and did not want to have to stay hidden for longer than was necessary, and poked her head through the brambles. She was behind the wildman who was bending over at his harvesting. She pointed at the wildman's hairy bottom and giggled. Peg then poked out her head and started giggling too. They may be the guardians of the wood, but they could not resist a spot of mischief if given the chance. Mog reached to her back and grabbed the tiny bow. She pulled a tiny arrow from its quiver at her hip and slid it into position. Peg gasped at Mog's tomfoolery but then nodded her head enthusiastically and urged Mog on. With a glint in her dark eyes Mog pulled back the string and let the arrow fly. It would not do much damage to such a large target, it would be not much more than a bee sting, but would be enough to startle the wildman from his foraging and would make a rather boring evening - for them - a little more entertaining.

As it hit its mark, the wildman bellowed and immediately swung his hand to his rump where the tiny arrow had embedded itself in his flesh. His hand scrabbled around and found the tiny weapon, which he pulled out and raised to his face to investigate more closely. Scratching his head again, he turned around to see what had caused him this small discomfort. There was nothing there of course.

Mog and Peg had watched as the wildman had pulled the arrow from his behind and had laughed and run off back into the darkness of the wood, leaving him to ponder on what had taken place.

XIII

When they awoke, they found a low mist enveloping them. The air was still and silent; not a bird could be heard, and it was very damp and cold. The ascent would indeed be difficult in these conditions, but climb they must if they were to keep to their deadline. Standing, Berowen yawned and as she stretched to bring her body to life she looked around her. She shivered and wrapped her cloak around her body. Her gaze briefly rested upon Thurstan who was crouching as he rolled up his bedding. Securing the roll, he rose, wrapping his cloak about him and walked towards where the horses were tethered. As he passed within a few feet of her he said, "Good morning my lady, I trust you had a restful sleep?"

"I did, thank you," she replied.

"And your mother, she has rested well also?" he continued.

"I am about to waken her, although I would wish her to rest for longer. I fear she is too frail for this journey and that she needs as much sleep as possible. I am concerned for her health," Berowen replied, turning to look at her sleeping mother.

"I sympathise with your concerns my lady, but we really should leave within the hour. You should wake her gently while I prepare your horses for the day ahead," he offered.

Aelwulf approached and laid his hand on his daughter's shoulder. He kissed her forehead affectionately. "Lord Thurstan is right child. Tend to your mother while I speak with our travelling companion."

"Yes father," Berowen replied as the two men walked out of earshot. She knelt down beside where her mother was now stirring, and gently shook her shoulders.

"Don't fuss child," came the gruff response. "I may be old but I am not so feeble as to not be able to get ready by myself."

"Of course you are not, mother. Let me get you some water," responded Berowen, lifting one eyebrow in her surprise at her mother's unusual sharpness as she left Ethwen to prepare herself for the day's journey.

As they walked towards the horses, Aelwulf spoke in earnest to Thurstan.

"What can we truly expect once we have crossed these hills?" he asked.

"We should be vigilant at all times my Lord Aelwulf," replied Thurstan. "Once we are over the hills we shall be in the realm of the Blue Wood, which is indeed a dangerous place to pass through, for it is a favourite with brigands. I have heard many a tale of travellers being waylaid; tales from those who make it out alive of course. There are others known to enter who have not been seen since. But it is no more dangerous than the rest of the road ahead.

"What hope have we then, of reaching our destination in good health? What chance have we of getting my daughter safely to Grimfell?" Aelwulf softly asked.

"Your men are hand-picked for their sword skills are they not?" questioned Thurstan.

"The very best my lord," answered Aelwulf . "I have overseen their training myself."

"Then you must trust in your teaching my lord and have faith in your men, for if they are true warriors of the sword then they will lay down their lives rather than see you in defeat."

Turning to look back at the camp, Aelwulf watched as his soldiers checked their weapons and prepared for the next stage of the journey. "Indeed I must trust in them," he whispered to himself.

As Thurstan had hoped, the band was ascending the hill within the hour. He led the way up the narrow track, between great boulders covered in moss. Droplets of moisture hung motionless from the scant bushes and the damp air made the path slippery for the horses as they scrambled ever upward, the sound of their hooves echoing with dull thuds around them in the mist. Alternating between riding and walking their horses, the party moved on until, as they had hoped, the higher the road took them, the clearer the world around them became. Looking back Berowen could see the mist clinging to the path from where they had emerged. She let her hood fall to her shoulders as the sun warmed her face. It was only then that she realised what a perilous journey they were embarking upon; just a few feet on either side of the path the ground dropped away sharply.

Leading his horse slightly ahead of the others, Thurstan stopped. Raising his hand to signal the others to halt he turned and spoke to his companions. "From now on the path descends into the Blue Wood below. The time has come to instruct your soldiers to keep one hand on their swords my lord Aelwulf," he said.

"Father," called Berowen from back in the line "Surely we can stop for awhile and let my mother rest?"

"We shall pause from our journey there, in the shelter of that tree," replied Aelwulf in agreement, nodding in the direction of a large oak that stood alone, its branches, bent by the winds, pointing downwards as if to mark their way forwards. Against its trunk rested a large boulder that seemed to be trying to uproot it and send it sliding down the path.

"I would strongly suggest only briefly," advised Thurstan quietly. "We are too exposed here to stay long."

Eneas dismounted and walked to where Thurstan had sat on the rock.

"Why is it named the Blue Wood? I must say that the wood does not look very blue to me," he said with a slight grin on his lips.

"In the months of spring it would seem that every inch of the ground is covered in a carpet of bluebells," replied Thurstan.

"Mmm an obvious answer for an obvious question it would seem," laughed Eneas. "But alas we have come upon it at the wrong time of year to see such beauty."

After about fifteen minutes, Aelwulf made as if to move.

"Once off this hill our formation shall be as on the grasslands," Aelwulf advised his small party. "Open your ears and eyes to every sound and movement. We must ride with caution. Come, we have rested enough, let us move on."

The tree line closed in around them as they descended the hill. Eventually the ground beneath them levelled out and they found themselves amongst the tall trees of the Blue Wood. The road ahead would take them through the centre, its path lined on either side by the ancient, gnarled trunks. The breeze rustled in the treetops loosening a flutter of the reddy-brown leaves, allowing them to float to the ground silently around them. Eerily, there was no bird song in the cooling autumnal air, the only sound being the muffled steps of the horses on the leafy ground.

Eneas felt a rush of air skim past his ear, accompanied by a low humming sound. Seconds later the soldier just behind him to his right made a gagging sound as the arrow struck him in the throat. He fell to the ground with a thud as he choked on his own blood. Instantly Aelwulf, his two sons Eneas and Amleth, and the other soldiers in the party had drawn their own weapons, and prepared themselves for the attack to come.

Behind her Berowen detected the sound of Thurstan's sword as it cleared its scabbard. In a second he was aside them, grabbing the reins of both Berowen's and her mother's horses. He pulled their mounts to the side of the road.

"Dismount and hide, both of you, down that bank," he instructed them hurriedly as his horse danced on the spot in agitation. Then he galloped off in the direction of the others.

The thunder of horses' hooves became louder and then, from around the bend in the road ahead, came twenty riders at full gallop, leaves and clods of mud being tossed up around the pounding hooves of their mounts.

Safely seeing her mother hidden in the shadow of the trees Berowen edged as far as she could back to the top of the ditch so that she could just see over. Ahead she made out the dark figures bear down on her companions. In horror, she witnessed one of the Brundannon men being felled from where he sat in his saddle. She watched Thurstan steer his horse into the melee with his drawn sword sweeping from side to side, slicing through the flesh of the ambushers one by one. It was easy to make out the opposition from that of her own kind for they seemed so much larger in stature, their long, red, straggly hair hanging in tails down their broad backs, their faces covered with bushy, red, plaited beards.

Their horses seemed huge against those of her party. They were heavyset beasts with broad girths and rumps, and had tassels of loose hair about their hooves. The horses appeared decorated with what looked very much like human hair, which hung from their bridles and saddlecloths, and swung in the air as the beasts tossed their heads and galloped. These horses also seemed much more armoured than the men themselves, each one having a face and chest plate, which had probably once gleamed when first sculpted by the armourer. Now, however, they were faded, and much dented.

Ethwen whispered to Berowen to come back down into hiding but Berowen replied in a low voice.

"Two women from our settlement have lost their husbands today, and I do not like to think how many children have hence lost their fathers. I cannot lie here cowering whilst more lose their lives."

"It is important that you reach Grimfell, Berowen. Then the women of Brundannon may sleep knowing that they have protection not just from their husbands, but by the army of Modig also. You owe it to them to survive."

Her mother, of course, was quite right in what she had said, but Berowen's blood was surging through her veins as she lay on her belly against the bank. She could not just watch as those around her lost their lives trying to protect her. She remained where she was, but promised herself that if needed, she would join in the fight. If she died then so be it.

Back on the road, the force of the blow from his attacker unbalanced Aelwulf and he fell to the ground. The enemy turned his horse and rode back towards the unseated man, but Aelwulf had regained his stance and was ready. The attacking horse bit and kicked at Aelwulf – these were obviously well trained horses for battle. With a heavy blow he knocked his antagonist from his horse in return, and was about to deliver the mortal strike when the man rolled over and jumped to his feet. Berowen watched in horror as they both fought hand to hand. Craning her neck further, she caught sight of Eneas, who was now also on his feet, but she could see no sign of Amleth from where she was lying.

"These men are like giants mother, they tower above father and the others by at least half their height. Who are they? Where are from?" asked Berowen, not really expecting her mother to know the answers.

Nearer to her, she saw Thurstan slide off his horse and run towards where Aelwulf and Eneas were fighting. Twisting and turning Thurstan wielded his great sword with skill, felling those that tried to stop him.

A few hundred feet in front of her, the soldier who had been leading the packhorses was now also on the ground, in hand to hand combat with one of the antagonists who was towering over the poor villager. The soldier, in turn, was struggling to keep his balance against the heavy blows. At this point Berowen could remain hidden for no longer. Another man would lose his life if she did not help, so taking a deep breath she inched up the bank on her belly as stealthily as she could, then rose to her feet and silently approached the pair. At the last moment, she raised her sword and with as much force as she could muster, sliced at his antagonist from the side, almost severing his left arm. This allowed the man from Brundannon to realign himself and separate the attacker's head from his shoulders with one blow. Berowen and the soldier acknowledged each other with a slight nod of their heads, and he rushed off in the direction of the fighting further up the track.

Holding her bloody sword in her shaking hand she stood in the middle of the road, her nerve slightly wavering, when out of the corner of her eye, Berowen saw the faint glint of metal. Looking to where she had left her mother she saw a figure amongst the trees approaching Ethwen, his great weapon raised above his head ready to strike. Her mother was standing with her back towards the path, her head and shoulders just visible above the bank. Berowen could see her mother's small sword raised in defence. She saw the figure lower his own weapon ready for the deathblow. The battle fever now began to stream through her body and Berowen ran down the bank, screaming at the top of her voice, both her hands holding the sword above her head ready to defend her mother. Her noisy ploy had worked and the enemy immediately turned his attention towards her, but not before pushing Ethwen to the ground with a mighty sweep of his arm.   Uttering a low growl, he sloped towards Berowen. Gulping hard as they came closer to each other she noticed the evil grin on his ugly, scarred face. As he swung his weapon she brought hers down to meet his with all her strength, the blades connecting with a screeching thud.

Back on the road, Thurstan crouched down dodging the blade of his attacker. One hand on the ground behind him he raised his sword with an upward thrust that caught the other under the ribs. Pushing the blade in with great force it exited through his opponent's back. At that moment, he heard Berowen's blood-curdling cry and turned his head quickly to see her disappear out of sight into the wood.

Aelwulf and Eneas also heard it but were powerless to help as they continued to fend off the last of their attackers.

"Thurstan!" Aelwulf exclaimed. "The women." With one foot pushing against the dead man's waist, Thurstan pulled his sword back backwards and as the body fell to the ground, he turned and ran back down the track to where he had left Berowen and Ethwen. He could hear the sound of metal on metal, and the desperate grunts of Berowen as she valiantly fought the man who overshadowed her small frame. Stooping beside the body of one of the ambushers, he grabbed the sword that lay beside it and rushed to the top of the bank. With his full force behind him, he leapt down upon Berowen's attacker, knocking him backwards. Jumping in front of Berowen he took up the fight, parrying the blows from the great man first with the sword in his left hand then with that in his right. He edged forward slowly, forcing the red-beard backwards with every step. The man however, soon regained his posture and stood his ground, bringing his sword upwards and knocking the weapon out of Thurstan's left hand. It flew through the air and landed point down in the soft earth where it rocked back and forth until its bloody blade slowly came to a standstill. It was now Thurstan's turn to retreat as the great man counter-attacked, reigning down terrible blows upon him, but Thurstan somehow managed to stay on his feet. He ducked and dived from side to side, trying to deliver a deadly thrust, his lighter stature working to advantage.

Bending his knees, he saw his chance and with a loud cry sliced his sword into the leg of his foe, causing him to grunt with pain. As Thurstan stood again, the other man responded with a sneering laugh as his blade glanced Thurstan's arm, cutting through the material and skimming the flesh. Thurstan did not seem to notice but responded with another lunge, this time to the great man's throat. The ugly face looked shocked, the evil grin disappeared from its lips, its eyes stared in disbelief at the mortal blow as the gurgling sound emitted from the gaping throat wound. The eyes then glazed over, and the body breathed no more.

Thurstan took an exhaustive step backwards as the great man fell to the ground. Returning his sword to its scabbard, he turned and walked towards the two women. When he saw Ethwen prone in her daughter's lap he fell to his knees, his laboured breathing slowly returning to normal, and laid the bloody fingers of his right hand upon Ethwen's neck to search for a pulse.

When Thurstan had leapt to her defence, Berowen had dropped to the ground, her sword falling from her hand. She had crawled on all fours to where her mother lay desperate to reach her. Unbeknown to Berowen, Ethwen - as she had fallen - had hit her head on the huge trunk of the tree they had sheltered behind, thus being rendered unconscious. Breathing heavily from her encounter and between the tears, muttering, "Oh no, no not my mother no," softly under her breath, Berowen gently lifted her mother's head into her lap, firmly believing that Ethwen was lost. On seeing her chest slowly rise and fall, Berowen sobbed in relief and sat stroking her mother's head.

In a daze, she knew that only a few yards away Thurstan was fighting for his own life as well as theirs, but she had no strength left inside her to move; she would have to remain where she was. She just had to hope that he would be triumphant, it was either that or she and her mother would die a bloody death along with him. Berowen began rocking slowly from side to side, humming the tune her mother had sung to her since the day she had brought her into the world. Everything in the wood was quiet again, the battle now over, the enemy vanquished. She could hear the faint sounds of the soldiers rustling amongst the trees searching for the horses that had scattered whilst the fight had raged.   As Thurstan knelt beside them, she watched his fingers search for the pulse and heard his sigh of relief when he located it.   In her confused state, she heard the sound of her father's voice as he descended down to where she sat. Eneas was already kneeling beside her, his mother's frail hand in his bloodied palm. Amleth was kneeling beside his brother, looking dazed. All of them were spattered in blood, their own mingling with that of their assailants. As Thurstan rose to take his leave, her head began to clear and Berowen raised her eyes and watched Aelwulf place his hands on Thurstan's shoulders, pulling him towards him and embracing him silently in thanks for the lives of his wife and daughter.

Ethwen stirred as she lay across her daughter's lap. Slowly opening her eyes she squinted at the sunlight that streamed through the trees. Groaning, Ethwen raised a hand to rub the back of head.

"Mother, you are back with us," Berowen spoke gently. "Father, come, she has awoken," she called to Aelwulf.

Helping her mother to sit up, Berowen moved to let her father sit down beside his wife. She then shakily stood and walked to where her horse had been left by the soldiers at the top of the bank, located her water carrier and returned to where her parents were, offering it to her father so that he could help her mother take a drink. Eneas rested his hand on her shoulder and smiled at her, "My courageous little sister," he said. "You are indeed a daughter of Aelwulf, stout of heart, if not a little reckless."

"Oh brother, but my recklessness nearly killed our mother. I should never have left her," Berowen replied.

"That foul-stenched creature would have still come upon you, even if you had stayed here. If you had not surprised him as you did then it could have turned out very differently sister. You have nothing for which to reproach yourself. You fought valiantly for your mother's life with no regard for you own."

"Aahhh, Eneas, but in truth I did not do so well did I? In reality my opponent was stronger than any I have fought before. I had thought myself a strong fighter but, alas, it is so different when fighting a real enemy. And this one was even bigger than any man should ever come across. I certainly have Lord Thurstan to thank for my life and that of our mother," she replied. "If he had not come to our aid when he did I know I would definitely not be standing here now. I must find him and give thanks."

She returned to the road, every muscle in her small body beginning to ache. She had never felt so tired and vulnerable.

Berowen found Thurstan as he and the surviving soldiers of Brundannon were dragging the eleven dead red-beards off the path and into the woods so their bodies would not be found should more of their kind come by this way. They found it difficult to drag them as each weighed more than any other man they had met and it took two men per body to carry out the task. Then the torn bloody bodies of the two men of the garrison who had met their death in the fight were taken into a different part of the woods, where their remains were covered by the dead leaves of autumn.

As she approached, Thurstan stood and pulled her sword from where he had tucked it into his belt.

"My lady, I believe this belongs to you. It is a fine sword and has served you well today," he said as he offered it to her. Taking it in outstretched hands, she looked deep into his eyes.

"Thank you my lord, but it was your sword which saved the life of my mother and me today and for that I thank you." Returning her weapon to its sheath, she shivered slightly in the cooling air.

"I desire no thanks Berowen, for none are needed. I fear though that you picked a rather formidable adversary for your first battle," he grinned trying to lighten her mood.

"I shall indeed try to pick someone smaller than myself next time," responded Berowen smiling weakly back. As she spoke, with great sadness he thought how pale she looked.

"Lord Thurstan!" called Aelwulf as he marched up the road towards the pair.

Clearing his throat and taking a couple of steps backwards from Berowen, Thurstan looked over her shoulder in Aelwulf's direction.

"My lord?" he replied.

"Have you any idea from where these fellows came?" Aelwulf asked, as he got closer.

"I have heard of such red-haired fighters before, yes. But this is the first time I have laid eyes on such men," Thurstan answered.

Her father had now joined them and Berowen took her leave to walk back to her mother, who had been reunited with her saddle. As she walked, Berowen passed Eneas. Her brother laid his hand on her shoulder. She clasped her own hand over his briefly before they walked on in opposite directions. Reaching Ethwen she threw her arms around her mother, and sobbed quietly.

"My dearest child," was all that Ethwen could say.

XIV

Eneas joined his father, brother and Thurstan. The latter was binding his arm wound with a strip of cloth he had torn from the clothing of one of the corpses. He took one end of the makeshift bandage in his teeth and the other in his free hand and pulled them both, knotting the cloth round his arm.

'I fear that these men did not just happen upon us?' asked Aelwulf of Thurstan.

Thurstan winced slightly as the bandage tightened. "On the contrary my lord, I believe that they did. They were not brigands, they were trained warriors, and trained warriors are enlisted for more purpose than to rob mere travellers. Someone has sent them on a different mission, but what that mission is I am unable to tell you."

Aelwulf nodded slowly at this suggestion. "We can assume, then, that as we killed them all we can proceed on our journey without fear of reprisal?"

"Not necessarily. If these eleven fighters were the only members of the mission, then yes perhaps. But if, as I am more inclined to expect, they are part of a bigger company, once they are missed we may become part of their mission. In which case, my lord, I fear that our arrival at Grimfell alive may become uncertain."

Eneas interrupted, "But we still have another four or five day's journey ahead. It is surely impossible for us to reach our destination now under such treacherous conditions?"

"We have no choice Eneas," responded Thurstan. "If we turn back then the alliance between Modig and us is lost and you can be sure that Modig would not let it rest there. He will send his armies after us and destroy Brundannon into the bargain just out of spite. No, we must reach Grimfell and your sister must wed Brack as arranged. The strong army of Modig shall then take Brundannon under its protection, rather than destroy it."

"We are down to fifteen men and two women, it is an impossible task," replied Eneas shaking his head.

"It may not be as impossible as it seems," offered Thurstan. "The journey would take an extra two days, but if you agree we could take a different route out of here."

"I am not aware of another route, where would it take us?" asked Aelwulf.

"Through the Forest of Whispers and then out on to the marshes of Wellonaw, by way of the caverns in the Dragon Hills," replied Thurstan. It is a roundabout way of reaching Grimfell, in fact we will approach from the opposite direction, but it should provide us with more safety. You will surely have noticed the hills on your own visit to Grimfell."

Aelwulf scratched his beard as he spoke, "Yes I remember the hills, but the caverns only exist in folklore. My father used to tell me tales of the dragons that dwelt there when I was a small boy."

"The dragons may well have long since passed into legend, Aelwulf, but I can assure you that the caverns do exist. No-one knows of the route for it has been well guarded in secrecy for many years."

"Then you must show us this magical place, Lord Thurstan, although if guarded in secrecy I am not sure how you should know of its existence. However, we have no choice but to trust you and besides, we should linger no more in this place of death."

Signalling to the soldiers to mount, Aelwulf and his two sons were soon in the saddle. Thurstan strode back down the track to his own horse where she stood patiently waiting beside the mounts of Berowen and Ethwen; the packhorses also safely rounded up and in the care of the man who Berowen had helped earlier.

Once astride his horse, Thurstan gestured to the women. "Ladies, it is time to leave this place, let us make haste," and he urged the great chestnut mare to take up the lead position.

Tightly grouped the party moved on through the Blue Wood until they came upon a fork in the road. To the left the path would take them slowly downhill and out on to the direct road to Grimfell across the plateau. The right hand fork would lead them deeper into the Blue Wood, the road descending more steeply until it left the trees behind and entered on to the grasslands that would take them to the Forest of Whispers. But first they would have to negotiate a narrow ledge that would take them around the side of the mountain. Turning his mount to the right Thurstan led the party on. The road soon became more difficult to traverse, and Thurstan slid down from the mare's back.

"We shall have to walk from here. For safety's sake we must keep to the inside of the path," he instructed.

Holding them on a tight rein, they led their horses on. The trees began to thin out and slowly the scene below them revealed itself. There before them was a great horseshoe-shaped chasm gashed out of the mountainside where overhead the buzzards screeched to each other as they circled around the rocky escarpments. There was a chill in the air and the travellers wrapped themselves in their cloaks to help shield the breeze that was stirring up from the deep valley below. Across the huge chasm, they could see three mighty waterfalls cascading down into the gorge below. Slowly their path thinned as it meandered downwards. Eventually it took them out on to a rocky ledge. The sound of rushing water deafened their ears, icy cold spray pricked at their faces. Keeping close to the side of the mountain they wearily and carefully urged their horses to follow where Thurstan led them.   The horses were scared; they nickered and snorted at the rushing sound of water. It took all of Ethwen's strength to keep hold of her horse's reins as it carefully picked its way along the ledge ahead of Berowen. Behind her, she could hear the packhorses scraping their loads against the rock. Looking over the ledge the ground fell away into the void below.

Ahead Thurstan laboured on with Ora, gently stroking her soft muzzle and whispering to her as he led her on. His ears had begun to ache from the sound of the water and the spray was so cold it stung his eyes as he squinted to look ahead, forcing him to keep his head down and the hood of his cloak pulled across his face.

Eneas could hear that the soldier, Oswald, who was travelling behind him, was having trouble keeping his horse in order. Its back legs were skidding along the ledge as it reared with fright and tossed its head in agitation. He heard a scream above the sound of the rushing water. Pushing his horse against the rock, he turned to see the soldier's horse disappear over the ledge. Oswald had been pulled off his feet as it fell, and he was now hanging from the ledge, his legs dangling in the air. Eneas gave his reins to his father's outstretched hands and carefully edged his way back to the where Oswald was suspended. Kneeling down on the slippery ledge Eneas reached and grabbed the arm of the petrified man. Gritting his teeth and using all his strength, he sat back on his haunches and tried to pull him up but the ledge was too slippery for his feet to get a grip. He noticed a small outcropping and pushing against it with his left foot he pulled hard again. The stricken man vainly tried to search for some leverage with his feet, but there was nothing below him and he swung in the air with one arm secured in Eneas' now weakening grip.

"I -will –not- let- you- fall," Eneas spat the words out between gritted teeth. With both hands round the other's arm, his face contorted with the effort, he pulled harder, his foot pushing against the rock. Slowly Oswald's shoulders cleared the ledge and he managed to grasp the rocks at its edge. Pulling backwards, Eneas finally managed to pull him up enough to enable him to crawl back on to the path.

Sitting back against the rock Eneas sat exhausted, his arms hanging limply in his lap. Oswald crawled on all fours and sat beside him, his chest heaving and his eyes wide with terror. As they caught their breath there was no need for spoken words, the look that passed between them was enough.

Ahead Thurstan had been unable to come to the aid of Eneas or the man, just as Aelwulf had been helpless to assist. They had called out to him but had had no choice but to stand powerlessly and watch it all unfold before their eyes. Ethwen and Berowen had stood motionless, their hands clasped together across the flanks of their horses, not daring to breathe as they watched Eneas. Their grip had tightened and their hands shook each other's when the rescue had been successfully accomplished and when both the men were safe again. Throughout the party the other soldiers nodded to each other, their faces etched with relief.

Recovered, the group moved on again and came upon a curve in the rock, around which the mighty waterfall came into view. Aelwulf watched in amazement as Thurstan walked behind it and disappeared from sight, pulling Ora after him. Moments later Thurstan emerged again and beckoned Aelwulf to follow. One by one, the travellers disappeared behind the rushing waters. As Eneas passed him, Thurstan gave him a pat on his shoulder in silent recognition of the brave deed he had just undertaken on the ledge. Aelwulf embraced his son and they walked their horses to the back of the cavern where Thurstan had left Ora.

Behind the waterfall, the cave opened up before them. The travellers gazed around them in awe at the great cavern stretching before them, and with the spray no longer able to reach them, they lowered their hoods.

"We shall stay here for the night," said Thurstan. Replacing his hood he returned to where they had entered, beckoning two men to follow him.

"Where are you going?" enquired Aelwulf.

"To gather wood for a fire."

"But surely you are not going back out there?" added Berowen anxiously from behind her father. "It is too dangerous a path to walk again."

"We shall be travelling the ledge again on the morrow my lady, but for now we shall tread with care and return before nightfall," replied Thurstan, and he disappeared out on to the ledge, the soldiers following.

In the time that followed, the horses were unsaddled and the packhorses relieved of their loads. Aelwulf embraced his wife and rubbed her shoulders and arms in an attempt to halt her shivering. He glanced across to where his daughter was tracing her fingers across the cavern walls.

"My poor Berowen," he sighed. "She goes to her destiny with such bravery. Am I such a bad father to send her to wed a man she has never met?"

"Husband," Ethwen replied stroking his woolly beard. "You could never be a bad father. You have done what you think is best for us all. Berowen knows you do not send her to this betrothal lightly and without feeling. She bears her fate proudly. Besides, it is a duty of many a noble father to arrange such a union for their daughter. You have merely followed in the footsteps of your father, and of his."

"But she is so sad these days. The Berowen I once knew no longer exists. She does not laugh any more. Dear wife, I cannot bear to look into her eyes for the emptiness I see there," he softly said.

"If you look into her eyes, Aelwulf, you will see the adoration a daughter has for her father. You have not lost her love."

Ethwen followed his gaze and they both stood in each other's embrace, and watched their daughter as she stood staring upwards at the great granite ceiling above her.

As the hours passed they waited for Thurstan and the others to return. Eventually the two solders reappeared, their arms heavily laden with wood. Berowen wanted to ask them where Thurstan was, but she was hesitant of displaying any concern in case it were to be taken the wrong way.

As they built up the wood to make a fire, one of the other soldiers asked the question for her.

"He left us to hunt for food back in the Blue Wood," was the reply.

"But that was hours ago," responded another of the men. "What if something has happened to him? How do we proceed from here?"

"I am sure that Lord Thurstan will be back soon," interrupted Eneas as he listened in to their conversation. "Let us get this fire lit, we need to make some warmth and it will soon be so dark in here we will not be able to see each other at all."

Eneas stood at the entrance where they had entered the cavern and looked back along the ledge. The encroaching darkness caused him concern for the safety of their guide and companion. He looked back to where the fire now lit the cavern and at the weary faces of his family, and fellow companions. The soldiers huddled around the fire wiping the dried blood from their blades with their dampened cloaks. Aelwulf tended to Ethwen as they sat together nearby. Sitting alone, his sister stared ahead of her, her chin resting on her knees, her arms wrapped tightly around them.

He heard a sound and out of the twilight came Thurstan, his dark cloak wrapped around him as he once more braved the icy spray.

Thurstan passed Eneas, the body of a small deer draped across his shoulders, "It is not much my friends, but the fading light was against me," he smiled. He tossed the animal to where the soldiers were waiting, their knives ready to carry out the disembowelling.

Skinned and gutted, the carcass was soon roasting across the fire. Whilst the deer cooked, Thurstan busied himself cleaning his sword and dagger, before replacing them in their scabbards. This done he undid the belt across his chest that secured his bow and quiver, laying them on the ground in front of him, and then removing his cloak, he spread it over a nearby rock to dry off. His hands were numb with cold as he unfastened the leather gauntlet that protected his sword hand, and unbuckled his belt, laying his weapons on the ground beside the rock. Thurstan then strode to the mouth of the cave, where he held his hands under the cascading water to wash away the dried blood from that morning's encounter, before he proceeded to unravel the bandage from his upper arm. Returning to the fire he again crouched down and began dabbing at the gash when, satisfied that the cut was clean enough, he edged just a little bit closer to the fire and commenced to rub his hands together in an attempt to bring his icy fingers back to life, before replacing the bandage.

Locating his saddle amongst the others where they had all been bundled up against the far wall of the cavern, he looked in his pack, and after a short search, he took out a small leather pouch from which he produced a needle and some thread. Oblivious to those around him Thurstan sat down again in the light of the fire and stitched up the tear in the ripped cloth, shearing the thread with his teeth when finished.

There was only one person who was really taking any notice of his actions. In the shadows, Berowen watched him with fascination as he tended his wound and repaired his shirt. He was clearly used to travelling and knew how to look after himself. For the first time since he had arrived at Brundannon she began to wonder why he was here. Up to now she had just assumed he was a traveller, albeit the nephew of a King from many miles to the north. She had presumed he was on a journey west for some royal business but had assumed that he was one of the courtiers she had heard tell of who fussed and fluttered around the court but would not say boo to a goose if a goose should have the audacity to bite him on the leg. However, after seeing Thurstan's skill in battle and his obvious skill at leading men, she began to wonder what else there was about Thurstan that she did not know.

Once he had tended to his work, he strode to where Ora and the other horses were tethered for the night. The light from the fire cast great shadows on the cave walls, seeming to enlarge the horses to twice their size. Thurstan talked quietly to his chestnut companion, tracing a hand from her neck to her rump. He gently stroked her muzzle and forehead, leaning his body against hers in the dim light. He felt down each of her legs in turn, making sure all was well with his beloved mare. She stood, head hanging in half-sleep as Thurstan blew gently into her nostrils and was soothed by his soft words, moving only to shift her weight as she rested each rear leg in turn.

When cooked, the food was shared fairly around them all and was soon despatched into their hungry stomachs, washed down with cupfuls of the pure water so readily to hand.

"This place is well hidden my friend," spoke Aelwulf to Thurstan between mouthfuls. "How do you come to know of it?"

"My mother told me of its route. She had cause to travel this road many years ago before my birth."

Aelwulf stayed silent expecting Thurstan to explain more, but upon no further information being offered decided that now was not the time to press their companion any further. The look in Thurstan's eyes told of a sorrow that he obviously did not wish to share.

One by one, the soldiers crept off to the far corners of the cave to their beds. Aelwulf moved to where Ethwen had already fallen asleep and affectionately replaced the blanket over her shoulders before laying beside her. Thurstan, however, remained seated by the fire staring into its flames.

Berowen could not sleep but lay staring upwards at the cave ceiling, watching the shadows dancing across its glowing expanse. As her brother tiptoed by her she whispered, "Eneas, why do we follow this man without question?"

Kneeling down beside her in the dim light her brother answered, "Our father trusts him and we trust our father."

She lifted herself on to one elbow, "But we know nothing about him. He is so quiet and withdrawn."

"I think that he is just not used to having travelling companions, Berowen. That is all. From what I have gathered, he has travelled in solitude for many years. Besides, think about it sister, if he had not been with us in the Blue Wood I am certain we should all be lying there now with our throats cut," said Eneas looking towards where Thurstan sat. "He is indeed a formidable fighter; I have not seen such a capable swordsman before. He has been well schooled."

"Indeed yes, that is true. He seems not to fear death either I suspect. But think on this," she said earnestly as she placed a hand on his arm. "How did they know we were coming, Eneas? Have you thought of that? Perhaps it was not us they were hunting.   Perhaps they were searching for him?"

"Berowen, why are you so against this man? He has saved your life today and that of our mother. I am sure your suspicions are unfounded."

"I hope so, Eneas. It is just ..." she paused. "It is just that I have this feeling that he will somehow change our lives forever. I am just not sure whether it will be for the good or for the worse."

"And this from the stubborn young woman who had to be almost dragged from the river to the safety of the castle walls when he first came into our lives," Eneas smiled.

Berowen smiled weakly back, "I know. I know. You are right. Perhaps I am just over-tired and see things that are not there."

She sighed, "I shall miss Brundannon so much Eneas."

"I know, Berowen, and Brundannon will miss you, but you must sleep now sister. Clear your head of such bad thoughts so that they do not cloud your dreams," he said placing a kiss on her forehead before standing and continuing on his weary way to his own bed.

As she lay once more staring at the shadows above her, Berowen was desperately resisting sleep. Her body ached from the encounter that morning but she was determined to make the day last as long as possible. To her, every end of the day brought her closer to the day of her marriage and although that day was inevitable, she would try to savour each day of freedom for as long as she could.

Thoughts of Thurstan came uninvited into her mind and she began to hold a silent conversation with herself.

"I shall get up and speak to him. Find out more about him…. but I have not the nerve to do so," she argued silently.

"Of course I have, I shall count to ten and then I shall go and do it," she promised herself and she began to count. Ten came and passed. "For pity's sake Berowen," she chastised herself. "Just do it – now."

Sitting up sharply, the fire was within her sight. Unfortunately, though, Thurstan was not.

Disappointed, and annoyed at her own dithering, Berowen lay back down. Her eyelids were getting so heavy now that she had to make a conscious effort to keep blinking them open. As her brain began to drift into sleep and her whole body began to relax, she could hear the faint sound of the horses nickering behind her, but sleep had taken her too far down its captive road for her to stir again that night.

XV

It would soon be the night of the tenth full moon of the year, the night when the man of the woods, the wood-walker, would begin his journey to spend another winter on the far side of the moorland. He would join the motley procession as he had done every year since the woods became his home. With luck, the pale disc would reveal herself in her full glory in the night sky, and bathe the land below in her pale, ghostly light.

His gnarled and worn out fingers plaited the stems of the ivy together to make the crown that he would wear on his head for the journey. There was no need to do this, it did not give him any special powers or protection, but it had been something that he had always done. It simply gave him pleasure to wear it, and although it became more difficult to weave the thin stems together the older and more inflexible his fingers became, he refused to travel on the long journey without one.

He became bad-tempered at his fumbling and started to growl under his breath at his shoddy efforts. His buttock was still sore from the odd attack he had received the day before, which made sitting down for too long uncomfortable. He felt a rage surging up inside him and he tossed the half-made crown aside in anger and frustration. Standing slowly, rubbing his buttock as he did so, he limped off deeper into the wood to search for more greenery.

Mog and Peg had been watching the wildman from their hiding place behind the upturned trunk. They could both see that the mischief making they had performed had obviously caused him much more discomfort than they had intended and they both felt remorse for what they had done. They couldn't help it, like the wildman could not his crown-making, and when the urge to commit such naughtiness surged within them they could do nothing but let it take its course. It was in their nature.

A short while later, the man returned to his spot outside his den, where he proceeded to make another crown. This was as unsuccessful as the first, and again he tossed it aside. His anger and disappointment this time, however, could not be placated by another trip for more ivy for it was becoming dark. He would have to wait until tomorrow and hope that his craftsmanship improved. He raised his hands to his face and shouted at them for their bad efforts.

He shouted into the dusk and his cry disturbed a myriad of animals, all of which scuttled through the undergrowth in fright. He picked up his two failures and ripped them apart in frustration before crawling into his den to sleep away the hours of night.

When he awoke and crawled out, he stopped suddenly. There, just outside the entrance, was a perfectly woven crown of ivy. He picked it up and looked at it closely, turning it repeatedly in his hands. He raised it to his nose and smelt it. He laughed. Then he dropped it, squatted and looked all around him.

The man picked up the crown again and placed it slowly on to his head. He smiled and began to dance around shouting and waving his hands in glee, his bad leg dragging slightly behind him as he circled around in his mirth.

Behind the trunk, Mog and Peg patted each other on the back, and - clasping their hands together - danced round and round in celebration of their cleverness.

XVI

Eneas shook his sister gently. "Berowen. Berowen. Time to arise sister."

"Another day already?" she asked yawning.

"Yes and you are the last to awake this morning. Even mother is ready before you this day," he grinned.

"Why did no-one wake me sooner?" she enquired somewhat tetchily.

"Lord Thurstan told me you were the last to fall asleep last night so father thought we should let you rest for as long as possible."

"And how could Thurstan possibly have known that?" she asked, her agitation clearly showing now. She stood up and brushed down her clothes. Looking around the cave, she observed the activity that was taking place in readiness for their departure.

Berowen was angry at not being woken sooner, and she hurriedly rolled up her bedding. She was embarrassed to think that Thurstan had seen her unrest the night before. Even though she knew he could not possibly have known what she was thinking, she felt that somehow he knew everything. With her bedding rolled and secured, she fumbled in her saddlebag to locate her comb. Unbraiding her hair, she glanced around the cave for Thurstan, but he was nowhere to be seen. She roughly combed through her hair, her eyes continually searching, before re-braiding it into plaits.

"Father," she asked Aelwulf. "Where is our guide?"

"He left to travel further down towards the valley just before Eneas woke you, presumably to scout ahead," came the reply.

"Hmph," replied Berowen under her breath.

Not hearing this, her father asked his daughter if she had slept well, to which Berowen replied that she had, well enough, considering. The packhorses had been loaded up once again, and the horses saddled and tacked ready for the day ahead.

"I do not know how we are going to get these horses to walk down that ledge again, Eneas," Ethwen voiced her concern.

"I am sure the ledge must be big enough mother, after all Lord Thurstan would not lead us this way if they were not," Eneas continued smiling at her fondly.

"I think, Eneas," cut in Berowen. "Mother wonders how our horses will cope with their surroundings not the size of the ledge. It is not a natural place for a horse to be after all is it?"

"Sister, you have woken with a sore temper this day," he said, one eyebrow raised. "What ails you?"

"I am quite well, thank you Eneas," she snapped back. "I just wish you had woken me earlier."

She snatched up her bedding and walked to her horse. Eneas followed her and, grabbing her round her waist from behind, tickled her. She brushed his hands away and tutted but he persisted relentlessly until she turned around swiftly and glared at him, hands on her hips. He immediately mimicked her stance and pulled a face at her. A smile slowly found her lips and she laughed. Berowen could never remain angry with Eneas for long, and as usual he had managed to lighten her mood. She kissed him on his right cheek and threw her arms around him. As she did so she noticed Thurstan re-appear through the waterfall. She pulled away from her brother and following her gaze, he turned to watch Thurstan approaching her father.

"Aelwulf, the path ahead seems safe. If we leave now we should reach the valley below by late afternoon. Are we ready to move?"

"We are ready Thurstan," Aelwulf responded.

Berowen followed Thurstan to the front of the cave where the early light filtered through the cascading water. She cupped her hands and thrust them into the icy cold downpour, drinking thirstily.

Behind her Thurstan kicked dust into the dying flames of the fire. Berowen went to the back of the caverns to fetch her horse.

"Come daughter," called out Aelwulf.

XVII

The travellers walked through the cascading water one by one out on to the ledge and, with Thurstan leading, they continued their journey down the slippery path. Now with one horse less, the luggage, food and extra equipment had been shared between three of the horses so that Oswald could use the other as his mount. The group hardly spoke such was their concentration in the difficult descent. They knew from yesterday how one false move could mean disaster and so most of their concentration was focused on where they put their feet, and in keeping their mounts calm.

They groped their way slowly down until at last the ledge became wider and the steep gorge grew shallower, and they at last reached level ground. It had begun to rain and all were relieved that they had reached the bottom as to have made that descent in pouring rain would have been even more treacherous.

Thurstan halted Ora. "We will rest here," he shouted to Aelwulf. "We are to travel across open ground again and need to gather our strength."

The party pulled over their hoods and prepared themselves for a damp journey in the open.

There was no argument at Thurstan's suggestion and everyone except Berowen sat down and heaved a sigh of relief. Berowen passed her water bottle to her mother and let her eyes wander over the landscape before them. She couldn't see much as the rain was now falling from the sky so heavily that anything from a few feet away was obscured. The heavy downpour caused Ethwen to voice her concern as to the safety of the luggage, in particular the delicate gown, but Berowen tried to reassure her that it should be perfectly safe from the elements. Much effort had been made to ensure that all baggage had been packed so that it would be safe from bad weather, but upon her mother's concern about the dress, it urged Berowen to check that her lute was securely contained where it hung from her saddle.

The water splashed off the backs of the horses and soon the ground around the travellers became a patchwork of muddy puddles and the hems of the two ladies' tunics became sodden. No-one from the group of bedraggled travellers looked forward to the road ahead in such uncomfortable conditions, but travel it they must for there was nowhere for them to take shelter where they were.

After a short while, the heavy shower eased off slightly and it became easier to see the landscape around them. It was then that Thurstan mounted his mare and suggested that they recommence their journey.

The shower seemed to be over as quickly as it had begun and it was not long before the travellers could remove their hoods and enjoy the warming sun again. The steam rose from their cloaks as the warmth evaporated the drops of rain on the sodden material. Thurstan urged his mare into a canter, and the remainder of the group followed suit.

Berowen could now see the landscape around her. It was not very different from the grasslands around Brundannon apart from the odd outcroppings of grey stones that broke up the starkness. There were a few scrawny looking trees dotted around and a few bushes, but other than that, they were completely in the open.

As they travelled further, the ground around them began to change in appearance and they were soon on open moorland. In the distance, they could see a range of hills and Berowen assumed that it was to these hills that they would be heading. The sun had begun its journey into the west and she supposed that Thurstan would be trying to get them to a more sheltered spot for their evening camp. However, Thurstan reined his horse to the left and Berowen realised that he had other plans.

XVIII

Mog and Peg did not like the rain. It made the hare pelts heavy upon their slight frames, so when the heavy downpour had commenced they had both huddled together under the large mossy rock that was Mog's nest. They sat and shivered as they watched the puddles splash into the stream beside them, and after a while they dozed off, snoring happily to themselves.

Further down the hillside, across the other side of the stream, the man huddled in his own den. Unlike the faeries, he could not fall asleep. Instead, he shivered in fear as he remembered the last time the rain had come to the Writhing Wood. His ears were constantly alert for the low rumble that could mean the beast was searching for him again. The occasion was so fresh in his addled mind that he overlooked the fact that it often rained through the trees without such a threat - to him the menace was too recent and the thought of a repetition terrified him.

When the heavy drops turned into a lighter shower, the man poked his head out of his den and sniffed the air. He scratched at the irritating itch that persisted to annoy him upon his left shoulder-blade but could not quite reach it satisfactorily so had no choice but to stand in the rain and rub his shoulder against the oak tree's rough bark. He sighed with pleasure at the relief and closed his eyes as he continued to rub up and down. It was always the same; once he started to scratch his back, he could never stop – there was always the need to repeat the process on the other side to ensure that the whole area of his back felt the same satisfaction.

Back under the rock Mog and Peg continued in their noisy slumber completely unaware that the rain had nearly stopped. It was a small herd of deer coming to the stream to drink that stirred them into wakefulness. They yawned, stretched their tiny arms and smacked their own lips together at the sound of the deer sucking up the water. Crawling out from the gap underneath the rock, they knelt down amongst the creatures and took a drink in their cupped hands. The deer took no notice of them and continued with their own business before the herd made its way back into the maze of tree trunks.

Looking down the stream, with a quizzical look upon their wrinkled faces, the two faeries watched as the man continued to scratch himself. They looked at each other and with a slight shrug of their shoulders, wandered off into the wood.

XIX

Thurstan knew that they would not reach the foothills before daylight failed them so he decided that they should rest at the ring of seven stones known as The Old Men of the Moor. Thurstan knew they would offer shelter, albeit with a small amount of comfort, but they would shield the travellers from any winds that may sweep across the open moorland during the hours of darkness.

No-one knew for how long the stones had been there, nor for what reason they had really been placed, although it was told by many that they circled a sacred site, built by earlier inhabitants of the area and used for sacrifice. Thurstan decided, however, that he would ignore such tales, and hope that nothing untoward occurred during their rest that night. These tales were, after all, mostly based on mere superstition.

The sun was almost gone from sight on the horizon by the time the party arrived at the place of their evening's rest. There was an orange glow to the west and a chill in the air as they approached the ghostly figures of the Old Men.

Several of the horses shied as they passed through the stone circle and followed Thurstan as he led them to a sheltered spot within the ring.

Berowen's father dismounted and approached Thurstan and spoke in hushed tones to him.

"My Lord Thurstan," began Aelwulf under his breath. "I have heard of this place. Why are we resting here? If tales told are true, then we are indeed treading on dangerous ground," he continued whispering so that no others overheard his anguished enquiry.

"There are many tales recited around camp fires, my lord Aelwulf," responded Thurstan in a quiet tone as he unsaddled his mare. "These very moors are said to be a fearsome place once the sun has left this world in the command of the moon. Tales are told for many reasons, and we should be choosy which tales we treat as mere yarns and which we treat as true."

"And you treat the tales of this great circle as mere yarns, my lord?" enquired Aelwulf. "I fear that you may be a fool if you do."

"I did not say that, sire – there could well be truth behind such recitals, but I have rested here on more than one occasion and have encountered no such reality. Call me a fool if you will, my lord, but I can only assure you that this is the safest place to rest on *these* moors".

Aelwulf turned to look at the others. "What, then, my lord, do you see upon the faces of these people, who seem even too afraid to dismount their horses?"

"I see fear in their eyes, Aelwulf. They clearly believe in their own heard tales, but.... and his voice trailed off when he saw the look on Aelwulf's face turn to one of disbelief and concern.

"There is one – who is not yet among them – whose look reveals something else," said Aelwulf quietly. Thurstan followed his gaze, and saw Berowen, and upon seeing her, he suddenly became uneasy with his decision to make camp where he had.

Berowen had reined her horse to a halt before crossing the perimeter of the circle. As the shape of the ring of stones had loomed out of the fading light, she had become uneasy. She knew not why, but a feeling of foreboding had washed over her, enveloping her in a cloak of mistrust and fear. She had felt unbelievably cold, as if the icy breath of some unseen being washed over her, and her skin had prickled with goosebumps that travelled across every inch of her skin.

"I have seen this place before, I am sure of it," said Berowen as her father and Thurstan approached, the latter placing his hands around the reins of her mount.

Thurstan shot her a puzzled look. "I thought you had never travelled this far before, my lady," he asked stiffly.

Both Berowen and her father were alarmed at the tone of his voice. "That is true my lord Thurstan, I have not, and yet I know I have seen this place." She searched in the back of her mind trying to remember. "What is its name, where are we?" she asked him.

"It is a sacred.....," began Aelwulf before Thurstan could reply, but Thurstan interrupted for fear of her father saying something to her that would either addle her thoughts or put even more fear within her.

"The place is known as The Old Men of the Moor; an ancient stone circle that has stood for many hundreds of years according to scholars and storytellers alike my lady," continued Thurstan.

"But something occurred here. It is so barren. There is a stillness here. A smell of death," continued Berowen.

Thurstan looked at her and did not respond to this statement immediately. He then insisted of her, "You must remember how you know of this place." He tightened his hand on the reins of her horse as if to prevent her from escaping his interrogation.

Berowen began to feel unwell and a wave of panic and a despair that she had never felt before began to overcome her.

"Your persistence is becoming irksome and worrying my lord. I tell you that I cannot remember and your questioning is clouding my memory even more," she retorted angrily. "Unhand the reins, my lord. I will not be tormented so by a man who I know not, and who has come upon our company as a guide with no proof of his real intentions."

"Daughter!" roared Aelwulf. "I shall not suffer such ill-manners from one so high born as yourself. Your tongue will remain still from further such outbursts."

"Father, you are bewitched by some sorcery from this fellow, methinks," replied Berowen completely unaware of her father's recent concerns aired to Thurstan in private. "He has brought us to this place intentionally I fear. He wishes some evil to befall us. We are not safe here – there is a curse amongst these stones, I can feel it!" she exclaimed, her eyes wild with a fierceness her family had never witnessed before.

She pulled backwards on her reins hard, forcing Thurstan to let go or be dragged off his feet by the suddenness of her movement. Eneas and Amleth looked at their sister with shock upon their faces at her sudden outburst. This was not the Berowen they knew.

At that moment a vicious wind blew through the stone circle and enveloped each of those within its confines with an icy grip. They all shivered and pulled their cloaks around them tightly, terrified at the wind's intervention. It blew out of the circle and beyond into the darkness of the moor.

Berowen looked almost feral as she sat upon her agitated horse; the cloak of her hood had fallen to her shoulders in the wake of the sudden gust of wind and her hair had loosened from its plait and tumbled freely down her back. Her face had changed from one of serenity to one of terror. Her once clear complexion became distorted with thin grey lines that aged her instantly as the air blew around her. Her russet locks greyed before everyone's eyes and she wailed, "Can you not smell the stench of burning flesh, or the roar from its gaping maw?"

Ethwen shuddered in her saddle at the sight and words of her daughter. Before her very eyes, Berowen had become possessed. This was no longer her child before her and she dismounted her horse and ran to her husband's side grabbing his arm in fear. Would her daughter ever return?

"Husband," she wailed. "What is to be done? Do something, Aelwulf!"

"Good wife, I know not……," stuttered Aelwulf.

Amleth urged his horse out of the realm of the circle. "Everyone…move out of its grip!" he cried. He reached Berowen and grabbing the reins of her horse he tried to move it further away from the evil that seemed to have come upon the wind from within the Old Men and had somehow entered into her sister's body. As Amleth tried to pull Berowen's horse round his sister suddenly drew the sword from its scabbard.

"You will not touch me!" she hissed, her voice low and menacing. "You will unhand me, or you *will* lose your hand." She glared at him from beneath the wild strands of hair that covered her stricken face. "You have been warned," she spat, thin strands of spittle hanging from her bottom lip as she spoke the words between clenched teeth.

Amleth withdrew his arm from the reins and pulled his own horse to a halt. "Sister," he shouted. "Tis I, Amleth, your brother. You would harm *me?*"

Amleth saw, with the utmost dread, that there was no recognition in those black eyes that stared back at him. His horse was agitated and would not stand still – it paced back and forth and round and round. As it swung around once more Amleth saw his brother, Eneas, at his sister's opposite side, just as he also saw the blade swing downwards and heard a sickening thud.

All at once he heard his mother scream and his brother shout "Noooo!" He too, heard himself utter that same exclamation. He saw his father running forward and Thurstan grabbing the reins of Berowen's horse.

Lightning crashed down from the heavens and landed in the middle of the stone circle, its place of impact illuminated by a bright white light. The patch of grass in the very centre flickered into life and a glowing blaze soon took hold; it remained in the centre and did not spread, but lit up the area, throwing eerie shadows across the seven stones. The smouldering earth created a cloud of smoke that spiralled upwards into the night sky.

XX

Mog blew her horn. The sound echoed through the creaking boughs and all those who would travel raised their heads. It was time.

The man heard the horn's call as he was quietly dozing, his back supported by the large rock. He jumped up as best he could considering his aching limbs, and raised his head to the call. Something within him urged him to answer the horn's call and he bellowed with all his might – his call echoing back through the trees. Gradually the whole wood became alive with the sounds of beasts answering Mog's summons.

As Mog stood upon her mossy rock, gradually others of her kind – including those she knew, but had not seen since they had returned to Writhing Wood the spring before - occupied the ground around her. There was Peg, Knot and Bark, Root and Sap, Piggle and Woggle amongst many others. Once upon a time creatures that only those that lived within the embrace of the wood would know, some perhaps too peculiar to try to describe to those ignorant of their existence, would have also joined them. But in recent years they had vanished one by one and this year it would seem that the latest disappearance were the group of man-horses that had dwelt in the deepest part of the wood. Mog knew why, but the other animals and birds were blissfully ignorant of such things, and were to remain so for the time being at least. It was not of their concern until if and when their time came.

The tiny glade was soon full of bodies of all shapes and sizes, all jostling for position to be at the head of the line, but all stood back when the sound of large paws rustling the dead leaves approached. They knew it signalled the arrival of the beast of the wood – the giant, pink tongue lolling from its large tooth-filled jaws, and the red eyes glowing as it scoured its surrounds for any available victim of its terror-filled growl. Scrimble's dark shape loomed into view and his presence brought a heavy silence amongst those already at the meeting place by the stream. No-one argued with Scrimble and everyone accepted his place in the hierarchy of the dark wood. As he paced around the area, marking his scent on every available bush or tree trunk, Mog jumped down from her rock and warily approached him. Placing one foot in front of the other, she stooped into a low bow before him. Scrimble looked in her direction, sniffed the air and continued with his business around the foliage.

The man made it his business never to join the main group of creatures and as usual at this auspicious time he held back in the shadows of the wood, and watched the proceedings from a safe distance, his crown of ivy firmly seated upon his head.

It was nearly dusk, and it would soon be time to begin the journey up the hill and over the tor to the moor and the safety of the Forest of Whispers beyond. The creatures by the stream jostled and fidgeted as they awaited the signal from Mog. It was all very precise – she would not issue the call to move until she deemed the time completely right. Mog and her kind would lead the way with lanterns in case the full moon should become shrouded in cloud and Scrimble would follow behind his bearers. Then would come the more lowly of the creatures of Writhing Wood. The man would follow at a safe distance behind. Those at the rear would be at the mercy of the pale light of the moon and if she should fail them, then they would stumble in the darkness.

XXI

As the lightning had fallen to the earth from the cloudless sky Berowen's horse had reared, unseating her. She had slid to the ground with a thump, but in her possessed state she had immediately jumped to her feet ignoring any pain that would have obviously ricocheted through her body when it met with the earth. Still holding the bloody sword she swung it around her head and then stood, with feet apart as if daring anyone else to approach, with both arms outstretched in front of her. The wildness in her eyes had not abated and she snorted with anger, more and more spittle oozing from between her clenched teeth.

Amleth lay where he had been felled from his own horse. The sword had cut into his flesh just below the shoulder and he remained on the ground not daring to move in case his 'sister' attempted another attack. Likewise his mother, father and brother dared not move to his aid for fear of an outburst of spite from the raging harridan in front of them.

They had all shaken as the light from the sky had struck the ground behind them. Instinctively they had crouched to the ground with their hands covering their heads. The horses had all scattered into the darkness, including Thurstan's Ora; she had broken loose from her tethering within the stone circle and had galloped off screaming in terror.

One of the soldiers whispered to the man next to him, "How come that there fire keeps alight? There ain't nothing to burn but damp earth." His neighbour shook his head and shrugged his shoulders nervously. "'Tis eerie magick," he answered. "And why don't it spread? 'Tis sorcery if you asks me. They say this place is bewitched by devils and after tonight I be of the same mind."

"It would be stupid for a man to make a fire that will set alight the very moor upon which he is to travel," came a voice from within the smoke. "What a great error of alchemy that would prove to be."

The two men did not move, but froze to the spot – the only movement being the wide eyes within their heads as they looked at each other in horror at the sound of the unknown voice behind them.

"Psst," said one of the men in the direction of Aelwulf. "My Lord, psst. There be someone else 'ere behind us."

"Psst?" repeated the voice. "A strange noise to utter from a man's mouth I must say. It is the sound of the adder that you make – are you an adder?"

"Who goes there?" shouted Aelwulf in the direction of the blaze. "Show yourself and declare your identity."

"Show myself and declare *my* identity is it?" the voice said in response. "You walk upon my brethren and it is *you* who demand *my* identity?"

As Berowen continued to twitch behind them, Aelwulf and Thurstan turned and walked slowly towards the fire, swords drawn.

"If I were you, I would watch my back," offered the voice. "*It* is not to be trifled with, as I think you may well have learned to your detriment this very hour."

The two men returned to face Berowen and discovered to their horror that she was moving slowly towards them, as if stalking her prey. Amleth instinctively curled himself into a ball as she stealthily walked past him. She looked down at him briefly and curled her lip, the sword in her hand lowering to prod him as she did so. But she left him alone from further injury, and her gaze reverted back towards Aelwulf and Thurstan.

"You require the assistance of this old man and his brethren, methinks," continued the voice as the two men walked slowly backwards towards the light from the fire. "It seems the time is nigh for us to rise and thwart this impending escape of the evil one."

Aelwulf and Thurstan continued to walk slowly backwards. The heat from the fire grew warmer as they approached it, and the voice became louder.

"Just keep walking as you are, make no sudden moves and pass by the flames," the instructions continued. "And everyone else remain rooted to the very spot upon which you stand as if the horned one was standing right in front of you. Utter no words and move not a muscle within your bodies. Above all else, all those present must … *will* … trust me."

As the two men passed the fire, an old man stepped forward. A cowl of grey linen covered his skeletal head. Two piercing blue eyes stared forth from the sockets that sat in the taut-skinned covered skull. A grey beard hung from his chin in a long plait and his bent body slowly crept forward through the smoke and flames. All could see that he was not merely old, but ancient. His bony hands hung from his tattered sleeves and his bony bare feet shuffled across the earth.

He began to chant:

> *"Seven brethren of the broken circle round,*
> *Here is your eighth to make your circle complete."*

A rumble filled the air and the earth began to shake as the stones wobbled in the ground. Berowen halted in her tracks and snarled at the old man. Her dark eyes turned red, her face grimaced and she cackled – the sound sending fear through everyone present, except the old man, who stood his ground and did not waiver from the beast before him.

> *"These past centuries have flown in peace*
> *But it was foretold she would come upon us*
> *The roots of your stones have held you fast*
> *Deep in the earth that hides its lair*
> *The lair you have guarded for days and nights uncountable*
> *But as was foretold she has come upon us*
> *Upon this eve of shadows*
> *When the night is thin and easily crossed.*
> *Make haste my brethren for the beast is out*
> *And a pestilence it will leave in its wake."*

There was an eerie silence that fell upon the circle, apart from the snarling and mad laughing from Berowen, but the vibrations deep beneath their feet continued.

> *"Seven brethren of the broken circle round,*
> *Here is your eighth to make your circle complete."*

"Do as I bid and arise!"

The old man walked backwards into the fire and stood amongst the flames. At that moment there came upon the circle a huge grinding sound as the stones began to move with more speed. It was if they were being pushed upwards from some great strength beneath the ground. The air was filled with dust and smoke, and Aelwulf and Thurstan began to cough as the dust began to penetrate their lungs. No-one dared move.

Then silence fell as the dust settled and the smoke dissipated to reveal the circle of stones flattened. The great slabs lay on the ground, their runic symbols pointing skywards. Sulphurous smoke began to rise from the symbols and the gaping holes left in the ground. Soon the circle was enveloped in a haze of yellowish mist. As it continued to rise the group saw figures that seemed to materialise from the within the smoke. They twisted and turned as if in their own private agony, writhing as the furls of smoke wrapped itself around their tortured bodies. From each of the seven dark gaping holes a tall figure took shape. All were covered with gowns of the finest black cloth, decorated with the same symbols that were etched upon the stones. Black cowls hung loosely over their heads and cast a shadow over their features.

Then, from out of the flames stepped the eighth and he positioned himself in the broken circle to make it complete.

Berowen moved forward, with her eyes glowering in her lowered head.

The eight figures slowly raised their right hands and as they did so, the cloth fell away to reveal that each carried what appeared to be a small pebble in their right palm. It was not until these pebbles began to unwind themselves that all present realised that they were tiny serpents. As they unfurled they coiled themselves around the wrists of those holding them.

The eighth began to chant in a foreign tongue, words that came fast and made no sense to any that were present other than the other seven figures, which all began to chant the same words in unison. The speech became faster and louder, and the serpents were raised higher and higher until all the figures stood with their right hands raised above their heads. The writhing forms hissed as they swung from the wrists.

Berowen screamed and ran towards them screeching something that seemed to be in the same tongue.

The eighth figure raised his left hand and gently lowered it, and as he did so the serpent released itself from its grip around his wrist. At the signal from the eighth, the serpents from the other seven brethren slowly uncoiled themselves and all eight dropped to the ground together. They slithered along the ground towards Berowen, who immediately came to a halt. They hissed at her and she recoiled slightly before raising herself to her full height and screaming. The serpents formed a circle around her where she stood and slowly began to wrap themselves around her legs, some of them climbing their way up her body, four remaining around her ankles. As she began to struggle, the creatures began to grow longer and their girth increased. The four around her ankles buried themselves head first into the ground and re-emerged on the other side of her foot and coiled themselves around and around, tightening their grip so she could not move. Those two around her arms dived head first into the ground and their strength pulled her downwards and secured her arms against the soil. She was now on her belly, one of the remaining last two serpents wrapping itself around her neck so as to keep her head steady.

At the sight of her daughter covered in the writhing creatures, Ethwen had to stifle her anguish as she remembered the old man's instructions. She had to trust him, she could do nothing else, but to see what was taking place before her was becoming unbearable to watch.

The remaining serpent dropped to the ground in front of the trapped girl's face. But Berowen still spat and snarled as it stared at her, a hair's breadth away from her nose. It flicked out its tongue and smelt the air.

The chanting had not ceased as the serpents performed their task and trapped Berowen in their writhing grip. As the remaining serpent had faced Berowen the chanting had increased, and then suddenly stopped. The horrified spectators watched as the head of the serpent began to change. Its skull grew in size and began to sprout human features until the ill-formed creature looked repulsive with its scaly body and the pale wraith-like head of a woman. She opened her mouth and uttered forth a low guttural sound as she closed it around Berowen's mouth and nose. The body of the serpent twitched as she inhaled deeply, its girth slowly growing larger as something seemed to enter into it. Berowen could do nothing in the grip of the creature that seemed to be sucking out her very being.

Ethwen could bear it no longer and breathed in sharply in shock as she had watched the serpent's head transform into the hideous head. She dropped to her knees and wailed.

The dark sky above suddenly clouded over, and a howling wind whipped around the feet of those standing watching the macabre events before them. It called for its victim as it wrapped itself around Berowen and the serpent-creature that held her in its grip.

Suddenly the head pulled away and Berowen fell silent. Her body relaxed and she fell into unconsciousness. The head shrunk in a flash, and the fattened serpent flicked its tongue once more in the air, before its body returned to its normal size and it slithered back to the eighth figure. The others released Berowen from their grip and they too slowly shrunk, before they returned to their masters.

Recoiled in the master's palms the yellow smoke returned once more and the figures melted back into the holes. The eighth figure returned to the fire, which flickered and spat as he entered into its centre. The smoke and dust returned and the sound of grating stone filled the air.

All became quiet again; the clouds left the sky, and as the dust and smoke cleared the circle of seven once again stood rooted to the spot as if they had never moved.   The beast had been returned to its lair among the roots of the stones and there it would remain until a chance once again revealed itself for its escape.

For the last time, the old man again stepped forth from the fire and clapped his hands as if to break a spell. "It is done," he announced.

Ethwen rushed forward to her daughter who had collapsed where she lay.   She was unconscious and was bleeding from her nose. She looked exhausted and pale, and Ethwen was relieved to see that she was still alive after her ordeal.

Eneas ran to Amleth to help him to his feet and to examine the wound that Berowen had inflicted upon her brother in her torment.

Aelwulf and Thurstan bowed deeply before the old man. "My deepest thanks," said Aelwulf. "I am not sure how we can repay you for your intervention upon this strange eve, sire."

"There is no requirement for repayment, my lord," replied the old man. "Other than to pay heed to tales that you hear in future, especially on such an eve as this."

Thurstan stepped forward and knelt before the old man.

"You have been travelling for too long, my lord Thurstan," began the old man. "You have slept upon the ground of my brethren on many occasions and they have cared for you and guarded you in your slumbers, but to bring others amongst them on this evening of the year was foolish. I can only assume that you had forgotten the day upon which you are travelling."

"I did, and I beg your forgiveness and that of your brethren," replied Thurstan somewhat sheepishly, in his embarrassment completely overlooking the fact that this old man knew his name and that he had camped at this place before, facts that at any other time would have shocked and worried him.

"I know not where you are travelling, Thurstan, but I would tread your path with care, for the young woman is obviously susceptible to all things unworldly. She has a power about her that she is clearly unaware that she does possess. This is a dangerous mix. There are many creatures out there who would take advantage of her openness with glee and misconduct. One such did this eve.   And as you saw, it had great mischief and malevolence about it. There are worse to be encountered if the traveller is not wary, Thurstan, believe me…much worse."

Thurstan rose to his feet and turned to look at the sleeping figure lying in her mother's lap.

The old man tapped him lightly on the shoulder with a bony finger, "If you would kindly humour my old curiosity, I would be interested to hear why you travel this road. There are not many who would travel this way, by choice."

"The girl is to be wed to Brack, son of Modig of Grimfell in the Wellonaw Marshes. I am riding with them as I was travelling the same road," explained Thurstan. "We have ridden from Brundannon, beyond the mountain and the Blue Wood."

"Wellanaw Marshes? Then why are you taking this road? It would, should it not, have been more prudent to have taken the more normal path out of the wood?" questioned the old man.

Thurstan continued, "We were attacked by a party of foul men that came upon us as we travelled the path through the wood. I have heard of their kind, but had never *seen* their likes before. Their appearance before us urged me to reconsider our route."

As Thurstan explained their arrival at the Old Men of the Moor to the old man, Aelwulf joined them and silently listened with interest.

"How so did they look?" enquired the old man, clearly intrigued by this snippet of information, so intent on the answer that he somewhat rudely ignored the arrival of

Aelwulf to their deliberations.

"Hair and beards as red as the embers in a dying fire with horses of great size to fit their riders' large countenance," replied Thurstan, himself slightly nodding his head at the other man's arrival.

"Hmmm," considered the old man, scratching his forehead. "Red you say….large horses. And did those horses have armour and trophies about their great bodies?"

Thurstan nodded. "You have heard of them too, it seems."

"Oh yes, indeed I have," nodded the old man as he tapped his cheek with one bony finger. "It seems you may have come across someone on your road that it would be far better not to have encountered. You were perhaps wise not to continue upon the more direct route."

"How so?" interrupted Aelwulf. "Who are they and from whence do they hail?"

"They are from the bog lands far across the sea to the west. Formidable and dirty fighters by all accounts – I am somewhat amazed that you all survived their attention," replied the old man.

"There were but eleven riders," said Aelwulf. "We lost two of our party, but they lost most of theirs. Those left standing retreated."

"Good fortune, then, rode with you," said the old man. "Or, perchance, something a little more," he continued as he looked towards Berowen.

"However, enough of this chitter-chatter," announced the old man suddenly, and he called out into the darkness. Soon the sound of hooves announced the return of the horses, Ora appearing first followed by the others. "Remember that these beasts are sensitive to evil, Thurstan. In future it would be wise to take heed of their warnings."

"But…" continued Aelwulf. "What more of these red-bearded men? Is our party in danger, more so than we had first imagined?"

"I can tell you no more, for I have no more information to tell," said the old man as he shuffled across to where Amleth sat while his brother tended his wound.

"You were lucky," he said. "She could have removed the head from your neck if she had so wished. The beast had not quite taken control of her completely or you would have been cut in two instead of just nursing a mere scratch."

He cast his hand over the wound and to Amleth's astonishment the stinging and discomfort waned until it had disappeared completely, along with the bloody gash.

"My thanks, sire," he stuttered in disbelief. "How did you ......?" he began.

"Bah," said the old man with a wave of his bony hand. "Do you really think I would tell?"

"I must leave you all now," and he walked back to the fire. As he passed Berowen where she still lay unconscious in her mother's lap he looked down and gestured something with his hand over her head, muttering words under his breath.

"Pretty young thing," he muttered as he stepped into the flames and disappeared.

XXII

To pass the time until Mog decided the moment was upon them to move, the faeries began to sing and dance. It was the same every year and they all knew that Mog could be awkward upon this eve. She was old, and she was cantankerous and she always wanted her own faerie way. If any creature took it upon themselves to begin the journey on their own accord she would become mean old Mog and throw stones, twigs or acorns at them – in fact anything she could get her tiny wrinkled hands upon. As Scrimble was beast of the wood, then Mog was faerie of the wood.

It would not be known by any, other than their kind, that the easiest way to tell the age of a faerie is by counting the wrinkles upon their faces. This exercise would never be easy for several reasons. The first being that they are born already possessing their first wrinkles – some more so than others, depending upon the amount of wrinkles that each of their parents had when the child faerie was born. Add to this the fact that it is a most tiresome way to spend one's time trying to count the wrinkles upon a face that belongs to one of the most fidgety beings in existence, so most give up after the fourth day of trying and go about their other business. There is more to faerie life than trying to ascertain who is the oldest anyway. It matters not in the grand faerie scheme of things.

Thus Mog had taken it upon herself to assume the position of Most Important Faerie of this particular wood and none of the others could really be bothered to challenge this call. Hence they found themselves having to endure such pedantic idiosyncrasies that Mog had adopted over the years such as making everyone wait until the 'right time' arrived. This 'right time' was, of course, merely when Mog decided it was the 'right time', and until then the gathering would have to wait.

So all the others of her kind had learned long ago that to ignore was the best policy and took up their own entertainment to while away the hours between the first call of Mog's horn and the final triumphant blow that signalled that she was now ready to lead them onwards.

Deep down they all loved Mog, and they knew that she was just full of her own importance, and a faerie of an uncertain age who is full of her own importance has to be tolerated rather than ignored, thus avoiding the sting and resulting bruise from a tossed stone.

So the singing and dancing took place. Of course, none of the other creatures understood what the little folk were singing about, but if they had, they would have heard:

Woodlewose Woodlewose
He has lost the gift of speech
Woodlewose Woodlewose
Words are always just out of reach
Woodawasa, Woodowoso
So he just grunts and growls
Woodawasa, Woodowoso
And in the thunder he just howls

And then they would all lie down on their backs, wave their little legs in the air, rub their tiny hands upon their stomachs, and giggle at the thought, before all getting to their feet again to continue their singing and dancing.

A little further away, the man continued to stand in the shadows of the trees where he watched the entertainment. He had no idea what the little creatures were saying – their voices were soft and the words in a jumbled up tongue – but the ivy crown upon his head slipped this way and that slightly as he nodded his head back and forth to the rhythm of their dance.

He *was* the wildman of the woods, he *was* the woodwose, but to him these titles meant nothing. He had no name that he called himself – he had no memory of such things and never thought of such things either. The name that the world around him saw fit to call him was nothing to do with him at all, and even if he had known, he would not have cared.

To others it would be plain that the faeries were making a fool of him, but to him they were just singing a happy song and dancing a faerie jig.

XXIII

The company were shocked and stunned by the recent events that had befallen them. Berowen was still deeply asleep, and Amleth was back on his feet after his peculiar and miraculous recovery.

Behind them the fire still burned brightly – it seemed as if the old man had graced them with one small last favour by keeping it alight. If he had not done so, then they would have been all plunged into darkness save for the silvery light of the fat moon that shone overhead. It was clear that they could not return inside the circle that night and it was obvious also that they could not wander too far on to the moor in the darkness. They had no choice but to set up camp as far from the circle as was feasible, whilst retaining as much as possible of the light it afforded. They built another fire and all but one of those still awake sat around it enjoying the warmth and welcome glow from its flames.

Thurstan kept himself to himself after the possible disastrous repercussions that could have arisen after the error of his judgement. This error could have cost the lives of all those with him, as well as countless other innocents if whatever evil that had possessed Berowen had been allowed to roam freely across the land.

He was deeply embarrassed and ashamed that his actions could have had such a horrendous result and he thought it wise to stay apart from the others. So he sat at the edge of the camp slowly smoking his pipe and staring into the heart of the fire from a distance.

It was Eneas who decided to break the cold atmosphere that seemed to share the fire with the travellers.

He stood quietly beside Thurstan and reached into the pouch at his side, retrieving his own long pipe. "The scent of your smoke is sweet my lord Thurstan. I do not think I have ever had the pleasure of tasting of its variety. May I be rude and request a nip to try?"

Thurstan, without a word, reached into his pouch and gave Eneas what he had requested.
"My thanks my lord," Eneas said as he packed his bowl with the mixture. "A light and I shall return to discuss with you its merits."

A few moments later he returned and sat himself quietly beside Thurstan and began to puff on the pipe stem.

"A word of caution, my lord Eneas," spoke Thurstan as he exhaled, his gaze still fixed upon the fire. "This variety is sure to be stronger than any you have tasted."

However, his words were too late. Eneas had taken a hearty puff as he was used to doing with his own mild mixture and began to cough violently as it burned and irritated his throat. He turned to look at Thurstan, his eyes watering with the effects of his discomfort. "You are not incorrect, my lord."

"It seems I was tardy with my words of watchfulness, for which I am sorry", Thurstan said in reply.

"No matter," responded Eneas, still spluttering. "I should have been more wary of a new mixture, but I am not one for treading carefully, my lord."

"So it would seem, my lord," agreed Thurstan. "But I do admit that it caught me out when I first lit a bowl."

Eneas laughed. "Ha, I do oft wonder whether to inhale the soothing smoke is really a good thing to do, for it does cause fits of coughing occasionally. But it does make for a relaxing pastime after a long day riding…..and fighting….and dealing with sisters who wield swords in a way that they really should not."

He laughed louder, "Upon my word, she will be beside herself when she awakes and learns of her abominable behaviour. She will be mortified to hear what an ill-headed flap-dragon she turned into."

Thurstan's gaze left the fire. "I do not think it was such a good game as to warrant such mirth, my lord Eneas."

"Ah, my lord," laughed Eneas. "It was not when it was taking place, but upon my weary soul, and in my beetle-brained head it is now it is over."

Thurstan half-smiled.

"Have you ever seen such a quiet lass suddenly turn into such an ill-tempered baggage as my sister did?" continued Eneas encouraged by the curl of Thurstan's lip, albeit a slight one.

"I am not convinced that your brother will see it in such a jovial way," stated Thurstan knowing full well what Eneas was attempting to do.

"Bah," answered Eneas. "He knows it was not his sister that wounded him and has already said as such. He bears her no ill-feeling."

"Your mother and father, I fear, have their trust in me lessened greatly now," continued Thurstan, not to be dissuaded from his melancholy.

"They are well aware, especially after what the old man told my father, that you have brought us all along this path for good reason. My father is old and therefore wiser than any of us, but he knows that what took place here was not of your making, nor your fault."

"He warned me of the dangers of the place, but I chose to think that I knew better, Eneas," explained Thurstan, digging the burning mixture in his pipe with his little finger.

"You were speaking of your experience of past visits here, Thurstan," said Eneas. "You can only tell people of what you know by your own experiences and therefore you did no wrong. My father was speaking to you of tales he had heard and you were speaking of the truth as you saw, and had lived it."

Thurstan began to puff on his stem again and blew out the smoke slowly. "What do you think of the mixture?" he said changing the subject.

"Its scent belied the kick of an angry boar, my lord," answered Eneas. "But it is pleasant enough if you like your throat scoured by a horse brush."

Thurstan laughed. And so did Eneas. Whilst Thurstan allowed the soothing mixture to slowly enter his body and fill it with a satisfying warmth, Eneas continued to splutter, choke, and laugh.

"By the by, my lord Eneas," announced Thurstan quietly. "In answer to your earlier question, yes I have met such a woman before."

Eneas looked stunned. Then let out a roar of laughter that cracked the silence around them. "Tell me more, my lord, I am agog."

XXIV

Peg cleared her throat as loudly as she dared next to Mog, but the latter just raised her head slightly and turned it in the other direction with her nose in the air. She stood with her arms folded across her chest and tapped one foot against the rock on which she was perched, as a warning to Peg.

As she turned, her eyes caught sight of Scrimble as he lay beside the stream, away from the others. His gaze met hers and she noticed the drool hanging in great globules from his large jaws. His tail twitched angrily and he half snarled at her, revealing a row of gleaming white teeth that seemed anxious to sink themselves into something soft and fleshy. Perhaps she was pushing her luck too far on this occasion. Even Scrimble had not been unknown to take full advantage of such a gathering and help himself to some easy pickings from amongst those lurking at the back of the congregation.

She jumped down from the rock and blew her horn, and the grand parade of different sizes and shapes cheered and started to follow the well-worn track that would take them above the treetops and to the tor. They were lucky; the moon was shining brightly and her light would aid them in their evening travels. After the faeries had led the way, all the others remained until Scrimble had stretched himself and had loped off after the leaders. They would keep a respectable distance from the great black wolf for they knew him to be unpredictable. At last, the wildman of the woods joined the end of the long line and bid farewell to the dark wood that had been his home for the past seven moons.

He reached the tor and the world around him opened up in the moonlight. There was a thin breeze that ruffled the ivy leaves in his crown, and his first reaction was to hold on to it for fear that it would blow away. He could make out the faint light in the distance ahead of him from the lanterns of the faeries and he began his descent from the tor over the rocky ground to the moor that spread out before him. He began to feel dread as he knew they would eventually reach the crossroads.

The cold metal of the frame, which hung from the wooden structure that stood menacingly in the centre of the meeting of the four roads, haunted his thoughts as he picked his way over the barren moorland.

He heard it before he saw it. The breeze had sent it swinging in the moonlight and the eerie sound of the squeaking of the rusty chains sent a shiver down his back. The noise echoed across the silence of the moorland and then the metal glinted in the silvery light. He hoped it would not still be there … the thing he noticed last time he passed. He didn't want to look but something would not let him pass without casting his eyes over the base of the structure. He knew the bones were still there – he could see the leg dangling through the bars, but this time it was stark and naked of all flesh and hair. The last time he had passed it, it was a mass of heaving worms and matted hair, the skull eyeless and the skin half eaten away.

Many moons before, when he had first seen the face in the stream when he had gone to refresh his thirst he had jumped back in fright. It had taken him a while to realise that the face staring back at him was his. Likewise, when he had seen the body in the cage on his return to the dark wood in the spring he had also jumped back in fright, this time when he realised that what was left of the body was just like him.

His eyes continued to search until at last they found it. It *was* still there. He shook his hairy fist at the moon for her daring to shed light upon the one thing he did not wish to see. Her pale finger of light cast itself upon the carving etched deep into the base of the scaffold; the crude carving of a man such as him, with a hound at his feet, its jaws firmly grasping his left leg.

It was as if the very moorland wished him to see it as a warning every time he passed by it from now until he no longer dwelt upon the land. The rest of the base was covered in lichen, which was slowly creeping its way up the supporting beam, but the carving remained untouched by its grasping clasp. It remained there for all to see. He shuddered and carried on his weary way after the others, the light at the head of the line faintly glimmering in the distance, and the sound of Scrimble as he occasionally stopped to howl to the moon.

XXV

It had been Thurstan who had awoken first just as the sun was beginning its ascent to the east. The fire in the ring of stones had not only gone out but all traces of it had disappeared completely. He had expected nothing less. The soldier who had taken the last watch had kept the party's fire fed and it still crackled and spat as Thurstan rose and walked to Ora. She was still half-asleep where she stood tethered, but upon hearing her master's gentle words of greeting she nickered and raised her muzzle as he gently stroked it. He saddled and pulled the bridle over her head before raising himself on to her back and urging her out of the camp and on to the moor. The sentry raised his hand in acknowledgement of Thurstan's leaving and settled back into his position where he could keep watch on the land around the camp.

Thurstan had slept fitfully and had decided to rise before the others and scout for a while on his own before the others were ready to continue the journey. The old man's words had un-nerved him slightly about the possible dangers ahead and he was aware that to make another foolish error would at best cause him to be cast out of the group or at worst would cause death to one of the travellers, Berowen being the most at risk.

He decided that he would ride Ora to the crossroads and then make his way back to the camp. If all looked well upon that part of the route he would encourage everyone to move as quickly as they could in order that they could cross that mark and therefore make the relative shelter of the Forest of Whispers before the next nightfall. The forest was by no means a safe place, but at least they would be under cover from spying eyes that could pick them out so easily whilst out in the open.

It did not take him long to reach the crossroads. Luckily their route did not send them across the middle of the moor, but off to the eastern side – a path that was relatively short to cross and if started early enough it could be achieved in a day's hard riding. His destination achieved, he dismounted Ora to stretch his legs and take a sip from his water carrier. Ora shied nervously away from the swinging gibbet and its occupant and placed herself a comfortable distance away from the abomination of death that sat awkwardly within the rusting cage. She grazed quietly as Thurstan examined the instrument of torture and inevitable cause of demise from this world. Its occupant was just a skeleton, the bones bleached by the recent summer sun. The bottom jaw hung down as if in a constant scream, and Thurstan pondered on whom the poor man had been and the nature of his crime that had inflicted such a foul punishment. He could only imagine how horrific it would be to find yourself placed in a gibbet without food or water, at the mercy of the elements and creatures that would wait by your side for the tasty meal that would be sure to arrive before too long. To sit and stare death in the face whilst those around you stared back, arguing amongst themselves as they jostled at the prospect of being first at the tastiest part, each silently marking their booty to themselves as the life ebbed away from you.

He assumed that eventually someone would come and take away the remains and dispose of them. Or perhaps they would stay there until a new occupant had been found to take up the lonely and desperate vigil of death.

There was something about the remains though that caused Thurstan some puzzlement. He didn't know why, but he paced around the metal cage trying to understand the reason. Then he looked down and saw the carving. Kneeling down he looked closely and gently brushed his fingertips across the figure. His fingers could feel faint indentations across the figure's body. He closed his eyes and as his fingers traced the marks he realised it was hair that had been faintly etched into the body. He knew then what the figure was. But why here? Standing up he looked again at the poor unfortunate seated within its prison. Was he really looking at a wodwos – a wildman of the woods?

There was not a man, woman or child who had not heard of such beings – they were the subject of many a yarn spoken to children and adults around campfires in settlements across the kingdom. It is not wise to wander too far into the woods on your own for fear of being killed and eaten by a wodwos. They ruled the woods and forests and did not take kindly to humans trespassing into their leafy homes. He had listened to many a tale about them and he had heard them called by many names, but wodwos was the name he had learned as he had grown up.

Forests and woods were their home…. and here he was leading a group of people into a forest. Did this creature in the gibbet before him once live in the forest to which they were destined? If so, would that mean they were safe from the attack from such a fearsome creature? Did he really believe in such tales? A few days ago he would have thought not, but after the events of the night before he began to doubt his views on the subject of yarns. Perhaps they were, after all, based on a truth, however ancient that truth may be.

He walked to Ora and raised himself into her saddle. As he rode back to the camp he thought about the possible discovery at the crossroads. Why would there be a carving of a wodwos on the very structure that held a corpse that indeed seemed to be more than a normal man? There was no settlement near to the crossroads so surely it could not be that of an ordinary felon –

why would it be placed so far from habitation? What warning could it possibly give to anyone situated at a place that is visited rarely by man? The four roads that meet at that place are ancient paths that led across the moors from the four points, but are not known to many people now.

However, if the wodwos did indeed exist in fact, and the corpse was once of flesh and blood then placing it there could well be a warning to all those others of its kind that may inhabit the woodland and forests to the edges of the moor. It must be so.

As the scenery passed by him as he rode, he wondered upon his next problem. Should he mention what he had discovered to those who followed his direction? They had put their trust in him to take them upon Grimfell and he had already almost failed them. If he was to hide the discovery from them and something did occur within the Forest of Whispers it could have disastrous consequences. However, if he were to tell them, would they wish to travel that way?

His early morning ride had posed him with a difficult problem it would seem. And he had no idea whatsoever how he would resolve it.

XXVI

The wildman had kept his distance from the others, but had managed to keep the lights in sight for the remainder of the journey across the moors. The sight at the crossroads had disturbed him greatly and he felt vulnerable in the open. He wished to reach the darkness of the trees as soon as he could, but he could walk no faster than he did. His leg was already aching from the continual marching and it would take many hours of rest to make him feel refreshed.

This annual journey was always one of those travels that were dependent upon the hours. When the moon had retired to sleep away the day it would be dangerous and foolish for any of the motley crew of creatures to be caught in the daylight out in the open. It would also be dangerous for those who may catch them in such a predicament. They would suffer the wrath and jaws of the great Scrimble if there were but two of them; if more then the faeries would have to take action, and no man would wish that upon even their worst enemies. Faeries may be sweet to look at with their tiny forms and happy disposition, but when angered they can be as fearsome as the darkest wolf. Fifty or more tiny beings crawling over you, biting, kicking and tearing at your skin is not the most pleasant way to end your days on this world.

Their wrinkled faces contort into fearsome devils and their teeth are as sharp as tiny, well-honed daggers. Their fingernails are long and pointed and their feet are powerful. They could rip at your flesh and literally tear you to pieces in moments – if they so wished.

But their kind did not like to kill unless they were forced into so doing. Thus the faeries at the head of the procession had increased their speed as a pale pink glow appeared on the horizon. The outline of the forest was in sight and it would not take them long to reach it, but the line of creatures was long and it would be well into dawn before the stragglers reached the confines of the dark boughs.

Mog crossed the threshold first followed by the other faeries. They stood and waited for

Scrimble to walk past and as he did so, they bowed before him. He halted and looked at their group fleetingly before loping off into the gloomy forest. One by one, the rest of the creatures reached the forest's edge and disappeared amongst its dark foliage. They would not be seen again until it was time to return across the moor after the winter months had past. Peg skipped off with the others of her kind and left Mog standing at the crossing place from danger to safety. She would not move on until the wildman had arrived. She became impatient with his tardiness, as she always did, but she knew he would arrive eventually, dragging his foot behind him.

After a short period of time she saw the figure looming out of the fading gloom. The wildman unknowingly passed by her on his way into the forest and grunted as he walked along. He did not know she was there for she kept herself well hidden. He stopped under the trees and sat down, and then proceeded to rub his tired legs.

She left him and ran off after the others, satisfied that all her charges had successfully reached their wintering grounds.

The wildman's eyelids became heavy and he began to drift in and out of a light sleep. He decided that he would rest in the shadows briefly before roaming off to find his den, hoping that he would find it as he left it and that another creature had not taken advantage of its warmth and protection in his absence. That had happened once before and there had been an almighty battle to gain back his possession.

He let his eyes close and was soon fast asleep, twitching in his slumber and occasionally moaning as his dreams took him back to the crossroads and the carving upon the wood.

XXVII

A wildman?!" exclaimed Aelwulf. "What do you lead us into my lord Thurstan? Is there no end to this?"

"My lord Aelwulf," began Thurstan. "I am sure…" but he was interrupted by Aelwulf who flung himself around to face their guide. He stood but not a hair's breadth away from Thurstan's face. "You are sure? What will you be sure about now?" he bellowed, his eyes gleaming with rage. "If I remember you were sure upon last night's eve that we would be safe," he ranted.

Thurstan stood perfectly still, although the poor distance between him and Aelwulf was greatly disturbing. He dared not move and did not wish to show any failings by doing so. A voice inside his head chastised him for telling the group the truth upon his return to the camp. He should have kept the discovery of the carving to himself and his thoughts that the corpse was that of the mythical wodwos – they would have seen the corpse in the gibbet but would have assumed that it was a felon who had met a timely end, and nothing more would have come of it. Now, because of his honesty and moral standing, he had caused the rage before him.

Aelwulf threw his hands in the air and turned on his heel to stomp away towards where his two sons were watching with horror and surprise upon their faces. They had never witnessed such a rage from their father, and were at a loss as to what to do. Should they speak to him and try to calm him down? Or if they were to do so would it cause the rage to be redirected at them? They both looked across to their mother who had been quietly brushing her daughter's hair when Thurstan had returned.

Berowen had awoken from her sleep and had apparently no memory at all of what had occurred the previous evening. Her mother, father and brothers had thought it prudent not to inform her of her actions and told her that she had fainted after a long day's ride when they had arrived at the ring.

Ethwen handed her daughter the brush and approached her husband, placing a hand on his right arm.

"Husband", she softly spoke. "I am sure the Lord Thurstan is not intentionally leading us into any sort of mischief. Why would he? Any conflict brought upon us would involve him also, would it not?"

"Perhaps you are correct in your observations, good wife," answered Aelwulf after a short while. "It just appears that ever since we trusted this man and took that fork in the road in the Blue Wood we have been beset with trouble, and now it seems there may be more to come. If legend is correct, the wildman of the woods is not to be trifled with."

"I have heard such as this, but a long time ago, Aelwulf," said Ethwen. "My brothers, sisters and I knew such creatures as the woodwose. Our uncle used to tell us tales of them when we were younger and it would put terror in our hearts to hear of the horror. He would tell us that there was a woodwose in the woods beyond the pastures and that we should never go there or we would anger him and he would bring bad fortune upon our settlement. We would lie abed at night not being able to sleep lest one would creep into our chamber, and steal us away and eat us. But that was long ago, Aelwulf, and they were but tales told to five young children whose imaginations were easily influenced by such stories."

"This place is full of mischief," announced Berowen from where Ethwen had left her seeing to her hair. "Can you not hear the voices that whisper on the wind?"

"What are you talking about, child?" asked Ethwen, somewhat troubled by her daughter's sudden outburst.

Berowen stared into the distance, seemingly completely unaware that her mother had spoken to her.

"Berowen?"

The girl shook her head slightly and turned her eyes to the direction of her mother's concerned voice.

"Yes mother?" she enquired. "I am sorry, mother, did you address me. I did not hear what you said."

"You were talking about mischief, sister," interrupted Amleth.

"Was I?" his sister asked quizzically. "I am sure I know not to what you refer."

"She must have hit her head harder than we thought when she fainted," said Eneas, trying to muster a lighthearted laugh. "You must have flummoxed your poor brain," he continued. "You will be saying you saw a faerie next."

Berowen looked confused and became pale. "Do you think I have injured myself beyond repair, brother?" she asked worriedly.

Eneas laughed loudly. "Sister, you are always so easy to tease. Hush now."

At this point Thurstan thought it would be an opportune moment to ask whether they were to continue upon their road or turn back and return via the cliff edge to the Blue Wood and resume their original path. Whichever was decided upon, they would have to leave soon for they had dallied far longer than he would have wished. Aelwulf grudgingly advised him that the former should be the choice; further delays were to be avoided as much as was possible.

The group moved on from their camp by the stone circle into the chilly air of the moor. Their journey was uneventful and they arrived at the crossroads with good speed. The men in the group could not help looking at the body that sat in the gently swinging gibbet but when Amleth and several of the soldiers halted their horses to take a closer look, Aelwulf announced that they should move on, "And leave the poor bugger to his peace."

Thurstan led them on for a little while longer before he signalled them to stop so that they could rest their horses and their own tired legs and backs. After a short break in their journey it was soon time to continue – the sun was now past its zenith and it was important that they reach the close cover of the forest before dark.

Ahead, in the distance, they could make something out on the rough moorland trail. As they approached they could hear someone singing heartily in a deep voice that, in all honesty, could not sing very well. Every time a high note was required, the voice would break up and the result was a bellowed screech being brought forth.

An old wooden cart trundled along the track, its wheels bumping over the ruts and stones in its way and the whole construction swaying from side to side in a rather disturbing manner. It seemed as if the next rock its wheels battered against would snap the wooden wheel and topple the whole construction over. As Berowen and the others came alongside it, the man holding the reins waved and gave them a beaming smile that revealed a dire lack of teeth. He was a plump man with a balding head and sported very red cheeks from the cooling air that swept across his face. "Greetings, fellow travellers," he shouted merrily. His excess flesh around his belly seemed to wobble beneath its tunic as the cart rocked back and forth.

"Greetings to you," shouted Eneas in return. "How does the day find you, fellow traveller?"

"'Tis a fine day to be travelling if not a little uncomfortable on this road, my lord," chortled the man. "Methinks I may need to find a wheelwright soon enough, but will have to hope that this old cart keeps body and soul together till I gets there."

"Where are you heading?" asked Eneas loudly over the sound of the rumbling wagon.

"Don't rightly know, me lord," came the reply. "I just harnesses old Bessie up, shouts 'walk on there', and leaves it to her. Best leave decisions to the womenfolk I always say." And he laughed again.

"Ah," laughed Eneas. "Then the wheelwright may well not be sometime soon then. But then on the other hand, if Bessie is clever you may even come upon him tomorrow."

"'Appen she is, and 'appen we may," he replied cheerfully. "You don't 'appen to know where nearest settlement might be, I be thinkin'?

"I know not, I fear to say," replied Eneas. "Our own path takes us through the Forest of Whispers, but I am not familiar with this moor so cannot tell you. How long have you been on the road, and from where do you hail?"

"Oh I been on the road all me life methinks, I ain't got no place to call 'ome no more. But you be goin' through the forest, you say?" enquired the jolly fellow, his face losing some of its cheer. "You would not be catchin' Bessie or me goin' through there by choice, traveller. Strange bein's in there so they say."

"Strange beings you say," scoffed Eneas. "You are referring to this thing known as a wodwos methinks?"

"Aye, yes one of them wildmen roams around in there, so I be told," answered the wagonmaster. "And maleficent faeries I been told too. No, you would not catch me in there I can tell yer. It not be called the Forest of Whispers for now't yer know; there be strange goin's on."

"Tales, yarns, stories to stir the blood and the nerves of children," Eneas responded boldly, although deep down he was no longer quite that sure of this bold statement.

"Depends what yer believe, methinks. But I would sorely consider takin' a longer trail if I was you."

The plump wagonmaster clicked his tongue against his teeth in order to persuade his horse to pick up her pace a bit. "Ger up old Bessie," he called. She was becoming a little apathetic in her plodding, and he did not want to have to camp for the night too near the forest.

Eneas trotted his horse to the front of the line, where Thurstan was concentrating on the horizon for any unforeseen and unwelcome company. Aelwulf rode silently just behind him, his own eyes checking for anything unusual also.

"Lord Thurstan," shouted Eneas. "If this man can take another path, perchance we should take it also and avoid the forest?"

"He is a wanderer, my Lord Eneas," replied Thurstan. "If he has no particular place to travel to, then it does not matter to him how long it takes to get there. We, however, cannot afford such a change of direction. He could well take in Grimfell upon his journey, but who knows how long it would take him to get there...if he is to skirt the forest then he will be travelling miles to the east or west before heading north again."

Aelwulf added, "Lord Thurstan is right in his observations, Eneas. We have no choice but to continue on our original path, although I do wish that we could follow the cheery fellow's example."

Eneas reined his horse to a halt and waited for the rickety transport to come alongside him.

"God's speed, fellow traveller," shouted Eneas as he waved at the man. "Who knows, we may meet again one day, when Bessie has made up her mind where she wishes to take you."

"If you is goin' into that forest, then it is you who may need God's speed," shouted the man in reply. "But fare thee well," and he waved an enthusiastic goodbye.

Eneas shouted as he wagon trundled off ahead of them and slightly turned right off the path. "What is your name, traveller?"

A laugh answered on the approaching dusk's breeze, "Don't rightfully recall, good sir. But those that knows me calls me Wanderin' Kipp."

At that moment the wagon dipped sharply into a rut and Eneas watched the figure sway side to side as the rickety structure righted itself, before Wanderin' Kipp and Bessie continued on their way into the distance.

XXVIII

Just as the sun disappeared over the horizon and left a pinkish glow in the sky, the party found themselves within the outskirts of the forest. As they had approached it, the outline of its canopies against the darkening sky looked foreboding. It was like a black gaping maw in front of them that seemed to be waiting to swallow them up, and digest them inside its very core.

It was the coldest night yet since the warming days of summer had faded into those of the autumn's cool. The group huddled together around the fire that had been built in the first glade they had come upon. It crackled with the dry wood gathered from the forest floor and sent tiny particles of blazing wood upwards into the clear night sky.

Everyone seemed slightly unnerved by their surroundings and no-one seemed able to relax completely, no matter how tired they were, or no matter how their muscles ached and longed to be stretched out beneath the covers of the bedrolls. The soldiers chattered quietly with each other in an attempt to take their minds off the eerie feelings that travelled up and down their spines and made the hair on the back of their necks and arms stand up. Occasionally the sound of a hoot bird calling to its kind made them jump – the haunting call not helping to calm their uneasiness.

Thurstan stared into the blazing fire and unconsciously stabbed at its heart with a stick, sending more embers upwards. Eneas puffed slowly on his pipe and Amleth sat under his bedroll that he had draped around himself while he constantly kept checking into the darkness beyond the glade in case of unwelcome visitors of man or beast. He wished he had been able to appreciate the pipeweed as much as his brother, but after several attempts at inhaling the smoke that his brother dubbed as a soothing elixir to calm the most addled brain, he had just ended up coughing, and spluttering. And upon the first occasion he had even emptied the contents of his stomach over the floor; a meal he had particularly enjoyed eating he had remembered afterwards and had been extremely angry and upset at Eneas in his offering of the substance in the first place.

However, now out here in the wilds and in the most unsettling place he had ever found himself, he could not but wish he had the comfort that his brother had as he silently puffed on the weed that sent such a glorious aroma around the campfire.

Aelwulf and Ethwen sat huddled together, Ethwen's eyes getting heavier as she cuddled into her husband's warmth. Berowen looked down at the ground, biting her bottom lip. Her mind was completely elsewhere as she thought about the day that loomed ever closer with each evening's fire.

The comment from Brago, the oldest and perhaps wisest of the soldiers, that he felt as if the gaze of a dozen eyes were upon him from somewhere in the darkness did not help quash the uneasiness that clung like a fog around the group.

And his observation was indeed true, and what is more, the watchers were looking on with great interest.

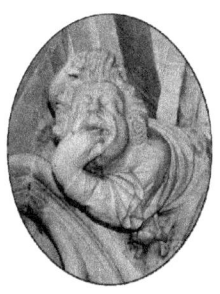

XXIX

It had been a long time since the forest dwellers had seen humans within their boundaries. They were used to the yearly visits from those creatures who lived amongst the wood across the moor, but these pale-faced, smelly, two-leggeds were much less known. They had occasionally espied them journeying along the rough track that ran along the wood's edge, but until now these travellers had always avoided actually entering into the darker depths beyond the treeline.

The creatures of the forest were bemused, angry and disturbed. This was the second time in the last few days that their home had been visited by such people. However, the first to come were much more frightening to look at than this group. They were tall, had red hair and beards and the creatures upon which they sat were fearsome as they trampled through the undergrowth with no care for the life that dwelt within it. These invaders had swept their destructive way through the low boughs, slicing the bark with their weapons and beating the shrubbery in their way with their heavily armoured boots.

However, this small group that sat together around the warmth of the fire seemed a little different. They did not seem to be hostile to their surroundings and seemed, to the creatures, to be slightly humbled by them. The watchers would speak with their like from across the moor to ascertain whether they had any knowledge of either kind of these visitors.

XXX

One by one, Berowen's escort gave into sleep and she soon followed suit. She had no idea how long she had been asleep but the sound of rustling nearby awoke her from her slumber. She lay perfectly still under her covers but strained her ears for any further noise that would perhaps make it clear as to what it may be. No other sound reached her ears so she assumed that it must have been perhaps a mouse or some such other tiny animal of the night going about its nightly foraging.

Then she was awoken again, and this time she recognised the voice of one of the soldiers quietly complaining that he needed to relieve himself. Looking up she could see that the first faint light of dawn was creeping upon the world. There were uninteresting grunts from a couple of the other soldiers at their companion's statement, and it seemed as if they all just turned over and went back to sleep.

"What a time to need a piss," complained the man.

"Just go and show the birds your dick, and don't get it bitten off by some wild beast," responded one of his comrades gruffly, obviously fully recovered from his own uneasiness of the place now that daylight was dawning. "Or do you want someone to come and hold your hand?"

"Bah, Thorgan, I had forgotten you are an irritable ill-headed bugbear in the morning. Go back to sleep and perhaps you will be more likeable henceforth," replied the man with the full bladder.

Berowen heard the man leave the camp and drifted in and out of sleep for a while. The early morning song of the birds was ever in her sleepy mind, and every so often she would open her eyes and wonder where she was. The dreams of waking she called them; those times when she would lay abed and change from sleep to waking, and in between she would dwell in a land of weird thoughts that never quite seemed to be dream or truth.

She cursed under her breath when she felt a twinge in her own bladder and knew that she would have to brave the forest to answer the call of nature herself. She sat up slowly and looked over to where the soldiers were sleeping. It was then that she realised that the soldier had not yet returned and it raised a feeling of fear inside her. She knew not how long it was since he had left, but gauging the time by the manner in which the light had increased, she thought that it must be at least a half of an hour.

She wriggled for a bit in the hope her desire would abate, but it was no good. She would have to leave the safety of the camp and venture into the forest – just a little way. As she left the glade the light faded slightly as the sun's rays could not permeate the thick mantle of the needle-like pine leaves. She found herself a spot safely away from the scrutiny of any eyes from the camp that may accidentally find her, but not far enough that a cry would not reach their ears if necessary.

She lifted her skirts and squatted, carefully avoiding any shrubbery that would scratch at her skin in defence of her audacity. As she emptied her bladder, she felt something wet drip onto her back as it soaked through the fabric of her dress. Her initial thought was that a bird had performed a similar task upon her, and she was reminded of the fable that if a bird shits on you it is lucky. She half-smiled when she remembered the first time she had heard her mother tell of such things. When her brother Amleth had been a young boy, one fine day in summer he had been sitting outside watching his father and the soldiers of Brundannoch practising their archery on the dummies outside the walls. He had been sitting enthusiastically eating an apple when a passing bird had decided to empty its bowels overhead and the resulting wet dollop had landed firmly on his head. He had made such a fuss that Berowen had had to take him back to the keep to their mother, who - whilst washing off the offending deposit - had told him of the saying.

Another wet plop and this time Berowen assumed that it might have begun to rain. Then another just as she stood up, this time causing the drop to fall upon her head. She felt it trickle downwards towards her forehead and, out of instinct, she raised a hand to wipe it off. It felt sticky and she instantly felt fear, although she could not explain why…until she looked at her hand and saw the red stain.

She gingerly looked up and reeled in disgust as she saw the origin of the falling liquid. Above her swung the recently killed body of a man; his stomach had been ripped open and his guts spilled out, dangling as his body twisted around on the rope that was tied tightly around his neck and had been winched against a branch, thus allowing the broken body to be raised high off the ground. A steady trickle of blood ran down his legs and dripped to the ground from his bare toes. Looking at the face – a face that had been disfigured by the sharp edge of a sword - she realised that it was the soldier who had left to answer the call of nature earlier.

She opened her mouth to scream but no sound came forth. She had seen many dead bodies but not one so suddenly. She had been completely surprised – it had been the last thing she would have expected to see. She reeled around and searched into the gloominess of the forest around her to see if she could make out any form in the vicinity. The kill was fresh and whoever had performed it would have had to act quickly and may even still be around. Was it the notorious woodwose come to get them as told in the tales?

As she circled around on the spot, she noticed a large thick bush shake slightly in front of her. Unfortunately, it was situated near where she had entered so if there was some malcontent lurking behind it then she was cut off from her escape. She quickly looked for another way out and noticed a faint track that had probably been etched through the trees by deer – that would be her exit if needs be. Yes, it would lead her further into the gloom but at least it meant that she would not be trapped.

Her gaze returned to the bush. It still shook slightly and she examined it more closely. Was that red she could see or was it just berries on the branches? She began to sweat, even in the damp air that enveloped her. Sense told her not to try to run past the bush, even though it was but a relative short distance to the camp. Those at the camp would not be prepared for attack and if there were to be something malevolent watching her, there was no way of knowing whether it was alone. If she screamed, it may well encourage whatever it was to attack her, so she decided to retreat backwards slowly, her eyes not leaving the spot. Intermittently she turned her head to establish the exact position of the track she would take in her escape, and when it was within her reach she turned and walked towards it.

It was then that a figure revealed itself from its hiding place and she saw, to her utmost horror, that it *was* one of the large red-haired figures like those who had come upon them in the Blue Wood. His hands were bloodstained, as was the sword he held, and it felt as if her heart sank to her stomach as the recognition dawned upon her that this was the murderer of the poor man who continued to swing in the tree above.

Berowen's gait increased and she made a dash for the track. The thunder of heavily armoured boots told her that he followed.

She ran and ran until she thought that her heart would burst through her ribcage. Her legs seemed that they would not support her body any longer and would collapse at any moment. She dare not turn around to see if her foe were closing in on her, but she could still hear the loud breathing and growling. She nearly tripped but managed to right herself before falling, and raised her skirts even higher to avoid such a disastrous and terrifying event occurring. Her chest hurt as the cold air rushed through her mouth to her lungs, and her nose and eyes were running with the rush of air against them.

The pine needles beneath her feet were soft against her burning soles that throbbed through her shoes. She had to duck through low branches, but in her speed she did not manage to avoid them all and she felt the sting of several as they gashed across her neck and cheeks. But still she ran on for she could hear the heavy thud of footsteps behind her and she knew he was still behind her. She began to despair that she would never shake off her antagonist and that she was doomed after all her efforts of escape.

She knew not where she was going, but kept running blindly through the trees. She came to a small clearing and a shadow loomed beside her. She instinctively flinched and expected a blow upon her person and veered to her left, catching her foot in a knot of roots, and falling to her knees with a thud. She raised her arms above her head in a bid to protect herself from the blow that she was sure would follow.

But there came no blow, only the sound of a heavy thud behind her and a low grunt. Still crouching, she slowly turned her head around.

XXXI

The wildman had heard the crashing of bodies through the undergrowth. His senses had been intrigued as to what the commotion could be about and he had followed the sound to find out. Out of sight, he watched as the woman ran passed him, exhaustion and fear etched upon her face. Then he watched the tall, red-haired figure follow, sword held high above his head ready to deal a deathly blow upon all that with which it came into contact. It was clear what was occurring, and some deep instinct told him that he should aid the woman against her attacker.

He had moved as quickly as he could from behind his hiding place, and had followed the two – his way hampered by his damaged leg. However, due to the low hanging branches, the red-beard's height was hampering his speed so the wildman managed to keep the antagonist in his sight. When the woman's attacker had stopped, he had managed to creep up behind him silently as his years in the woods had taught him. Slightly ahead, he could see the woman had fallen and was on the ground. Instinctively, he knew this was the time for him to act and he moved himself closer to the figure. Unfortunately, he trod on a dry twig and the noise of it snapping diverted the attacker's attention to himself. The wildman grabbed the sword arm and wrenched the sword from its grip – the surprise enabling him to achieve this without too much effort. The red-beard glared and snarled but the wildman took no notice and swept the sword down across the other's shoulders. The face's expression did not change, the eyes did not blink and then suddenly the body fell to the ground with a thud, the head lolling to one side where it had not been completely detached.

The wildman bent down and finished the job at hand and, releasing the weapon, raised the decapitated head in his left hand, and danced and shouted with glee.

With her eyes wide and her breath laboured from the battle with the trees and undergrowth in her escape, Berowen watched the events unfurl before her. Blood was clotting in the gashes caused by the sharp pine needles and thorns of undergrowth but she could feel no pain; her body was still full of the extra energy she had found to escape the red-beard. Tears of fear had left trails down her cheeks; they ran over the tiny clots like rivulets over stones and she wiped them away with her hand.

She dare not move. What stood before her was a figure covered in a fine down of hair. Was this really a wodwos in front of her? Had a wildman of the woods saved her? He was not as she had expected him to be from the tales she had heard. She had imagined a figure beyond that of an ordinary man; taller, and more frightening, but here before her stood an old man, slightly bent over with age and thin like a reed.

Berowen stared at him, not quite knowing what to do. She stood cautiously and walked backwards until she felt the trunk of a tree against her back. She did not know whether to run or stay in his company. Yes, he had killed her attacker, but was she to be his next victim or had he, out of some instinct, dealt with her prospective killer on her behalf? As she watched him, he watched her and cocked his head from side to side, scratching his beard as he did so, almost as if the sight of her had sparked some recognition in him.

"Thank you," Berowen ventured softly. It seemed rather odd to speak to such a creature, but on the other hand, it seemed the most polite thing to do. At her words, the wildman looked at her even more quizzically. Somewhere in the recesses of his mind, the words seemed familiar to him, and yet he had no real knowledge of what they meant. The sound that came forth from her mouth reminded him of his far past. He opened his own mouth and tried to make a sound but all that came out was a low grunt. He was confused, and this confusion made him scared. He began to feel agitated.

It was the voices behind them that completed the transition from a vague recognition to madness. He roared and tossed the head into the air, then turned clumsily on his heels and limped back into the forest as fast as he could.

Berowen watched as the head rose in the air before its descent began, and it eventually plummeted to the ground with a thump and rolled slightly towards the trees. She did not notice, however, the tiny figure that crept from behind a tall trunk.

Mog sliced off some of the red hair and placed it in her pouch. She grinned from ear to ear and ran off.

XXXII

Berowen heard her name called and recognised the voice as her father's. She remained completely dazed by the recent events and found herself still shaking from the exertion of her escape from death. However, she mustered enough energy to call out in response to her father in as strong a voice as possible in order to belie her true feelings.

Aelwulf, Thurstan, Eneas and two of the other men – Brogil and Finn – arrived in the small clearing and stopped short of the decapitated body in front of them.

"Daughter, what has occurred here?" enquired Berowen's father. "We discovered you missing and came upon a horrendous sight in the trees just outside our camp. We feared the worst, and have been searching for you. It would seem that our thoughts were not entirely ill-founded," he continued as he looked at the body in front of him, slightly nudging it with his left foot.

"Are you injured sister?" soothed Eneas as he came to her side and hugged her.

"I am quite well, thank you, although I am shaken." Berowen explained what events had led her to the spot where she was now standing. From their response, it would seem that her father and the others had assumed that a wildman had attacked her after she had come upon the evil deed stricken upon the other of their party. When she had explained the true story, whilst they seemed to accept that the body before them had been the murderer of the soldier, they did not seem to believe that he had been dispatched by a creature that, to them, sounded all too like the fabled wildman. If, indeed, a wildman of the woods had killed her antagonist why had it not then attacked her?

She stood amongst them as they reached the opinion that their calls for her had disturbed him in his vicious plans, and would not listen to her appeals that it would seem that he had not any intention to harm her, for he would have had ample opportunity, and time, so to do before her rescuers had arrived. She also pointed out that he had not taken the sword, but had dropped it as if it burned his hand – as if it was a bad thing rather than something to be used to carry out further destruction.

But they would not hear of it and after Brogil and Finn had rifled the clothing of the deceased for any clues as to his presence there, or his origins, they escorted Berowen back through the forest to where her mother, Amleth and the others were waiting.

The look of relief upon Ethwen's face was blatantly obvious when her slightly bedraggled looking daughter returned to the camp. Amleth ran to his sister and hugged her before Ethwen took her away to a quiet spot so that Berowen could tell her what had happened.

"It is clear that we shall be foolish to try and continue our journey through this forest," stated Thurstan. "Where there is one of those red-beards there must be more, and we have no way of knowing whether they are still within this place or have moved on. I doubt, though, that they will be far."

Aelwulf nodded slowly. "It seems that we should have taken heed of the traveller after all, although for different reasons."

"I suggest that we should return to the moor and take his route to the west. It is, however, your decision my lord," said Thurstan looking at Aelwulf. "What say you? It is perhaps possible that we could send one of your men ahead of us to announce our difficulties. It will then leave us with four less escort, but I cannot see another solution."

"Two or three days added to our journey, you think?" responded Aelwulf.

"I would anticipate such a delay, yes my lord."

"If we were to continue our path through the forest, how long would that take?"

"We have lost time, my lord, but if we left immediately we should reach the other side by nightfall. However, if you are thinking..."

"I do not know what I am thinking, my lord," interrupted Aelwulf. "I am just trying to get my daughter safely to her marriage with as much speed as possible. This journey has already proved more hazardous than I would have ever thought possible."

"I appreciate your concerns, my Lord Aelwulf," continued Thurstan. "But I would seriously suggest that we do not continue on our present path. We are not enough to fight off another attack methinks and in a place such as this, ambush would be an easy weapon against us."

"Eneas?" asked Aelwulf. "Your thoughts?"

"I feel that Lord Thurstan is correct, father. At first we merely had the fable of a wildman to contend with. Now we seem to have another enemy who may be lurking to prevent our arrival at Grimfell, for whatever reason they may have."

"I will think upon it," announced Aelwulf as he turned and walked towards his wife and daughter.

"Do not take long on your deliberations, my lord," offered Thurstan. "Our day is getting shorter by the hour and we need to move in one direction or the other as soon as we can."

"Get the horses and men ready to ride, my lord," responded Aelwulf without turning around. "We shall then be ready for whatever I decide. Eneas....follow me."

Thurstan bowed his head in acknowledgement of this request and signalled to the men to begin to dismantle the camp and prepare the packhorses. Eneas looked at him as he moved to follow his father and shrugged his shoulders as if to acknowledge what Thurstan was thinking at his father's singular reaction to what was – in his own mind – a perfectly easy and sensible decision at which to arrive.

As the family of Brundannon stood together, clearly discussing what was to be done, the packhorses were loaded, and the other horses were saddled and prepared for the ride ahead. Eventually the head of the family returned to Thurstan and announced that they would leave the forest and take the longer path to Grimfell. He agreed that one soldier should be sent ahead, and Brogil was chosen as the messenger.

The decision made, all mounted their horses and Thurstan turned them back towards the marshes. Berowen had recovered from her experience earlier and sat upon her horse with straight back and stared ahead of her, no emotion whatsoever shown upon her scratched and slightly bruised face.

They followed the track along which they had watched the traveller disappear into the distance the day before, and their horses picked their way across the rough terrain. Brogil travelled on ahead, his horse now being able to move at its own pace and he was soon out of sight. At last the forest was behind them and the moor opened up. The ground began to descend slightly and soon they came across a maze of streams that had split from the main as it navigated itself around the tussocks, and the ground beneath their horses' hooves became more boggy and difficult to traverse. The rough track continued upstream, presumably to a ford or bridge for wagons to use; it had been well used lately by the look of the disturbed soil, but Thurstan led the party through the waters and boggy banks to save time in trying to locate the easier route.

It was apt to be dangerous ground for laden horses, so Thurstan suggested all dismounted and lead their mounts instead. Thurstan went ahead, followed by Aelwulf and both helped Ethwen and Berowen across the wider parts of stream, the waters of which raced beneath them with such clear water that the submerged weed could be easily seen as its roots strained to keep it from being uprooted in the current. The horses stopped to drink from the noisy flow and the party waited patiently for them to quench their thirsts before leading them on further through the boggy ground.

Berowen ignored her dampening feet and looked upwards, watching a buzzard make its lazy way across the sky in search of its next meal. With her back to the stream, all around was quiet. When she turned around, however, to follow the bird's journey the busy din from the rushing waters was deafening to her ears. The noise cut through the silence and she was surprised as to quite how much sound the water made, so much so that it made her jump slightly as she was not expecting it and thought something had crept upon her and made a loud noise.

Looking to her left, she saw a tor on the skyline, its summit having rocky outcroppings that seemed to be broken in the middle leaving a gap in its centre. At the moment she looked towards it, the sun seemed to be shining its rays straight through this gap and she shivered as if this spectacle somehow meant something to her. The whinny of one of the horses broke her musings, and she returned her gaze to the events around her.

She became aware of an itching sensation upon her bare arms and realised that a swarm of gnats had begun to circle around her – in fact they were everywhere, obviously attracted by the presence of fresh blood. Everyone was scratching periodically and swatting the insects when they could. There were always more, and it rapidly became an impossible task to rid themselves of the irritation. The only solution was to move on as quickly as possible and leave the dank area behind them.

Eventually they managed to leave the stream behind, and the ground became more solid beneath their feet so they remounted and continued on their way – still itching from the tenacious attacks from the flying insects. Berowen's arms were covered in tiny red blotches where she had fallen prey to their hungry onslaught and although she tried not to, she could not help herself continuously scratching at them, causing temporary relief before beginning to irritate again within a few minutes.

They all rode mostly in silence, the soldiers who were left in the party muttering to their horses every so often. After a short while Eneas urged his sister to play her lute to help pass the time, but she was reluctant so to do as her mood was not one of making music.

"The movement from my horse would encourage me to drop a note or two, brother," she explained. "And there is nothing worse in my mind than a dropped note or even one missed. No Eneas, I feel that it is not the time for my lute to see the daylight."

"A song then, sister," urged Eneas.

Berowen shook her head. "My voice would waiver with the pace of my mount."

"Bah," replied her brother. "There must be some sport that can be played to break up this dire monotony. Amleth....have you a thought?"

Amleth shook his head. "I fear not brother. A race would be good sport, but methinks our father would scorn if we tried."

An idea made Eneas smile from ear to ear. "Father," he shouted. "Methinks that Amleth and I should set about hunting some rabbits with which to feed our stomachs. We should not be gone long and would not travel far."

Aelwulf considered this request for a moment before replying to his son. "One hour Eneas and I shall expect you back in line. I need not stress upon you that we are sorely unguarded as it is, but I shall agree to your request as we do need to replenish our food stores."

Eneas beamed with delight and, nodding to his brother, they both steered their horses to the right of the party and were soon mere dots on the horizon.

Berowen watched her brothers ride away and felt a tinge of jealousy that she could not join them on their hunt. She knew full well that the subject of food was a cover for what they both really wanted – to get away from the group and burn off some excess energy in both themselves and their mounts. How she longed to be riding with them with the wind rushing against her skin – freedom from all the burdens upon her heart if only for a fleeting hour. She looked across at her mother, who was dozing in her saddle. She wobbled back and forth in her seat, her chin bouncing gently off her breast and was oblivious of her sons' departure. It was probably just as well, Berowen thought to herself, for if she had known she would have been worrying – continually and vocally - until they returned.

The hour passed quite slowly, as did the journey, but at last two small figures appeared in the distance and gradually made their way towards the small line of travellers. Aelwulf stopped those behind him and they all waited patiently for Eneas and Amleth to come alongside. Unfortunately, Ethwen was still asleep in her saddle so Berowen had to make a mad scramble to get hold of the reins of her mother's horse and pull it gently to a halt. The sudden movement caused Ethwen to awaken from her slumbers and she looked around her with a look of confusion upon her tired face.

Before she could utter any concerns at the lack of the presence of her two sons, they both appeared alongside the group, each bearing three rabbits strung across their saddles.

"A successful trip I see," called Aelwulf to the two young men. "Supper will be slightly tastier than of late then it would seem. Did you see anything, or anyone, on your hunt?"

"No-one father," replied Amleth. "The moor seems deserted of anything other than rabbits and birds, although there are well-worn cart tracks that cut across to the west."

"I had wondered whether we would come across the traveller we saw yesterday – his mare was slow and the cart near to broken. There was no sign of him?" asked Thurstan.

"Ah yes, Wanderin' Kipp you mean," answered Eneas. "There was no sign of him at all, but there was no reason to believe that he would be travelling the same way as us. If he spends his days roaming he could have headed off in any direction."

"That is true, Eneas," Thurstan replied. "But he was heading to Grimfell I am sure of it."

"He was indeed," offered Berowen quietly.

"I do not remember him saying as much, sister. In fact I will wager what paltry coins I have left in my purse that he didn't," Eneas laughed. "Methinks you are imagining it Berowen."

"Perhaps we are merely going the wrong way, brother," was her reply. "For I can assure you that the traveller was heading to Grimfell."

Eneas was a little taken aback with his sister's curtness at the last part of the sentence, but she had been acting very unlike herself ever since the incident at the stones a few days before. He decided to ignore her brusqueness, but did wonder whether her comment about being on the wrong path might be a sensible suggestion and urged his horse forward to come alongside that of Thurstan.

"I think that perhaps my sister has made a relevant point," he said as he rode next to their guide. "Are you certain that we travel the correct path to Grimfell? I do not mean to doubt your directions, but, if I am correct, you have not travelled this way often and are perhaps not familiar with the road?"

"We are on the correct road, my lord Eneas," replied Thurstan. "It may well be that the traveller went an alternative way to avoid his ramshackle cart being pulled across such a rough landscape. There may well be a longer road that is more suitable for his failing wheels."

Eneas thought for a moment. "Hmm that is quite possible, my lord. However, you did not enter into the suggestion that he may not be travelling to the same destination as us."

"That is because he *is,* my lord," was the reply.

"I am beginning to think that it is my hearing that is amiss here," laughed Eneas cheerily, not wishing to doubt their guide, and yet still slightly bemused by the firmness in both Thurstan's and Berowen's assertions.

Thurstan kicked his horse into a quicker pace and shouted to those behind him, "We need to make that small lake by dusk." As he spoke, he pointed towards a small clump of trees in the near distance. The sun is falling quickly now and we have yet to build a fire. If I may be so bold I must urge you all to make haste."

XXXIII

The man had retreated far into the depths of greenery and had secreted himself in the shadows away from the sound of the approaching voices. He had more voices in his head – shouting at him, goading him, nagging him. And he wanted to scream for them to go away and leave him alone to his solitude. He bit his lip so hard that he made it bleed and he scratched at his arm so hard that he scraped off the top layer of skin, along with a clump of matted hair – but he did not notice the pain, or the blood that trickled down his chin. He was in his own pain – a pain known only inside his head. He slapped his head with his hand and then knocked it against the heavy tree trunk beside him. Nothing worked – the voices were still there.

And then a new voice – a softer one than of late. It etched itself into his psyche and repeated the words repeatedly. "Thank you," it said in the soft, gentle voice of the figure he had just seen. He swayed from side to side and moaned. Somewhere in the far reaches of his mind he knew those words, but could not remember from whence they came. He had lived for so long on his own under the shelter of the trees, but they were familiar to him. A flash of lightning raged through the front of his head – in his eyes as they were closed. A figure stood before him – a figure like that he had just witnessed. A different form, a different shape in different clothing. A soft voice. Mother. The word flashed in his head. MOTHER. He sobbed into his hands and fell to his knees before lying embryonic upon the pine needles.

Exhaustive sleep took him, but the voices did not leave him in his slumber. They became louder and took on shapes in his eyes. He was there and saw it all before him with clouded eyes as the form of an arm thrust itself towards him. The hand grasped him on his shoulder and dragged him towards the body that had identified itself as mother within his memory. It hugged him closely and he could smell the familiar scent of warmth, love and security. Then he was thrust backwards and through hazy eyes he could see tears in the eyes of the figure that looked towards him.

In the distance he could hear the rhythmic sound of a beating drum – pounding out a solitary note every second. Voices – faint then loud – shouting, angry voices.

The hand grabbed his own and dragged him across the ground – ground that had been cultivated with plants that were shooting through its muddy confines into the open air above.

His bare feet squelched in the mud as he was dragged through it. He looked at his arms – they were bare and he could see the flesh pale and unblemished save for a few well-healed scratches. There was no visible hair covering them and his hand was large in that of the figure that pulled him along. He could hear the voice urging him to hurry.

Then the familiar sight of the wood reached his vision. The figure dragged him into its darkness and then it knelt before him. Recognition exploded in his subconscious. This was his mother – her soft brown eyes, her soft skin and her soft voice. With a hand on each shoulder she urged him to stay out of sight. "You must stay here, Walt. They have come for you and I will not let them take you." The words echoed through his mind. "You are my dear, sweet son and what you did was not your fault."

The man started to cry in his sleep and his body twitched as his arms stretched out into the night as if to embrace an invisible entity.

"I will come and find you, Walt. But you must stay here until I do. Do you understand?"

The man nodded in his sleep.

The woman leant forward and kissed him on his forehead before standing and returning back the way they had come.

Then silence – a silence and loneliness that had lasted for many years hence.

XXXIV

Berowen approached Thurstan as he sat by the fire, having positioned himself at a slight distance from the others. As was usual every evening he sat cross-legged and smoked his long pipe slowly. He spoke very little to anyone around him, and seemed always intent upon his own thoughts as if something heavy weighed upon his mind that was so burdensome that it would not leave his consciousness.

"Do you mind if I sit with you for a while, my lord?" she asked hesitatingly. "I have a question to ask of you if I am not disturbing you."

"You are most welcome, my lady," he replied as he exhaled a thin trail of grey/blue smoke. "If, that is, you are not offended by my pipe. I have been informed on more than one occasion that its aroma is rather pungent."

She sat beside him and wrapped her skirts around her ankles. "Not at all my lord. But you seemed intent upon some question of your own, as you appeared deep in thought, and I have no wish to trouble you."

"They are thoughts that can be put aside, my lady. They are ever present, but their resolve is used to being delayed after all these years of such dallying on my part."

The notion came upon Berowen that this was the first time that she had studied the features of the man who had become their guide. Her mind had been elsewhere since he had arrived all those days ago at Brundannon, and indeed still was, but after the recent events in the forest a burning question preyed upon her mind, and she reasoned that the man before her may well be the best to answer it.

This man who sat cross-legged before her was supposedly the nephew of a king although he gave no impression of being high born. He gave not the appearance of royal birth, but one of a man who wanders the land. His dress was not rich in colour or cloth and his demeanour was not one of pomposity or particular grace, although his manners were impeccable, and his humility towards her father was ever apparent.

Thurstan was quite aware of her examination of his person, but continued to stare into the fire – his only occasional movement being his hand as he moved the pipe slowly back and forth.

His wavy black hair was speckled with grey and fell to his broad shoulders. His eyes were dark blue, the midnight blue of a summer's night sky, and glinted in the light of the fire. His face had the look of someone who had seen frequent days in the sun, with the russet cheeks of a man who worked among the fields. His long fingers were unadorned by jewellery but around his neck she could make out a chain, shining in the firelight; any pendant or jewel hidden under his shirt. His legs were long and slim and his boots had seen better days, their soles being worn through in places – again not the apparel of one who is a nephew of a king. Her study of him brought more questions to be asked, but she dared not broach such a subject for fear of offending him.

Berowen picked a blade of rough grass and toyed with it between her forefinger and thumb, not quite knowing how to begin her questioning.

Thurstan sat silently and continued to smoke his pipe. He said nothing to her and waited for her to begin, although it was obvious to him that she was having difficulty commencing the conversation. He had no desire to urge her into speaking - that was not his way. If she were ready to talk then she would do so, without any assistance from him. Her presence before him affected him not, and she was more than welcome to sit in perfect silence for as long as she wished. He had an inkling as to what subject it was that she wanted to question him about, but it was completely up to her to begin; he would offer no information unless pressed.

Berowen searched in her mind for the right words to say. She had no desire to make a fool of herself, and yet she had a desire to know the truth.

She cleared her throat and Thurstan's attention turned towards her, expecting this was the signal to the commencement of her enquiries.

"I am confused, my lord," she began. "I had been led to believe that the wildman of the woods was an evil creature, but my meeting with him today did not give that impression. He appeared just a man, although he had wildness in his eyes."

"The wodwos has many tales told about him, my lady," replied Thurstan. "They are based upon tales handed down over years and no-one knows the real truth. There are many woods and forests that are supposed to be home to such creatures."

"But are there tales of them having harmed travellers, my lord?"

"I have heard tell of such tales, my lady, yes," responded Thurstan. "But I have heard tales of dragons also and have never seen one, nor anyone else who has. But then I would not have heard of such if the witness had been dispatched by such a terrible creature, I would add as a probable explanation of this," he continued with a soft smile.

"Indeed," replied Berowen with a reciprocal smile. "Then for all is to be known the wildman is just a man who lives wild?"

"You seem to have your own thoughts, my lady, from the way that you speak," queried Thurstan.

"I only know that the creature I saw was as familiar as a man to me as you, or my father, or any other man I have seen, my lord. The only difference was his stature and his nakedness save for an animal skin around his loins and hair that covered his whole body. I perceived that he posed no threat to me and when I spoke to him, he seemed to recognise what I said, although..." and here she paused.

Thurstan drew on his pipe and waited for her to continue.

"And yet he did not seem to be able to respond," she carried on. "Although I was close enough to him to see the look in his dark eyes – there was a sadness there and also a look of emptiness."

"And what does your instinct tell you of his appearance before you?" quizzed Thurstan.

"My instinct?" Berowen asked with a frown of query upon her brow.

"Let me say it this way, my lady. My gut reaction in the forest was that we should not continue to travel through its boughs. You have encountered a possible wodwos. Many would automatically have called upon the hunting dogs to flush it out, much as they may have been called down upon the creature whose body languishes in the gibbet perhaps. But you, it seems, have other thoughts."

"Gibbet?" gasped Berowen. "You are telling me that the body in the gibbet was that of a woodwose?"

"I believe it to be yes," replied Thurstan almost wishing he had not admitted such a thing. "The inscription carved into the wood below the frame seems to intimate such."

Berowen fell silent for a few minutes, as if mulling over this information in her mind. "I do not understand, my lord," she ventured at last.

Thurstan cocked his head to one side. "Understand what, my lady? The beliefs of the people of the land? Or that people can be so easily led by tales?"

"I understand neither of those, my lord," replied Berowen. "The man today saved me from certain death at the hands of that red-bearded beast. Methinks the people of this land should rather hound them than those that live quietly in the forest."

"Hmmm," began Thurstan exhaling a puff of smoke slowly into the night air.

"I know nothing about the origins of the tales of the woodwose, my lord Thurstan. I only know that the man I came upon today was not violent towards me. If he was a woodwose, then I am happy to retell the tales and portray him as good rather than evil. In fact I shall compose a song about him methinks."

Berowen stood up and dusted herself down. "Thank you, my lord, for your council this evening."

Thurstan brought himself to his feet and bowed before Berowen. "You are most welcome my lady. I am happy to have had the chance to speak with you. It has been a pleasure. Although I fear that is has not brought a resolve to the question you asked."

"Indeed it has not, my lord, but it has brought a resolve within me that I shall praise the help of the fabled woodwose in song for all to hear, and perhaps it will change the view of some who doubt in future."

Thurstan watched Berowen make her way back to her bedroll before he bent down and tapped out his pipe on the stones that had been placed around the fire. As he did so he felt something behind him and an icy cold breeze embraced him. He turned around but nothing was there.

It was not the first time that this had occurred, and as usual he pondered upon its origins. The iciness was acute and the malevolence that travelled with it was intense, but it always passed quickly and nothing ever happened upon its passing. Not usually. However, upon this night he noticed Berowen shiver and pull her cloak about her tightly as if something cold had passed over her. He watched as she looked about her nervously, before she lay down and settled herself for sleep.

XXXV

The Forest of Whispers stretched deep into the crook of a horse-shoe shaped range of hills. The path the travellers would have taken would have guided them towards the belly of the forest before turning sharply to the east to take them out on to the marshes. No-one had ever ventured into the deepest heart of the forest of pines. Or if they had, they had never returned to mankind. Only the creatures of the woods dared tread that path and even then only upon invitation by the one whom dwelt there.

Mog and Peg, and their kin had often paid homage to The One and they dreaded and loathed the occasions. They feared, like all the other creatures, the one who had made their home there centuries before. This being could take life on a whim and had no qualms on doing so. It was the personification of evil and delighted upon issuing punishment. It was also the embodiment of good, and equally delighted in giving care for those who honoured it.

In a few weeks, it would be time to pay her respects – she had already received the summons. Mog had been working hard since their last visit to the forest and had now to just put the finishing touches to the work she was undertaking. It had taken months to collect the various locks of hair that bulged in her pouch and she was particularly pleased with the lock of thick red hair she had managed to obtain from the body the wildman had killed. She felt sure that when her item was finished it would appease The One and thus would ensure that Mog and her kind would secure a future within the forest for winters to come. The task that she had been set the previous winter had been an onerous one, but she knew that if she had not succeeded it would mean retribution of the most horrendous nature.

At Yule she would present her gift and at Yule she would either return to her kith and kin or she would be lost forever and they would be banned from existence itself under the wrath of the most terrifying evil. Not only did her very life depend upon her skills, but that of her whole race. So many other races had passed into myth when they had failed to meet the requirements laid down by The One.

Mog had risked her life on many occasions in her search for the contents of her bulging pouch. She had left the confines of the wood and had travelled by the light of the moon to those places inhabited by the humans. On successful trips, she had left a special mark of thanks after her visit and she had dealt a fierce retribution on those that had been unsuccessful.

Those who had awoken not noticing that they were missing a few locks of curly or straight hair would go outside to find their horses manes in delicate plaits. Those who had found their chickens dead would still have all their hair and would instantly blame the unfortunate event on the foxes. However, Mog would sport a feather in her hair for the rest of *that* day.

Mog was fleet of foot and sleight of hand and could gather her supplies with ease if the time was right. She teased the dogs and played with the kittens in the barns, made faces at the cows and grunted at the swine and danced along fences, stopping occasionally to pee in the wells and water troughs. She would have great sport with the humans who unknowingly gave up their hair to secure her future. Occasionally a young human would awaken when she was about her business and she would play a game of hide and seek with them under their covers. She would scuttle across their pillows going about her task as she went, and would dance upon their bedclothes. They would giggle and clap their hands in glee at the little creature that performed before them, before they fell slowly back to sleep. And when they told their mothers and fathers the next morning, they would tell them that they had dreamt about the faerie folk and that they had been blessed to have done so.

She had managed to fill ten pouches worth of hair and had stored it all in the intricately carved box that The One had given her last winter. This she had guarded vehemently and would be relieved when all was done, and she could relinquish the task of constantly keeping it hidden. The box unnerved her. The carvings upon it unsettled her. They were carvings of all the races that had disappeared since she had been visiting The One in the deep of the forest. Was hers to be next?

XXXVI

It was dusk nearly on the next day, when the wedding party came across a troupe of musicians and dancers. The music wafted on the breeze long before they had come alongside them. But it was the cart at the rear of the parade that caught everyone's eye first. It was the unmistakeable rickety construction of Wandering Kipp's. Ahead of it, they could see a long line of figures that danced and skipped their way along the track.

"Hail!" shouted Eneas as he drew up beside the wagon master.

The jolly man laughed and waved his hand. "Greetings young sir," he shouted above the music. "It is a good day is it not? I be glad to see you and your fellow travellers again. Did that forest spit you out?"

"All but one of us, my friend," said Eneas sadly.

Kipp's expression grew serious. "I be sorry to 'ear that and offer sorrow to 'is family. Which creature did for him?"

"None of which you will know, methinks," replied Amleth who had come alongside his brother. "Unless you have heard tell of red-bearded warriors of great size."

"Nay, sire," responded Kipp. "I not be 'earing of such."

There was awkward silence for a few moments before Kipp continued, "You see Bessie 'ere picked up some cheerie companions?" He laughed again and urged his horse on with a quick shake of the reins.

"Indeed," laughed Amleth. "Who are they and where are they heading?"

"Oh I never ask no such questions," chortled Kipp. "I be satisfied that Bessie 'ere is 'appy to follow so we will find out in the end no doubt. They be from other parts though, that is for sure, for I cannot understand a word of what they is saying," he bellowed with laughter.

Eneas offered loudly, "I'll wager I know where they are going."

The wagon master eyed him curiously. "And where might that be?"

"Grimfell," Eneas responded. "That is where our journey ends also – we are taking my sister there to be wed."

"Ah, that could well be the truth young sire," agreed Kipp. "However, from what they 'ave told me with a spot of waving 'ands an' all that, is that they be from a land across the waters and 'ave never been in this land before."

Eneas looked at him. "Which means no-one would know about 'em," continued Kipp. "Methinks they just wanderin' like me and Bessie 'ere, and will follow any road to see where it takes 'em. So makes sense they could end up at Grimfell, but only by fate's will."

Berowen was amazed at the gaily-coloured clothing and admired the musicians' craft as she rode passed them. They played their instruments as they danced along, some of them turning in circles as they did so. They slowly made their way along the path twirling and dancing as they went – the music inviting all who heard it to join in the fun. Even Berowen could not help but tap her feet slightly in her stirrups.

The girls were darker skinned than she had ever witnessed before and all had raven black hair that shone in the sunlight and loosely flowed to their waists and beyond. They all seemed so young, and they all seemed so happy with their world. Their feet wore no shoes as they happily danced along the track apparently not noticing the rough ground across which they were travelling. In their hands they carried garlands, and around their ankles were small circlets of bells that tinkled and rang sweetly in the air with every movement. As they danced they weaved patterns in the air with the ribbons, which coiled around akin to brightly coloured serpents about their heads.

They all had fresh faces of the most delicate beauty; their complexions were smooth, and their eyes dark. Berowen smiled to herself as she noticed both her brothers turning their heads to watch them with a look of instant adoration across their faces.

They sang as they went, in a tongue that Berowen did not recognise. All were smiling and their eyes shone with delight at their music-making. She smiled at them with envy as she passed. How she wished she could stop her mount and join in their merry journey.

The music slowly faded behind them, as the wedding party moved on towards Grimfell. But Kipp and the others were never far behind, for the walking pace of the horses and the dancing pace of the troupe were not that different. As Berowen turned in her saddle, she could still make out the gay colours behind them. A hope began to take seed in her mind with the twilight.

"Where shall we camp for the night?" she queried. "Would it not be good to camp with our fellow travellers?"

Thurstan thought for a moment and it came to him that Berowen's suggestion was perhaps a sensible solution. They were out in the open and there was the added security of safety in numbers. He reined his horse to a halt and the others did likewise.

Aelwulf was not so sure, however. Whilst he agreed about the added numbers, he was not certain whether it would be safe to camp so near to people about whom they knew nothing. Eneas and Amleth were only too eager to suggest that the proposition was an excellent idea, but they obviously had other motives on their minds. Eneas, with a hardly disguisable enthusiasm in his voice, pointed out that Kipp had obviously been with them for a few days and had been perfectly safe amongst them, so there was no reason to believe that they would not be.

The troupe caught up with them again, and as they passed by the wedding party, they waved.

It was Berowen's mother who voiced the doubt; a doubt that niggled at Aelwulf also, but the voicing of which he had no idea how to approach. When his wife spoke, he realised that he should have left it up to her in the first place, for he remembered that Ethwen never skirted an issue and always went straight to the point. He cringed as the words came forth from his wife's mouth, but also smiled inwardly at her outspokenness.

"Their skin colour is not natural – look how dark it is," whispered Ethwen. "The girls have their hair loose and look unkempt, and look.....their arms are painted with patterns." She so wanted to point at one of the girls as an example, but even Ethwen knew that that would not be becoming of one so noble as herself. "I do not think we should stay near to them. And the men look like thieves and brigands with their dark hair and eyes. A bunch of ruffians if you ask me; they were probably exiled from their own lands for some deed against others."

"Oh mother, you should not judge people by the way they appear," scolded Berowen almost impatiently. "I feel sure that to make camp with them would put us at no danger whatsoever. They are perfectly trustworthy. You make it sound as if they would murder us in our sleep and steal our belongings; what little we have."

Ethwen huffed and ruffled herself in her saddle. "Look at those eyebrows – they are much too closely set together and you know what that means......"

"Mother!" Berowen said with raised voice. "You are becoming unsettled. I insist that you relax your composure for now, before you say something that is overheard by someone. And if they had committed some crime in their own land, I am sure that exile would not have been the first choice open to their accusers. Methinks they would be not breathing the air of our lands if found guilty of any wrong deed against others."

"Bah", retorted Ethwen getting more and more anxious. "The accusers were probably fooled by their beauty. You know how that turns the heads of weak men."

Aelwulf let out a load roar of laughter. "Wife," he shouted. "You may not be a fresh, crisp apple any more, but to me you are a plump, round delicious windfall and always will be. You must not be so critical of young women – it is not becoming and you must remember that you were once the most beautiful woman in all of Brundannon. Does that make *me* weak?" He looked at his wife, and the look on her face was enough to encourage him to mull over his last words. It was clear by her expression that he had said something to upset her. When the realisation of his error dawned upon him, he swiftly remedied it with a quick clearing of his throat. "As indeed you still are, my love."

Ethwen fiddled with her wimple and tutted to herself as her cheeks reddened with prickled indignity. "An old windfall am I? Riddled with maggots too I presume."

Berowen could not help but giggle at her father's ineptitude at romance and her mother's bristling annoyance at the perceived insult. "Your words are definitely honeyed, father. They deserve to be immortalised in song from this moment on. Methinks I shall have to pen a verse or two and match them to some music that will be remembered from this day forth."

She began to sing words as they came to her mind:

> *"My sweet, sweet love, the wind did blow*
> *And knock you to the ground*
> *Your skin took on a wrinkled glow*
> *But my love for you holds no bound"*

Then she laughed more than she had laughed in a long time. She could not help herself, especially when she saw the looks upon her parents' faces; her mother glowered and her father blushed. But her singing gained the attention of the musicians and slowly one instrument after another began to play. This made Berowen laugh even more for she knew that the troupe knew not of what she was singing. She dismounted and sang the verse twice more before slightly curtsying to the musicians and remounting her horse feeling slightly guilty at taking advantage of the difference in tongue, but also feeling elated at her triumph.

Berowen dearly hoped that they could make camp with the travelling musicians. She longed to play her lute and sing, and to have such company would be most welcome. She had no sense of misgiving about so doing, and found herself unreasonably angry with her mother for suggesting otherwise. She too had noticed the patterns painted on the girls' arms, but rather than instantly despise them for such a thing, she was intrigued with the images.

Thurstan had thought it best to keep quiet whilst the family continued their strange conversation. He could not quite fathom as to why the dialogue had turned into such a peculiar exchange of words, but had sat upon his horse and watched the events as they unfurled.

He was surprised at Ethwen's reaction towards the fellow travellers for he deemed her observations slightly harsh, but then he was used to travelling and, hence, with making passing acquaintance with many different people. When Berowen began to sing her little song, he watched her performance with veiled amusement and a certain amount of delight that she seemed to be enjoying herself for the first time since he had first met her. He knew that the weight upon her heart must be heavy and the journey unbearably onerous in its ending. He thought, then, that it would probably be a most beneficial course for them to share camp that night. If only to ensure that one of Berowen's final evenings on the trail would be one that she could fondly look back upon as at least one shining light in her last days of freedom from her vows.

Thus it was this that he spoke about quietly to Aelwulf when the marital squabble had abated between Ethwen and her husband. Aelwulf considered Thurstan's words carefully, Berowen's happiness being of the utmost importance at such a time. He considered his wife's observation also, although he had to admit again that he had thought along similar lines for a short time, and could not really accuse her of being over-suspicious of the troupe under such circumstances. If he were wrong, the wrath of Ethwen would know no bounds, but if he were right then his daughter would be able to enjoy herself at least one more time before entering into the arrangement that Aelwulf still felt guilty about. So, to both his sons' and daughter's delight - and to Ethwen's obvious chagrin - it was decided that the camp that night would, indeed, be with their fellow travellers.

XXXVII

When the man awoke, his sleep's thoughts were still with him. They were so vivid within his mind that when he first opened his eyes, he thought that he was still huddled in the bushes where his mother had settled him. He could almost feel the dampness left by the soft caress of her lips upon his forehead. After all these years alone in the woods, the sight of the woman in the clearing the day before had unlocked a part of his memory that had long been firmly closed. He had once been a part of the outside world; he had had a mother and she had taken him to the woods to hide him from the voices that came for him. He had no recollection of why she should take and abandon him in such a place, nor what happened to her and why he had not seen her again. But the urgency in her voice and the way she had dragged him from their home brought a sense of fear within him.

He remained for some time curled up on the soft bed of pine needles, hesitant to move. Part of him wished to return to sleep in the vain hope that he could dream further; now that the door was slightly ajar he wished to sneak in and see if he could learn more of his past. However, at the same time the thought of doing so was extremely worrisome for he feared that he might gain knowledge that would prove too painful for him to bear. Even after last night's discovery, he felt a deep sense of sadness within him. He did not know what exactly this feeling was; only that it caused him to hurt deep inside himself – in his chest and in his stomach.

No, he would not let himself fall asleep again.

He rose from his resting place and hobbled off further into the forest in search of food for his empty stomach, and water for his nagging thirst.

Deeper in the belly of the forest, Mog had been working since the sun had first arisen in the sky, and her fingers were tired and sore from the toil she had been undertaking all day with the tufts of hair from the box. On several occasions, Peg had tried to persuade her to join in a spot of trickery with the hares in the forest. Hares were such easy prey to tease and worry – they fretted about almost anything and it was always great fun to watch them freeze and then thump on the ground with their back legs before scuttling off into the undergrowth with their scut signalling danger to all that happened to be behind them. Mog was usually game for such japes, but she was shrouded today under a cloud of anxiety and irritability as she sat with her head down in concentration, and her tongue clenched between her teeth.

Peg had often noticed Mog retrieving the mystical box from its hidden confines. She always knew where Mog had hidden it, but she never once went to take a look. Mog had reappeared with the box last winter when she had returned from the bowels of the forest, and the visit with The One. Her face had lost its usual rosy cheerfulness and the smile that usually stretched from ear to ear was absent for the whole evening. She had refused to speak of the meeting other than to say that a task had been given her to perform before the following winter, and Peg had not pressed her. It became obvious over the months that Mog was collecting something, although Peg had never actually witnessed her during the act. And there had been many evenings when Mog had disappeared into the darkness for hours upon end, obviously upon some mission on behalf of The One and the task laid before her.

Peg had a natural curiosity as do most of her kind, and it had been extremely difficult for her not to be nosey and to take a peek at the box. Once she had accidentally sat upon the clump of grass under which it was hidden, and Mog had thrown such a vehement rage toward her that Peg had jumped up in haste and had run off into the nearest thicket to hide from her friend. She was so scared of any retribution that Mog may throw down upon her, for - when angered - Mog can be a dangerous faerie and that is a fact not to be argued.

So Peg had left Mog to her task and had wandered off in search of some of their kin to see if any of them were up for a game of hare-harrassment. She did not have to search for long, because it was the faerie way to play at such games.

Mog scowled as Peg left, and muttered under her breath. She wanted to join in the fun, but the days were passing rapidly and daylight was at a premium, and although she still had a few weeks yet to complete the undertaking, she wished to finish it with plenty of time to spare in case there was a need for more supplies. If there were, it would indeed be more difficult to obtain them and may mean long travels under darkness to find a suitable source, something that she did not wish to do if such a task could be avoided.

XXXVIII

During the talk around the campfire, Kipp mentioned that a rider had passed them by that same afternoon. He had been travelling at great speed and did not stop to exchange pleasantries, but kept his horse at its fast pace. If nothing else, he prided himself on his counting skills and he had noticed that one rider was missing from the wedding party – not including the poor man who had met his end in the forest.

Wandering Kipp was not one to keep himself to himself and he chatted away well into the night, his rosy cheeks glowing in the firelight - it was as if he was catching up with all the days and nights that he had been travelling on his own. The words poured out of his mouth and it was a hard task for anyone to get a word in – even in reply to any questions he might ask. He did not give anyone a chance to respond, but continued chatting about anything that came into his head, even if it was completely at odds with what the question had been about in the first place.

Ethwen nodded off with her head on her husband's shoulder, not out of rudeness for the jolly chap's bantering, but out of extreme exhaustion. The journey was beginning to catch up on her, and she would be very glad to reach their destination, even though it would mean that she would give up her only daughter into wedlock and would say goodbye to her a few days later. These days in the saddle had given her buttocks a rough time and she could hardly walk properly, let alone sit down for long before they began to ache. She was used to riding, but not at this hard endless pace.

Eneas and Amleth had both wandered off in the vague direction of the musicians and dancers, as was perhaps to be expected. They had stayed with the others for a short while before making excuses about having to stretch their legs or have a piss, but had not returned. Berowen had thrown them a look of knowing when they each took their leave, and had sighed to herself at having to remain seated next to Kipp as he gabbled the minutes away.

The aromas of cooking that had wafted over from the other camp had reached her nostrils and had made her most unsatisfied with the usual meal of hare stew that had been slopped unceremoniously into her bowl by Finn earlier. The sweet scent of herbs and spices that tickled her senses from their camp companions impelled her to try their taste, for she had not smelt such before, but she had had to be satisfied with her meal.

Thurstan smoked on his pipe as usual and her father seemed to listen with intent to Kipp, although she noticed eventually that his eyelids too had closed, although he remained sitting as if still listening. Berowen even began to feel a bit sorry for poor Bessie at having to keep company with Kipp day in and day out. No wonder she plodded with drooped head.

Laughter reached her ears and she could make out the guffaws of her younger brother, mixed with the giggle of female voices. "This is not fair," she said to herself as she fidgeted with exasperation. "It is insufferable that they should have all the fun all the time," continued her private conversation. She smiled at Kipp and nodded her head in agreement at whatever it was that he was saying. In truth she had no idea what had just been uttered forth from his mouth as she was too frustrated to listen. She craned her neck to the right so that she could peer behind him. In the background, she could see the flames of the other fire, but could only make out shadows of figures. She bit her lip and glanced back at Kipp, who seemed to have paused as if waiting a response from her. Embarrassed, she offered a definitive "Yes, indeed."

She heard Thurstan splutter and cough as if he had inhaled too deeply. She turned around to see him throw back his head and roar with laughter, spluttering as he did so. She looked quizzically at him and then returned her gaze to Kipp, who looked slightly aghast and crestfallen. Suddenly she had the feeling that she had said something out of turn and became worried as to what she had agreed with her reply. She felt her cheeks redden and turned again at Thurstan in the hope that he would enlighten her.

"My lady," Thurstan said, still coughing up the smoke that he had inhaled too deeply. "Kipp enquired as to whether he was talking too much as is his wont. I think your reply may have been a bit too honest, my lady." And he roared again.

"Oh!" she exclaimed. "I...I...I...Not in the least Kipp," she ventured hurriedly, completely ashamed at her behaviour, and the resulting misunderstanding.

"My dear Kipp," added Thurstan. "Please forgive my lady, but she has her mind on other things of late. In a day or two - if we are lucky in our travels - we shall arrive at Grimfell where she is to be joined in wedlock. I am sure you can understand that her thoughts are elsewhere at this time."

Kipp nodded in sympathetic agreement. He had no way of knowing the exact truth behind the forthcoming nuptials, but was under the personal assumption that the idea of wedlock in general needed the solemnity of a sympathetic nod, rather than an enthusiastic one. He had never entered into such a union himself, and had no expectations of ever doing so.   He laughed. "'Tis alright me lord," he said. "I knows me mouth talks too much. And methinks my ramblin's have rambled a bit too long on this night. I takes no offence, me lady," he said looking at Berowen. "You's a young'un and it must be a bad time you be 'avin' on this 'ere journey."

Berowen looked down at her hands that were nestled in her lap. "I am sorry, Kipp. Please forgive me for my poor manners. My attention was diverted by my brothers' laughter."

"Nowt to forgive, me lady. Why don't you go an' join 'em over there. 'ave a bit of fun before your journey's end," replied Kipp winking. "Tis time I laid these old bones down anyway and rested meself."

Berowen stood and turned again to Thurstan, who had at last regained his composure. She bowed her head slightly at him in acknowledgement and thanks for his intervention. She was taken aback slightly when he returned her smile and threw her a quick wink.

"I think I may join you for a short while," he said as he tapped out his pipe. "If that is agreeable my lady. It seems that everyone at this camp has, or will, be asleep before too long and I still have a small breath of wakefulness within me."

"Please do, my lord Thurstan," said Berowen. She was aware of the various snores from around the camp and became conscious that it was indeed just herself and Thurstan who seemed to be awake still.

"Aye," mumbled Kipp from under his cloak. "That's what me babblin' usually does. Sends folks to sleep." And he laughed. "Even ol' Bessie nods off while she's a'walkin. I shall greet you on the morrow."

As Berowen and Thurstan approached, Amleth and Eneas removed their arms from the shoulders of the girls they had draped themselves around and looked slightly abashed as their sister appeared before them.

One of the men gestured at the two with beckoning hands and a broad smile on his face. He said something to them, but they did not understand, although it was obvious that he was welcoming them to the camp.

There was a pot still bubbling over the fire and the aromas made Berowen's mouth water with expectation. She walked over to it and inhaled deeply.

"I have no idea what it is, but it is delicious sister," said Eneas.

One of the girls offered Berowen and Thurstan a bowl each and nodded towards the pot. Although Thurstan's hunger had been satisfied, he knew that it would appear rude not to accept the offer, so he took the bowl and ladled out a helping first to Berowen and then to himself.

Berowen seated herself next to her brothers and Thurstan sat at a slight distance. Berowen looked around for something with which to eat the stew.

"Sip from the bowl," offered Amleth.

Berowen did so, raising the bowl to her lips. As the stew met her tastebuds, she was not disappointed. It was indeed delicious.

One of the girls began to sing in a soft voice, the notes dancing in the night air. Berowen was at once annoyed with herself for forgetting to bring her lute, but when she saw that the musicians did not take up their instruments she relaxed and listened to the sweet voice. She could see from their faces that all loved this song – perhaps it was a song regularly sung in their homelands. The men and other girls started to hum softly under their breath as the girl sang. She had such a beautiful clear voice and she walked amongst them as she sang, touching their shoulders as she went. Some of them started to cry, their tears rolling down their cheeks slowly. Oh how Berowen would have loved to know what the words meant, for they were so clearly very special.

When the girl had finished her song, she sat down and one of the men began to croon a different tune. His voice was deep and the others fell silent and listened intently to his words as they rolled off his tongue in a language that was richer than any Berowen had heard before.

When the song had finished all remained silent, everyone seemed to be lost in their own thoughts – perhaps of a land far away and lost in time.

"A lullaby, sister?" asked Eneas, his own eyes seeming to glisten with tears. "A sweet lullaby to end the evening?"

Berowen all at once realised that this would most likely be the last time that she would sing for her brothers. The thought saddened her deeply and she was not sure whether she would be able to sing for fear of her voice waivering with the melancholy. "I am not sure that I can, dear brother," she replied.

"Please sister. One last time; sing for us before we are parted," pleaded Amleth as if he had read her mind.

"I shall try, sweet Amleth."

And she took a deep breath and began to sing the lullaby so familiar to her family. Everyone listened as her voice filled the air, and by the time she had finished there were tears flowing down everyone's cheeks.

Apart from those of Thurstan, that is, for he had left the camp the moment that Berowen had started to sing.

XXXIX

The marshes spread out before them as they began their day of travel. The travellers had awoken to a dull day – the sky seemed to hang low with foreboding with great swathes of grey clouds. A well-worn track stretched out before them, the ground on either side of it becoming more and more waterlogged as they went. Large clumps of bull-rushes and tuft weed wafted in the wind that gently blew across the open space around them. There was nothing to stop its progress save for the odd tree that clung to life in solitude, their trunks and branches bent tellingly in one direction as if pointing the way for the wind to go. Ever since they had been saplings, the wind had moulded them in its wake and now they all leaned north. It was an eerie sight and Berowen became morose as she realised that this land around her was that which she was to live within for the rest of her life. Gone were the green pastures of her home – a barren, gloomy land was to replace them, land that seemed to breathe despair over whoever traversed its landscape.

It was important that all kept to the path, as the marshes were full of pits that would suck even Kipp's dilapidated wagon into their depths. They followed two abreast at most, and a silence befell them. Even the troupe had temporarily lost their gaiety and love of life. There was dampness in the air and the earth around them smelt of decay. And then it came. Without a sound, a low mist rolled across the landscape devouring the ground around them. It wrapped itself around the travellers who soon found themselves enveloped in its damp grip. As its tiny droplets settled in the fabric of their cloaks that they had pulled tightly around them, the mist seemed to take on shapes and perform a dance of death as if attempting to lure them off their path.

As the wheels of Kipp's wagon crunched the stones as they rolled across them, the sound seemed to echo around everyone in their murky shrouds. Everyone's mood fell to despondency and all rode or walked in their own silent contemplation. Berowen rode next to her mother, and occasionally she would glance across to see her muttering incantations under her breath, followed by a frantic crossing of herself.

On one occasion Ethwen seemed so beside herself that Berowen reached her hand out, which her mother immediately clasped tightly in return; so tight was her grasp that Berowen felt as if her own bones would be broken. She winced and shut her eyes against the discomfort; the muttered words of her mother resounding in her brain until they seemed to blot out her own thoughts. Berowen had never heard her mother recite such words and their meaning was completely unknown to her, but to her utmost dismay, she found herself reciting words under her breath in unison with her mother. But they were different words – almost as if in competition with those of her mother. The grip on her hand loosened immediately as the words came forth with unexpected ease from her lips.

A hoarse croaking cry of 'kaugh' silenced her. Berowen opened her eyes to see a raven flap its dark way over her head. It flew so low over her that she could feel the air from its wing beat. It flew slightly ahead, circled around and flew back towards her – its cry eerie in the mist. As it passed her, she could see its brown beady eye staring at her from its glossy black head. However, she did not flinch but sat with her back rigid in her saddle.

The travellers tried to shoo the bird away. It was clear that the reputation of the raven was rife in the homelands of the troupe for the girls began to wail at its appearance and the men, although obviously as disturbed at its arrival as their womenfolk, tried to comfort them.

"A portent!" wailed Ethwen. "Death awaits someone here."

"I believe not, mother," responded Berowen with a knowing firmness in her statement.

"Ravens are bad omens, daughter, you know that," replied Ethwen.

"Not always, mother," answered Berowen as she watched the bird fly into the distance ahead of them.

"You know not of what you speak," said Ethwen.

"I know not of what I speak, mother. But I know that what I speak is true."

"You are babbling daughter. You speak no sense."

"There has been a lot that has not made sense upon this journey, mother. But the arrival of the raven is not one of them."

Ethwen stared at her daughter for a moment, trying to hide the look of mistrust that suddenly surged within her. She crossed herself frantically and her incantations began again.

The mist seemed to abate slightly and ahead she could see Thurstan riding unerringly on. He, alone, appeared to be the only person who, like her, knew the sudden appearance of the raven not as a portent, but as something far more *potent*.

The brief respite did not last long and the grip of mist encircled them again, this time seemingly more intent upon leading them astray into the boggy earth around them. It became denser and at one point Berowen could not even see her mother clearly, as she rode alongside. It was at this moment that the distant thud of heavy hooves reached everyone's ears. It was impossible to discern from which direction they approached. Was Ethwen's warning coming true after all? And was Berowen – and perhaps Thurstan - completely wrong in their own interpretation of the raven's appearance?

Were they, after all these days on the road, destined to now be cut down by an invisible enemy, and their corpses left to sink into the depths of the marshes? In her mind's eye, she could see the ugly, pock-marked face of the red-beard who had chased her through the forest only days before. Her right hand clenched itself around the cold, wet hilt of her sword that hung at her side.

The sound of hoof beats ceased. A voice boomed into the mist and she jumped in her saddle from the sudden outburst that had been most unexpected.

"Hail there, travellers! We are sent from Grimfell to search for Aelwulf of Brundannon and his party to give them safe passage. Upon the orders of Lord Modig. Are you they?"

Berowen's grip relaxed. She heard her father reply in the affirmative.

"A soldier by the name of Brogil arrived at Grimfell this morn with tales of terror upon your travels."

Berowen heard the other soldiers welcoming the news that their companion had arrived safely, and she too was relieved that no harm had befallen him. But a wave of despair washed over her at the arrival of the escort for it meant that her destination was near. Suddenly she felt vulnerable and the sense of fear of what awaited her – something she had managed to keep under reasonable control over the past days – overcame her. She wanted to scream and urge her horse onwards into the gloom in the hope that she could disappear under its cover. The notion gnawed at her very bones; her grip tightened on her reins, and the muscles in her thighs tightened against her horse in preparation for her flight.

Then sense returned to her and she remembered the dangers that lurked not a step or two away from her in the marshes of the Wellonaw. Was it a fate worse than death that she was riding towards or would death really be a better escape? There was a definite result from death but the fate may not be as she perceived. Even she had to admit that, even now as she pondered on her next possible move.

The mist clearing again, she saw the shadowy shapes up ahead next to her father and Thurstan. She could make out at least ten other riders. Eneas walked his horse slowly back towards his mother and sister. "My father requests your presence at the head of the line."

Ethwen and Berowen followed Eneas to where Aelwulf and Thurstan had halted their horses.

The man who was in conversation with them bowed his head at the two females as they approached. "My ladies," he said. "My Lord Modig sends his highest regards and looks forward to your arrival at Grimfell, as does his son Brack. He is sorry that you have encountered such a dangerous journey and wishes now that he had dispatched an escort earlier."

"I am sure he would not have thought that our journey would be so perilous," responded Ethwen. "And he should not reproach himself for the lack of escort."

The man scrutinised Berowen from behind the visor of his helm. His first impression of his lord's new daughter-in-law was that she was unkempt, dirty and had a wild look about her. Her clothes were soiled from the travelling and her hair dangled limply from beneath her hood. She definitely had no look of nobility about her, and he wondered whether there had been a mistake made. However, he was taken aback slightly by her curtness when she spoke.

"Sire," she said quietly. "To whom are we addressing if I may be so bold to ask? Your appearance here on this road under such conditions concerns me, and the safety of my mother. Father, did you not ask his name?"

Aewulf shot his daughter an angry look at her audacity at questioning him. Tempers were frayed he realised, but her attitude was not befitting of her status. She continued before he had a chance to reply.

"Sire. Please forgive my impertinence, but I feel under the circumstances it would be gracious of you to remove your helm and show yourself before us," she said, her confidence gaining. The notion had come upon Berowen that her future status over this man should be put to good use, and that in demonstrating her position now would benefit her in future and show these particular men that she was not to be trifled with. They could then pass on this information to others in the garrison; she would not entertain the thought of anyone treating her as a mere chattel now, or in the future.

Disgruntled by her manner, the man hid his ire; he was intelligent and wise enough to realise that to cross the future daughter-in-law of his master would be a great mistake. After all, in doing so could incur a wrath upon him that would ruin his career within the hierarchy of the garrison.

He bowed his head slightly and raised his hands to remove his helm. "I offer my apologies for this oversight, my lady." She watched as he eased the helm from his head and sat with it balanced across the front of his saddle. "I am called Earh, my lady."

Berowen nodded her head in greeting. "And what, pray, is your status?"

"I am a Captain in the garrison of Grimfell, my lady," he responded.

Berowen noticed a slight puffing of his chest when he announced this and she could not resist saying, "And very proud of such a position it seems."

She was well aware that she was taking out the unhappiness of her situation on this man before her. However, she had taken an instant dislike to him for reasons unknown, apart from the fact that she found his stance to be arrogant.

But then, as Earh sat astride his horse before her, she began to feel her resolve slip away. She found herself feeling guilty at taking out her frustration on him, however much his presence irritated her. Berowen began to question herself about her determination in making sure that these men before her acknowledged her status, and that she was to be treated as well as her forthcoming position deserved. Perhaps, in her efforts, she had been too harsh, and had merely given the impression of being rude rather than commanding. It would certainly be better to attain respect from Earh by displaying her rank over him more subtly and thus avoiding making an enemy of such a man, which would be a foolish thing to do so early in her life at Grimfell.

She heard her brothers stifling their mirth behind her, and, out of the corner of her eye, noticed Thurstan half-smiling. But she noticed, too, her father glowering at her impudence and heard her mother chuntering under her breath. Her nerve suddenly evaporated, and she decided to end the matter. And so in response to his revealing his position, she said as sweetly as she could, "And so you should be, Captain Earh, for it is an esteemed position to hold I am sure. Your family must be very proud of you."

Thurstan took this opportunity to change the subject and enquired as to how far away Grimfell was, and how long it would take to reach.

Earh turned in his saddle and pointed down the road from whence he and his men had ridden. "When the mist clears, my lord, you will see Grimfell in the distance upon the hill. I would have suggested that we ride on in haste in order to reach the walls tonight, but it would not be prudent to attempt such a journey in these conditions. We shall make camp a little further, and hopefully be able to arrive sometime on the morn."

Earh urged his horse to move further down the line of travellers to ascertain how many there were to escort. He scrutinised each member of the wedding party with an air of authority, but the disdain he held for the troupe of musicians, dancers and old Kipp was more than obvious when he came upon them at the rear of the procession. He reined his horse sharply to a halt and ordered them to move on. "Be off with you – keep to the path and you will undoubtedly reach the walls before nightfall. If you do not stray then you shall not come to harm from the terrors of the bog. I can, of course, not be responsible for any accidents that may befall if you should lose your way."

The members of the troupe did not understand a word of what Earh was saying to them. They looked at each other, some shrugging their shoulders, while others shook their heads. Some talked amongst themselves in apparent confusion, but Kipp it was who spoke from the midst of them. "They do not understand you, Captain, and although it is as clear as day to me what you saying, I be thinkin' it would not be a good idea for us to agree to your instructions."

"You *think*, do you?" responded Earh, eyeing the rotund traveller with contempt. Not known for his cool temper, the words spat from the captain's lips seeped in sarcasm and belligerence.

Thurstan had followed Earh down the line of travellers, and quickly intervened, "They are with us." Continuing firmly, but graciously, he added, "They will arrive at the walls when we do. They will not be moved on."

Earh turned his head, much as a cat does when it espies something tasty out of the corner of its eye. He stared at the man who had just spoken. "And who might you be?" he asked curtly, thrusting his head forward as he spoke. Earh was not accustomed to having his orders challenged, and Thurstan's intervention had caused his mood to darken even more.

"That is of no matter Captain. I have been your new charges' guide since leaving Brundannon, and that is all you need to know. I am sure Lord Aelwulf would concur with what I have said."

In truth, Aelwulf had no care one way or the other, but for the sake of preventing the flare of temper within the Captain of Grimfell burning even stronger, he acknowledged that what Thurstan had said was true, and with a nod of his head, he responded, "Indeed, that is so."

The bedraggled travellers followed Earh and his men for about about half-an-hour but the ever-thickening murkiness seemed to cling to them. They found themselves eventually making camp in the thick fog, and were all glad when it was time to bed themselves down out of the cold, damp air.

XL

When Berowen awoke the next morning, the woolliness of the sounds around her confirmed that the fog had not lifted during the night. She had lain awake for most of the dark hours, wrapped within her bedroll. She assumed that her parents had suffered a restless night also from the constant sounds of restlessness that arose from their direction. There were odd sounds emanating from the bog all through the dark hours, of creatures chirruping and squeaking. However, she had eventually fallen into a fitful sleep and had been awoken by the activity around the camp as the soldiers of the escort and those of Brundannon prepared to make everything ready for the last part of the journey.

The morning of her arrival at Grimfell had dawned and there was nothing for her to do but put a brave face upon the whole thing. She would be changing her travelling clothes before starting out that morning, and wearing something a little more befitting her station. She did not relish the thought considering the coldness in the air, but she could not arrive at the fortification in the clothes that she had been wearing since leaving her home. A gown, shoes, gloves and cloak had been carefully packed for this last part of the journey, together with a fresh gown for Ethwen, but neither her or her mother had checked upon their condition since leaving Brundannon. She could but hope that they had not suffered any mishap.

Ethwen had had the same thoughts during the night as she lay trying to get to sleep. She had worked herself up into a panic at the idea that they would unpack the items from the saddlebags to find they had been ruined by the weather, or had been eaten by those creatures that flittered around the braziers at night. They flirted with the flames and many a time one fluttered too close and met its death in the fire.

∞

Moths. They were the bane of Ethwen's life. Or so Ethwen was often heard to exclaim. She would rush down the stairs and fling a garment at her husband accusing these tiny creatures of ruining her gown, and exclaiming that she now had nothing to wear at the banquet that evening. Aelwulf would usually examine the gown and notice nothing until Ethwen would snatch it away and then thrust it under his nose, her finger pointing to a tiny hole or two. "There. You see? It is ruined."

"But they are but small holes, wife. Surely you can stitch them," Aelwulf would say, for he never learned his lesson from the time before.

"Stitch them. Stitch them!" she would cry as she ran off to find Morgen, the seamstress. "As if I have the time to sit and stitch, with a banquet to organise. You must rid us of these pests, husband."

∞

Berowen arose from her bed, such that it was, and stretched before quickly wrapping herself in her cloak once again. She poured some water from her water carrier into the palm of her hand and quickly splashed it across her face. There was not much of it, but it would suffice to wash away the remaining sleep from her eyes, and the coldness of it jolted her into full wakefulness.

She could hear the girls singing as they went about their business in the separate camp behind her own, and admired their cheerfulness at such an early hour and in such dismal conditions. Her father and brothers were already up and talking to Earh and she noticed that Thurstan's bedroll had already been packed away. However, she could not see him and wondered where he had gone.

Her mother was sitting up, still wrapped in the bedroll and her cloak. Berowen felt sympathy for Ethwen – the journey had been hard on her in her advancing years. As she watched her, Berowen felt a tinge of great sadness within her heart. Her mother looked so tiny as she sat shivering in the early morning chill, her grey hair bundled upon her head and secured with a bone comb. She would miss her mother terribly and feared that this may even be the last time that she saw her. There was still the return journey to Brundannon, and Ethwen's frailty was more apparent with each passing day.

Berowen approached Ethwen and held out a hand to help her mother to her feet. Ethwen looked up at her daughter and smiled, despite the glistening in her eyes. She turned her head and wiped at her eyes so that her daughter could not see her sadness. Taking the offered hand, she got to her feet and brushed down her dress.

"Daughter it is time we were brave and gave our gowns the sight of the day, as miserable as it is." They walked arm in arm to where the two bags lay. Berowen knelt down and unfastened the buckles on both bags before opening each one slowly. Ethwen was relieved to see nothing moth-shaped flew out. Out came Berowen's shoes and gloves, which she gave to her mother to hold while she pulled out the cloak. She stood and shook it to let its shape fall loose before handing it to Ethwen. Then it was the turn of the gown. Gently pulling it out of the bag, she stood with it and gently shook out the creases.

"I do hope that this weather improves, Berowen, for I fear that by the time we reach Grimfell these clothes will be in as bad a state as those we are wearing now."

As she handed her mother the gown Berowen nodded in agreement, "I am afraid you may be right, mother. But there is nothing that we can do about this disagreeable weather."

Berowen then pulled out her mother's gown from the other bag. Shaking out the creases she smiled and said, "It would seem that your fears are allayed, mother. Everything seems to have endured the journey well." She looked at mother who had fast disappeared under the pile of clothing draped over her. She laughed lightly. "Mother, you look like a washerwoman on wash day."

Ethwen laughed. It was as if the two had suddenly become friends after all the years they had been together, rather than just mother and daughter. A different bond had seemed to stretch between them that had not been apparent before. Perhaps it was because Ethwen realised that the girl before her had become a woman in her own right overnight in the face of what was to come. She sighed, but was determined not to let gloom overshadow the day and quickly laughed again.

Ethwen called for Aelwulf to come to their assistance. He made his excuses to Earh and strode towards his wife and daughter.

"We find ourselves in a predicament, husband," began Ethwen as he neared them. "We are to change our clothing for the final stage of our journey but have no privacy. Are we to strip ourselves naked in front of all these prying eyes?"

Aelwulf scratched his beard, as he was wont to do in times of deep thought. "Hmmm." He really had no idea whatsoever what to suggest in order to save the blushes of his wife and daughter.

Ethwen eyed him impatiently as if expecting him to come up with a solution forthwith. She handed Berowen the clothes that she was still clutching to her breast and put her hands on her hips. "This is most unacceptable, husband," she began. "Do you expect us to arrive at Grimfell dressed as we are? What will Modig think? And Brack ... will he think he has been duped when he catches sight of his future wife appearing before him like some serving wench from some inn of ill-repute?"

In her present anxious state, Berowen was not very happy with her mother's description of her appearance. Did she really look like some ale-swigging whore from a grubby tavern? She was shocked at the thought and felt immediately angry, embarrassed and extremely self-conscious.

"Mother!" she exclaimed. "Please tell me that you are exaggerating in your observations of my current appearance."

Ethwen hardly took a breath and replied hurriedly with a wave of her left hand, "Yes, yes, yes, of course my dear. Think nothing of it."

"But how could you....." started Berowen with tears in her eyes. This was not the day for such harsh words. Her mind was already full of misgiving and insecurity and it was not fair for her mother to have been so thoughtless as to say such a dreadful thing. Still clutching the clothing she ran off in the direction of the troupe's camp.

"Tut," huffed Ethwen. "What is wrong with that girl?!"

"An insult is bad enough, dear wife, but one spoken from her own mother's lips is unforgivably cruel," replied Aelwulf in answer to her question. He stared in disbelief at his wife's outburst. He knew she was under much strain of late, but this was going too far.

She had not meant to say such a thing, of course, and after her husband's verbal admonishment, she quickly felt great guilt wash over her. "I am sorry, Aelwulf," she quietly said.

"It is not me to whom you should address this apology, Ethwen, and you know that," answered Aelwulf gruffly.

Ethwen turned to offer the apology to her daughter, and was surprised to see that Berowen was no longer standing behind her.

Aelwulf said nothing but simply lifted one arm and pointed in the direction of the camp to where his daughter had fled in her distress. Ethwen nodded and began to walk away in the same direction.

However, she had only gone a couple of steps when the unmistakable rotund shape of Kipp appeared. He shuffled towards them, his large girth undulating beneath his jerkin. "Greetings of the morning on this auspicious day," he cheerfully said. His eyes were sparkling and his wide grin revealed the large gaps in his top jaw where teeth should have been. He seemed completely oblivious to the stilted atmosphere that clung to the couple as they watched him approach.

"The matter has been resolved to great satisfaction, methinks," he announced proudly.

Ethwen stood in stunned silence; Aelwulf narrowed his eyes as he enquired, "The matter?"

"Aye", he replied. "The matter. You know ... the ladies... flesh," and he laughed almost boyishly as if the last word had triggered some childish delight of saying such a 'dirty' word aloud. As he laughed, his own flesh jiggled even more violently under its tight cloth restraint.

Ethwen grimaced as she watched the fastening at his widest part stretching to the point of threatening to detach itself. And then to her dismay that is exactly what happened. The material could take the strain no longer and flew apart letting a large dollop of white belly flesh flop loose.

Kipp stopped laughing for a minute and looked down. "There it goes agin!" he exclaimed merrily and continued to laugh even more raucously.

"Your resolve to our predicament, Master Kipp?" interrupted Ethwen as loudly and forcefully as she could, all the while attempting to hide her impatience regarding the problem at hand, and the irritability she suffered at the man's cheerfulness.

"Yes, my lady, yes, yes." Kipp spluttered. "Follow me."

Ethwen could see the circle of girls, each of them holding a blanket between them and their neighbour, this circle only broken by the wagon where it acted as the temporary storage place of the clothing. Along with the cloaks, the gowns were spread out on a blanket, and dangled over the edge of the wagon, just above ground level to avoid any stains seeping into the fabric. This was really quite a rather futile act as the hems of the gowns were bound to absorb some moisture once adorning the women, but that could not be helped.

The girls were all facing outwards and just within the circle, Ethwen could make out the head and shoulders of Berowen. She had to admit that it was a very clever idea and definitely served the purpose at hand. She was a little concerned, however, when Kipp continued to walk towards the circle. He seemed to have no awareness that if he was to get too close that the whole attempt at shielding Berowen would serve no use at all. She cleared her throat and stopped in her tracks. He lolloped on.

"Master Kipp," she said loudly. "Methinks that perhaps you can leave now. My thanks for escorting me here, and for your arrangements in finding such a perfect resolve to the problem."

Kipp stopped and looked at Ethwen. He beamed and bowed as far as his belly would allow and hobbled away.

All the girls were busy chattering to their companions and laughing and giggling in delight at their special role that morning. Berowen noticed her mother arrive and turned her head in the other direction – she was still smarting at the insult tossed at her, no matter whether or not it had been delivered without contempt. And, unfortunately, at the moment Berowen saw her mother, Ethwen was still wearing a dark look upon her face from the mixture of annoyance at Kipp's seemingly total oblivion of manners, and his vexing habit of always seeing the bright side of everything.

This did not help to lift Berowen's mood and she wondered upon the correct way of approaching the situation.

Ethwen was perplexed at the morning's unfortunate events also, but there had to be a resolution, and she continued her pace towards the circle. The delicate business of lowering one of the fabric shields to allow Ethwen to speak to her daughter was avoided as Berowen was only in the process of changing her footwear. She sat upon an old milking stool that had been placed in the ring by the thoughtful Kipp; he travelled with many such odd items in the back of his wagon.

Ethwen placed a hand on her daughter's shoulder and stood for a moment in silence. Berowen stiffened under the touch. "Daughter, I am ashamed at the words that uttered forth from my mouth earlier. They were not intended to cause insult, but I can understand now that they were ill-chosen. They were the first things that came to mind when trying to impress upon your father the urgency of our dilemma and the importance of our arriving at Grimfell not looking like common people."

Berowen inhaled sharply and cringed. Common people. It was just as well that those around them could not understand their words for to hear such would have offended them greatly no doubt. In her mother's eyes, though, a definitive line divided the accidents of birth. Either you were born to nobility or you were born to 'the rest'. The rest. Those who toiled the land, fought in armies, worked in the kitchens. All without whom the nobility would not be able to survive. But, Ethwen had always been kind to those who worked behind the scenes at Brundannon in order to ensure that her home ran smoothly, and she thought highly of her seamstress Morgen.

Berowen thought of little Beatha, Morgen's understudy. Being born to lowly labourers had marked her as not to be important, and she was made to feel grateful that she was able to study under the auspices of one such as Morgen in order to learn a respectable trade. Perhaps that is why Berowen had no generous thoughts about Morgen. She was not in those fixed areas of class in which her mother believed, but had become betwixt and between nobility and 'the rest'. Berowen had long been aware of that misty area between them both – those who had worked their way to the top of *that* other class. They were of course, to be commended for their tenacity and hard work, but purely because they were privy to the inner sanctum of nobility, they thought themselves to be better than their peers. Morgen treated little Beatha abominably and made her feel that she was beholden to the old woman for having given her the privilege of 'bettering herself'. This in itself was no bad thing at all, but Berowen did not like the manner in which it was made known constantly, and openly, to the young girl.

When she was young, Berowen had played with children of Brundannon. They had been no different to her other than they had poor parents. She had grown up with them and up to the day she left her home, she always spoke to them as she always had done, and had treated them as friends.

Eahr was one of the Morgens of her world and she had taken an instant aversion to him for it. She knew that her reaction to him the previous day was borne purely out of this instant dislike. She had since questioned herself as to why she could possibly feel such a deep aversion for the man, but as was usual she failed in an answer. It was a feeling that she had experienced on the odd occasion in her life and had realised that there was no answer to the query. It was just that

– a feeling deep within her, almost as involuntary as smell, sight, taste, touch and sound. It was part of her, and she could do nothing about it; she had always just assumed that everyone else was the same, and had never spoken of it to anyone.

Tugging on her second shoe, she decided for the sake of peace between her and her mother that she would ignore the whole affair and accept her mother's apology with good grace. There was no point in arguing with her for she knew she could not win – her mother was set in her ways and had been brought up to think the way she did. Nothing could change her now, and never would.

However, she made up her mind then that she would demand of her new husband that Beatha should be escorted to Grimfell, and that she would look after the young girl and teach her as much that she could in all manner of things.

XLI

Thurstan had arisen earlier than anyone else had, and after saddling his mare and packing his belongings, he decided to ride on ahead for a short way. The fog had not deterred him for he was used to travelling in all weathers, but he still let his mare make her own slow way down a more well-beaten track than of late. The last weeks' interruption to his journey and personal affairs had been interesting, if not a little peculiar. His own passage would now resume but he was not sure whether to stay for a few days at Grimfell to rest in comfort before continuing, or to leave now. His position as guide was now over and there was no real need for him to linger. However, he was at a loss as to why he had been led into the arrangement. To him there was always an explanation for everything. He believed that whatever happened did so for a reason, but he was completely oblivious as to why these last weeks had occurred in the manner in which they did.

What exactly had he learned from the journey? That there was a group of red-bearded soldiers who seemed intent upon causing death to the party? That there was perhaps a real wodwos at large in the Forest of Whispers? To what purpose was either of these pieces of information? He could find none. He had no idea why the red-beards were on their mission – perhaps they were just renegades who enjoyed their sport; he had never heard of them and the only one who had, had been part of some ancient magick and would not speak further of it. He had the sense though that the appearance of the raven was not so hard to explain, and it was this – and this alone – that decided him upon travelling to Grimfell to stay for a few days. Just to prove if his theory was correct. Only then would he leave.

XLII

"W alt. Walt! Come here boy!" came the call. "Where you got to? You being lazy again?"

The 19-year-old lad heard the call and ground his teeth, mumbling to himself as he did so. He sat in the tall grasses at the edge of the pond and rocked back and forth slowly as he intently watched the shiny black beetle tumble its way across the ground. He had spotted it when the sunlight caught its shimmering back and became instantly fascinated with its precarious journey over the small clumps of dry earth in its way. He even helped it in its journey by occasionally removing some of the arid soil from out of its way. His eyes glimmered in delight at his intervention, and he laughed quietly at his benevolence towards the little creature.

It had been an extremely dry summer and the pond had almost dwindled to nothing more than a large murky puddle. But there was still life that breathed amongst the weeds within it and flowers that grew around it. There was the occasional flash of blue as a butterfly fluttered past erratically before landing on the petals of a flower, where it would slowly fold its wings tightly shut whilst it unrolled its long proboscis into the depths of the flower's centre. Then it would slowly open its wings again and flutter off in no particular direction.

Once when he had been sitting very still a frog had sprung on to his foot and had sat there with chin undulating. Walt had imitated the action for many minutes before the little creature hopped off back into the undergrowth.

There were no frogs now – the water had receded to such an extent that they had all gone away. He found himself left today in the company of the beetle, and the occasional butterfly, but both had caught his attention avidly. So much so that he eventually lay down on his belly and watched the beetle as closely as he could without his nose touching the tiny bug's body.

"WALT!" came the call again, this time with anger in its tone and a lot closer than before. Walt flinched and realised his hiding place was soon to be discovered, but he refused to move until it was necessary.

A foot came down in front of his face and landed on the unsuspecting subject of Walt's interest. He had been so close that he heard the scrunching sound of the beetle's demise. He growled softly.

He felt two hands grab the material of the cloth around his neck as he was hauled to a standing position.

"You lazy simpleton, why I ever agreed to your mother's request I will never know," said the man in front of Walt. "You are worthless and deserve to sit in the corner of a locked room away from everyone."

Walt just stood with hunched shoulders in front of the man he knew as Eadric. He was becoming used to the vicious sounds that were slung in his direction from the mouth of this unpleasant man standing before him.

"Your mother dumps you on me every Monday and Friday so she can go off to the market place so that you can help me round 'ere, but you never do nowt."

Eadric was a short stout man with balding hair and dark brown eyes. His face had a dark look upon it and his facial hair framed a tight mouth that hardly ever smiled, with the beard closely cut to his chin. His belly flopped over his hose due to an excessive liking of ale. Although Walt overshadowed him by quite a few inches, Eadric had no fear of insulting his unfortunate charge.

"Go milk the cow like you was asked hours ago," he barked and pointed in the direction of his unfortunate beast. "If you don't the wife will get on at me, and then I will get on at you." The words he spoke meant nothing to Walt.

∞

In the silence within his den, the man stared into the world around him as these memories whirled around in his mind. They came to him as if they had only occurred yesterday, for they were clear in their imagery. He could see Eadric as if the man were standing right before him, here, now, in his sanctum. The sight of him made him angry and upset and he wrung his hands in irritation.

If there was any sensation given by these recent small snippets of memory, it was definitely one of loathing for men. The only sensation of warmth had come from the visions of his mother while asleep the evening before.

A disturbance outside of his den gained his attention and he crawled towards the opening and peered into the dappled light outside. There appeared to him to be an altercation within the thick greenery of the trees, but he could not see the creatures responsible for the dispute. His eyes searched around the vicinity until movement caught his attention in a tree to his left. One of the boughs was shaking violently about five feet from the ground. Then he saw what appeared to be a pair of short legs dangling from the bough – they had fallen into sight and were treading the air. Then the tiny body to which they were attached appeared in view and was obviously hanging on to the branch by the small arms that stretched above its head. From the very faint sound of laughter that reached his ears, it did not appear to be in any distress as such, but almost seemed to be enjoying the whole thing. To the man's astonishment, another body appeared above the other, but this one was upside down, as it clung to the hands of the former. Scratching his head, and with his curiosity pricked, the man approached the tree and peered upwards. The bodies swung in front of his head and occasionally a small foot tapped his forehead. He could see that the figure hanging upside down had wrapped its legs around the branch at the knees and was hanging only by the strength within them. As soon as the creatures saw him, the first one dropped to the ground, followed swiftly by the second whose fall was broken by the first. They turned to look at him and beamed from ear to ear, their pointed ears poking through the mass of tangles of their hair as they did so. They ran round and round him, occasionally tugging at the hair on his legs. This made him dance in discomfort as he tried to avoid their attentions. Soon all three were part of a strange woodland dance as they reeled around on the bed of pine needles until all three of them collapsed on the ground out of dizziness.

Root and Knot were the youngest, and hence the most naughty, of Mog's kin. She would not be pleased to hear that they had shown themselves to the man of the wood. So they made a pact to keep it a secret, but also swore that they would revisit their hairy protagonist again and tease him some more for they had not enjoyed themselves so much for a long while. They had no idea that their futures, and indeed their very lives, depended upon Mog's success in her toils, only that they had the freedom of the forest and that much fun and mischief could be had.

They got to their feet, each poking the man once again for luck, and then darted off into the undergrowth, their tiny bodies shaking with mirth.

The man lay where he had spiralled to the ground out of dizziness and felt confused about what had just occurred.

XLIII

After they had finished their transformation from weary traveller to groomed visitor, Berowen had individually thanked each of the girls for their help. This had proved slightly problematical to begin with, as they did not understand what she said, so she took each girl's hand in both of hers and thanked them while smiling and nodding her head. She had no idea whether they knew what she meant, but she could but hope that they did.

The girls ran off and commenced helping the menfolk in their group in packing up their camp. Most of it was seen to already, and soon they were ready to move on.

Berowen and Ethwen picked their way carefully back to their own camp, where their horses were ready for them to mount. As they walked, they lifted their skirts in order to prevent as much of the moisture from the dank ground as possible oozing its way into the fabric of their hems.

Aelwulf was relieved to see his wife and daughter return seemingly at peace with each other after the earlier events and he kissed both of them on their right cheeks upon their arrival back at camp. He helped them both mount their horse and stood for a moment in quiet contemplation at his daughter as she sat in her saddle. He realised that most of her body must be quaking in anticipation of this last part of the journey, but was full of admiration for her in not showing any such feelings. She looked serene and peaceful as she stared ahead.

"We are ready?" called out Earh.

Despite her outward appearance, Berowen was feeling acutely nauseous. She was also sensitive to the fact that Thurstan was missing from the group, and this troubled her. Whilst she was aware that his presence over the last weeks had been solely to guide them to Grimfell, she had not thought that he would just leave without saying goodbye. From what she had observed, this would not be the action of one such as him, but she had to accept the fact that he *was* absent and this both confused and upset her.

As it rose higher in the sky, the sun had been filtering its way through the fog and was slowly winning the battle over the murky vapours. As the motley line of characters made their way along the path the world around them became more visible and it was not long before they were travelling in full sunlight, the warmth of which shone upon them, and they soon forgot the miserable atmosphere that had greeted them upon their awakening.

In the distance, they could make out the shape of the fortification of Grimfell on the top of a hill that rose from the marshes around it. The last remaining remnants of fog continued to cling to the battlements and gave the impression that a shroud of perpetual gloom enveloped the buttressing. This appearance did not improve Berowen's mood, and sent her deeper into her private world of despair.

Whilst she could not deny that she felt much better after having discarded her travelling clothes, she had to admit to herself that in an odd way she had been sorry to swap them for the garments she was now wearing. She had taken much pleasure in the sense of freedom she had experienced on her journey and, although tinged with fear and sorrow, her travels in the wild had stirred within her a desire to do such again. She had always escaped to the world outside the confines of the walls she used to call home, but that world was still secure – it was well-known to her. The world in which she had been travelling was very different and it intrigued her greatly. Unfortunately, these observations and desires just reinforced her view that she was destined to be no more than a captive within the fortress that loomed ever nearer in her sight.

Earh led his party on with pride. Only recently had the rank of Captain been endowed upon him, because of the death of old Vodlig who had held the position for many years. Vodlig had been one of the captains that had led Modig's army to quash the invasion almost thirty years before that had threatened to march on Grimfell and destroy it and everyone who dwelt within it. As Modig's father, Morgil, had grown older, he had become complacent and had allowed his lands to fall into disarray, thus tempting those with their eyes on a bigger prize gradually to form their own alliances in an attempt to overthrow Modig. There had been two main parties – Thordan and Lofa – who had planned to oust him and split the land between them. However, they had not bargained on the son of Morgil's strength of character, his army, or his natural aptitude for the tactics of war, and he was quick to crush any hope they had of destroying him, or carving up the lands of his ancestors between them. They were rewarded for their efforts by having their heads placed upon spikes that stood outside the gates of Grimfell as a warning to all who may dare wish try a similar act of treachery in the future.

However, with armies came taxes, and although peace had been established on the borders, the price of protection had risen and there was great unquiet amongst the peasants who lived in and worked the settlements under the banner of Grimfell in the Wellonaw Marshes.

As such, Earh was taking his position with extreme seriousness. He was intolerant of those who dare cross him and he would allow no-one to question his orders. The fact that Thurstan had over-ruled such the day before in front of his men had irked him greatly and he was glad that the former had taken it upon himself to leave the party of his own volition.

He was not, then, pleased, when the sight of a stationary horse and rider came into view ahead on the path, especially when it became apparent that it was in Thurstan.

Thurstan had halted his journey at a fork in the track. It had loomed in front of him through the grey haze when he was almost upon it and had taken him by surprise, and it had been here that he made the choice of either going west to continue on his own business or eastward into the chasm that were the gates of Grimfell. There was an old weathered stone leaning backwards and at an angle due to the erosion beneath its base. At first, he had presumed that since travellers had first trodden that way, they had formed the well-worn tracks to the east, west and south of it by happenstance simply by walking around it. There had been a gradual incline in the road leading to the stone, culminating in it being situated on slightly higher land than the marshes around it, and the soil was less boggy. In fact, all three tracks that led to it dropped away from it on its elevated position. This was either one of those strange coincidences of nature or the stone had been placed there deliberately for whatever reason. Gold and green lichen covered the face of it, much as the support of the gibbet was covered, and the elements had worn it down erratically; there was nothing to stop the wind in this forsaken place and over the years, the stone had been attacked relentlessly by sun, rain, wind, snow and sleet.

He had dismounted and inspected its form closer. It was very loose in its earthly socket, and upon laying a hand on it, the stone moved easily under his touch. His tongue instinctively worried the tooth in his jaw that had become loose of late. The movements were so similar – the stone in the ground was like a loose tooth in the mouth of the great mother earth. Trying to ignore the nagging ache in the right side of his lower jaw that his unconscious action had awoken, he ran his fingers over the stone to try to pick out any carving that may have be hidden beneath the thin grasp of lichen. First the front of the stone and then the back, along the sides and the top. Nothing. He found himself strangely disappointed at finding that this stone appeared to be a natural inhabitant of the landscape and had probably stood there in solitude for centuries amid the boggy marshes around it.

Its appearance and position though still nagged at him. There was something not quite right about its situation and he set about searching the area around it to see if anything else could shed light on its existence. The ground, although less boggy, was still soft underfoot – the earth seemingly held together by the roots of the matted grasses. He trod warily and his left foot hit something firm just beneath the soil's surface. 'Probably just a rock,' he thought to himself, nevertheless he stooped to take a closer look. Pulling back the matted grass, he saw what appeared to be another slab of stone, and he tugged at the grass until he had uncovered most of the hidden slab. From the shape of its uneven broken edge, it was clear that it had once stood atop the stone behind him – the edges were a near match apart from the general erosion of the part still fixed, albeit precariously, in the ground. If there was anything on this half-hidden remnant he only hoped that it was on the surface rather than on the reverse, as there would be no way that he would be able to lift it by himself without the aid of some kind of pulley and rope – neither of which he had in his possession. He suddenly thought of Wandering Kipp and a wry grin crept across his face as he mused that this fellow may well have such items in the back of his wagon amongst the strange assortment of items his poor horse Bessie pulled along day by day.

He bent his head down to look closer; luckily the nagging ache in his jaw had at last ebbed so he could bend his head without encouraging a more oppressive ache. He cursed himself for worrying the offending tooth in the first place. He knew that this would cause discomfort but could not resist doing so at times – it was a habit, almost a dare to the tooth to cause him such pain – and the tooth consistently obliged in varying degrees of intensity.

The lichen had not taken so much of a grip on this portion of the stone and it was easier for him to trace his fingers across its surface. From the look of the erosion on the piece that still clung on to its vertical position behind him, the parting of the ways had occurred many years before and in his mind's eye he tried to visualise how it had come to be broken in the first place. It could not possibly have been a natural occurrence. It must have been a deliberate act performed by either man or magick. The former would have the tools of masonry and the latter would have the tools of something higher.

Now on his knees in the damp grass his fingers caressed the cold, uneven surface of the stone. The fog around him was beginning to thin, but his solitary presence in this lonely place was eerie and he could not shrug off the feeling that someone was behind him, watching his every move. Every so often, he would turn, but could make out no shapes in the receding murkiness.

And then he found it - under his fingertips an indentation was carved in the stone. He reached back into his boot for his dagger and gently scraped away the covering of lichen to reveal the semi-circle that his finger had found. Continuing to remove the lichen, he gradually uncovered a crudely carved circle. Slowly he uncovered the whole area around the carving and sat back on his haunches to study it. It made no immediate sense to him, but it was obvious that it must have had some meaning to someone once. No-one would take the time, trouble and effort to carve such an intricate design for no reason. There must be an obvious solution to the enigma before him.

Returning the dagger to his boot, he wished he had a fire to light his pipe. A long smoke of some of his aromatic weed would help his concentration but alas, he would have to make do without. Besides it being unlikely to find the correct kindling, it would be unwise to light a fire in such an open position, especially as the fog was now lifting more rapidly and he could feel the faint rays of the sun upon his back.

Thurstan stood up and, walking around the stone, looked at the carving from different angles to see if an obvious solution appeared miraculously before him. Nothing. It soon dawned on him that the others may well arrive at the spot at any time. He had no idea how far on the path they were, but he felt it important that they should not know of the carving, especially Earh. He would have to come back at another time, preferably under cover of fog so that he could build a small fire, smoke his pipe and study it in more depth. At this time of year, the thick grey vapours often fell upon the earth and the marshes were the ideal place on which it could cling with its cold damp fingers.

As he quickly covered the stone with as much of the grasses as he could, he could make out the faint sound of horses moving toward him. Wiping the dirt off his hands onto his hose, he mounted his mare and waited for the arrival of the rest of his travelling companions.

It was thus that they came upon him. It was not hard to escape the look of loathing upon Earh's face when he noticed Thurstan. He caught the eyes of Berowen's brothers and they both smiled and raised a hand in greeting as they rode passed. Aelwulf was indifferent and Ethwen did not seem to have even noticed he was there. Berowen however looked at him with what he could only describe as a look of hope in her eyes. As always she rode next to her mother, but when she saw Thurstan she reined her horse to a slower pace and as her mother's mount moved on, Thurstan drew his own horse besides Berowen.

"I thought you had left without saying farewell, my lord," said Berowen quietly. "I did not think that you would do such a thing and I am glad to see you again."

"Forgive me, my lady," replied Thurstan. "But I have to admit that I had intended to leave until I came across this fork in the way."

Berowen looked slightly shocked at this admission and asked rather curtly, "And what occurred to change your mind my lord?"

"The raven," he said and did not elaborate further.

"The raven?" Berowen asked suspiciously. "I am sure that I do not understand what you mean." She knew what he meant, but she was not going to admit to anything further until she knew she could trust him.

Thurstan looked across at her. "You, like I, did not see its arrival yesterday as an ill omen," he stated.

"Pray explain your words," she responded, still suspicious of his questioning.

"My lady," began Thurstan. "I have noticed certain things about you whilst we have travelled together. After the incident at the stone circle the seed was sown within my head that you and I are, as my dear late mother would have said, cut from the same cloth."

She eyed him nervously.

He continued, "You and I see things differently to others. We have an opposite view of the earth than others around us. We hear, feel and see things that others do not. Would you agree with this?"

"You talk of things that can be dangerous to speak aloud, my lord," whispered Berowen. "On hearing this, some would kill you and some would use you. You know that."

"Indeed, my lady. That is true. But that in itself does not make it go away. You, like I, were born with it within, the only difference between us is that you are only just beginning to learn its true self. It is only just awakening within you."

"And the raven?" she asked deliberately avoiding a response to the previous statement.

"I think you know, my lady. However, we shall find out before long as we shall soon arrive at the gates of Grimfell."

Berowen turned her head towards the hill and there before her was the now unshrouded shape of the fortification that would be her new home. Its forbidding stone slabs loomed over her and cast a shadow down upon those beneath its walls as they approached the great wooden gate.

"You should arrive with your mother, my lady, not one such as me," Thurstan said as he reined his horse to the left.

"But....you are staying awhile my lord?"

"For the time it will take to refresh my body and horse my lady, yes. And then I shall leave to follow my own path. Good luck to you my lady."

And he turned his horse away and rode to the back of the line of travellers, behind old Kipp who gave him a typical cheery smile and wave as he passed by.

Berowen watched him go and urged her horse to quicken its pace in order to catch up with her mother, who had – as usual – nodded off in her saddle.

XLIV

Mog stamped on the ground with her tiny foot. Her face was red and her eyes were black with anger. A faerie in a rage is not a pretty sight. And Mog was in such a fury that had never been witnessed before and it was sorely hoped by Peg that she would never witness it again.

Mog screeched words to anything that could hear – words of terror and words of death. Peg had heard the sounds and had rushed through the forest to investigate. She found Mog lying on her belly, thrashing the ground with her fists and her feet in a temper so foul that birds flew out of the treetops, and the deer stampeded away into the shadows.

Peg noticed the obvious cause of the terror that raged from Mog's very being. The delicately carved box lay open next to her on the ground where she had tossed it aside. It was empty. Peg still had no idea what Mog hid in the box, but she had always known that it was important.

She sat cross-legged on the ground in front of Mog as she thrashed on the ground. It was no use trying to communicate while Mog was in such a state so she decided to wait until the wrath had subsided.

It took a long time – in fact, it took several hours and it was well into the night before Mog finally became still and silent. Peg, still sitting cross-legged in front of her, patted Mog's head softly in comfort and Mog raised her blotchy wrinkled face and looked at her. She got to her feet, and sat next to Peg and wrapped her arms around her neck. She babbled the whole story to her friend. She told her about the task, the collection, the fate of their kind if she failed to produce the item to The One and how, while her back was turned, something had sneaked up and had stolen everything. They were all undone. There was not enough time to start the collecting again – it would be an impossible task. Mog slapped herself in frustration of her stupidity. Her eyes began to turn black again, and Peg saw the rage threatening to return.

Peg rocked Mog backwards and forwards slowly and patted her head. She spoke quietly to her and managed to sooth her to sleep. All through the night, Peg thought hard on a possible solution. Did whatever, or whomever, that had stolen the contents know of their true value? And had they taken them out of some abhorrent spite, or had they taken them purely because they liked them? If the latter then there was some hope of locating both them and the culprit, but if the former then Peg feared they were completely lost and after Yule their kind would never be seen again wandering the woods and forests. Perhaps even, out of some spiteful trick, The One had arranged for them to be taken. Whatever the reason for their disappearance, the consequences of failure in finding them were devastatingly final. They *must* be found, and she *had* to find a way, although she did not know how.

Scrimble.

The name brought a shudder through Peg's body as she realised that the great beast may be the one who could help. He was a tracker by nature – a solitary hunter who could sniff out his prey with ease. The challenging question was, however, how could he be persuaded to use his keen sense of smell to the two faeries' advantage? Why would he come to their aid? They were of no consequence to him – he merely endured their presence as he did any other creature of the woods and forests, in fact even more so for they were not even part of his normal menu and were of no personal use to him whatsoever. He endured their existence in his world purely because they were there, for no other reason at all. He would have no care whatever, even if he did know of the pressing urgency of the location of the missing items. In truth, he would probably be pleased to learn that they would no longer be a part of his world.

However, he was not the only one of his kind to wander in the shadows of this world. Peg had no way of knowing whether he had already had an audience with The One or if this dubious pleasure had yet to be bestowed upon him. If the latter, then perhaps it was time to divulge the secrets of the darkest part of the forest as a warning. Yes, that was it. Perhaps they could come to some 'arrangement'. If he helped them now, when it was his turn to defend his own then they could help him; a secret alliance of their own.

Therefore, a plan had formed in Peg's mind. This then was to be their first step and it all depended upon whether The One had already demanded his presence. It also depended upon whether they could find him amongst the tangled roots and boughs of the forest. This was Peg's next dilemma.

Peg sat with a smug look on her age-weathered face, rather pleased at her extreme cleverness in possibly solving the grave crisis. If there is one thing - and there are, in truth, many things - that faeries are not, it is being modest about their talents, or rather their perceived talents. They do possess a rather over-inflated view of themselves in all things.

Peg gently shook Mog's shoulders to waken her so that she could tell her the news. Mog was impressed at her friend's idea and a grin spread across her face with delight. Mog enjoyed intrigue and secrets, and the thought that they could share such a delicious agreement with Scrimble of all creatures was an absolute joy. Gone was the desperation of the evening before and the natural optimism of Mog had returned in an instant.

Root and Knot would know where Scrimble was – they always made it their business to know where everyone and everything was. Being the youngest of the kin, they spent all their days roaming the forest for they had nothing better to do, and got bored very quickly when allocated a task by one of their elders. They were always getting into trouble, and it had long been the policy of the elder faeries to ignore their pleas for assistance when some creature would come calling with complaints. If they were clever enough to make the trouble, then they were clever enough to suffer the consequences and resolve the problem they had brought upon themselves. This was another trait of faeries – their intolerance with the younger generation.

When summoned into Mog's presence, Root and Knot immediately assumed that chastisement was to befall them for doing something wrong. It was rare for them to be summoned into her presence for anything else, so they dragged their feet slightly on their way to see her, in anticipation of a fierce ticking off. By the time they got to her, she was not a little impatient, and the dark look upon her wisened features merely appeared to confirm their earlier suspicions. Knot looked at Root and Root looked at Knot. They winked at each other and immediately placed one hand each behind their backs and proceeded to cross their middle and forefingers. To nullify their deceit, this was their usual trick.

They were amazed when no admonishment rained down upon them. They had performed many a woeful trick on a number of creatures recently, and they were surprised that none had complained to Mog about their behaviour. As Mog explained what was required of them, they listened intently and beamed with delight at the task set before them. To hunt down Scrimble would be entertaining and it would show off their prowess for tracking in front of the two most esteemed members of their kin. They had seen him only the day before snoozing whilst his stomach digested the meal he had recently eaten. The luckless hare had wandered too far across his invisible boundary and had paid the most final penalty – unlucky for the hare but deliciously lucky for Scrimble.

Mog and Peg would follow them through the forest and would present their proposal to the great hound if, and when, Root and Knot located him. The two youngsters glowed with pride and imagined that wonderful tales would be told of their hunting of the great beast, and even a song or two may be written of their epic adventure. As youngsters, they did over-emphasise their importance, and by the time all four of them were ready to leave on the great hunt, Root and Knot had egos the size of the quarry itself.

It had not crossed their excited minds to query the exact motives behind the location of Scrimble, and even if it had, they would not have dared to do so. No-one questions the motives of Mog. The four ran through the trees, under bushes, around trunks and jumped over roots in their way. Their tiny forms made hardly a sound as they scrambled through the forest and with luck, the hound would not sense their arrival until they were upon him.

As she ran, Mog recited the words she would say in her head. It was a long time since she had used the tongue of the creatures and she hoped that she had remembered them correctly. The language was taught to the elder of all the different races of creature in order that they could communicate with each other in times of importance. Mog had been taught the tongue many moons before, but she had only had cause to use it at the times of emigration from their seasonal homes. And even then it was just rudimentary speech; this conversation would be more intricate and would have to be worded with extreme care.

Knot's nose was the more sensitive out of the two youngsters. He stopped and raised his head to sniff the air. Raising a hand in signal for all to remain quiet, he pointed towards a glade to their left. They all looked, but could see nothing but the rays of the sun streaming through a gap in the canopy above them. Mog turned to Knot and shrugged her tiny shoulders, and the latter returned her signal with a nod of his head. Scrimble must be there somewhere, hidden in the undergrowth.

Mog took a deep breath and with a series of nasal sounds and tongue clicks began to speak the language of all creatures. No shape came into view and the silence of the forest around them was only broken by the occasional answer of her call from a bird in the boughs above them. This was not an ideal situation – the area would have to be cleared of all other creatures; the meeting with Scrimble should not be overheard. Mog spoke again and the forest floor immediately became a hive of activity as creatures of all descriptions vacated their hiding places and left the area. Root and Knot were impressed with Mog's omnipotence over the other beings that shared their wintering quarters.

Signalling Root and Knot to remain where they were – safely out of sight and hearing distance - Mog and Peg ventured forward into the openness of the glade. There was a peculiar silence around them now that all the others had left. The sounds that became common in everyday life, and therefore largely ignored, were distinctly obvious in their absence and an uncanny quiet befell them. Mog tried calling for Scrimble again. She was beginning to think that Root and Knot had not led them to him after all, but then a movement behind her attracted her attention. Turning she saw the great black head of the hound emerging from a thicket. His ears were down on his skull, his eyes were dark pools of cunning and his lips wrinkled against his shiny, long, white teeth. It was evident that he was displeased with the interruption into his day exacted by the faeries that stood before him.

Mog stood on a fallen trunk that lay in front of her. Its demise was of advantage to her - if only in her own mind - for to stand upon it elevated her a foot or so higher. In situations such as this, her lack of height was infuriating and she needed to appear as important as she possible could, especially in front of one as formidable as Scrimble. A thought crossed her mind that she should perhaps have brought some kind of gift for him, and for a brief moment she thought about instructing Root and Knot to fetch some delicacy for him, but decided that this would be too obviously a last minute consideration.

By now, Scrimble had emerged completely from the thicket and was slowly walking around the fallen trunk on which the faerie stood. He did not avert his gaze once, but fixed it upon her as he circled her, drool hanging in slippery threads from his maw. Peg stood slightly quaking on her spot on the forest floor as the beast walked just behind her. She could smell him, and the fresh smell of blood upon him. She stood as still as she could and shut her eyes as she heard him softly pad past her.

His circuit of psychological terror completed, he stood before Mog and demanded why she was standing before him.

She explained that she was hoping for his help in a matter of life or death. He seemed uninterested and completely unimpressed when she went on to elaborate that the very existence of her kind was at stake. His response was along the lines of why that would bother him. At this point Mog was hesitant as to whether to go any further or to just give up and make her humble excuses and retreat. She began to question whether it was the best course to continue and ask if he had ever met with The One. It was Scrimble, however, who pressed it further when he enquired as to exactly what she meant by 'the end of her kind'. His first reaction had been to be secretly pleased at the prospect of being rid of the tricksters that shared his home, but had then wondered how, with his aid, he could help them prevent such an exacting extinction, and how she had even come to this conclusion.

He had to admit that over the years he had noticed that several races of creatures had not returned over the moor after wintering in the forest. None of them really concerned him, for they were not on his usual menu, and he was only alarmed if it affected his dietary requirements. However, he had heard of a being known as The One, but had always shrugged off the rumour as exactly that – a mere rumour that had spread as a story to induce fear and respect for the forest.

Mog told him about her visit to the darkest part of the forest and her meeting with The One. Scrimble sat on his haunches and listened intently when she reached the part of her story where she told him that the disappearance of races was due to the failure of them to fulfil the task laid down by this being. His ears pricked up when he learned from her that one winter it could well be his turn to go before The One. He did not know whether to believe her or not, but he was keenly aware that if she spoke the truth a secret pact of aid would be a definite advantage. If, however, it was just another trick played by the faeries, he could easily inflict his own wrath upon as many of them as he wished in payment. He decided, therefore, that he would help them seek what it was that had been stolen, in return for their help if and when the time came for him to perform a task for The One.

The deal made, Mog signalled for Peg to produce the box and lay it before Scrimble. He eyed the carvings and a realisation came upon him that everything he had just heard was true. Peg opened the box and the great hound sniffed it. There were many scents within its stark interior; a mishmash of scents of various items that had been collected over the years, but he concentrated on the strongest. Mog had handled her own collection many times, so her scent was strong, but just to make certain – and to Mog's discomfort – he approached and sniffed her too. She had never been so close to that slathering maw before and it filled her with a fear that she found hard to suppress from his view. Instinctively she held her breath while he inched his nose around her frame, and when he had finished she exhaled with loud relief.

Scrimble would now try to hunt out Mog's missing possession and would inform her when he had located it.   The meeting closed, Mog and Peg bowed deeply before Scrimble as he left the glade. He would make his way back to their part of the forest and would begin his hunt from there. Mog and Peg both sat down to gather their composure before returning – Root and Knot joined them and demanded, out of their natural childish curiosity, of the outcome of the meeting. Mog informed them of its success but refused to go any further, despite the expectant looks upon the faces of the youngsters. They had to be satisfied both with their success at locating Scrimble and with the fact that all was well within their world – as far as they saw it.

XLV

T he fortress of Grimfell was built on a hill that rose starkly up from the marshes. As the travellers approached, Berowen stared at the great battlements that towered above her. The drawbridge of the barbican slowly descended with a loud scraping sound. It appeared to take so much effort to drop that the impression was given that it was something that did not occur often.

The procession briefly left the sunlight as they rode through the small building. The sentries on duty stood to attention as the escorts and wedding party clattered slowly through the barbican. However, upon the arrival of the troupe they stood at ease and gawped at the young women as they passed by. Each had their own thoughts, and there was no doubt that these opinions were to be shared amongst each other later in their billets. Pretty girls always sparked off such discussions, and ten of them arriving at Grimfell would cause a dialogue that may well last long into the early hours.

Behind her, Berowen heard the drawbridge screeching shut, followed by a loud thud as the opening to the outside world was sealed off. Heraldic trumpets announced their arrival as they emerged from the barbican into the small community that sprinkled the foot of the hill within the outer and inner walls. The dilapidated buildings huddled against each other in the shadow of the outer wall where some of the workers of the fortress and the families of soldiers appeared to survive in less than ideal living conditions. What could only be described as a well-worn track to the main gate was crowded with the inhabitants of the settlement, with people jostling each other in the cramped space to catch a glimpse of the new bride. The women gazed open-mouthed at the beauty of Berowen's gown, children ran through the legs of the inhabitants and chased each other – and the odd wayward hound - giggling, and shouting as the procession made its way slowly up to the castle gate. The tattered and dirty material of heraldic flags fluttered in the light, late-morning breeze from atop the two turrets that flanked the gatehouse; their golden backgrounds edged in the deepest blue, each bearing the outline of the castle keep and two golden dragonheads.

First appearances were not at all welcoming and gave the feeling that Grimfell had seen better days. At least entry through the portcullis, which would give them access to the bailey, was unmarred by an unwelcoming closure. It was only shut at night or in times of threat but as she passed underneath she looked up at its metal teeth that, in her mind, threatened to fall down upon her at any moment, pinning her to the muddy ground below. Again, the trumpets sounded as they crossed through under the drawn portcullis into the bailey beyond. A page ran up and took Berowen's reins as she dismounted. Ethwen was soon at her side to adjust her daughter's cloak and dress before they embarked upon the long climb to the keep at the top of the hill, thus gaining entrance to the great hall itself. Satisfied that all was well Ethwen nodded to her husband and Aelwulf held out his arm for Berowen to take as they began their ascent, Earh leading the way.

Berowen suddenly stopped. She had noticed the absence of Thurstan, and the musicians and their group from the bailey, and enquired of the captain as to where they had been sent.

"They are without the gatehouse my lady," he replied.

She noticed an attitude of self-satisfaction within his tone.

"I hope that they will be looked after well and shown the hospitality of Grimfell as befits those called upon to perform their skills at the forthcoming marriage," she asked, glancing at Earh in response to the self-righteous look upon his face.

"I know of no such arrangement, my lady," responded Earh churlishly.

"The captain seems not to believe me, father," said Berowen to Aelwulf, as she looked intently at him in a desperate attempt to send him a signal to unite with her in her duplicity.

Earh looked at Aelwulf and waited for his response. He knew, before Aelwulf spoke, that the woman before him had once again won the argument. Even if she had just made the explanation up, there would be no way that her father would refute her statement in public. So it was with a silent curse and visible nod of acquiescence that Earh acknowledged Aelwulf's "It is indeed so, Captain, and I would be grateful if you would see to it that their needs are attended to and that they are not treated as mere travellers."

The way up to the keep was steep, broken occasionally by well-worn steps of stone, and it was as much as Ethwen could do to keep up with the others at times. Her sons supported one of her arms each in theirs and helped their mother make the arduous trip up the hill. At last they reached the great wooden doors that overshadowed those who stood in their outline. Berowen turned to look back down the slope they had ascended and her eye caught the view that opened up below her. She had not realised that they had climbed quite as high as they had, and the vista that met her eyes was, even she had to admit, a breathtaking sight. The marshes spread out below them and she could just make out the outline of the forest against the horizon in the far south.

Thurstan had remained with Kipp and the others, and was helping them set up some sort of camp. They had attracted much attention from the children, who had collected into a small group and watched intently as the colourfully dressed men and women went about making their stay as comfortable as possible. None of the children had ever seen such brightly coloured clothing before and many stood with their eyes wide open in fascination at the sumptuous shades of red, yellow, and orange. They pointed at the anklets of bells around the womens' ankles and were delighted at the delicate tinkling they made as they moved. Some of the little girls jumped and danced around imitating the sound as if they adorned their own ankles. Gradually mothers collected their offspring – some of them indifferent to the source of the attention and some of them voicing concern at the apparent waywardness they perceived from the troupe. Others just called out in loud voice, and some did not bother to reclaim their children at all. They would wander home when their stomachs told them to.

At the keep, Aelwulf, Berowen, Ethwen, Eneas and Amleth waited for Earh to escort them through the great wooden doors into the great hall beyond. Berowen just wanted this first meeting to be over and done with, and became impatient that Earh dallied at the entrance. The longer she had to wait the more wild her imagination became. She knew not what would greet her once those doors were open, and her mind spun with different pictures. She recalled the descriptions of Brack that her father had told her many months before, but all she could visualise was a bloated, balding old man, with leering eyes, rotten teeth and breath and body odour that would be so intense as to knock down a bullock in a field a mile away if caught downwind of the pungent aroma. She began to fidget – why was Earh taking so long to open the damned doors?

She looked up as she squirmed with anticipation of the horrors that awaited her. The keep towered high above her – there must be at least four levels in all, maybe even more. The afternoon sun was high in the vivid blue sky and she had to squint as it shone in her eyes. She could make out a shape on the top of the building, but could not make out what it was in the sunlight; it appeared to be black and seemed to be bobbing up and down. She raised her hand to try to shield her eyes against the glare and realised that the shape was moving closer towards her. As it did so she heard the unmistakeable 'kaugh' call and as it became clear what the shape was, it flapped its black wings and landed on the stone wall next to her, its iridescent black plumage shining with a blue tinge in the sunlight. Just at that moment, the great doors were pushed open from the inside and Earh led them across the threshold. Aelwulf had almost to drag his daughter through as she craned her neck to look at the raven as it stood and ruffled its feathers on the wall. Out of the corner of her eye, she saw her mother crossing herself and wailing quietly under her breath. But all Berowen could do was smile at the bird and its most welcome appearance. As she disappeared into the hall it opened its beak and let out a loud 'toc-toc-toc' sound as it bobbed its head up and down, with its elongated throat feathers splayed beneath its beak. When the last of the party had entered into the keep, the raven hopped on to the ground, and with the ungainly gait of a bird more at home in the air, it lolloped behind them, unnoticed in the shadows of the doors, and secreted itself in the darkness of a corner.

It took a few minutes for the visitors to adjust their eyes to the dimness within after the brightness outside. The hall was double the size of that of Brundannon and they stared in awe at its vastness. However, in contrast to its size, the decor was on par with the dilapidated buildings they had passed on their way to the gatehouse from the barbican. The walls were draped with what must have once been the finest tapestries, but which now hung worn and grubby, some with large holes where someone had once worked intricate embroidery. Large candlesticks stood along the long tables that ran the full length of the hall on each side of the aisle. The tallow candles had oozed their melting fat over the sides, which had settled into large dried yellowing pools on the wooden surfaces. In the middle of the hall, a huge fire roared in the great brazier, where two large, lean-looking hunting dogs sprawled in front of it soaking up the warmth; half-chewed bones littering their immediate vicinity. They just lifted their heads lazily to inspect the visiting group, before flopping them back to the floor and returning to their dozing.

Earh led the party towards the end of the hall to where Modig was sitting. Beside him sat the man Berowen presumed was her future husband. Both figures stood as the others approached. Earh bowed, turned and began his walk back to the entrance with an arrogant strut. As he passed Berowen, he eyed her with disdain and a sneer crept across his lips. Their mutual dislike of each other was obvious, and Berowen returned his gaze with a cold stare as she silently wished upon him the misfortune of falling upon his supercilious face and wiping away the sneer that dwelt upon it.

"Lord Modig," Aelwulf began. "I present my daughter Berowen."

Before he could proceed any further with the introductions, however, there was a noisy crashing sound behind them and the unmistakeable resonance of Earh's voice as it cursed loudly. Everyone turned to look in the direction of the racket and saw the captain sprawled on his stomach on the floor, one of the hounds loping off down the hall with a bone in its jaw. Eneas and Amleth had to stifle their laughter while Ethwen uttered words of concerned surprise at the man's misfortune. Berowen, however, looked around her rapidly and although extremely amused at the event, she could not but ponder upon the coincidence of such a thing occurring after her silent wish only moments before.

"Cursed, flea ridden cur," shouted Earh as he rose to his feet, brushing himself down as he did so. "Fuckin' animal ran straight in front of me to get its fuckin' bone. I hope it fuckin' chokes on it," he raged. He turned and stared at Berowen, blood trickling out of his nose, with a look of malice in his eyes. "It's broken my fuckin' nose."

At this statement, Eneas could not help but snigger loudly and had to thrust his fist into his mouth to stop any sound uttering forth.

Berowen was still stunned at the timing of the accident that had befallen Earh and then she heard a faint rustle of feathers in the gloom to the side of the hall. No-one else seemed to notice it, but as she stared hard into the dimness she could just make out the shadow of a black bird. And then she understood.

"Captain," she stated calmly. "By your insolent stare as you said that, you seem to be directing a veiled accusation at me for being responsible for breaking your nose. You will accuse me of bewitching the hound into tripping you next no doubt."

Earh thought for a moment. Had she said that out of some attempt to hide the truth or was she just goading him in his discomfort? She seemed intent on questioning his authority and of embarrassing him at every opportunity ever since their first meeting.

"That would be a very foolish and unwarranted accusation, my lady," he said after a short silence. "After all, to undertake such magick would require a very special talent, and it is obvious that you possess no such thing."

He paused for a few seconds to let the insult sink in, before adding innocently, "You are much too young to have learnt such a skill - spell-casters are invariably bent with age and possess a look of madness about them."

A deep, sinister laugh behind Berowen resounded around the hall. Modig called to Earh, "Methinks you should take yourself to visit the chiurgeon instead of standing there bleeding in my hall."

"My lord," Earh said as, taking the hint to leave, he bowed and left the hall, clutching his hand to his nose.

Ethwen had been astonished at the exchange between her daughter and the captain. She was mortified that Berowen had spoken in such a way after only just being introduced to her future father-in-law. She had shown no respect at all for his status; in fact, she had changed greatly in her general attitude as their journey had progressed. Ever since the incident at the standing stones, Ethwen had had the nagging feeling that her daughter had become more like her own sister, Eda, as the days drifted passed and it concerned her greatly.

∞

Eda had been Ethwen's younger sister; they had been two girls with six other siblings, all boys. Eda had been a pretty child with flaxen hair that framed her heart shaped face and tumbled in curls down her back. She had the most beautiful eyes the colour of a cloudless summer sky, with a turned up nose and pouting lips. They used to play together in the halls and grounds of the manor they called home and spent days on end laughing and tumbling in the pastures. When in their lessons, however, Eda would often stare out of the small window as if off in some place of her own. But it was not until she was thirteen that things changed dramatically and Eda would go off for hours on end on her own, or sit in a corner and recite words to herself in some strange tongue.

She became intolerant of interruption when disturbed by her siblings in their attempts to encourage her into some merriment. She would speak sharply to them and changed from a quiet, well-mannered child into a terse and sometimes rude young girl. Ethwen remembered her parents' dismay at their younger daughter's manner. It was not until the arrival of Sebbi that her mood became calm again – for a short while.

Sebbi was one of a litter of kittens that were born in the stables. It seemed that the moment that Eda and he first laid eyes upon each other that they became inseparable. She would spend most of her day in the stables whilst Sebbi was weaned from his mother and once he became independent of her he would follow Eda everywhere. He slept on her bed at night and wherever Eda went, Sebbi was there at her side. He had been the runt of the litter and never reached the usual size of a normal cat, being small in stature with short stubby legs. He always looked slightly emaciated, although he ate well and never went without. He was black with four white paws and a white blaze down his nose and chest, and Eda adored him.

For two years, they were never apart and although Eda became calmer, she was often to be found talking to him as if he was human, which alarmed those around her. He would sit by her side, looking attentively at her as if he understood every word she was saying. She would say something to him under her breath and he would saunter off only to return later with what could only be described as a smile upon his feline face, and she would sigh with obvious delight at some secret success that no-one else knew or understood. Strange occurrences took place to others around the manor, hence rumours soon began to spread that Eda, and Sebbi were somehow responsible for them, for whenever a mishap occurred, the cat was always seen in the area.

Ethwen's parents, Elfec and Maudrid, took what they thought was a sensible action to restrict this unhealthy relationship between their daughter and Sebbi and decided to keep them apart as much as possible. But alas, it only made things worse and more and more misfortune began to fall upon those in the household of the manor, from scaldings to accidents with farming implements, which left one peasant unable to work in the fields for weeks.

Ethwen's parents had decided to consult Old Nen, a wise woman who lived in a nearby village, and upon her arrival at their home, Old Nen immediately informed them that their daughter was bewitched with a great power, not unlike her own. Unfortunately due to her young age and lack of instruction she had no idea how to apply this gift and was thus using it to ill-effect. The arrival of Sebbi as her familiar spirit had empowered Eda greatly, but the gift was enveloping her and there would be dire consequences if she were not to be correctly tutored. Sebbi would do as Eda instructed to serve his mistress, and she merely had to idly think of something and he would do as she bid, whether or not it had been just a passing thought or a real wish. There was no doubt that Eda, in her frustration and un-schooling, was causing the mishaps around the manor. Old Nen was surprised that Maudrid had had no idea of her daughter's gift, for it would run in the female line of the family – on the mother's side. "It must be yer sister then, you got sisters?" she had enquired.

Maudrid had nodded sombrely. Yes, she had a sister, but she had been sent away many years before when Maudrid was eight years old. She could not recall any details of this banished sibling but she had been told that she had been sent to a nunnery. Somehow, the real reason for her sudden disappearance from the home became perfectly clear. It must have been her sister who had the knowledge that had seeded itself in her youngest daughter Eda.

Old Nen had offered to take Eda with her to try to school her, but they were fearful of releasing their daughter's care into the hands of the wise woman and of what would become of her. The old woman seemed kind enough in her explanation, but she was old, bent and, from the look of her clothing, obviously poor. She had wild, staring eyes and seemed to possess a manner about her that they did not wholeheartedly trust.

They had refused the old woman's dubious offer, had thanked her for her visit and dropped a few coins into her palm before sending her on her way, with the half-hearted promise that they would call upon her again should they need her advice or help.

Ethwen remembered watching the old woman shuffle down the muddy track back towards her own village. As she had passed Ethwen, Old Nen had given her a cold stare, followed by a slow wink, as a sly grin crept across her face. It had made Ethwen shudder with fear and disgust and was relieved – at that time – that her parents had made the decision they had.

It had been later on that evening when lying in her cot that Ethwen had heard the sound of muffled footsteps along the corridor. They padded passed her door quietly as if attempting to hide their existence, and she saw the flickering light of a candle beneath her door as it passed. Then she had heard muffled screams and the sound of a cat spitting and growling. She had jumped from her bed and had run to her own door, and – pulling it open – had seen two hooded figures run back down the corridor, their figures casting misshapen shadows on the walls. One of them was carrying a writhing, hissing sack and the other held the candle that the rush of air eventually extinguished as they ran out of sight. The aroma of melting tallow was strong as they passed, and Ethwen felt slightly nauseous as she inhaled its reek.

There had been wailing and screaming from Eda's room. Ethwen knew immediately what had occurred and she ran to her sister's cot to comfort her. Eda was sitting on her bed, thumping it with her hands and feet much as a child does when having a fit of temper. Her hair was a mass of tangles and clung to her face where she had been crying. As Ethwen had attempted to embrace Eda, her sister had turned to face her, and the look in her blue eyes had startled Ethwen, and she had drawn back for a moment. Looking at that face, contorted with anger, fear, and madness shocked Ethwen. She knew not what to do. Sebbi had been taken violently from her sister, and it seemed that Eda would never recover from the loss.

Ethwen had sat with her sister for the rest of the night, and as dawn's light had crept through the window, it had shed its golden rays upon the two figures sitting next to each other on the bed. One of them was rocking back and forth and the other was clinging on to her, smoothing her hair and humming gently in comfort.

Eda's mood grew worse with every new day after Sebbi's abduction on that night. She stayed in her room most of the time and grew wilder and more unpredictable in her mood, until it was eventually decided to keep her under lock and key with only occasional visits from a maid – under guard - to see to her needs. Not even Ethwen was allowed to venture into her room.

She could only lie in her own cot at night and listen to her sister's incantations. The words made no sense, but still they came forth and it seemed as if Eda never slept.

No-one really knows how she managed to escape that fateful night. The maid had entered to take Eda her supper as she did every evening, although the food was never touched. The guard had stood at the doorway to ensure that nothing unfortunate occurred should Eda be in one of her more aggressive moods. Somehow, Eda managed to flee her confinement and amidst a flurry of shouting, and orders to stop her, she managed to escape the building. As she had run through the door at the front of the house, the skies had become brooding and let loose a barrage of hailstones on the earth below. The darkness swallowed her up and she disappeared from sight. Finding her that night had been a fruitless task and it was not until morning that her body was found as it floated face down in the river some distance from the manor. It had become wedged between two large boulders, the only mark upon it being the large bruise on her forehead where she had presumably dashed her head against one of them. No-one knew whether she had taken her own life or whether she had slipped and knocked herself out on the rocks, but she was gone.

Ethwen knew that it had been the power of the bewitchment that had killed her sister. And to see her daughter now it brought back the terror of Eda's enchantment, and that terror seeped into her very bones as she looked upon Berowen after her outburst.

XLVI

Hearing a chastening tut from under Ethwen's breath, Berowen looked back at her mother and lowered her eyes from the concerned stare given her in return. She felt uncomfortable under her mother's gaze and knew that Ethwen had been disappointed with her for her outspokenness towards Earh.

"Come friends," called out Modig. "Let us leave Earh's clumsiness to the concerns of our healer." He waved his hand to the group, ushering them to follow him. "My son is eager to meet his new bride."

"He may well be," thought Berowen to herself. "It is sad that the feeling is not mutual." But she took a deep breath and, again with her hand on her father's arm, she allowed Aelwulf to lead her towards her future husband.

Brack bowed his head as they approached. He was tall, and as thin as a barren twig. He had long brown hair of no particular attraction or style as it hung limply to his shoulders. As he raised his head and looked at Berowen she hesitated in her step slightly. His dull eyes looked her up and down and she shrivelled under his examination. His bony fingers constantly wove themselves around each other as he stood before her – fingers adorned with rings whose gemstones had long lost their natural beauty and were now faded through time. That is exactly how she felt at that moment – as if her natural sparkle had instantly dulled upon meeting him.

Amleth and Eneas looked at each other with sadness and dismay when they saw the listless looking man who was to be their future brother-in-law. The fate of birth had made their sibling female and thus, in front of them stood the penalty of such an origin. Unbeknown to each other, they both had inwardly shuddered at the thought of those long, bony fingers touching their sister.

Had her father deceived her? Aelwulf had spoken often of Brack's good nature and high standing in the months approaching this moment, but she had not quite grasped as to how much older this man was who stood before her. His tight lips pursed under a long, beaky nose and occasionally his tongue would poke between his lips to moisten their dryness. He looked like some awful weird bird just waiting to feed upon her flesh. His dull, sullen eyes stared out from under thick eyebrows, and his shrunken cheeks seemed to sag against his skull.

It was clear by both his and his father's dress that Modig and Brack felt more about their own appearance than that of Grimfell and its other inhabitants. Both men were adorned with jewellery and their clothing was of the highest quality and style.

Berowen's hand gripped her father's sleeve and he patted it with his other hand in reassurance. However, when she turned to look at him and he thought that he saw the accusation of betrayal in her eyes, he turned away feeling utterly wretched for what he now saw was a diabolical pact to have made. Months ago when he had visited Grimfell to arrange this union, he had been full of his obligations to his family name. Although he had suffered back then over the task that he recognised was the hardest thing that, as a father, he had ever had to perform, he had convinced himself that it was the proper action to take. Now, on this day, presenting his daughter into this household he realised his grave misjudgement and knew he had betrayed her trust and most probably, her love also. His heart was heavy and he could not look at her out of the shame.

XLVII

The wildman had lain for quite some time after the incident with the little people who had danced him into dizziness with their teasing. He would have to slate his thirst and satisfy his growling belly soon enough, but for now, he preferred the comfort of his contact with the forest floor. He lay on his side and watched the various bugs going about their business across the fallen cones and needles. He became mesmerised by two lines of ants that passed nearby. One procession all carried tiny packages between their strong jaws, the occasional little body having difficulty carrying its load and sometimes crashing into things in its way. The other procession travelled in the other direction with empty jaws. Their antics were soporific and his eyelids soon started to droop. He heard the voice of Eadric barking at him.

"Walt!"

He could feel the soft skin of the cow against his cheek as he pushed himself into her haunches, his hands working nimbly on her udders as he squirted the milk into the wooden bucket. Her scent was comforting and behind him, he could hear her chewing the cud as he milked her. Occasionally she would flick up a hind leg to shake off a fly and once or twice, her tail would swish into his face. But he did not mind for she was a dear old thing and he enjoyed his moments with her – she had no malice within her and stood patiently as he performed his task.

On hearing Eadric he had looked up and seen his neighbour approach. "You done milking that beast yet? Your mother is 'ere to take you 'ome."

He shook his head in reply.

"Bah," grunted Eadric. "Hurry up then."

179

He had not really understood exactly what the man had said to him and had only recognised the words 'mother' and 'home' as well as his name, but he assumed that he was to finish his task as quickly as possible.

Once done, he stood up and stretched his back. Bending over to milk hurt his long back and large shoulders. He patted the cow on her rump and stroked her before picking up the bucket and ambling off to the house, where he knocked on the door and waited patiently for the woman to open it.

The door flew open and a plump, angry looking woman stood before him, with one hand on her hips and the other grasping a broom. Her fat cheeks were red and glistened with sweat and strands of hair protruded from beneath her grimy coif. "'Bout time me lad," she scolded, and snatched the bucket from his hand. "'Now be off with yer." Again he did not really understand what she had said and remained standing at the doorway. She scowled at him and waved the broom-held hand in his direction. "Be off, be off." And she slammed the door shut in his face.

It was his mother calling him that took him from the door, and he turned towards the direction of her voice. She was standing talking to Eadric; he could hear them speaking, but the words were lost on his ears. She smiled at him and stood on her tiptoes to kiss his cheek. "Hello Walt." He smiled back and bent over to return the kiss, and then grabbed her hand and held it tightly in his.

They walked slowly home, his mother singing softly and sweetly as they made their way along the track and over the fields. He walked in his own silence and listened to the melodic sound that came from his mother's lips, his hand not once leaving hers.

He could see the familiar small building he knew as home in the distance as they walked through a field of yellow flowers, all waving their heads gently in the afternoon breeze. It was a hot afternoon and the golden rays of the sun glinted on the small flowers and made their petals even more yellow. He used to pick flowers such as these as a child, when his mother had shown him how to wave them under her chin to see if its colour glowed on her skin. It had taken quite a while for him to understand what she meant, but once he saw the glow he had giggled in delight, and had made it a daily routine to insist that she sat down while he looked for that golden glow. When the plants died off at the end of the season and no longer produced the flowers he was sad and looked forward to the next summer when they would cover the field again in their golden hue.   As they neared the cottage, he suddenly stopped and his mother waited patiently while he stooped down and picked one of the flowers, and smiling, waved it under her chin. She laughed and, taking the flower from his hand, did the same to him.

Their own cow was munching on the grass as they neared home, and lifted her head slowly to eye the approaching figures, but lowered her head and resumed her foraging when she recognised them. The scrawny hens scratched about the yard, clucking softly to themselves and paid no attention to the return of the man and his mother, but continued on their ever present desire to look for anything to satisfy their hungry crops.

As his mother opened the door, he felt a nudge in the small of his back. In his half-dozing state, he thought it was the cow come to welcome them home, but upon opening his eyes to reality he realised that there was something else snuffling around behind him. He slowly turned over and his eyes met those of Scrimble. He lay perfectly still and watched the hound as it sniffed around his person and scratched with a large, deadly paw in the thin layer of pine needles. Scrimble curled his lips to reveal his shiny white teeth, and snarled at him. The man snarled back, but the hound merely eyed him with total disregard before sauntering off into the forest - what he was searching for was not at this place.

His memories once again disturbed, the man stood and wandered off in the opposite direction to search for water and food.

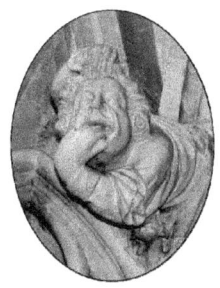

XLVIII

Thurstan sat hunched in the quietest spot he could find between the walls, and pondered on the stone. As he puffed slowly on his pipe, he tried to make sense of the carvings he had seen. He could make no sense of them whatsoever and it had begun to annoy him that the answer to the puzzle constantly eluded him.

A small boy came and sat directly in front of him. His big brown eyes looked out from a dirty face but no sound came from his lips. His just sat...and watched. Thurstan took no real notice of the boy and continued to think upon his puzzle, although it did occur to him that this boy seemed to have no real purpose in placing himself where he did. After about an hour, a flaxen-haired woman came scuttling over to where the two sat facing each other. "There yer be," she hollered. "I been lookin' for yer everywhere. What yer doin' 'ere annoying this man?"

"Not doin' nowt," came the quiet, if not a little rebellious, reply.

"My pardon, sire," said the woman to Thurstan. "I hopes the little squirt ain't been annoyin' yer."

"He has said not a word, nor has he moved a muscle for the last hour," replied Thurstan. "So no, in that, he has not been annoying me, good woman."

She laughed. "Good woman! You be not knowin' whether I am bad or good woman methinks."

"Then it is my pardon that I offer. I had no wish to offend by my friendly greeting."

"No offence be taken sire. Just call me Lin, everyone else does on account of they can't manage to say me full name – Llinos," she laughed. "Me 'usband is one of soldiers 'ere. I ain't seen 'im in ages. He stays up there in garrison and I think he's avoidin' me," she continued with a sly wink.

Thurstan bowed his head slightly at the woman and deliberately avoided the last part of her sentence as he had no wish to get embroiled in the affairs of her wedlock despite the jovial way in which she had introduced the subject. He turned his attention to the boy who was still sitting cross-legged in front of him. "And to you, young man, I give my thanks for your fine company this afternoon. However, if I may be so bold as to suggest such a thing, perhaps next time you will venture to utter at least *one* word so that we may base a conversation around it?"

The boy raised his eyebrows and his huge eyes looked at Thurstan, and then with a cock of his head looked to his mother as if searching for some assistance.

Thurstan grinned. "What is your name, boy?"

"My name is Eni and I am six," was the bold reply as the boy raised two hands and showed six fingers to Thurstan.

"Well Eni, who is six, it has been a pleasure to have met you. I believe your mother wishes you to go with her now, so I shall bid you farewell. Perhaps we shall sit together again soon."

Eni stood and ran off, waving as he went. Lin picked up her skirts and ran after him. "That boy will be gettin' into more mischief if I don't catch up wi' 'im. Where's 'is bloody father – he should be 'ere 'elpin to raise 'im instead of 'iding up there in garrison drinkin' 'imself silly! Farewell sire." And she disappeared out of sight.

Thurstan took a long puff on his pipe and pondered on the strange interlude. There had been no reason for it at all, or had there? It seemed that the event might have left him with another puzzle.

XLIX

During the introductions in the hall, Modig's wife had joined them. She had been previously engaged in a dispute with her seamstress over the modifications to her own gown for the upcoming occasion and had been unable to join her husband and son earlier. She had entered the hall flushed with anger at her argument with the needlewoman, and with frustration and embarrassment at not being present when her new daughter-in-law and family had arrived.

In contrast to her husband and son, Aubreda was not dressed quite so elaborately. Her obvious rush to be present had caused her to be still fussing with her wimple as she entered the hall, but by the time she had come upon the group she had presented herself in good dress. She quickly brushed down the front of her skirt and curtsied slightly to her guests.

"Welcome to Grimfell," she gasped still slightly out of breath after her rush to the hall. "I have heard of the trials of your journey and I am glad that you have arrived safely. And this is Berowen I presume," she continued without pausing, looking at the girl stood before her.

"My lady", said Berowen curtsying.

Totally ignoring Berowen's acknowledgement, Aubreda continued chattering.

"Well, well, I am sure that you must all be exhausted after your journey. I will call for young Alric to take you to your chambers," she said as she clapped her hands loudly.

There was no response. "Alric!" she shouted as loudly as she could, which startled the group of travellers somewhat.

Eventually a skinny little boy emerged from the shadows and ran towards them. He was dressed in very ill-fitting livery and looked completely out of place in his station. It was obvious that he been interrupted whilst eating something because there were crumbs around his chin, and he was still half-chewing when he arrived at the group.

Aubreda gave the youngster a cuff round the head and he winced. "You have been feeding your face again I see," she said sternly. "Perhaps it is about time that you earned such morsels. Take our guests to their chambers and return to me immediately for I am sure there is something else I can find you to do that will keep your fingers away from the pies."

"We shall eat when the bell strikes nine times," she called after them as they climbed the stairs at the back of the hall. "And then you shall meet my elder son, Oswald. He has been out running family errands but will have returned by then."

"Collecting taxes no doubt," whispered Eneas to his brother. "After all, I noted a finger on Brack's left hand which seems to lack adornment."

Amleth nodded at his brother's sarcasm and grimaced as he continued his way after the others. As the party disappeared, there was a faint rustle of feathers in the corner of the room as the raven hobbled closer to the stairs.

The church bells had struck seven by the time the drawbridge screeched its way downwards and let Oswald and his men back into the fortress on the hill. Their horses' hooves threw up clods of soggy earth as they trotted from out of the barbican. A few dogs barked as the beasts took their riders at a slower pace up the track that led to the gatehouse and it was this sound that alerted Thurstan to the activity and urged him to take a look at the new arrivals.

"That's Lord Oswald," said a female voice he recognised. "Lord Modig's oldest son. Nasty piece o'work by all accounts," continued Lin, who had appeared at Thurstan's side. "'e left yestermorn tax collecting from the poor bastards that live out east ways."

Thurstan raised an eyebrow and nodded in acknowledgement. "Bet those saddlebags is carrying a lot less coin than expected," continued the woman. "And I'll wager a good many of those coins is stained in blood."

Thurstan bent his head further towards her to hear more.

"Those lands is becomin' barren so I 'as 'eard. The peasants plough the land and each year they get less for their trouble. Been that way for nigh on two years. But each year the taxes go up and each collecting day there is less coin to give. Me 'usband 'as been on many of those trips and he told me it is bad. Poor bastards got nothin' left to give, but still Oswald comes. There's many a family lost everythin' and moved on."

As the party entered through the gatehouse and out of sight, Lin continued, "That land used to be rich, worth a lot of coin. Then somethin' odd 'appened and nowt much grows no more. I reckon I knows what it is though. If you asks me its summat to do with those holes in the hills."

"Holes in hills?" enquired Thurstan, his interest in what Lin was saying increasing.

"There be a range of hills east ways and they has big holes in them. I reckon summat lives in those holes and has poisoned the land or summat like that anyways."

Something inside Thurstan's mind clicked, and suddenly part of the carving on the stone made perfect sense. The wavy lines with circles in must be the very hills about which this woman was talking. Part of the puzzle had clicked into place – caves in the hillside.

"Lin, you have no idea how much that information means to me. It has aided me greatly in my own journey and I thank you most gratefully."

"Oh," she said beaming. "I be glad to 'ave been of some 'elp."

"Tell me, *good* woman," began Thurstan smiling at the use of his wording. "Is there anyone here who has dwelt here for many years and may know of old tales and legends?"

Lin smiled back and thought for a moment. "You should talk to the apoth'cary. 'e bin here for years so I understand. Name is Cynefrid. Alas, you will need coin yerself to pass through gatehouse, and good reason for doin' so I'll be warnin' yer."

"Warning noted and my thanks, friend."

She laughed airily and walked off whistling happily.

Tomorrow he would find the apothecary, but for now, Thurstan decided upon an early night's sleep and he wandered off to find as cosy and quiet a place to bed down that he could.

L

As soon as Berowen had been left alone in her chamber she had thrown herself onto her cot and sobbed. As she lay prone, she heard the bell strike four times. Five hours before she would have to see Brack again and she would cherish every passing minute before the fateful hour. Her worst fears had become true; he was loathsome and she felt physically sick at the thought of her union, which would take place before the week was through. She felt utterly betrayed by her father and although she loved him dearly, she found it hard to forgive this act of treachery. How could he say that he loved and cared for her and then send her into the waiting arms of this odious creature?

She lay in silence. In the background, she could hear the life of the fortress carrying on its daily business, but here in the closed solitude of her chamber she felt safe from that world outside. She became aware of a faint tapping sound. It persisted in its regularity and became louder and she realised that it was coming from the other side of her door. She leapt from her bed, opened it and looked down. The raven hopped in and she closed the door quietly behind her.

"I am glad you are here, friend raven," she said as she knelt down and smoothed the feathers on his head. "You are most dearly welcome."

He flapped his wings and cried "kaugh" and she raised a finger to her lips. "Hush now, raven. Yours is a call that is not easily mistaken and in this place it would be most unwise to be heard."

Berowen returned to the bed and sat upon it. The raven flew to the end and sat perched on the wooden casement. They studied each other until Berowen broke the silence by saying: "Odi, I shall name you Odi. I trust that this name meets with your approval dark bird of the skies?" The raven cocked his head to one side and then bobbed his head up and down as if in agreement. "Good, Odi it is then. Welcome Odi," and she stood on the bed and curtsied deeply before the raven. Unfortunately she lost her balance and crumpled in a heap upon the coverlet and for the first time since her arrival at Grimfell her spirits lifted, and she laughed at her misfortune. Odi's head bobbed up and down again and intermittently he flapped his wings to raise himself a short distance from his perch before descending again and tapping the wood with his beak.

The bell rang six times but Berowen and Odi did not hear it for they were both fast asleep. However, upon it ringing seven times Berowen awoke with a start and leaping from her bed began searching her bags for her quill, ink and parchment as if possessed from the visions she had seen whilst in her slumber. As she scribbled a note, Odi sat on the window ledge watching her intently. When she had finished, she lay down her quill and blew across the parchment to dry the ink before folding it up as tightly as she could. "Odi, I have a task for you. You know to whom you are to deliver this, and I think you should find him somewhere within this fortress' walls." She handed the note to the raven and he took it in his beak. "Now let us see if this ill-fitting window opens," Berowen said as she struggled with the latch. It had not been opened for a good while and it took quite an effort for her to turn the latch, but eventually it opened with a squeak that seemed to echo all around her. "There, freedom for you my friend from this gloomy room, but I hope that you will return soon after a successful delivery."

With a jump into the air and a great beat of his wings, Odi took flight and Berowen watched him soar downwards towards the castle walls, using the torches that lit the steep stairs as his guide.

Thurstan was just settling himself into a comfortable position in his bedroll when he heard the flap of wings above him, and a tightly folded scrap of parchment fluttered down and landed near his head. His hand reached out to retrieve it. He left his resting place and moved towards the fire that burnt steadily near the camp of the dancing musicians, unfolding the parchment as he walked. Angling it so he could see the delicate script written upon it, he read the words "If my messenger has found you, it seems we are indeed both of the same minds after all". It had been signed with a flamboyant 'B'.

Refolding the message and placing it in the pouch on his hip, Thurstan smiled and returned to the shadows. A dark shape stood by his bedroll, and watched Thurstan rummage in his saddle bags. After a short while, he pulled out a small leather pouch and handed it to the shape that took it in its beak and flew upwards, back towards the keep.

Berowen was still leaning out of the open window, her eyes scanning the immediate vicinity for any sign of Odi. It seemed like an age before she saw him flying towards her and she sighed with relief when he landed on the ledge and dropped the small pouch into her hands. Moving back to the bed she pulled it open and turned it upside down. Out fell a signet ring on to her coverlet. She picked it up and examined it closely to find an ornately etched letter 'T' upon its face.

She smiled as she returned the ring to its pouch. "Odi, my dearest feathered friend. I am so glad that you are here."

LI

As the bell tolled its ninth, there was a knock at Berowen's door followed by her mother's voice softly reminding her that it was time to return to the company of their hosts and dine.

Berowen was as prepared as she could be and acknowledged her mother telling her that she would be but a moment. And then she turned to Odi, who was still sitting on the window ledge eyeing the world below him.

"Odi my dear friend, you will have to remain here, although your presence at table would be most welcome, though not possible."

The bird bobbed his head up and down slowly and tapped the windowpane with his beak.

"Ah yes, of course, you wish your freedom," Berowen said as she fiddled with the latch once more. As the window screeched open, a gust of cold wind entered the room and Berowen shivered against its penetrative blast. The bird ruffled his feathers against the chill and launched himself off the ledge and into the darkness once more. She watched his form flit by the torches as he descended the steps. Closing the latch behind her, she walked to the chamber door and out into the corridor, where her mother and father patiently awaited her presence.

If she had squirmed under the gaze of Brack, then Berowen wished that the ground would open up and swallow her when she came under the scrutiny of his brother, Oswald. He was shorter than his brother was, and much more portly in stature – more like their father. He had a balding head and round cheeks with deep-set grey eyes that scrutinised everything in their view. As he looked her up and down Berowen felt a deep disgust and felt naked under his gaze, and she was glad that it was not he who was destined to be her husband in a few days time.

She had been placed next to Brack on the long table with her father on her left seated next to Modig. Her mother was on the other side of Modig next to Oswald. Whilst Brack hardly spoke a word or paid her any attention, Oswald would constantly lean forward to look in her direction and leer openly at her. With his fat cheeks and balding head, he reminded her of a swine as he chewed on a chicken leg with its fat dripping down his chin. His long-suffering wife sat next to him and seemed oblivious to his leering, or was merely used to his wandering eye. It was probably a very good – if not quite accidental – seating arrangement, as she had been sat between her husband and Eneas, the latter of whom made it his business on any day to make amusing conversation especially when in the company of the opposite sex. Amleth faired a little less better as he had been seated next to Modig's wife at the opposite end of the table. It was she who appeared to be doing most of the talking and by the look on her brother's face, Berowen assumed that the conversation was not of much interest.

"Shall I meet your children on the morrow, my lord Brack?" enquired Berowen in an attempt to open a dialogue with her future spouse.

"Most likely, that will be the case," came the stunted reply.

"And what of their ages?" she continued, determined to make him speak more on the subject.

"The boy is ten and the girl is seven," came the reply.

Berowen had hoped that by mentioning his offspring it would spur him into animated conversation. After all, most people were usually eager to talk about their children. However, he seemed disinclined to elaborate further and continued picking at his chicken with his long, greasy fingers, lifting tiny morsels of flesh to his dry lips. Although annoyed by his lack of speech, Berowen felt unenthusiastic to ask further questions and returned her gaze to her food.

"You are not eating Berowen," boomed Modig. "Does the food not meet with your satisfaction?"

"Oh...yes ... it does my lord, it is just that I find that my stomach is not as empty as I had first imagined," replied Berowen slightly shocked at the sudden question and quickly having to find an excuse for her meagre picking at the food upon her platter.

"Just as well," Modig guffawed. "I would not wish to have to beat the girls in the kitchens for not pleasing their new mistress."

Somehow, deep down, Berowen did not think this last statement was necessarily a joke. She could well believe that the girls lived under such oppression in this household, and perhaps even more where Oswald was concerned.

"Indeed not I would think," replied Berowen with a look of mock surprise on her face. "I would not expect such a severe reprimand to be given for such a mild offence should one have been made. The preferences of my palate would not be known to those who do not know me my lord."

"Ha perhaps," replied Modig with a wave of his hand as he picked up his mazer and slurped the mead from within it.

"My lord," began Berowen taking this opening in dialogue with her future father-in-law as an opportunity to enquire further on her union with his son. "You may know that my family arrived at Grimfell in the company of a group of musicians and dancers....."

"Indeed I do," he interrupted. "The details of their presence has been widely reported amongst the garrison so I hear. Strangers in our land it would seem, with skin as smooth and brown as ripe acorns."

Oswald chuckled at his father's observation as he himself took a long drink from his mazer and wiped his lips with his sleeve. "Very smooth by all accounts," he leered.

Berowen cleared her throat and hid the disgust she felt from her face at the obvious meaning behind the comments made by Modig and Oswald. "I was wondering whether any entertainment had been arranged for Brack and my union later this week," she continued.

Modig laughed. "Entertainment eh?" He scowled across at Berowen. "You think we have coin for such frivolity as entertainment?"

"Oh, forgive me, my lord," began Berowen. "I only assumed that such an event would merit some kind of festivities through the fortress as it did at home..."

Again Modig interrupted her. "This is your home now, pretty lass, and we do not usually partake in such tomfoolery here at any time. Your union with my son is a pact of alliance, nothing more. Your lands are now joined with my lands."

Berowen balked at his rudeness and shortness. She saw her father straighten in his seat at this last statement. It was painfully clear by the look on his drawn face that her father felt betrayed. Whilst he had assumed that the marriage union would pull together both the forces of Brundannon and Grimfell in a stronger force against those who had ideas of invasion, it would seem that it was merely a way of increasing Modig's personal riches. It became clear that it was Modig's intent to make Brundannon his own in the near future but at what cost to her family?

She squeezed her father's hand under the table. Her anger at him at once dissipated upon her horrific realisation of his innocence in the arrangements that brought her here at this moment. He had been duped, and he knew it only too well. And there was absolutely nothing to be done, for to renege on the arrangement would be not only seen as the utmost insult, but it would also be seen as a slur on the Brundannon family name. It was clear that Modig would not take the matter lightly should the marriage not take place – there was nothing else left but to withhold the treaty.

Aelwulf squeezed his daughter's hand in return and looked at her with melancholy in his eyes.

The pregnant silence was disturbed by Oswald. "However father," he grunted between mouthfuls of food and mead. "Surely if this pretty bird desires some amusement her wishes should be met. After all it would seem that it should be extremely entertaining with such an *interesting* group of strangers." And he winked at his father slyly. "I am sure the great hall of Grimfell would welcome such a pleasure."

Modig gnawed at a chicken bone, sucking out the marrow with much delight and furiosity. "You are right Oswald," he spluttered as particles of food flew from his mouth. "So be it, the lady shall have her wedding entertainment and we shall all enjoy it greatly no doubt."

Berowen was not as content at the result that she should have been, purely because she knew the reasons behind her wish being granted. Modig and Oswald just wished to ogle the pretty girls – or worse - and she suddenly became wary of involving them in the events at all. But the deed was done; they were expected and she could only try to warn them of the preying nature of their hosts, and only then, with the help of Kipp and his hand signals.

Berowen studied Oswald's wife closer as she sat between him and her brother, Eneas. This woman's life here in the claustrophobic, grimy fortress of Grimfell must indeed by grim. She was a plain, thin woman of an unidentifiable age due to the life of drudgery she obviously endured as Modig's eldest's wife. She was adorned with the plainest jewellery around her neck and her fingers wore no rings apart from a single thin band of metal that acted as her wedding ring. Her clothing was ordinary and slightly worn, and her dull brown hair hung in a single plait down her back. Even though it was evident by Eneas' cheerful face that he was engaging her in some light conversation she showed no outward acknowledgement. Her mouth remained tightly shut in a miserable droop, and even when Berowen's brother laughed at something he had said that he deemed very funny, she did not respond with a reciprocal smile.

Berowen then turned to look at Brack who sat quietly staring at a serving boy as he scuttled towards the table struggling under the weight of two heavy tankards of mead. The look upon her future husband's face was unsettling as he watched the youngster place one on the table in front of him and remove the empty one and then totter down to the other end of the table to repeat the exercise. His face alluded to something she dared not wish dwell upon and she frowned her disconcertment towards him. He caught her look and averted his eyes to the food upon his platter, which he had only half-eaten. Picking up the half-eaten chicken carcass, he tossed it over the table towards where the hounds lay awaiting their evening meal of leftovers and bones.

The two nearest to where the carcass had fallen squabbled and growled at each other in their attempts to claim the offering as their own. Their lips curled over their teeth as they both held it in their jaws and thus began a short tug of war as each tried to win the prize. Berowen watched in horror as the two beasts put their weight behind them and pulled hard. Eventually the flesh began to give way and with a final pull, the largest of the hounds managed to part the rest of the carcass from one leg, leaving the smallest to have to be satisfied with the meagre morsel. The prize was instantly taken into a corner from where the sickening sound of tooth grinding against bone could be heard.

Soon the floor was littered with chicken carcasses in varying degrees of demolishment as Eneas and Amleth joined in on the feeding of the hungry canines, and each of the six hounds were soon hungrily feasting on the leftovers. One carcass remained lopsidedly lying on the floor where it had been thrown, where it would wait until claimed by the first mouth that finished its meal amongst those that chewed hungrily in the background. Berowen, her mother and her father chose not to follow suit in the lobbing of the contents of their platters. Their decision was soon over-ruled when Brack leaned over rudely, and grabbed the remains of the chicken from their platters one by one and tossed them to the floor in front of the table.

Modig picked at his teeth with the point of his dagger before thrusting it into an apple that sat on a platter in front of him. She watched the juices erupt from the point of entry and dribble down the sides of its shiny green skin.

She could bear no more. Standing, she pushed the chair from beneath her with her legs and made her excuses to leave the table of depravity. "I am sorry, my Lord Modig, but I am feeling tired and unwell. I shall retire if that is acceptable to you all."

"But of course, my dear," replied Modig whilst holding the apple in one hand and slicing off segments with his dagger and thrusting them in his mouth. "Your family and I have other matters to speak of and your presence is not required, along with that of your mother's. Please both take your leave and have a pleasant night's rest."

Ethwen grunted under her breath at this announcement, but like her daughter, she was very pleased to be able to leave the table. As she arose from her chair, Aubreda and Oswald's wife also left the table, each wandering off in different directions into the shadows of the great hall, with Oswald slapping his wife's bottom harshly as she left his side. Berowen took her mother's arm in hers and both ascended the stairs to their respective rooms. She could feel Ethwen tense under her support. Ethwen wanted to apologise to her daughter for the doom that awaited her due to their haste in securing the boundaries of their ancestral home. She wished her daughter to know that what they had done had been for the best reasons and that if they had known exactly what lay ahead they would not have agreed to such a union in the first place. She was in total shock – Aelwulf had reported such good things about Grimfell, but he had obviously been tricked by their false hospitality on his first visit those months ago.

Berowen knew her mother was agonising about the situation before them. "Mother," she whispered as they arrived at Ethwen's door. "I do not blame you or my father for the position in which we now find ourselves. These people are cruel, heartless and despicable human beings. It is clear that father was given a false impression when first he visited. What we shall do I know not, but we are under a contract that cannot be broken I fear."

Ethwen looked at her daughter with great sorrow and pity etched across her tired face. Berowen embraced her, "Mother, I shall survive in this pit of wickedness. Have no fear for I know I shall rise above their lecherous, evil ways. Do not reproach yourself." She kissed her mother on her forehead and opened the door for her. "Sleep mother, for we have busy days ahead and we shall need our strength for them, and for the future."

LII

Scrimble had slouched off well ahead of Mog and Peg after their meeting, and Root and Knot had disappeared into the forest on errands of mischief of their own. Mog had cheered up slightly, but she was still not certain that Peg's idea would work. Something was not right with her world; she sensed big changes to come and knew not what they could be. She wanted her possession back and she wanted rid of that box. It was like a heavy weight around her neck and had been all year since The One had presented it to her with its orders. She despised the creature that held so much power over those of the forest, but she despised whomever or whatever had stolen her collection even more at this time. If she did not get it back then it would be the end. She was sure The One would not be impressed with sorry tales of how her work had been stolen from right behind her back. That would simply not do.

The meeting with Scrimble had been fearful; he was a foreboding beast and had made perfectly sure that they all knew how easy it would be for him to kill them if he so wished. And now the matter was down to him and his nose to solve on their behalf. As they ran along, Mog became aware of the songs of various birds from high up in the treetops, and it suddenly dawned on her that if such a creature had taken her assortment of hair they would most likely never find it. She voiced her opinion to Peg, who simply shrugged her shoulders and relayed the platitude that she was sure that this would not be the case.

They eventually came to the clearing where Scrimble had investigated the forest floor around where the man had lain. The two knew that this was where the man lived for they had often seen him here and they could smell him. There was nothing quite like the smell of man, and the aroma was quite strong to their sensitive nostrils.

Mog had first come across this man many moons before when she had found him, huddling in the undergrowth. The shouting of men had drawn her to that part of the wood and she had found him cowering and jibbering under a bush. It had been plain to see that he was hiding from those behind the angry voices and Mog had fully expected the humans to come crashing through the undergrowth at any moment. However, they did not come, and soon the voices faded into the distance. She had sat some way from the man and wondered why he did not return to the world outside the trees when it had become quieter. She had sat with him as the darkness came upon the wood and was still there as the sun rose in the east the next morning. After three days it was clear that this man was to become a part of her world, for no-one had come to find him, and he would not leave.

Eventually he had crawled from beneath the bush he had been hiding under ever since she had first found him. To attract his attention she had rustled the leaves in front of him and by this method managed to lead him to the nearest stream for him to take water. He crept along on all fours deeper into the wood after her, not knowing that she even existed, but his curiosity kept him following the sounds she made with the leaves, until the smell of fresh water had entered his nostrils and he had leapt towards it's source and gulped as much of the clear liquid as he possibly could.

There had been nothing more that Mog could do but hope that his hunger would eventually lead him to the fruits of the bushes and roots of the few flowers that grew below the canopy of woodland. And so he had grown in the woods over the many years that had followed, eventually discarding his clothing and growing hair all over his body. He became the wildman of the woods to all who glimpsed his shadowy figure in the outside world, but to Mog and her kind he was just another outcast from his own world, whom they would watch over in their position as guardians of the wood. They judged him not for his apparent madness – in their eyes all humans were touched with a similar affliction. On the whole they left him alone to his business, although the elders knew that the youngsters of their kind often took it upon themselves to play tricks on him. Mog herself, of course, had teased him occasionally but that was only when she was bored. Boredom and faerie folk do not mix – it is a dangerous combination and usually culminates in faerie magick of the utmost trickery.

On this day, however, as Mog and Peg returned to their own dwellings in the forest, the wildman was not at home. Mog was sure that Scrimble had already been there, but she had to check herself that the wildman had not taken her goods so she crept into his den to look around. The only possession she could find in the dark den was the faerie wreath that she and Peg had made him before their travels across the moor. It had been placed on a bed of pine needles in the farthest corner of the hovel, these needles clearly gathered especially for its resting place. Satisfied that he was not the guilty party she scuttled out of the darkness to find Peg blocking the way. Peg was moving slowly backwards into the hole and Mog immediately grew aware of an odour she had not smelt before. It was disgusting and very strong. She backed up and let her companion enter the hole beside her. Peg had a look of apprehension upon her small wrinkled face, and she pointed out into the clearing.

Screwing her eyes up against the light that streamed through the tree boughs, Mog could make out the figures of two large beings coming towards them. Mog and Peg pressed themselves up against the side of the hovel in the darkest place they could scramble to. This was not good. They both smelt danger in the appearance of these two figures. They could hear the clank of armour as the feet stomped closer. One figure stood right outside the opening and they could see the deerskin boots clearly. Huge boots on huge feet. The two faeries clung to each other in fear. Faeries do not like being trapped, and that was the situation in which Mog and Peg had suddenly found themselves. There was nowhere for them to run and all they could do was sit and wait for the figures to carry on their journey, hopefully without discovering their presence.

But it was not to be. The figures remained where they were, and Mog and Peg could hear their deep guttural utterances as they spoke to each other in a language completely alien and unknown to the two hiding right behind them. They both jumped and clung to each other more tightly as a sword was suddenly thrust into the earth next to the feet. It swung slightly from side to side as it settled itself in the sod. They fully expected a giant hand to thrust itself into their hiding place and yank them out one by one by the neck.

The nicker of horses reached their ears, followed by the heavy fall of hoof beats, and even more rattling of armour. More were coming. Mog and Peg were beside themselves. If these beings remained where they were, then the faeries were captives by default. The feet in front of the opening turned around to face them. Then a rapid stream of hot steaming liquid sprayed into the hole and on to the ground. Mog and Peg looked at each other. The smell of the liquid was over-powering and disgusting, and they could not believe that they had narrowly missed a shower from one of these creatures relieving themselves.

The guttural voices continued to speak to each other as the two-leggeds seemingly began to be settling down for the coming night. Mog and Peg listened as a fire started to crackle and the smell of singeing flesh reached their nostrils on the early evening air. Some unfortunate forest creature was being roasted over the fire and Mog and Peg turned up their noses in disgust at the odour.   The two legs eventually moved from the opening slightly and the observers watched the heavy body flop to the ground on its rear. It was then that they could make out the flaming red hair as it fell down the being's broad back and they knew that they were in grave danger if discovered. Their only salvation was the fact that these creatures were far too large to fit into the hole so they knew they would be safe from discovery as long as they kept quiet. They would just have to wait the night out and would hopefully be able to escape their prison when the red-hairs moved on in the morning.

Mog was annoyed at herself for her curiosity. If she had just left the idea in the back of her mind that the wildman may have stolen her collection, then they would not be in this predicament.

On the other side of the clearing, the wildman watched the imposters quietly. One red-beard he could tackle but a group of eight would not be possible. He eyed them with mistrust, but like Mog and Peg, he would have to wait until morning in the hope that they would move on. Only then would he be able to go home and immerse himself once more in his solitude.

He curled himself up in the thickest bush he could find in case the red-beards awoke before him and discovered him asleep. The twigs scratched at his skin through the thin covering of hair on his body, but he could do nothing but endure the irritation in his bid for safety. The man took some while to fall asleep in his uncomfortable 'bed', but in time his eyelids grew heavy and he fell into the land of dreams.

∞

He was asleep when a crash of thunder brought him to his senses with a jolt. Then a flash of lightning lit up his tiny room throwing shadows across the walls. He sat up in his cot and opened his mouth to scream, but no sound came forth for he could not make sound of any kind other than a guttural grunt in his throat. He had always loathed storms and the malevolence they spread across the land. He kneeled at the foot of his cot, and looked out of his small window and watched the rain lash against its grubby pane. Every so often the land around was lit up by the lightning and he closed his eyes and covered his ears when the thunder came before the next flash. He heard his mother come into his room and felt her sit beside him. Her arms wrapped themselves around his shoulders as she comforted him whilst the storm raged outside. With her there with him he did not feel quite so afraid of the storm and they sat together and watched the rain beat down in torrents on to the sun-hardened soil outside.

It was during a particularly bright flash of lightning that they both noticed two figures making their way towards their cottage. With the next streak of white light they were closer. He had felt his mother tense as they drew nearer, and then she stood and left the room. He went to follow her, but upon reaching the door, she put up her hand to signal that he should stay where he was. Then she went to the front door and opened it. Two men stood before her and he could see them talking and gesticulating with their arms as they did so. He saw his mother shake her head, but they pushed her into the room and walked in, shutting the door behind them.

He watched through a crack in the door as the men started to push his mother further into the room. He had no idea who they were – he had never seen them before, but by their actions, he knew they had come to do his mother harm. The storm continued to rage outside and seemed to have entered his home as the men began to push the meagre furniture around the room. One man picked up a chair and threw it against the wall, where it smashed into splintered pieces of wood. His mother was cowering against the other wall under a hail of blows from the other man. He pulled at her hair and slapped her round the face, and was yelling at her, although the words meant nothing to the watcher in his room.

Quietly he opened the door a bit more and when he saw that both men had their backs to him, he crept into the room. He picked up a splintered piece of wood that had once been a chair leg, and rushed at the man who was attacking his mother. He heard his mother cry out his name. "Walt!"

At this, the attacker turned around just as Walt thrust the jagged edge of wood into his face with all his force. The man screamed as the wood pierced his skin, leaving bloody gashes on his cheeks and forehead. The other man lunged at him, but Walt managed to sidestep him and hit him hard on the head with the wood several times until he lay prone on the floor.

The bloody-faced man who had been attacking his mother then made a grab for Walt's arm, but Walt was too quick for him and hit him hard across the face with the wood, this time piercing an eye with the splintered edge of the chair leg. The man fell to his knees clutching his eye, the blood oozing through his fingers. "Walt!" cried his mother. But he took no notice. Something inside of him had snapped. All the bad things done to him by Eadric over the months of him looking after Walt whilst his mother had gone to market came forth in acute anger. This man kneeling before him was attacking his mother for a reason he did not know, but he knew that there would be nothing that she had done to deserve such treatment. In his anger and frustration, he continued to hit the man as he knelt before him.

His mother grabbed his arm and he stopped and looked at her for a minute. It was just enough time for the man to get to his feet and try to grab Walt's other arm. Walt snapped both arms away, and ran to the other side of the room and stood with legs apart and the chair leg in his hand daring the man to come forth and try to take it from him. His face covered in blood the man did just that. This simpleton was not going to get the better of him. As he lunged forward again, Walt heard his mother yell his name. "Walt! No!" But it was too late. Walt thrust the broken chair leg into the face of the man again and this time it made a deep gash in his right cheek. The man fell to the floor in agony, but Walt kept on hitting him until the man lay still, the life gone from his body.

Walt slid down the wall and slumped to the floor. He looked at his bloody hands and then up at his mother who stood frozen in fear and disbelief at her son's explosion of ferocity. The man who had been knocked out began to stir back into consciousness, and slowly rose to his feet. But Walt did not move to stop him as the man looked first at the body of his acquaintance, and then at both Walt and his mother before he ran out of the door as fast as he could into the storm that still raged in the darkness outside.

His mother stood and covered her face in her hands and sobbed. Walt watched her for a few minutes and then slowly got to his feet and, picking up the dead man's feet, he started to drag him across the floor towards the open door. Once outside he pulled him to the corner of the yard and let go of the feet. Then he returned inside to his mother and gave her a hug. She continued to sob and he heard her say his name over and over, along with other words he did not understand.

After a while she stopped crying and looked at him. The storm had moved on and the cottage was entombed in silence save for the slow methodical drip of the rain falling from the cottage eaves. She bent over and picked up the bloody piece of wood and gave it to Walt, signalling for him to take it outside and hide it. Then she went to the bucket of water and soaked a rag in it, wringing it between her shaking hands before kneeling on the floor and wiping away the bloodstains as best she could, for some had already soaked into the wood. When Walt returned she was moving the table back from where the other man had toppled it over on its side. She pulled it across the stubborn stain in an effort to disguise it, but she knew it was hopeless.

Daylight filtered through the small windows and shone on the faces of the two figures standing in the room. She was waiting for what she knew would come. He was waiting for her to make him breakfast. She smiled softly at him and smoothed down his hair. She could not be angry with him for she knew that he had done what he had done out of protection of her. He knew not what crime he had committed in doing so, but she knew that they would come for him and that she would have to be ready to hide him if she could.

And they did come.

∞

And now he awoke in his uncomfortable place of sleep to the daylight that seeped through the treetops. He closed his eyes again for a few moments as he chased the dream that had just left him, in the hope that he could catch up with it again. But it had gone and it left him with the memories of how he came to be in the woods alone. Why *hadn't* his mother returned to find him?

The smell of burning embers reached his nostrils and he remembered where he was. He listened hard for any sounds that may give away the presence of the red-beards, but heard nothing but the sound of birdsong and the occasional rustle of undergrowth as a creature went about its early morning business. He slowly rolled out of the prickly bush and edged his way towards the clearing. There was no-one there, just the dying embers of the fire that had not been completely put out. He heaved a sigh of relief that the red-beards had gone, and made his way slowly to his den.

Mog and Peg were no longer there – they had made quick their escape as soon as the red-hairs had left.

LIII

Thurstan arose early and prepared himself for his visit to the apothecary, Cynefrid. Lin had warned him to have a good excuse and the fact that the nagging ache in his jaw from the loose tooth had begun to force itself into his consciousness again seemed a perfect solution to the problem. He strode purposefully towards the gatehouse and was not surprised to see the raven sitting atop the structure staring down at him.

A surly guard stepped out to stop his progress. "Halt. State your purpose, traveller."

"I wish to visit Cynefrid, the apothecary. I am hoping that his herbs may cure the ache in my tooth."

The guard snorted loudly. "Coin?"

"I have coin, sentry, yes. The price?"

"Two silver, traveller," and the sentry held out his hand.

"One for the purse and one for you I'll wager," thought Thurstan as he dropped two silver coins into the waiting hand.

The sentry withdrew to the side and Thurstan made his way through the gatehouse. "Which way?" he asked of the sentry who nodded his head to the right. "Up hill and turn right. Can't miss it – always smoke coming from chimney and a foul stench of weed with it."

Thurstan raised an eyebrow and continued on his way up the hill. Sure enough he spotted a small cottage clinging to the side of the hill, with a steady stream of thick smoke puffing its way skyward. He knocked on the door and waited; a gust of wind blowing down the smoke briefly making him cough from the potent scent carried with it.

The door slowly creaked open and a scrawny man stood before him. He was dressed from head to foot in a black robe, its cowl disguising most of his face apart from the nose that peaked out from its shadows. "Yes?" the figure asked.

"I am here to seek out Cynefrid. Are you he?"

"And what do you want with him?" came the reply.

"A poultice for my aching tooth, and some information on the legends surrounding Grimfell. I have heard tell that he is a man with great knowledge of such things," answered Thurstan.

"You may enter, traveller with a bad tooth; I have just the remedy for such things. As for information, it depends on exactly what you wish to know."

Thurstan ducked his head as his crossed the threshold into the tiny cottage. Looking around he could see every corner full of books and every surface covered in bottles, vials and piles of strange looking roots, and bits of dead animals. The walls were covered in bunches of hanging herbs, and flowers and over the fire a cauldron bubbled furiously sending up the offending spirals of smoke that fled to the skies through the chimney above. His eyes immediately began to sting and became watery from the potent mix churning over the fire.

"Wirt! Wirt! Boy where are you?" shouted the hooded figure. A scuffle and crash in the corner followed this cry, and a young lad emerged from the gloomy spot, with tousled hair and sleep still vainly trying to keep his eyes firmly shut.

The apothecary's apprentice, Wirt, was in his 19th year. He was always out on collecting trips around the marshes and the edge of the forest gathering supplies for his mentor. However, it was not a rare event for him to be missing for hours and to return with an empty bag, or quite often no bag at all, for his mind wandered easily. He was a handsome young lad with longish black hair that he always kept tied with a thong and fashioned in a tail down his back. He knew much about the wildlife of the area but also, unfortunately, was ever swayed if a serving girl about the fortress threw him an alluring look. Then, without question, the task at hand would be forgotten in an instant. The apothecary despaired of his young charge, but at times found Wirt's attempts at wooing amusing and had found himself, on more than one occasion, having to turn his head away from the young lad's view, for fear the smile across his lips would give away his delight at the boy's clumsiness.

Upon Cynefrid's call, Wirt had jumped up from his stool where he had been sitting, whilst dozing with his head on his chest. The suddenness of his movement had caused the stool to topple over on its side, crashing into a pile of books that had been stacked beside it. They had all tumbled to the ground with a resounding thump.

"Asleep again?" enquired Cynefrid of his assistant. "You should reserve the evening hours for such basic necessities, rather than use them for entertaining your young flibbertigibbets. How is that serving wench Pip anyway?"

Wirt scowled at his master. "I have not spoken to her for many moons, master. She is too ...." and he scratched his head searching for the word.

"Worldly?" offered Cynefrid with a grin.

Wirt yawned and scratched his chest in earnest as if being bitten by a plague of bed bugs. "Perhaps that is the word, master. You have a task for me?" he continued rapidly seeing an escape from the line of questioning about his personal life that he found painfully embarrassing.

"Ah yes. Let us see if any of my teachings have sunk into that young brain of yours. This man has an ache in the jaw from a troublemaking tooth. Make up a powder, Wirt."

The young man looked across at Thurstan and then nodded his head and replied with a slight waiver of self-doubt in his voice. "Y-y-y-es master".

Thurstan became slightly concerned that the soothing of his ache was to be left in the hands of this young man. He could only hope that no poisonous plant would accidentally make its way into the hands of the drowsy fellow.

As Wirt shuffled sleepily off into the maze of vials and books, the hooded figure beckoned Thurstan to sit with him by the fire. It was then that he threw back the cowl and revealed his features. The left side of his face was grossly disfigured; his eye was half closed and drooped into the area where a cheek would have been, and the corner of his mouth drooped downwards. He had no hair at the temples and this whole side of his face gave the impression of a wax effigy that had half melted before setting forever in this gravely misshapen form. Thurstan had not expected such features and could not help but stare, if only briefly, when Cynefrid pulled back the hood.

"My everlasting reminder of an accident with some volatile concoction when I was but Wirt's age," he announced with no emotion. "You would not imagine that a plant that is harmless on its own could react in such a way when mixed with a root from another, but – alas - it is in the quantities of such that you have to be wary of. A sorry tale of a young lad misreading the inscription on the vials mixed with the same young lad falling asleep whilst the concoction was brewing. But we learn by our mistakes, do we not?"

Thurstan was amazed by the man's apparent flippancy of his maiming, "We do indeed apothecary, we do indeed and I beg your pardon for the rudeness of my stare."

Cynefrid waved his hand in dismissal of the statement. "Think nothing of it, stranger. If nothing else it taught me, and I teach others like Wirt here, that not looking where you are going whilst carrying any remedy is a foolhardy and often dangerous pastime." Cynefrid sighed. "I awoke with such a start at my master's bidding that I grabbed the brew and ran with it to him, tripping over his cat as I did so, thus falling and spilling the liquid over my face. This is my legacy. Never run and never trust a cat," and he laughed aloud at his amusing anecdote.

"Can't find the beetles, master," came a shout from the farthest point of the room. "We got any?"

"Ah Wirt, he is such an amenable young lad, but quite hopeless at this time in the morning," said Cynefrid quietly to Thurstan. "They are there lad. I know because I boiled them up only a few days ago. Next to the frogs if my memory serves me well," he shouted back to Wirt, raising an eyebrow in frustration at Thurstan and rolling his eyes to the heavens.

"Ah yes found them!" came the reply. "Three males and one female by the looks of it."

"Yes, yes lad, I am sure you are right," responded the apothecary wearily waiting for the obvious next question.

"Which shall I use, master? Male or female?"

Cynefrid chuckled at the confirmation of his thought. "It matters not Wirt."

Turning his attention back to Thurstan, a serious look crossed his face. "So you wish information? You have perhaps chanced upon some evidence that the marshes are not as they first seem?"

Thurstan eyed him cautiously. Evidence? Was he referring to the stone and its carvings? Or did he have something else in mind?

"I have come across something, yes, but I am not sure whether it is that to which you are referring."

"And there is no way that you could possibly know to what I am referring of course. You are cautious in your words traveller, and that is to be quite expected. You do not want to reveal anything you may have found in case I use it against you perhaps. There are people here that do not look kindly upon those that speak of signs, portents or suchlike."
Thurstan stared into the fire, and was surprised by Cynefrid's next question.

"Is the raven yours?"

"I do not believe such a creature could belong to anybody, apothecary, and if there is one here then it certainly does not owe me any allegiance."

"Aha, so if it does not answer to you, then it must answer to someone else who arrived at Grimfell yesterday, for it has not been here before. But no matter, we are digressing slightly are we not."

"Can you tell me about the hills to the east way?" asked Thurstan tentatively.

"You have been talking to Llinos it seems. She is certain that something in the hills is causing the death of the farming land over that way is she not. In fact, there may be some truth in what she says. There are tales of creatures that once used the caves in those hills as their homes."

"Creatures?"

"Fearsome beasts that once roamed the land and skies around these marshes, but legends such as these are often spread to scare, and are often not true."

"But you believe that what Lin thinks has some sense to it?"

"It would make sense if the creatures were still there. But I do not believe they are. You have to remember, traveller, that these marshes were once the home of a very ancient race. There are signs all over of their habitation if you know where to look. Much has been destroyed by those who do not believe, and who do not wish others so to do."

"So the carvings I found do indeed date from many years ago as I thought," stated Thurstan.

"Carvings?"

"I located a standing stone with strange carvings, not far from the gates of Grimfell. It had been broken in two, the carved section laying covered by undergrowth."

"Fascinating. Not far from here you say?" continued Cynefrid with a look of great interest in his eyes. "And what were the carvings, can you describe them to me?"

"Alas I cannot sir, apart from one set that seem to depict the caves in the hills. I have been pondering over the others since I first saw them yesterday. I plan to revisit the stone in the next few days to take a longer and closer look."

"Hmm, well I'll wager that the forest will be depicted and perhaps the ring of stones to the south," offered Cynefrid.

"I have knowledge of them both, for we stopped during our journey at the stones and attempted to make our journey through the forest, but unfortunate events dissuaded us from continuing further."

"We?"

"I accompanied the future wife of Lord Brack and her family here to Grimfell," explained Thurstan.

"And what, pray, led you to attempt to traverse through the Forest of Whispers? It is not a place that would be chosen by most sensible travellers."

"We were beset with problems on our journey not the least being two attacks from ferocious warriors of an unidentifiable race, and we attempted to avoid further attention from them by taking such a route. But the red-beards were already there and killed one of our party and almost succeeded in killing Brack's future wife," explained Thurstan.

Cynefrid immediately leaned forward in his chair. "Red-beards you say?"

"You know of them?"

"Indeed I have heard of such warriors, but their presence in these lands has not been known for decades. It surprises me to hear that they are blighting our shores with their devilry once more. It also concerns me a great deal."

"In truth you are the first person who has knowledge of them. From whence do they hail?" asked Thurstan sitting forward in his chair and resting his arms on his legs.

"I have lived at Grimfell for nigh on sixty years. I was born here and was employed as apprentice to the apothecary at a young age. He himself had been born and raised here, and knew of many things. It was from him that I learned most about the legends of the Wellonaw Marshes and their surrounds. The red-beards hail from across the wide waters to our north. They were renowned for their ferocity and tenacity in hunting down whatever, or whomever, they were seeking. They took no prisoners and never gave quarter. It was told that once, many years ago, they came in great droves in large ships across the water in a great invasion but were thwarted in their attempts by the great armies that stood together to repel them. They never really forgave our people for this great defeat."

"Perhaps then, they are planning a return battle after all these years?" offered Thurstan. "But this time they are sending out groups of warriors to spy on the defences of the land first. They are well trained in the use of their weapons, and well armoured. Their mounts are well-trained also and are adept at biting and kicking on command."

"Ah yes, that was always so, I believe. Vicious animals trained for despicable acts upon the flesh of unsuspecting people; those who are usually so trusting of such beasts. We must be vigilant. I trust that you have informed Lord Modig of such warriors?"

"He is aware of their presence."

"Good, if he has been alerted then he will have no grounds for complaint if they were to attack one of his weekly tax collections."

Thurstan could not fail to notice the dull barb of sarcasm in Cynefrid's voice.

"As for the carvings, traveller, I suggest that you try to make a sketch of them and bring them back to me. I may be able to aid in the deciphering if you would be willing to allow me so to do."

Thurstan nodded in agreement. "Indeed I shall endeavour to do this as soon as I can. My thanks, apothecary."

Wirt reappeared with a tiny vial of powder of the most peculiar colour and handed it to Cynefrid. "Powdered beetle, newt and carrot, master," he proudly pronounced.

"Excellent Wirt, there is hope for you yet, it seems," responded Cynefrid with a smile on his warped face. Handing it to Thurstan he added, "Wet you finger and dab it into the powder and rub on the gum around the troublesome tooth, traveller. Do this frequently and refrain from spitting out the foul tasting powder and with luck it should ease your discomfort."

Thurstan took the vial gingerly and examined it closely. The quoted ingredients did not sound palatable in the slightest but he vowed that he would give it the benefit of the doubt and would try it in the hope that it performed its allotted task with satisfaction. He stood and made ready for his departure from the cottage.

"My thanks again to you, apothecary. It has been a most interesting morning. And my thanks to you, young Wirt, for the potion." Reaching into his money pouch he produced several silver coins and placed them in Cynefrid's palm. He walked across the room, avoiding the piles of books in his way.

"One thing. You did not ask me my name," he said, turning, as he opened the door to the path.

"And you did not offer it," replied Cynefrid. "Besides it is not of any consequence. Names are merely given us by our parents to call us by when we are wanted."

Just as Thurstan was about to close the door behind him, he heard Cynefrid say, "The raven is a bad omen to many, traveller. You should warn whoever has brought him amongst this place to be wary, for his presence here – and that of his master or mistress - will not be tolerated if he should be seen. That is, of course, if you are aware of whom this person is."

Thurstan bowed his head and walked out on to the path. His physical irritations were relieved when the cooling fresh air hit his face and eyes. He had not gone far when he heard his name called from behind. Recognising Berowen's voice he stopped and turned around to see her walking carefully down the muddy path towards him. "My lady," he bowed deeply.

"Thurstan, I am so glad to see you," panted Berowen after her efforts of concentration in not slipping over. As they slowly continued down the hill towards the gatehouse, she told him all that had occurred the previous night. Thurstan listened intently, but there really was nothing he could say. It was very clear that the contract could not be broken now, at such a late stage. He sympathised with her and her family, and truly meant what he said, but felt hopeless as to a resolve of the situation.

As Berowen passed through the gatehouse, the sentry stood to a lazy attention, and looked at

Thurstan with a disinterested glance. As they looked for Kipp, Berowen explained the predicament in which she had found herself after asking that the troupe of musicians and dancers perform at the forthcoming wedding. Thurstan nodded slowly as he listened; it had not taken him long to realise upon his arrival at the fortress that not only was Grimfell not as formidable on the inside as it appeared to the traveller on their approach, it was also clearly corrupt within its walls and its halls; it was riddled with the disease.

They found Kipp gnawing at a piece of stale bread as he sat with his plump legs dangling over the edge of his cart; his face not as flushed and cheerful as it usually was. He remonstrated about the exorbitant amount of coins that he would have to hand over to the wheelwright to have his cart repaired, and despaired as to how he could possibly afford such a necessary restoration, especially after having to hand over most of the coin he had towards the stabling of old Bessie. He was just going to have to forego the repairs until his next stop in the hope that the cart's wheel managed to keep itself together until then.

There was not much Berowen or Thurstan could do but sympathise with the old man as he continued to complain under his breath - whilst he continued to chew his paltry breakfast - at the proposed thievery at the hands of the wheelwright. Sweeping his hand broadly in the direction of the performers he told the two that he, and they, would most likely move on as soon as they could. "Tis only for dear ol' Bessie that I be stayin'. One more day and she should be rested enough. Then we'll be movin' on methinks."

"Oh," muttered Berowen. "I had hoped that you would stay for a few days, at least until my marriage. I had come to visit you today to ask of your health and that of the others and to enquire as to whether they could play music and dance on the day, as well as inviting you to attend."

Kipp swallowed the last piece of bread and coughed slightly as its dryness made it stick in his throat.   "That is very kind of you, m'lady," he spluttered between clearing his throat. "I had not thought that you would do such a thing as invite ol' Wanderin' Kipp 'ere to such an auspicious occasion."

"Nonsense," responded Berowen with a smile. "Why wouldn't I? We have travelled together for only a few days it is true, but during those days I would like to think that we had become friends. You do not share the road and a campfire without forming some kind of bond with your fellow traveller."

Kipp looked slightly embarrassed as if he was not used to such kind words.Usually being a solitary traveller by nature, he was not accustomed to forming any bonds, other than those with his ale-drinking companions at oft-visited ale-houses once or twice in a year when they happened to be there upon his visits. The meeting with the performers and the travellers from Brundannon had been an uncommon one, but he had to admit that he had enjoyed it immensely - perhaps in his ageing years the time had come when he needed a morsel of company on his path.

"I had wondered whether you would be able to try and explain to the music-makers that it would be my pleasure if they could attend and show off their skills. However, it would only be fair to explain that upon agreeing to such, to my utmost disgust and horror, my future male kin displayed a rather un-gentlemanly reaction with regards to the dancing," continued Berowen. "So much so that I have since regretted suggesting the girls' presence as I have fears for their safety amongst these men."

Kipp raised his eyes to the heavens and growled. "Hmm I think I be understandin' of what you mean, m'lady. I have noticed some rather lurid attention from some of the garrison 'ere as they have passed. In fact I reasoned that they seem to be passin' a bit too often if you ask me, and gawping as if they had ne'er seen a pretty lass before."

"Can you explain thus to them, Kipp?" enquired Berowen. "Although I do not know how you will."

"Ol' Kipp'll find a way," he winked and patted Berowen on the arm. "I be likin' a challenge to ease the hours away," he chortled. "And I am sure Thurstan 'ere will 'elp me along. Eh, Thurstan?"

"Alas, Kipp, I am not certain that I shall be staying here myself for too many more hours," came the reply from the man beside Berowen.

"But Thurstan," she exclaimed turning to him. "You surely will not be leaving before ..."

"I am not sure that I can witness a free bird become caged, my lady," he interrupted. "And I cannot watch the parents' pain in seeing the wings clipped before their eyes and the freedom plucked from its body. From what you have told me, the life is sapped out of the women who dwell in the lofty hall. I am not certain that I wish to see the light dim in your eyes Berowen for I fear that is what will happen as soon as Brack's ring is placed upon your finger, and you have wandered the damp corridors in your solitude and despair."

"The light will not dull, Thurstan, as long as those I hold dear are there to witness the moment. If I am to suffer such a capture without the company of my friends, then I will not have the courage to survive for, although I know that my family has been tricked, I am the prey they unwittingly offered. And prey needs hope to survive. You, Kipp and these men and women here are my hope. If you desert me now, you will take that spirit to survive from within me. You cannot leave – not yet – please tell me you will stay."

"So, by your words it is *you* who wish to hold *me* captive?" Thurstan asked, a wry grin forming on his lips.

Berowen bristled slightly. She deemed Thurstan's words harsh and was not sure whether he was playing with her; she noticed the grin, but could not decide whether or not it was bolstered with sarcasm. "I wish to hold no-one captive, my lord Thurstan. You are, of course, free to do as you so wish. I would not presume to hold you to ransom. I merely would ask that you might consider staying for a few days more. But if you wish to leave, then that is your privilege and, contrary to what you seem to hint at by your statement, there is nothing I can do about it, or would wish to do about it. I have no desire to further delay you from your own business."

Kipp had remained sitting on the edge of his cart, and had begun to feel awkward in his position right in front of the two as they held their slightly barbed conversation. He had commenced picking at his nails and wished that he could think of some task to undertake that would take him away from the immediate vicinity, but there was nothing he could think of other than perhaps taking a walk around the outer wall, which he balked at doing for several reasons. One, he could not walk very far before getting out of breath and two, if he went in one direction he would come across the small township of villagers whose homes nestled against the walls and if he chose the opposite direction he risked having something disgusting landing on his person after it was lobbed from the walls above. It was an unwholesome pastime walking alongside that part of the wall as it was, primarily due to the various revolting aromas and suspiciously soggy earth. The guards that patrolled the walls were not the most polite people when needing to relieve their ale-sodden stomachs from the night before by heaving the contents over the side. Nor were they shy on relieving their full bladders - or worse - whilst on duty. So he chose to remain where he was, albeit feeling conspicuous at so doing.

Kipp had sucked in a sharp breath of air as Thurstan had replied to Berowen's plea to remain at Grimfell until her marriage. 'Those words were not well chosen. And he had started so well,' he had thought to himself as he noticed Berowen flinch with irritability at Thurstan's apparent accusation. In his opinion, her retort had been well-founded and to himself he silently praised her. Whilst he was sure that Thurstan had not meant it in the way the words had come forth, he cringed at the bad timing of the attempt at joviality – if in truth that was what it had been.

"My lady, I had no wish to cause you anger or despair with my words. They were not well chosen, or timed. My own affairs can wait until I am ready to deal with them. You have no need to hold me captive, for I will stay under my own volition and would be honoured so to do." Thurstan had had no intention to offend the woman before him – his aside had been purely to attempt to lighten the moment. He was sorely aggrieved that he had upset her. In truth he had a habit of doing such in instances such as this. As a defence of avoiding awkward moments he would always try to make light of it and had oft upset people in the past. Usually he did not really care that he had offended, but to do so to this woman before him was the last thing he would wish to do. However, he found himself not being able to resist another attempt at making Berowen smile.

"Besides, my lady, would I dare to leave knowing that there is a black bird circling overhead at this moment ready to peck out my eyes at a moment's notice should you wish to command it so to do?"

Berowen looked up and laughed. "How did you know Odi was there?" she asked.

"Simple my lady. Wherever you are, then so is he."

Kipp looked up also and then back at the two before him. The omen bird circled lazily high above and he shuddered at its appearance, and was momentarily suspicious of the calmness of Thurstan and Berowen. "Sorcery is afoot, it seems," he proclaimed suddenly clapping his hands in delight when the true meaning of the bird's appearance had sunk into his ageing brain. "I have 'erd tell o'it but never seen it wi' me own eyes."

"And you must tell no-one of such things either, Master Kipp," instructed Thurstan seriously.

"Bah, me lips is sealed. You can trust ol' Kipp 'ere." There was a pause before Kipp spoke again and with a wink said, "Reckon you can get it to persuade the wheelwright to lower his prices?"

LIV

With a new day upon him, Scrimble continued his search for Mog's missing items. He had been successful in locating a trail in the small clearing where Mog made her home. He had commenced tracking it until nightfall when he had become sidetracked by the scent of hare, which had made the juices flow in his stomach. He had left one hunt to commence a different one and soon he was feasting upon the warm, freshly slaughtered carcass of the unfortunate beast that had interrupted his tracking of Mog's stolen belongings.

It had been the crashing of something moving through the undergrowth that had awoken him that morning. It would seem that whatever it was it had no apparent regard for anything that was in its way. Accompanying this was a pungent aroma that he had never before experienced. It was man of sorts, but something else was mingled with it and he could not identify this added ingredient. He could smell horseflesh and indeed he could make out the unmistakeable sound of their hoof beats as they plodded on the bed of pine needles. The sound of armour alerted him to the danger and he hid out of sight as eight great horses slowly made their way passed the dense thicket in which he was laying. He eyed the riders with mistrust. The smell became overpowering as they passed and he watched with keen eyes as they hacked their way through any low branches that drooped in their way, the dappled sunlight glinting on their great swords as they did so. A sleepy roost of birds soared upwards into the sky; their cacophony echoing through the thick trees as the riders disturbed their peaceful wakening. The great hound growled as he eyed the fur around the boots and helms of the riders – fur he recognised as from his own kind.

The rider at the back of the group must have heard him, for the great beast beneath him was pulled to a stop. It swung round and its eyes rolled in its head from the painful pull on its bridle. Scrimble watched the boots kick it to urge it forward and it approached him, snorting with anger and malice. The great sword swung down upon the greenery that shielded him from sight and sliced away the top twigs, and he edged himself backwards slowly. The figure sniffed the air and Scrimble watched the head as it moved from side to side, its eyes searching through the leaves and boughs. A hare dashed out from behind him and the figure's attention immediately turned to the movement and the direction from which it had appeared. The sword came crashing down just in front of Scrimble's nose as it penetrated the earth before disappearing upwards again. Scrimble waited for the next thrust but could not move for risk of revealing his position. The metal pierced the earth just to the side of his head. It was too close for Scrimble's comfort.

With a loud deep growl in the bottom of his throat he lunged from beneath his cover and launched himself at the throat of the horse. It shied away and screamed at him, raising its forelegs and rearing sharply, almost unseating its heavy rider. The surprise attack had sufficiently thrown the hunter off guard, and as quickly as he had appeared, Scrimble ran into the cover of the forest, but not before he heard an arrow cut through the air beside his head. It knicked the edge of his right ear before embedding itself into the trunk of a tree just to his left. The scent on the arrow was strong as it had flown passed. It was not a scent he would forget, and the owner of the arrow would rue the day that he crossed the great hound of the forest. That would be certain; Scrimble would return to leave his own mark upon the unwelcome and uninvited hunter in the forest.

Scrimble had not halted in his escape until he was certain that he was no longer under threat. Then he slowly and cautiously made his way back to pick up the trail he was originally following. His ear smarted from the sharp edge of the arrowhead and this made him even more sour tempered than usual. Once the task at hand was complete he would track his antagonist and await his moment of retribution.

Following the trail, he found himself in a large, long-dried up gully. He sniffed around the roots of the trees until at last he found an opening. Whatever had stolen Mog's items had dragged them underground through this hole. There was no way that he could squeeze into the hole and he knew by the scent around the burrow that the creature that lived below would not appear until nightfall, and the sun had not long been in the sky. Should he wait or should he return to Mog and Peg, and bring them to the location and leave the collection to them?

The intervention in his work that morning had been ever-present on his mind, not the least because his ear still throbbed from the wound he had suffered. He made his way back to find Mog and Peg in order that he could relinquish his part of the bargain and continue with his own search, and the ultimate resolve of the evil doings of that morning. He suspected that the arrow bearer would be in possession of a fine liver and the thought of the warm, soft, and bloody morsel was a high priority on his mind, upon meting out his reprisal.

Mog and Peg would have hugged Scrimble if they had dared, but his bad temper was evident when he had arrived and informed them that he had completed his part of the bargain. They noticed the bloody nick on his ear but thought it best not to bring the subject up. Scrimble was not one to be trifled with at the best of times, and this injury was obviously souring his mood more than usual.

They dutifully followed him to the burrow and thanked him, assuring him of their allegiance in the future if he should find it his turn to be given a task by The One.

Although he knew that a tasty morsel could be had if he waited for the creature to appear from its underground home, Scrimble left to resume his own business. Then Peg tried to squeeze into the burrow. It had been easy until her hips had become lodged in the opening. She became completely stuck and Mog found it amusing to see Peg's legs treading the air in frustration, the rest of her body immersed in the earth. Peg, however, did not find it funny. She began to panic, not only with being stuck but also by the overpowering smell of whatever animal it was further down in the underground tunnel. What if it should come charging at her with teeth bared and sharp claw? Her feet frantically beat the air outside – she could not call out for help; Mog would not hear her and whatever had made this their home might well do. So she could just continue to waggle her legs until Mog realised the predicament in which she had found herself and helped to pull her out.

This Mog eventually did. She tugged and tugged on Peg's feet until suddenly she flew backwards and Peg tumbled out on top of her. Both scrambling to their feet, Peg stood facing Mog and angrily wagged her finger at her and shouted at her for not helping sooner. Mog could do nothing but laugh even louder at the sight of Peg's face covered in speckles of mud and pine needles. She even had a worm wriggling in her hair, which suddenly raised itself skywards and probed blindly at the air. It lost its balance as Peg jumped up and down in fury and fell down her forehead on to her beaky nose before dropping silently to the ground and wriggling off as fast as it could.

As happens with all faeries that lose their tempers, Peg's eyes grew darker and darker until they were but tiny black buttons within her wrinkled and anger-ridden face. Mog stamped her foot and imitated Peg before poking her long black tongue out at her friend. She lay down again and rolled over on to her belly before kicking her legs in the air. Peg's anger dissipated as she watched Mog flailing around on the ground. She began to realise how funny she must have looked and soon started giggling before throwing herself down on to her back and laughing loudly at her own recent misfortune – all the fears and perceived dangers gone from her mind.

It began to get dark and colder. Mog and Peg took up positions around the burrow. Mog sat atop the root that overhung the entrance, whilst Peg sat opposite it covered by a mass of fallen foliage to disguise herself. She had pulled the hare's skull fur over her head and all that could be seen was the glint in her eye as she watched the hole for signs of activity. Even through their coats of fur both the faeries could not help but shiver in the cold night air. They had to wrap their mouths under their coats to stop them sending up the tell-tale puffs of vaporous breath.

Mog heard the rustling first beneath her. Then Peg saw the winter-white face appear at the opening of the burrow followed by a long thin white body. Once outside it raised itself tall on its tiny back legs, before flattening itself to the ground again. It sniffed the air, not sure whether it was safe or not; he had a feeling something was not quite right. He stood perfectly still until his eyes became accustomed to the shapes around him. He thought he could make out a hare in the near distance. Hare was delicious and he could not believe his luck at finding one so near to home. He stood tall again and began his dance of war. He jumped and twisted his body, turning as he did so to hypnotise his prey into watching him perform his weird dance. And then suddenly he leaped upon the hare. Peg screamed as the creature sank its teeth into her neck. She leapt up and threw it off. It was only then that the stoat realised his mistake as the hare suddenly grew in size before him and shouted at him in a raging voice.

He recognised the shape of the form that stood before him and he tried to make a dash for his burrow only to find another of the same standing in front of the hole, blocking his way in. Mog eyed him with caution - stoats were well equipped with sharp teeth and claws. She spoke to him in the language of the forest and demanded of him his name and status among his own.

"Cob, if it is any of your business," had been the curt reply. "My status is irrelevant."

"Well Cob," began Mog. "Unless the hierarchy has changed within your breed, you are merely an underling. Am I correct in saying that Oram is still the Queen among your kind?"

"She is."

"And did she send you out to steal the contents of the box?"

"What box?"

Mog laughed. "Now, now Cob. Do you think we came across your burrow by accident? The nose that sniffed out you, and the contents of the box that are still below ground, belongs to one that you would not wish to cross. He would be here except that he had other matters to attend to."

Cob twitched his whiskers slyly. "I know of nothing about a box," he insisted.

"We can always ask Scrimble to come back tomorrow and persuade you to tell the truth if you so wish," explained Mog, as she leant back against the side of the bank.

At the sound of that name Cob began to look about him earnestly. Scrimble was well-known among his kind – many a kin member had become a meal for the great hound.

"I see the name means something to you," said Mog smirking. "So will you return my belongings now and avoid a revisit from Scrimble?" She hoped that this would not be necessary as she was not at all sure that she would be able to convince the hound to return to this place and help them again.

Cob stood tall. "She made me do it and I can understand why," he admitted.

"And why is that?"

"She wanted rid of you faeries that is why," he replied spitting the words out between his teeth and grinning inanely. "She knew you had seen The One last year and she knew what would be your punishment if you did not manage to comply with its wishes," he hissed. "It was her turn the year before and knew how much those things meant to you and your kind."

"And why would she want rid of us?" asked Mog somewhat surprised at Cob's candidness. Her eyes began to darken and she stared at him. And he saw the malice within that dark stare. "She took my collection out of spite knowing full well the consequences that the action could have resulted in, didn't she? I wonder what other creatures have suffered as a result of her malevolence."

"I-I-I don't know, I swear," spluttered Cob as he began to run round and round in circles in agitation. His own safety had suddenly become more important than the trick his Queen had played upon the faeries. He may well be able escape her wrath, but he knew he could not flee from the faeries for they would hunt him down until they could tear him limb from limb. He had heard many tales of how vicious they were when crossed. And they had the allegiance of the great hound of the forest too. He crouched down before Mog and put his front paws over his head in shame.

Mog had the cowardly stoat exactly where she wanted him. "I will let you go unharmed if you fetch my belongings now, Cob."

The stoat lifted his head and looked at her, the slyness returning to his eyes.

"However, if you trick me, I *shall* send Scrimble back to you," she continued as she noticed the change of his mood.

She stood aside and he scuttled into his burrow. Here was the gamble. Would he return with her things or would he stay below ground and call her bluff?

Moments passed and Mog was beginning to think that he had taken the last choice, when he suddenly reappeared with her samples in his mouth. She snatched them from him quickly. "Now Cob, you had better warn Oram that her plan has been foiled and that she is now under my watchful gaze. If The One is not interested in her trickery, then I know Scrimble will be. She had better watch her sly step in future."

The conversation over, Mog beckoned Peg to follow her. They both left the stoat mumbling to himself incoherently. Peg saw the anger still in her fellow faerie's eyes. She asked Mog to explain to her what had occurred – the dialogue had been quick and she had only managed to decipher one or two words. When Mog explained why the samples had been stolen, Peg was astonished. When she asked Mog if she was really going to let the matter lie there she was not surprised to hear Mog tell her that Oram would pay dearly for such a trick.

LV

Ethwen had taken to her bed and refused to come out of her chamber since the night before. She was deeply upset at the realisation that Modig had used her daughter as a pawn in his quest for more land and riches. Aelwulf, however – although also mortified at his stupidity – had had no choice but to attend the hall and be social with his host. Eneas and Amleth, however, had escaped the walls and were out hunting together on the marshes.

After instructing Odi to make his presence scarce, Berowen had returned to the keep alone and had immediately gone to her mother's side, and it was here that she stayed until she was requested to attend the hall where she was to meet Brack's children for the first time.

They were two of the most sullen children she had ever met. She could not but help compare them with her niece and nephews back at Brundannon and they were nothing like them whatsoever. Whilst her niece Eadlin was happy, outgoing and never went anywhere without a smile upon her sweet face, Brack's seven-year-old daughter, Alodia, smiled not once upon their meeting and sat with a constant scowl upon her gloomy face. Her eyes were dull and shadowed by dark rings, and her skin was blotchy as if she had been crying all morning.

The boy, Cnet, was an angry ten-year-old who sat with his arms crossed tightly across his chest, and glared at Berowen from under thick dark eyebrows. His lips were pursed together tightly and he just grunted when she asked him the simplest question. Both were dressed in clothing that obviously needed a good wash, as did their tiny bodies. She was clearly not going to have much joy with these two offspring of Brack's and after about half an hour she gave up completely in trying to have any kind of conversation with them, and - leaving them to their sulking – she returned to sit with her mother upstairs.

When Eneas and Amleth returned from their small hunting trip they stopped at the dancers' small camp and handed them the few hares that they had managed to catch. Kipp waddled up to greet them and once again told the story of the wheelwright and his attempt at thievery with regards to fixing the wagon's wheel. Both the young men liked Kipp, but their real reason for stopping was to be able to spend time with the pretty girls and although they listened patiently they both wished that the old man would return to his own business and leave them to theirs.

The gift of the hares was received with gratefulness, and would be eaten with relish that evening. Although an invite to stay was offered to the two young men, they had to refuse with as much politeness that they could manage to impart through signals, smiles, and shakes of the head. They would have dearly preferred to spend the evening with the troupe rather than have to endure another meal in the hall with Modig and his family. But, out of loyalty to their sister, and respect for their parents, they waved goodbye to Kipp and the others and proceeded through the gatehouse. The sentry slouched lazily and did not even stand to attention as they walked their horses through. The brothers – in turn - could not be bothered to challenge his laziness, but just cast him a disparaging look as they passed.

At the last moment Kipp poked his head around the gatehouse corner and called out to them, "My soft brain nearly forgot; please tell your sister that her offer has been accepted – with great delight!" And he waved again cheerily before disappearing around the corner again.

LVI

Mog was relieved when she returned the hair samples to the wooden box and, making sure there was no-one watching other than Peg, hid it inside her den. She would be glad when Yule came so that she could be rid of it finally – it was becoming both tedious and worrisome trying to keep it hidden and was a great weight on her mind whenever she left her camp. Once she had completed her task, she would seek out Oram and perhaps even manage to obtain a splendid new fur coat from the meeting - the white fur would be so resplendent that she would be the envy of all her kin and *that* she would enjoy so very much. For now she would continue to make the required offering, and whilst doing so she would form a plan in her mind on how to trap the treacherous creature that had caused her so much anxiety over the last few days, culminating not only in the fear of extinction, but also in having to demean herself by having to make a pact with Scrimble.

The same creature had unintentionally ensnared Scrimble by her deceitful ways. He was now on his own mission of retribution towards the two-legged that had caused him pain. He too, no doubt, would be interested to learn of Oram's part in the trail of events that had led to his receiving such a near miss with death.

Of course it was not only Oram and Mog, but also the red-beard – and he who would feel the wrath of the great hound - that were intertwined by fate by one particular act of treachery by one particular creature of the forest. Fate did work her tricks in the most peculiar ways sometimes.

The wildman of the woods was completely unaware of the twists and turns that Oram had effected within his world. He was only concerned with his own peculiar existence and the once long-overgrown path of enlightenment that the woman had cleared when she had stumbled into his domain. He now knew his name and how the past had flung him into this shady world of trees and undergrowth. What he would do with this information he knew not, but it came as some odd and quiet relief that he at least understood his existence amongst the creatures of the forest and wood.

Scrimble had encountered no problem at all in tracking his assailant – the stench was as ripe to his sensitive nose as a week-old rotting carcass; all he needed to do now was await his chance. That was the most difficult and potentially treacherous aspect of his retaliation. He needed to get the two-legged on his own and thus he may have to wait, watch and stalk for many an hour before this opportunity revealed itself to him. However, he had all the time that might be needed for he had nothing pressing to attend to other than to feed his stomach and sate his thirst occasionally. Time was on his side and he settled down to wait on his moment of vengeance, and dwell upon how divine that would be.

LVII

Berowen awoke on the day before her wedding to the sound of Odi tapping at her window. The dawn was still at its slow and lazy battle with darkness as it pushed it over the horizon and covered the sky in a hazy red glow.

"You have arisen early, dear friend," Berowen said sleepily as she fumbled with the latch in the half-light. As the raven hopped in through the window, she smoothed the feathers on his head gently. "My last day of freedom, Odi. I wonder what I can do to make it enjoyable. From the colour of the sky it would seem that it may be a bright day and I would welcome some of that brightness in my heart."

Odi cocked his head from one side to the other and flew to the tall back of the wooden chair, where he settled himself down to some early morning preening. Berowen remained where she stood against the ledge of the window and peered out into the morning. She was temporarily oblivious to the cold bite in the air as it blew its way passed her face into the room. The flame from the single candle blew out in its wake and a stream of grey smoke wafted upwards to the ceiling. As she heard Odi caw to her, an idea came to her mind. She looked across at him. "Yes my friend, it is indeed a good idea for a day in the saddle and it seems that you may have something in mind?" The raven looked at her briefly and with a soft cackle he resumed his preening.

Berowen shivered and closed the window, before proceeding to dress herself as warmly as she could for the day ahead outside. She was aware that she should tell her family of her plans for they would be concerned when it was discovered that she was missing, and this she would do in order to avoid such worries. However wonderful it *would* be for her future husband and his kin to wonder whether she had decided to escape the grasp of wedlock, it would also be unkind to incur any wrath towards her parents from Modig. Besides, she knew full well that there was no earthly way that she would be able to leave the fortress without her actions being well noted by the guards on duty.

She let Odi out of the window and made ready her day of escape from the gloom of Grimfell. There would be days aplenty ahead of her to suffer such a doom and she was eager to leave it behind for just this one day. It was too early to awaken any of her kin, so she hastily wrote a note and slipped it beneath the door of her parents' room as she made her way down the corridor. She knew not where she was heading, but would go where her companion directed her.

The stables were quiet save for the occasional snort and foot stamping of one of its occupants. She found her mare and proceeded to saddle her as quickly as she could, for she was not sure when the stablemaster would arrive for his daily duties. She wanted to avoid as much human contact in Grimfell as possible, for she did not want to risk ruining the chances of being able to make this day hers. As she passed the bridle over her horse's head she heard a rustle behind her. Turning around she could see nothing but the pile of straw that stood precariously in the corner, complete with the menacing looking pitchfork embedded within it. Shrugging her shoulders she assumed that she had disturbed a mouse, or even a rat, from their bustling return to their daytime dens, and returned her attention to preparing her mount for the day ahead. Another rustle, then a sneeze and this time Berowen realised that *that* was no rodent. Turning again she backed up against the shoulders of her mare and searched the immediate vicinity for signs of a human form intently. She could see nothing until slowly a small, fair-headed head poked up from within the mound of straw. She sighed with relief when she realised that it must only be the stablehand waking up and she watched with interest as the scrawny figure stood slowly with its back towards her, and stretched itself totally unaware that it was being observed. It looked like a tiny woodland creature coming out of its warm nest after its annual sleep.

The waiflike figure began to scratch all over his body and spent some time scratching the hair upon his head, before stretching his arms again. They she heard a loud yawn and a fart and had to stifle a giggle before uttering forth a soft "Ahem".

The boy swung around with a terrified look upon his dirty face. He looked in all directions as if trying to locate the safest and quickest route of escape. Berowen saw the look of panic in his large brown eyes and smiled softly at him. "I am sorry if I awoke you," she offered quietly in the hope that it would relax him. His face began to wrinkle and his little turned up nose began to twitch. She at first thought that he was going to burst into tears, but suddenly he threw his head forward and a loud sneeze uttered forth from his tiny frame. He wiped away the snot that oozed from his nose with his left arm and looked at her again. "What is your name? No.. no.. don't tell me," Berowen said. "I shall call you 'Mouse'. Good morn, Mouse," she continued with a small curtsey to the young lad, who stood completely stunned at her words and actions.

"Aha it would seem that the cat may have got your tongue, Mouse?" enquired Berowen.

 The boy began to jiggle on the spot and a look of urgency appeared upon his small face. Berowen smiled at him, "It seems you are adept at the bladder dance, young Mouse."

"If it please, I need to take a piss milady."

"So I see," laughed Berowen. "Off with you, young lad. By the look of them, I am sure those pants will not do with a soaking."

The young lad made a quick bow and ran off in the direction of the stable doors, his hands holding onto his crotch as he did so as if the action would prevent his full bladder from emptying itself before he reached his destination.

Berowen led her mare out into the daylight just as the boy was returning to the doors. She tousled his hair as he stopped to look at her. "Me name's Col," he mumbled.

She put her foot in a stirrup and hoisted herself into the saddle. "I shall see you upon my return......Mouse." And she laughed and urged her horse into a walk and made her way to the gatehouse; the scene of her first trial into leaving the fortress. Would the sentry let her pass without ado?

The gatehouse was quiet – the sentry who was supposed to be on guard leant against his halberd and both were propped up by the wall. The faint aroma of ale wafted from his person as Berowen walked her horse through and on towards the barbican. The situation was much the same here although this time she had no choice but to awaken them from their boozy dozing, for without them the drawbridge would not be lowered. She sighed loudly. Nothing happened. She coughed and again nothing. She drew her horse towards one of them and once aside him she leant down in the saddle and poked him on the shoulder. He muttered something under his breath and cuddled up closer against his halberd. His breath reeked of ale and she withdrew quickly from the nauseating aroma. Her patience waning she had the urge to kick him hard in the stomach with her foot, but did not want to risk having him empty his stomach contents over them.

"Soldier!" she shouted with all her might.

Still in his sleepy stupor he retorted "Shut yer mouth, wench! Get me another ale and be quick about it or I'll ......"

Dismounting sharply, Berowen gave him a hefty swipe on the cheek. "Or you will what, soldier?!" she exclaimed.

The man nearly fell over with the shock of being struck out of his dream. He looked with glazed eyes at the woman standing before him and screwed up his eyes to try and focus on her face. Her identity then dawned on him and he scrambled to some excuse of attention. "My lady," he said, bowing his head.

"You had better awaken your comrade and get that drawbridge open soldier, before I report your behaviour to Lord Modig. He will, I am sure, be very interested in hearing of how you just spoke to his future daughter-in-law. Not to mention that you are both drunk on duty."

The sentry eyed her with caution and then decided that it would be best to do as she bid without further question. He wondered where she was going and also whether he should allow her to leave the confines of the fortress walls, but her threat and his and his fellow sentry's obvious guilt was paramount to imprisonment or worse and avoidance of such was a high priority. He staggered over to where his comrade was still dozing and shook him violently by the shoulders. As Berowen re-mounted her horse she could hear them muttering under their breath to each other, every so often shooting her a malevolent glance. Eventually, they moved to their positions and began to heave on the heavy wooden wheels to drop the bridge.

Without a word to either man she rode out into her day of freedom only to find a rider waiting for her down the hill. Thurstan sat with his arms crossed across his saddle and when he heard the sound of the horse trotting down the hill he looked up, and watched Berowen approach.

"What took you so long?" he enquired.

"How... why are you here?"

"I was awoken early this morning, as I see so were you," came the reply.

"The guards did not mention another had left this morning."

"Hah, well I threatened them with a report to their superiors and no doubt they had forgotten all about it going by the shape they were in when I passed through."

"As did I," she laughed. "My temper got the better of me though, I am ashamed to tell. And I actually slapped one of them hard to awaken him."

Thurstan laughed loudly. "I would have slit their throats if I could have managed to lower the drawbridge by myself. I am sure that their presence would not have been missed."

"Odi would have enjoyed his breakfast of fresh eyeballs, no doubt," laughed Berowen in return. She heard a familiar call and looked skywards to see the dark shape winging its way towards them. Odi circled them a couple of times and then headed off in the direction of the fork in the road where Thurstan had found the broken stone.

But as to where their destination was, was anyone's guess, but they followed the raven without question.

Odi took them along the west road of the fork and the path soon took them away from the inhospitable fenland as it led them up a steep hillside and out on to a plateau of green grass. It was if they had crossed an invisible border, for where there had been a lack of birdsong in the marshes, here it was alive with chattering and calls. It was rich with deer that bolted for the cover of the bare trees of a tiny copse as the riders approached. The shadowy outline of Grimfell's turrets was swallowed up in the hazy distance until eventually they could be seen no more on the horizon. As they descended slightly the babbling sound of a brook reached their ears and the sunlight caught its fresh clear water as it cut its way through the soil. Odi landed briefly before heading upstream, his body flying close to the ground. The faint scent of woodsmoke wafted downwind and they could hear the soft tinkering of bells and a man's voice. As Odi disappeared from view, a great cacophony of squawking filled the air and the curiosity of the two travellers turned into caution. Under the leafless wintery boughs of a great oak tree they watched as the man cavorted around the small fire, waving his arms in the air as he went. He had long spindly legs that looked as if they would snap at a moment's notice if he were to lose his balance. His hair was a tangle of copper-coloured waves and his beard hung down from his chin in a dishevelled plait. Upon his feet were pointed shoes of gold and his breeches were patterned with gold and red diamonds. His shirt was golden with blue dots and its sleeves billowed around his arms as he waved them around. His doublet was stitched out of different coloured materials, which had once been vivid, but over time had faded into drabness. A curious looking fellow indeed, he at first seemed totally oblivious of the two that came upon him.

The sound of the squabbling, shouting birds above him in the branches of the tree was almost deafening. The tree was alive with the black forms and Odi had become invisible amongst them, under their blanket of dark iridescence. Berowen tried calling him through her mind but there came no response. She then called his name aloud and this time she received a response, but not from the quarter that she had expected.

"The raven is not yours to be at your beck and call," announced the wiry figure, halting suddenly in his capering to stare long and hard at her with deep blue eyes that peered out from his freckled pale face. "They belong in the trees, the fields and the sky," he continued with a sweep of his hands skyward before suddenly seating himself cross-legged on the ground. Then dramatically posing his finger against his chin and leaning his head to one side he continued, "However, they may lend a hand if they are so disposed for they are much kinder than crows. But do not rely on a rook for they are too self-opinionated."

Berowen was confused. She sat upon her horse and looked across at her companion, who merely sat in his saddle and watched the figure before them with great interest.

"I am the watcher of the ravens and the possession of the cat. Am I the maven who wears the pointed hat?" continued the strange man.

"You talk in riddles sir," Berowen said. "I know not of what you speak. Odi found me – I did not seek him out. It is he who has led us to you today. But for what reason I know not."

"The world is round, but the earth is flat; the fire below continues to wane as the moons above continue to wax, and there is nothing more than that," stated the man, ignoring her explanation. And then he jumped up and stood on one leg, with his suspended foot resting on the side of his shin.

Berowen sighed. It was obviously a hopeless task trying to obtain any sense from this odd person. Again she looked at Thurstan for some kind of support, but this time he lifted a finger to his lips to quieten any words she may wish to utter. She looked quizzically at him and with a furrowed brow turned her attention again to the peculiar individual before them.

"If the flames go out then all things will change - but not necessarily for the better."

Berowen looked up and noticed that the winter sun had already begun its afternoon descent into the west.

"Thurstan, we must take our leave. The sun will be nearly set by the time Grimfell returns on the horizon I fear. We must hurry or we shall be late and then I shall be admonished by my mother. And yet, on such an eve as this I cannot say, with truth, that I would think that bad of her."

Her companion looked up at the sky and then at her, "We have a little more time, I believe, before we must leave. However, if you are eager to return now, then we shall go."

"I am not eager, my friend Thurstan," replied Berowen. "Tomorrow will not be a day of celebration for my family or me, as you are aware," she added with a sad smile. "However, there is much to do this eve and I also wish to ensure that I do not arrive back to coincide with dinner. I have not eaten at table since that first night, and have no wish to be trapped into doing so tonight either. If I can arrive well before, then I may be able to sneak up to my chamber without being seen."

"One more question, my lady, and then we shall leave. Tell me riddler," addressed Thurstan to the man, who was still balanced on one leg. "What of the forest. Do you have words to weave about that?"

"A tapestry complete could well be woven. The forest stretches from afar to here and deep within its boughs, tooth and claw are both well honed."

At that moment the blanket of black lifted as one behind him with a cacophony so loud no-one could hear themselves think let alone carry on a conversation. "She heard me it seems, and they heard her response," said the riddler, deep in thought.

"Who heard you?" queried Thurstan. "And what did the ravens hear, for no sound came to my ears before they took flight."

"That is something which is not for me to say, but for you to find out yourself if you so wish," replied the man.

"But surely you cannot finish your explanation there," stated Berowen.

"And why not?"

Berowen did not know quite what to say to this question. It was not the reply she was expecting and she remained silent.

Slowly, the birds returned to roost and Berowen looked amongst them once again to try and spot Odi, but as before it was a futile attempt.

"If you can find him in the roost, then maybe he will follow," stated the man watching the woman. "But return after your union and perhaps that will be a better time, for he may be more content to come to you then."

"How did you know about that?" asked Berowen astounded that this complete stranger seemed to know about her forthcoming marriage on the morrow.

"As I said, I am the watcher of the ravens. They tell me all."

"But Odi is not just a raven, good sir," said Berowen. "There is more to him than …."

"There is more to many of them, my lady. Did you not know? Did you think you were special? I see that you did," interrupted the watcher.

Still balancing on one leg, he pulled out a thin, slightly battered, flute from his doublet pocket and flamboyantly raised it to his lips. Over-emphasising his intake of breath, he theatrically flexed his bony fingers before beginning to play a quick, shrill tune. Then he placed his raised leg to the ground and pranced over to where the riders sat on their mounts. He played another tune as he danced precariously around Berowen, interspersing the notes with peculiar words. "Shapes are shifting. Shadows lifting.   Black to grey and grey to white. Changing within sight," he chanted.

"I think it is time for us to leave, my lady," said Thurstan. He had understood the peculiar fellow's last words perfectly, and hoped that Berowen had not yet worked them out. Even though she had every right to know sooner or later, Thurstan did not think it was the time nor the place.

"As you suggested, I am sure we shall return after the events of tomorrow," Thurstan said, partly to interrupt the performance of the man dancing around Berowen, and partly to ensure that Berowen could return to Grimfell as she had so wished. "But for now we must bid you our farewell, for we must begin our return journey to Grimfell. But we thank you for your information."

"Grimfell's walls are not that strong, Grimfell may well fall before too long," whispered the man to himself as Berowen and Thurstan turned their mounts homeward.

As they rode along, Berowen looked at her companion and said, "Well that was a most peculiar meeting."

"Peculiar perhaps, but most interesting," answered Thurstan.

"How so? He made not much sense to me at all," replied Berowen.

As they continued their journey towards the marshes, Thurstan explained to Berowen about the stone that he had uncovered and the engravings upon it. Some of the engravings had become more clear in his mind now that he heard the – although strangely delivered – words from the riddle maker.

"I am glad that he has helped you, my friend. For me though, it seems that I have forfeited my new companion, which I find both upsetting and unsettling."

"Only until after tomorrow, it would seem Berowen. I do not understand why Odi would not be with you tomorrow, but I am sure there must be some reason that we have not yet thought of. Perhaps something will reveal itself tomorrow as to why he would not be here with you."

"Perhaps, although I cannot imagine what."

"My lady," began Thurstan tentatively. He had noticed since their arrival at Grimfell, that although Berowen was subdued with regard to her forthcoming marriage, she did not seem as upset that he thought she would be at the prospect of taking a husband she had only just met, and who – by all accounts – was less than wholesome. Her attitude about the whole affair had changed and she seemed more relaxed about the prospect than she had been at the beginning of their journey. "If I may ask you – and please forgive me if I am being too bold in my enquiry – but you seem almost unperturbed by tomorrow, other than being a little impatient of the whole affair."

Berowen smiled at Thurstan. "I am indeed impatient – I wish only to get the ceremony over and done with. After meeting Brack I know that the marriage is purely one of convenience for the house of Grimfell. And I feel that my future husband has no interest at all in taking a second wife, for – if I am correct in my observations these last few days - his attentions are diverted elsewhere. I am only truly and deeply sorry for my father and my family for it is they who will suffer more than me after tomorrow."

"And that must weigh heavy on your mind," nodded Thurstan. "And it is for them that you have not made your flight today no doubt, as you would have had an easy escape due to the poor guarding of Grimfell's sentries this morning."

"It would have been so very easy, yes, my friend. But I would not have liked to test the temper and power of Modig. I fear that my family would have suffered dearly for my transgression should I have chosen that path."

Thurstan's mind worked quickly and although he would never admit his thoughts to Berowen, he knew that even though the union may well take place, the health and safety of Berowen's family could still be at risk. Once she was married to Modig's son, she would be a valuable asset indeed for his staking a claim on the land of her forefathers. All he would have to do was eliminate the rest of her family and she would automatically become heir to Brundannon and by default so would his son – and him.

Once the celebrations were over, Berowen's family would return home with the remnant of their guard. If they left alone they could be ambushed, but if they were to be given an escort this may well have been instructed to ensure that they never reached Brundannon. They were in a hopeless situation, if indeed what Thurstan believed may happen turned out to be the truth.

He had become silent in his thoughts, and Berowen noticed that his deliberations were causing him distress when she looked at him and saw the concerned expression on his face. He knew that the engravings on the stone were important and he somehow felt that the caves in the hillside were a key, but there was not enough time to work out the puzzle. Berowen's family must not leave Grimfell – yet. He would have to seek council with her father and explain his thoughts to him and hope that he accepted the possible danger that may well lie ahead. But how he would be able to approach him was another matter – he would not be allowed into the keep until the union and then it would be difficult to take him aside. He could ask Berowen to arrange a meeting, but he wished not to burden Berowen with his thoughts. Hence it would have to wait until the morrow and he would have to ensure that he had time enough alone with Aelwulf, at least to arrange a meeting with him after the ceremony was over.

"You are deep in thought, Thurstan," enquired Berowen. "Is there something that I may help with you with? I do not like to see that look on anyone's face, let alone that of my friends."

"There is nothing, my lady," he replied. "I am just dwelling upon my own path. Please forgive me for my selfishness on such an eve as this."

"There is no need to ask forgiveness, Thurstan. We have taken you away from your own business for far too long and I wish you to know that we all thank you for your assistance over the past weeks. We could never have arrived here safely, methinks, without such aid."

"I am not sure that my success in aiding your arrival here is something to be proud of, my lady. Perhaps if I had taken you a longer route, we should not yet have arrived and this day would have been delayed for longer."

"Delay would only have served to prolong the agony that would come with the wait, Thurstan. And that, I feel, would have been worse in the long run. No, you did as you had been charged and I thank you for it. I only hope that you do not rue the day that you rode upon Brundannon."

They were now nearly at the fork in the road and the dark shape of Grimfell loomed ahead of them.

"Let us make the tongues wag and arrive at the gloomy gates of Grimfell together," said

Berowen with as much joviality in her voice that she could muster. "I am sure it will spread like wild fire amongst the garrison and it would be amusing to see how long it takes to reach the ears of Modig."

"You are a puzzlement, Berowen, that I can say. One moment you are showing a resigned despondency over your forthcoming marriage and the next you are making a game of it," said Thurstan as he glanced at the childlike expression upon her face.

"A game? Yes I imagine it could be referred to as that, but it is the only way I can force myself to journey into the jaws of imprisonment. So, shall we have some sport Thurstan?"

Thurstan grinned at her. "If it be your wish Berowen."

"Then let us race from here and laugh and shout as we do so. We may even be able to crumble a few of the dour walls with our false gaiety!" shouted Berowen as she kicked her mare into a gallop.

Thurstan shook his head from side to side and tutted to himself. "You are indeed pixie-led my lady and may it serve you well these following days." And he nudged his own horse into action and was soon on her tail.

The sentries eyed them both with the expected suspicion, and with surreptitious glances to each other they waved the two into within the walls. Upon passing through the gatehouse, the sentry tried to halt Thurstan's progress and demand the usual fee, but a swift glance from Berowen caused his hand to withdraw immediately and for him to step aside, allowing them passage through to the stables.

Once inside Berowen looked around for her 'mouse', but she could not see him. In fact the stables seemed quite deserted - even its four-legged inmates seemed slightly thin on the ground. She was sure that there were more in residence when she had left that morning, and she just assumed that maybe another tax collecting trip was underway. She even allowed herself a small selfish thought that perhaps a hunting trip for venison had been undertaken for a sumptious meal the next day. But that notion soon passed.

"What was that noise?" asked Thurstan.

"Noise? I heard nothing."

"A muffled sound. It seemed to come from the far corner of the stables," and he went off to investigate, leaving his horse half untacked in the process. He had not long left her when Berowen heard a gruff male voice behind her. "Didn't hear you come in. And didn't expect you back either," it said.

Berowen turned to face the man, whom she supposed was the marshal. She looked him up and down quickly and his demeanour immediately served to irritate her, and she took an instant dislike to him. He was a broad-shouldered figure, with greying hair and sallow pock-marked skin and did not look trustworthy in her eyes. His eyes had a cruel glint in them and his false smile was menacing.

"I am not sure what you mean, marshal," said Berowen, eyeing him closely.

"They went out looking for you," he continued. "They thought you and him had run off together and that you would not be coming back to fulfil your part of the bargain."

"My part of the bargain?" asked Berowen curtly. "And what quite do you mean by that? I know of no *bargain*. Mere tittle-tattle spread by the idle wasters of Grimfell, I surmise - an aspect of the place that seems to be rife by all accounts."

The marshal looked over her shoulder and she turned around to see Thurstan returning with the young stableboy, Col, tucked into the crook of his arm. Berowen heard the marshal grunt behind her - presumably out of some sort of disapproval.

"Boy's been beaten," Thurstan announced as he approached. He did not see the marshal at first, but when he did his words petered off.

"Beaten? Why...." exclaimed Berowen as she rushed forward to inspect the boy's injuries. Col had been crying and his tears had run down his cheeks, cutting through the dirt as they did so, leaving smudgy trails on his face, but there was no mistaking the mark left by the hand-print across his left cheek. Thurstan indicated with a slight nod of his head for Berowen to look at Col's back. Another darkening mark.

"My poor Mouse, who did this to you?" soothed Berowen as she smoothed his hair. Col buried his face into Thurstan's shoulders and would not speak. Thurstan just stared at the marshal and at once Berowen realised that the dealer of the punishment stood behind her. She swung around and demanded to know for what reason the boy had been beaten.

"Master's orders," came the nonchalent reply.

"And what was his crime?" enquired Berowen, angered by the uncaring manner in which he had replied.

"Not reporting your leaving my lady," sneered the marshal. "Boy should have alerted the guard."

"Not reporting my leaving......," repeated Berowen increduously. "And did the sentries also receive a beating for their blatant lack of duty whilst quite clearly with the stench of ale upon their breath?"

The marshall simply shrugged. "Just doing what was asked of me. No more, no less. I know nothing of the sentries. Not my business."

"And let me guess whose business that is," added Thurstan. "Earh no doubt."

"That would be right I would think. He is in charge of the guards, I am in charge of this waste of space here," said the marshall pointing a finger in Col's direction.

"And you clearly hold no loyalty towards this young boy under your care and tutelage. Did you not even question the punishment?" enquired Berowen eyeing the marshal with disgust.

"Not my place to question now't. I do my job and do as I am told."

"With too much pleasure in the more questionable orders it would seem," continued Berowen as she handed the marshal the reins of her horse. "Here are my orders - please ensure that my horse is unsaddled and cared for - I shall inspect your efforts later. I trust that my orders will be complied with as efficiently as your master's? And whilst you are about your task please see to my friend Thurstan's mount as well. I am sure he will join me later in inspecting your work."

She walked purposefully passed the marshal and called to Thurstan, "Bring Col and come with me Thurstan, you are about to have the pleasure of meeting my future father-in-law."

The marshal stood aside as Berowen brushed passed, and watched the trio leave the stables. He snorted to himself and cursed under his breath. He would have said the words out loud, but something within him warned him not to for he did not wish to risk the woman hearing him and incurring her wrath even more. There was something about her eyes that troubled him – he could have sworn that as she got angrier they had darkened until almost upon the brink of becoming completely black.

Once they were well out sight he set to bedding the two horses down for the night, knowing that with the encroaching darkness the others would soon return and that he would be at the stables well after his normal working hours due to Col being taken away, and him having to do all the work himself. This annoyed him and he cursed even more that his visit to the alehouse would be delayed. But he satisfied his ire with the pleasant thought of the serving wenches who would see to his every need once he did eventually get there.

LVIII

The effort of the steep climb to the hall did not seem to affect Berowen; if anything it seemed to spur her onwards and she reached the top of the uneven steps long before Thurstan and his charge. When he joined her at the doors she looked almost wild and he grew concerned at her appearance. "Methinks you should take a few breaths to compose yourself, my lady," he suggested noticing the darkness in her eyes. "If you are to present yourself in any worthy manner before Modig, then I beseech you to calm yourself before doing so."

"I am so angry, Thurstan, that this poor child was punished whilst those who were really guilty seem to have avoided any such remonstration."

"Hmm, I know Berowen. I can, quite literally, see the anger in your eyes," responded Thurstan.

Berowen had no inkling of exactly what he meant, but she knew that her rage would not set her in good stead should she present herself before Modig in such a way.

Col started to fidget in Thurstan's embrace. It was clear that he was nervous at being brought before Lord Modig and pleaded to be let alone to go back to the stables and his work. He was afraid of what the marshal would do to him for allowing his injuries to be discovered by the two who stood with him at the door to the hall.

"My little Mouse, you should not have been beaten and I can assure you that the marshal would dare not touch you again with regards today's events. And if I have my way, he will never lay a hand on you again. You must trust us. Do you trust us?"

Col looked first at Berowen and then at Thurstan and slowly nodded his head.

"Good boy. Now come. Let us get this done." Taking a deep breath, Berowen pulled open the doors and crossed into the darkness of the hall, Thurstan and Col following closely behind. She strode down the centre of the hall with a great purpose in her step towards the shape of Modig, who – as usual – was slumped in his seat.

"My lord, an injustice has been done," she began as she walked straight up to him and stood in front of where he sat. "It seems that either the note that I left my parents went astray or that the contents of it were not taken as truth by you. I would be surprised if the former was the case for my mother is very fussy about such things, so I must assume that the latter is the reality. And in doing so, then I am deeply wounded and angered by such an action on your behalf."

Modig was stunned into silence by his future daughter-in-law's tirade.

Berowen continued, "What is more I hear that the stableboy – Col, who I have brought before you, was ordered to be punished for not alerting the guard that I was leaving the confines of Grimfell this morn. Is this true, my lord?"

"The boy was lax. The punishment was fair," replied Modig whose hackles were beginning to rise at this woman's impudence."

"So the marks left on his body were fairly dealt out? I think for one so small they were overly unjust," pointed out Berowen as she beckoned Thurstan to let the boy down and come to her. Modig barely gave the boy's bruises even a cursory glance.

"And is it true that his small frame has taken all the blame? Is it true that none of the sentries on guard this morning have received any punishment for their lax behaviour? Are you in fact aware that they were on duty whilst still under the influence of ale? Has your captain informed you that they had to be awoken to lower the drawbridge?"

"The affairs of the garrison are of no concern to you," snapped Modig, rising from his seat.

"I disagree, my lord," countered Berowen. "It is the sentries' duty to ensure that no-one unauthorised enters the fortress by any means. If they are asleep, how are they to accomplish this simple task? If this is to be my home, then surely I am entitled to sleep in my bed knowing that Grimfell is guarded well?"

Modig stood in front of her, his nose almost touching hers. She refused to be bullied into submission by this stance and stood perfectly still. The atmosphere around them suddenly became ignited with mutual hatred and Thurstan breathed in sharply as he watched the two test each other's courage. Col became unsettled; he began to cry and Thurstan pulled him towards him and wrapped his arms around the boy's shoulders. He watched as Berowen's slight frame stiffened; he could see her shoulders tense and watched her clench her fists by her side. He knew she was desperately attempting to keep her unguarded self under control – this other side of her that had become more apt to erupt as the days wore on. She was undergoing a change in personality as her unseen power strengthened within her. He knew not what the eventual outcome would be, but he hoped that it would not be at this moment that it would manifest itself in its true form.

Berowen wanted to tear Modig's eyes from his head, his tongue from his mouth and his heart from his chest. She wanted to take her dagger and rip his skin into shreds and feed it to him before she finally slit his throat from ear to ear in one long slow sweep of the blade. She was only just holding on to reality; she knew that her thoughts were out of control and she realised that she had to keep them buried – for now. She was well aware that she could kill him if she so wished, with not a touch of the hand but only with a mere passing thought in her mind.

Modig stood his ground and stared at her. He did not show his increasing uneasiness at the sight of her eyes darkening as she met his stare. He could not admit his fear of who – or what – stood before him, but whatever or whoever it was, it had begun to slowly eat away at his nerve. This woman before him had dared to challenge his authority and to back down now would be a show of submission that he wished not to contemplate, but her stare was powerfully intimidating. He could look at her no longer and took one step backwards. Thurstan breathed out slowly in relief at Modig's apparent submission, but Berowen either did not notice, or chose not to for she remained where she stood, her gaze still fixed upon Modig. He had not forgotten the look upon her face the night they had arrived at The Old Men of the Moor, and it was gravely disconcerting to notice that her face was beginning to form a similar expression.

Thurstan gently moved Col to one side and strode quickly towards Berowen and putting a hand on her shoulder he stood in front of her, as if to break the gaze between her and Modig. He then raised one hand and held it over her eyelids, and gently closed her eyes. He kept his hand in this position for as long as it took for her to take in a deep breath and relax her body again. When he felt her shoulders droop he removed his hand from her eyes and nodded his head slightly, smiling softly at her.

Berowen felt exhausted and somewhat confused. She stood slightly swaying, as if she had taken a drink too many from the mead bottle.

Without turning he spoke to Modig. "I am sure your future daughter-in-law would be pleased to learn that you will look into the business of the poor behaviour of your sentries, my lord. For now she is going to seek out her kin before retiring to her room for she is tired and needs to prepare herself for the day ahead tomorrow."

"The woman is possessed with a madness," began Modig.

"And you are not sure whether tomorrow will take place after all?" continued Thurstan, still with his back to Modig.

There was silence behind him for a few minutes, but he could almost hear the wheels in motion within Modig's head as the man thought of the consequences of calling off the intended betrothal. If it were not to go ahead, then his plans for widening his control over the lands would be dashed. Thurstan smirked knowingly as Modig eventually replied, "I am under the impression that Berowen is tired and stressed over the arrangements of the morrow, my lord Thurstan. I am sure her behaviour can be easily explained under the circumstances. I am certain that a good night's rest will make her feel much better and that such an outburst will not be seen again once the betrothal as taken place."

"So the ceremony will go ahead, my lord Modig?"

"Indeed it shall. Now please escort the good lady to her mother's room. There is much I need to do."

"And shall I summon Earh to your presence on my way out, my lord?"

There was an angry growl behind him. "If you please," came the reply eventually, and, as Thurstan could hear, delivered through clenched teeth.

Thurstan smiled slyly again. Beckoning Col to follow, Thurstan took Berowen's arm and led her towards the back of the hall to the stairs to the upper chambers. As he did so he watched Modig walk quickly to his chair and pick up the mazer that sat on the small table next to it. He could not hide his obvious agitation as he downed the drink. As they reached the foot of the stairs Thurstan muttered under his breath and smiled as he heard Modig spluttering behind him as he seemingly swallowed a mouthful the wrong way.

LIX

Berowen awoke with a start from her dream, and noticed that she was drenched in sweat. She had dreamt of fire – great golden flames that had eaten away at every piece of wood, cloth and flesh within the fortress of Grimfell with relish upon its flaming lips. It had licked its way from building to building until nothing but stonework remained; great stone walls that encircled burning embers and the smell of burning flesh for those unfortunate enough to have been caught in its hungry grasp. She had been alone and somehow she had managed to escape – she knew not how – but was on the outside of the fortress looking in. As quickly as she awoke, so did the dream begin to fade from her memory, but just as it was all but gone, she remembered looking down and noticing that she was wearing her wedding gown.

As she lay in her bed, she wondered whether this was an omen for the day ahead. She still felt out of sorts with herself after the events of the last evening, and the dream had not improved her disposition. Her family had chastised her for venturing out of the fortress the day before; they had suffered greatly with accusations from Modig of broken agreements. Even her beloved brothers had not been pleased with her and whilst she had expected some kind of reprimand from her parents, she had not expected both Amleth and Eneas to take their side. She had retreated to her chamber completely exhausted and bewildered about the day's events; the expected joy of freedom from Grimfell had turned into a day of puzzlement and bad temper. And she missed Odi terribly and was bereft without his company.

The winter sky was lightening as dawn slowly broke.

She had always supposed, up until she had arrived at Grimfell, that this day would be one of celebrations throughout her new home. Even though she may have no joy within her own mind for such an event, she assumed that she would be made to feel welcome and that the event would be one of festivity within the walls. When she had first caught sight of the fortress looming skywards she had also assumed that it would be more hospitable within its confines than it had turned out to be. Once she had met her future kin, and saw the dilapidated state of the structure she soon realised that this day would be just like any other day, apart from a brief departure whilst vows were taken. There were to be no other guests to witness the event and she wondered whether it was even worth wearing the dress that had been so painstakingly made by the seamstress at Brundannon. The only small glimmer of enjoyment ahead lay in the troupe performing their dances and songs. But even that would only last for a short while, before darkness fell again over the Wellonaw Marshes and all became still.

There were a few hours yet before she would have to make her entrance into the great hall so she decided to remain under her covers, in the hope that should at least drift in and out of a light sleep until it was time for her to arise and dress herself. Was this how a felon felt hours before his execution - listening to the minutes pass away within his head before he met his doom?

She fell back into a dreamless sleep and was awoken by the sound of knocking on her door. It was her mother come to help her get dressed and Berowen called for her to enter, whilst scrambling out of the warm comfortable bed into the icy cold room. She stood shivering as Ethwen entered with a look of apprehension on her face. She had no idea in what state she would find her daughter on this day, and she was hesistant to enquire. However, Berowen's countenance was calm, almost serene, and Ethwen felt extremely proud of her daughter's strength and nobility on such a day.

But then Berowen announced calmly and without expression upon her face that she would not be wearing the dress that had been so painstakingly made for the occasion. Ethwen was mortified that after all the trouble Morgen had undertaken to ensure the gown was ready was for nothing. She briefly had the thought of arguing, but dismissed it immediately knowing full well that once her daughter had made up her mind, there would be no chance that she would change it. There was no time to question her decision anyway; they were already late in their descent into the hall, and Ethwen – however angry, upset and confused she was – had to put a brave face on the situation.

So be it.

Ethwen assisted Berowen in dressing into her chosen gown but was somewhat surprised at the design chosen. She complained that such a brown plain cloth was surely not fit for such an occasion, but Berowen insisted that the colour matched it perfectly. It was a dowdy gown for a somewhat dreary day. As mother and daughter left the chamber, Berowen's appearance was greeted by silent stares from her brothers and father, but she paid them no heed. She walked down the corridor to the stairs and slowly descended to the waiting group below. She smiled at Thurstan and Kipp but the smile left her lips when she looked at the members of her future family. The priest bowed his head low as she approached and she slightly inclined her head in acknowledgement. Brack looked as ineffectual as ever and merely stood fiddling with a strand of hair that hung limply from his forehead. Most did not at all seem to have any views on Berowen's chosen gown, other than Modig and Oswald's wives, who stared at her briefly before bringing their heads together so that they could exchange views on such a poor choice of dress. Had this young woman no taste at all? Was the house of Aelwulf really that short of coin that she could not have been given a more fitting robe for such an occasion? Brack's two sullen children completely ignored the entrance of their future step-mother and were more concerned with gaining the undivided attention of the two women, who – in turn - ignored their pestering for as long as possible so that they could continue their verbal assassination of the newest member of the household.

As was to be expected, Berowen's reason for wearing the dowdy gown was completely lost on those awaiting her entry into the hall. Her own kin were baffled, and all but Ethwen assumed that it was because something dreadful had occurred with the original dress.

Berowen stood beside Brack and the priest began to recite the vows slowly and precisely. "Hurry it up, priest," urged Modig. "We do not have all day. Speak the words, seal the vows and let us eat and drink. My stomach is empty and my thirst is keen for mead."

"And dancing girls," added Oswald slyly.

"Ho yes indeed," guffawed Modig in reply to his son's eagerness to ogle the pretty girls.

The priest cleared his throat in disapproval at the talk taking place before him. He did not wish to hear of the sins of the flesh and hurriedly continued with his service. For his part Brack was not thinking ahead to the joys of watching the young girls dancing, but of the serving lads who would be attending the table. He was so lost in his thoughts that he did not hear the priest ask for the ring until the second asking when the priest repeated his request with a loud "The ring!" Brack fumbled in his pouch for the metal band, and at first could not find it, bringing out a handful of coins and clumps of dust in his fist. Modig sighed with impatience as his son searched again, this time with success and producing the metal band prepared to place it on Berowen's finger. She, however, was not going to make it easy for him and instead of outstretching her hand for him to slip it on her finger, she kept her hand by her side and he had to wrench it forwards in order to complete the wedlock.

Modig then sighed with delight as part one of his plan was finalised. However, his delight was soon replaced by something much more terrifying when there was a loud bang on the great doors. The sound echoed throughout the hall and the candles flickered. Berowen's hair stood up on the back of her neck and a shiver ran down her spine at the sound. Unbeknown to her, Thurstan experienced the same and he stepped closer towards her. Another loud rap on the wood, but no-one moved to let the caller into the hall. The dogs began to snarl and the candles flickered and snuffed out. In the gloom of the darkening hall another knock on the doors ricocheted around the walls.

And then the great doors flew open with such force it would seem that an army were behind them. A wind blew through carrying with it the dead leaves of autumn that it had scooped up in its way, along with dust and grit and anything it could carry in its grip. It gushed down the hall and as it passed by them, each brazier spluttered and was extinguished, such was its force. The dogs were half blown off their feet as they jumped up from their sleeping positions and, whimpering, scuttled off into the farthest corners they could find to seek shelter from the unwaivering strength of the wind.

As the gust reached the wedding party, those who were able to keep their eyes open against its gritty force saw a head transform before them; a great beast's head that opened its mouth and blew an almighty breath upon them, causing all present to nearly topple over in its wake. Ethwen was already on her knees, with her hands tucked over her head in sheer panic. Both Modig and Oswald's wives had run screaming from the hall, dragging Brack's sour children with them as soon as the doors had swept open, and the men had all drawn their swords in a futile attempt to defend themselves against such an apparition.

The priest crossed himself and shouted, "What in God's name is occurring?"

No-one answered; no-one could hear him in the gale that blew around them all. He raised his arms to the heavens and shouted something to the wind. And all watched in disbelief and terror as the wind circled around him and lifted him high off the ground, swirling him around until it loosened its invisible grip and dropped him on to the floor, where he lay prostrate, gasping for air and with a look of sheer horror upon his face. He crawled underneath the long table to escape any repeat attention.

Modig leant against the table and stabbed his sword at the head. The blade went straight through as if a wraith it was that floated before him, but still he jabbed and poked. The wind continued to shape itself as it weaved its way around everyone, including under the table to where the priest was curled up in a ball. It whipped around him and he crouched with knees shaking. The beast's nose grew longer and developed huge nostrils, from which the wind whistled, and every time it opened its gaping maw a terrifying gust blew forth.

Whilst everyone around was in panic both Berowen and Thurstan stood perfectly still and watched the mayhem before them. Whatever magick was presenting itself was powerful indeed and they knew that to question or argue with it would be both foolish and pointless.

"I do beg your pardon," shouted a voice from the doorway. "My travelling companion does like to make as dramatic an entrance as he can, whenever possible."

The wedding party and guests, such as they were, looked in the direction of the voice.

"I see that we come upon some special occasion and once again I apologise for the interruption...or should I say disruption," continued the visitor. As the figure walked towards them each of the braziers that had been blown out so furiously a few moments before, ignited themselves again as it passed them.

"And who the devil are you, and how did you get passed the guards? How dare you present yourself in such a way," shouted Modig.

"I can assure you that I am not the devil, although I feel that this place could well be a very welcoming resting place for him on his travels. As to how I passed your guards, well I can only suggest that you address them the question yourself once they have awoken. As for your third statement, I can – and will – present myself in anyway I choose so to do."

As the figure drew nearer, Berowen heard Thurstan breathe in deeply and she saw the look of recognition pass across his face. This acknowledgement of Thurstan's was confirmed when the man looked towards them both and said, "Thurstan, my dear boy. There you are. I have been searching for you for weeks, nay, months."

Berowen looked quizzically at her friend, who looked embarrassed and even slightly angry, as if being discovered was not something that he wished to have happened.

"Oh forgive me," continued the visitor, taking off his hat and turning it upside down. "Beodin! Quieten and cease your torment of these poor people."

At this command, the beast's face dissipated and the wind immediately turned towards the man and blew into the upturned hat, which the man then replaced on to his head, patting it down with his hand and chuckling.

Once he was sure that the beast had gone, the priest crawled out from beneath his hiding place and standing up, brushed himself down and tried to compose himself.

"Ha!" cried the man. "Now I see. Beodin has a certain dislike of priests you know. I am not sure why he has taken such a stance, but they do rile him so. My apologies to you priest. I trust that you are none the worse for his attentiveness upon your person?"

The priest stuttered and replied that he would be as right as rain as soon as his bruises had faded and his fright had left him. "Good, good," nodded the man. "Bruises you say? You were lucky," and he laughed. "There was one priest who ended up with a broken leg after the cord around his habit broke when Beodin had left him dangling by it up in a tree, causing the hapless priest to meet the unforgiving ground with a bone-smashing crash."

"I fail to see the funny side," commented the priest rather shocked at the casual admission of the strange fellow. The tone in his voice irritated the visitor and in a darker tone of voice the mysterious caller added, "And there have been worse, good priest, on account of the corruption within the churches around this sorry kingdom. But such a subject has no place here methinks at this time. Beodin has his reasons for his actions and I must admit that most of the time I am not surprised by his behaviour."

The uninvited guest turned his attention back to Thurstan.

"And this must be the one who took Namon into her body at the standing stones on the edge of the moor?" he continued, looking across at Berowen. "I sat awhile amongst the guardians there and they told me of such a to-do many nights ago. I thought it was you Thurstan, who had rested there, for you are always one to test those that dwell in the half-world."

"I had intended no such thing, Felagin," explained Thurstan, revealing the visitor's name. "I would never deliberately displease such beings. You should know that."

"Ah, so it is true what the guardians said then. They told me that you seemed not aware of the woman's possible appeal to Namon and her kind."

Modig interrupted the conversation with a curt request of introduction. Felagin turned his head slightly and merely stared at him with contempt, before returning his attention to Thurstan and Berowen. Now with his back turned towards the lord of Grimfell, he raised one eyebrow when Modig repeated the demand.

"So I presume that the dark cloud of ravens that are circling the keep at this very moment are there at your bidding, young woman?" continued Felagin grinning.

"I know not of what you speak," answered Berowen with a questioning look upon her face.

"Is that so?" enquired Felagin. "Hmmm, then I wonder.....ah the watcher I presume."

"You know of the watcher of the ravens?" asked Berowen completely surprised that this stranger should know of the skinny man.

"But of course, it is my business to know of all such people," replied Felagin.

"I did have a raven but he returned to the roost yesterday," explained Berowen.

"As I thought," nodded Felagin. "One such as you would have such a companion; I was certain of that."

"Excuse me," said Berowen as she left the group and ran towards the doors and the fresh air outside. Looking up she saw that what the man had told her was true. There above was a dark mass of black iridescence as hundreds of ravens flew round and round the keep. She laughed and waved at them. She knew one of them was Odi, but still could not make out for sure which one he was.

"This is intolerable!" shouted Modig. "I demand you inform us of your name and from where you are from, old man."

"Old man! Old man is it?" responded Felagin as he spun around to face Modig. "I shall tell you who I am when I wish so to do." And he pointed a long finger at Modig, who immediately began to scratch furiously at his arms. "What is this trickery?" demanded Modig. "You have cast a spell, I swear you have. I shall order you taken to the dungeons."

"A spell, Lord Modig? I think not. Methinks you have fleas that is all. After all, this place is running with them. They must smell your sweat my lord, it is quite overpowering."

Modig glared at Felagin's insult, but he dared not utter another word.

"Thurstan, I shall wait for you outside the main gate. I would stay here but I feel that I may have outstayed my welcome," Felagin said with a wink. "Do not keep me waiting long, for you and I have much to do."

Thurstan nodded, "Tomorrow Felagin."

"Very well, tomorrow it will be. You were always impetuous Thurstan, but did you really think that you could manage on your own?"

With that Felagin tapped his hat once more and turned on his heel and walked back down the hall and out to where Berowen was still watching the ravens in awe.

"Found him yet?" he asked cheerfully.

"The watcher told me that I did not own Odi. He said that he would not be here today so I can only assume that not one of those that fly above is he."

"You may not own Odi, but neither does the watcher. Odi will do exactly what he wishes to do, that is the manner of the raven. If he wished to come here today, then believe me, he would have so done."

"They all look the same," sighed Berowen.

"To the untrained eye, yes perhaps," said Felagin. "But have you *really* looked?"

Berowen looked at him, not quite understanding what he meant.

"Be quick now. Use your inner eye and look. The others will be out soon and then you will have lost your chance."

"My inner eye?"

"Concentrate, girl, concentrate," urged Felagin. Berowen looked up again and stared at the birds overhead. Eventually all around became hazy and her gaze seemed to concentrate on one particular bird as it flew round and round. "It is he!" she exclaimed pointing upwards.

Felagin laughed. "I cannot see anything but a mass of black feathers. But if you are sure then he will come to you I am certain."

No sooner had he spoken than a flurry of feathers and squawking plummeted from the mass of darkness overhead and landed with a heavy thump on the wall.

"Aha," chortled Felagin. "Odi I presume. Pleased to make your acquaintance," he continued with a low bow before the bird. Odi bobbed his head up and down and flapped his wings, elevating him slightly from his perch.

Felagin waved to Berowen and made his way down the precarious stone steps, the sentries slowly waking up as he passed them, relieved of the spell cast upon them on his arrival.

As he had predicted, it was not long before Berowen could hear the others nearing the great doors. Odi took off with a loud call and joined his brethren above the keep and in a flash they were all gone, winging their way back towards the camp of the watcher. By the time she was joined by Thurstan, her family and the owners of Grimfell, she was by herself, and no-one was the wiser about the recent visit of Odi.

LX

Scrimble was as patient as any cat, if not more so. He did not let his prey out of sight for longer than was necessary. If he needed to drink he did so as quickly as possible before returning to his stalking spot. He had foregone food for that took longer to organise and he wished not to miss a chance at dealing out his punishment on the creature that had wounded him. The wound had healed; it was after all merely a scratch, and although it had left a slight nick in the top of his ear he felt nothing. However, no-one or no thing dealt out such harm to Scrimble without him taking revenge.

The red-beard was completely unaware that he was being stalked. He had no reason to believe that such would occur. He had been greatly aggrieved that his arrow had missed his target for he admired the fur and was in need of replacing a bare patch on his boot - the legacy from a tussle with a wild boar; one which the boar lost, but one in which his boot was also ripped by the beast's powerful tusks. But it was of no real matter, for he was sure that he would be able to repair it eventually.

Scrimble watched as they sat around the fire and ate the meat from the deer that the hunting party had returned with earlier on in the day. His prey had remained at the camp, but unfortunately for the hound, so had two other red-beards, so there had been no hope of acting then. His mouth salivated as he smelt the meat on the faint breeze and his empty stomach rumbled in anticipation, but it would have to wait.

It was during the hour just after midnight that his chance arrived. He had been lightly dozing with his head resting on his front paws when he heard footsteps crashing through the undergrowth. This event had occurred on more than one occasion since he had taken up his place, but it was always one of the other red-beards, none of whom he had any interest in. The tell-tale rip in the fur on the boot alerted him as it smashed down just in front of his nose. The scent was just confirmation that the two-legged was at last within his reach. Scrimble remained very still and waited for the figure to pass before he slowly crept his way in the same direction. He kept his body close to the ground and almost crawled on his stomach. There could be no mistake - he was determined not to be seen and to be successful in his hunt.

He kept the two-legged in his sights and at a safe distance so as not to risk being heard or seen. He watched as the figure squatted down to relieve himself in the shadows. He listened to the grunts from the red-beard and prepared himself for the attack. This was perfect for him, the two-legged was in a vulnerable position and would find it difficult to defend himself from the onslaught of the great hound's weight and, more importantly, his jaws. There was a half-light shining through the tree tops from the moon – her silvery glow forcing its way through the thick clouds and into the darkness below. Scrimble moved as silently as he could and did not once take his eyes off his crouching prey. Normally he would attack from behind, his usual prey being easy to kill with a sweep of his paw and the firm grip of his jaw around the back of the neck, but he wanted the flesh around the throat of this being.

He was close and he could almost make out the whites of the red-beard's eyes in the pale moonlight. He waited. But he dare not wait for too long. Hesitation would be the end of the hunt - failure.

The red-beard stretched and let out a grunting yawn, but still he crouched. This was Scrimble's chance – he could see the flesh of the throat before him underneath the red-beard. He launched himself from the bushes and before the two-legged could move, Scrimble's jaws were embedded around his throat. The force of the great hound's weight from the leap toppled the figure backwards and he fell to the ground, Scrimble's teeth cutting into his skin. The hound tasted the blood on his tongue and he bit harder. He stood over the figure and had him pinned to the ground as the red-beard thrashed around, his bare legs flailing in the air.

At last the two-legged gained his senses and he put his hands around Scrimble's throat and squeezed as hard as he could. The hound knew his prey was stronger than he was, and he could not let him get the upper hand in this battle to the death. There would be no doubt that a weapon would be about his person somewhere and if he was allowed to draw it, then Scrimble could lose the fight.

He shook his body to try to release the grip around his throat, the action in so doing tightening the grip of his jaw. He felt his teeth sink in further. He felt his victim weaken below him and knew from the great spurt of dark blood that he had at last found what he was seeking. The blood pumped out from the red-beard's throat and Scrimble saw the fear in the eyes. There was a gurgling sound and the body beneath him continued to become weaker. With one last squeeze of his jaws the great hound managed to rip open his prey's throat and it lay lifelessly on the ground under him.

His revenge was almost complete. All that was left was the prize. Ripping open the body's stomach with his teeth he located what he was seeking. The liver was still warm, just how he liked it. Before he loped off into the forest he sat on his haunches and threw back his head, and let forth a blood curdling howl that resounded throughout the forest. Its sound sparked a rapid exodus of creatures on the forest floor, as they darted into cover. Around the campfire, the sleeping red-beards did not hear the howl of victory and continued to snore loudly completely unaware of what had occurred deeper in the forest.

Mog, however, was overjoyed. She could not resist collecting another sample especially as it was so easy to obtain and before long the deceased red-beard had been shorn of most of his thick red hair. His plait would add the finishing touches to her crafting and she was delighted with her idea of finding Scrimble, and then staking out his prey with him – albeit at a safe distance.

LXI

O nce back inside the great hall, Modig signalled to the servants who stood waiting patiently for instructions for the food to be served, and before long the table was covered in food and great flagons of mead. The two women had already returned with the children once they knew that the coast was clear and that the apparition had left the confines of their hall. They both offered conciliatory smiles to Berowen and showed a mild courtesy towards her own kin as they made their way to the table. Berowen and her mother held back from rushing to the table as much as they could; it was an occasion they had both dreaded and were loathe to seat themselves until the last possible moment. Brack, however, had already placed himself and had set to ripping off a great chunk of bread and thrusting as much of it as possible into his mouth in one go. As Berowen approached, he patted the seat next to him in a signal for her to sit there, but he did not once stop chewing or even stand as she walked behind him to seat herself. Her mother sat as she had done on the first night in between Modig and Aelwulf. Brack's offspring were seated between Oswald's wife and Modig's wife and were – as usual – gaining absolute attention by refusing to eat what had been placed on their plates and demanding that they be excused from the table as they were not at all hungry and did not wish to sit with the adults at such a boring occasion. They wished to be at their more commonplace game of tormenting the hounds or searching for spiders to catch.

The food did not last long; Modig and his two sons soon saw to that. They ate as if they had not eaten for days and whilst the men in her own family managed to satisfy their own hungers, Berowen and her mother only ate a mere morsel each. The last things on their minds at that moment was feeding their stomachs – Ethwen's was threatening to empty itself of whatever food remained from the night before and the recent happening in the hall had caused Berowen to lose all her appetite and she wished to do nothing but seek solitude to think upon the events.

The ring upon her finger was ill-fitting and kept slipping down to her knuckle. She was unused to wearing such an adornment on that finger and looking down upon it she thought how ugly it was in its plain appearance. She knew she would have to tighten it somehow or she would lose it – but then again perhaps that would be no unfortunate thing although she assumed that her father-in-law may be less than satisfied with such an event occurring. She had a sneaking feeling that Brack would care neither one way nor the other and would probably not even notice if she no longer wore it.

As she sat waiting for the so-called festivities to begin, she held her hands in her lap and constantly fiddled with the metal ring. At one point it fell off and she panicked slightly for although she didn't really care, to lose it on the first day would be more than careless. She searched blindly in her lap and sighed quietly with relief when she felt its shape in the folds of her heavy gown.

Thurstan and Kipp had left with the priest, the last of whom made a quick exit as soon as he could after his ordeal with the ethereal creature. He would normally have endeavoured to secure a meal after such an occasion as he had just presided over, but he had been so afraid after being attacked that he had soiled himself and was eager to leave the hall before the discovery of his accident was made.

Unlike Kipp, Thurstan had had no preconceptions of being invited to stay to share the celebratory meal. The two of them had remained at the doors when the party had returned inside and made their way down the steep steps to the habitation below. Thurstan was content that he had managed to arrange a meeting with Aelwulf later that evening so that he could relieve himself of the burden of his thoughts of the questionable safe return to Brundannon.

Kipp, on the other hand, was most disgruntled at missing a meal. "Stingy bastards," he complained as he hobbled down each step in the most ungraceful manner. "Not even one leg o'poultry to spare. Hospitality is definitely not one of Grimfell's good points. You'd think they could spare some tiny morsel for an empty stomach."

Thurstan just shrugged his shoulders. He had had no expectations of being invited to stay, and whilst he could sympathise with Kipp over his disgruntlement, he could only ponder on why the rotund fellow should have anticipated such an invitation in the first place. As they descended the steps they noticed a distinct change in the weather from when they had ascended but an hour or so earlier. Whilst it had been relatively calm then, they could now feel the sharpness in the air as it had picked up speed and raced around the keep. They could smell the dampness upon their nostrils and knew rain was on its way. In the distance the sky was a dark foreboding grey, with thick clouds that appeared so low that they seemed to brush against the earth beneath them. A storm was definitely approaching and would be upon Grimfell before darkness fell.

Berowen and her mother were both relieved when all the food was gone – whether via the mouths of those in attendance or the hounds that loitered, ever present, just out of sight in the shadows. Soon her friends would lighten the approaching evening with some song and dance, and although the merriment would be short-lived it would do a lot to lift her mood, if only for that short while.

One of the small servant boys was dispatched to run and open the doors in order that the 'entertainment' could enter. As the great doors opened slowly with much complaint in their hinges due to the onset of the damp weather, the small musical troupe entered into the hall. They came in slowly, the men first walking slowly two abreast to a slow beat from the instruments, the pace of which increased as they neared the wedding party. By the time they had reached the long table the pace was rapid and the men were spinning as they played. Berowen's eyes opened in amazement to see the clothing they were wearing, which she had never seen before. Instead of the usual bright coloured cloth they were adorned with deeply coloured brocades and silks. Upon their heads, the men wore strange conical hats with fur trims that sat snugly upon their skulls. Embroidered richly, they were adorned with tiny bells that shook as the men spun around as they approached, their light movement filling the air with their tinkling sound. The instruments were issuing forth such music that seemed to dare anyone within hearing distance not to tap their feet to the rhythm.

Behind the men, the women's arms weaved their ribbons through the air as they sang. When she saw the women clearly, Berowen looked across at Modig and Oswald and smiled to herself. Gone were the bare ankles and feet – in fact gone was any sign of bare flesh apart from the pretty faces looking out from underneath headdresses of delicate intricately woven lace and the hands that swung the ribbons in time to the music. The two men looked slightly disappointed as the women danced and sang in front of them and it pleased Berowen greatly to observe their frustration. The women's bodies were completely concealed beneath gowns that flowed in a straight line down from their shoulders and their delicate frames were completely disguised from view. Berowen clapped and laughed aloud in her satisfaction that the dancers had foiled the lurid thoughts of both Modig and Oswald. She caught the eye of one of the dancers in particular – a face she did not remember noticing before – and the recipient slowly bowed her head, smiling to show a perfect set of white teeth, before continuing to spin around delicately weaving her ribbons in the air. How she could have missed such a beautiful vision before was a mystery. The girl was stunning, and in the short time that Berowen caught her eye she noticed a stray ringlet of bright red hair protruding from beneath her headdress. This Berowen did think strange, as all of the others in the group seemed to have either black or very dark brown hair. The sight of the recalcitrant ringlet had the effect of causing Berowen to shudder involuntarily as she remembered the last time she had seen such a colour upon the head of her attacker many days before.

There was definitely something not quite right with the sudden appearance of this girl amongst the group. Berowen considered it carefully for a few moments and came to the conclusion that there was always the possibility that she had not met all the dancers before – after all one may have been unwell and had perhaps been lying concealed from the others. But that did not sit right with her at all. They had travelled upon the road together and she would have noticed such a dramatic hair colour. No....there was definitely something odd at hand here.

However, she was determined to enjoy the spectacle played out in front of her and put the matter of the stranger amongst them to the back of her mind. There was bound to be some obvious answer and she left it to be investigated upon the morrow, before Kipp and the others departed Grimfell.

The music and dancing played on for almost two separate tolls of the hour bell in the tower. After the conclusion of their performance, the group bowed as one to applause from Berowen and her family, and half-hearted one-handed taps on the table by Modig and his sullen brood.

The group left the hall, the red-headed girl fiddling with her wayward ringlet in an attempt to conceal it beneath her headdress. She seemed agitated to discover it dangling to the side of her forehead and appeared to be pushing it as quickly as she could out of sight. No-one other than Berowen seemed to have noticed, however, and if even they had she suspected that there would be no reason for them to think anything of it. After all, if she had not endured such unwarranted and evil attentions from the red-beards, she would, herself, not have thought anything strange about the girl's hair either.

As the great doors closed, and the hall was once again enveloped in an uneasy stillness, Berowen looked up and down the table at those seated around her. She wondered what was to happen next, but did not feel inclined to enquire. Her family seemed to sit in an awkward silence.

No-one seemed to want to say anything and the atmosphere began to feel most uncomfortable. It was, however, the weather that broke the awkwardness. A loud clap of thunder broke overhead and all within the keep were shocked into sudden animation. The two children squealed in fright and dived into the bosoms of the two women for reassurance, whilst the hounds began to bark furiously at the sound. Berowen had been so lost in her own thoughts that the sound had made her jump in her seat and for a second or two left her wondering what had cast its evil spell upon them, fully expecting to look up and witness some evil apparition amongst them.

There were few windows in the keep, but there were enough to allow the flash of lightning to send its glow into the hall. They could not hear the rain through the thick stone walls, but all assumed that there was a deluge outside falling upon Grimfell and the Wellonaw Marshes. Unbeknown to those ensconced in the relative safety of the great hall, those at the foot of the hill were preparing for another deluge. If the rain did not abate in its severity, it would not be long before a river of mud and detritus would wend its destructive way down the hill towards the small habitation. Those that dwelt in the few shoddy buildings huddled around whatever warmth they had at their disposal and waited for the inevitable flood that would wash under their wooden doors and into their homes. There would be nothing they could do to avoid the destructive, and invasive rush of water as it cascaded down the hill. Outside, those who were unlucky enough to have no walls to shelter behind made the best of what protection from the rains that they could find.

The gloaming was darkened by the storm, making sunset turn to night without the gentle sleepy transition between them. Behind the storm followed the wind, a wind so fierce that it howled as it clung to the top of the keep of Grimfell in a vortex. The storm seemed unable to move on but appeared drawn to the circling of the wind, and the sky above the fortress darkened so deeply it was as if a heavy black curtain had been suspended above it. As the battering wind circled, so also did the tempest; mercilessly tossing great torrents of rain upon the habitation beneath. For those below, looking up at the keep, it was as if the heavens were raining down punishment to all within the stone walls. A streak of lightning struck the rotting wooden pole that brandished the heraldic flag of Grimfell. With an ear-splitting crack the wood split in two vertically and the sliver that held the banner toppled and fell down towards the ground; the wet material wrapping itself around the splintered wood as it descended to the steps, where it lay impotent upon the wet stone.

No-one inside the keep was aware of the events occurring outside for within those heavy walls, nothing of the outside world could be heard apart from the crashing of the thunder and the faint whistling of the wind that slipped its way through any available crack in the badly fitted windows. The two children still clung to their sheltering and comfort in the arms of the two women, but the conversation had begun to flow generally again once the sudden impact of the first crash had dissipated. Berowen dearly wanted to leave the hall and retreat to her chamber, but she was well aware that she was now a married woman and as such the property of the weedy and repulsive man who sat beside her. She glanced sideways at her husband and watched as he picked his teeth with his dagger – something he had begun immediately on finishing eating and even now was still avidly wielding the blade between his rotting teeth. She looked at his wiry fingers grasping the hilt of the makeshift toothpick and felt suddenly nauseous at the thought of those same fingers on her flesh.

Her only salvation would be that he had emptied mazer after mazer of mead and she could but hope that he would collapse into a drunken sleep as soon as he lay down. Whenever he did utter forth into any conversation with his father or brother, his words were slurred. His eyes seemed to have a mind of their own, and gave the effect of rolling around in their sockets as if on strings. In fact she wondered whether poking around in his mouth with his dagger, when under such an influence, was a good idea, but she was not concerned enough to implore him to cease in such a potentially hazardous pastime. After all, if he were to befall some kind of accident, she would have not a care; in fact she had rather hoped that he may.

She watched him as he poured himself another drink and lifted it shakily to his lips. The thick honeyed liquid oozed over the sides of the cup and dribbled down into his beard. Once he had swallowed as much of the liquid that his mouth managed to catch, he thumped the mazer down onto the table and belched loudly; his body swaying back and forth in his seat as he did so. She cringed. Then, with his elbow on the table he resumed his tooth picking, and she found herself imagining him passing out and falling forwards on to his dagger, the consequences of which would probably make her a wife and widow all in one day. She checked her thoughts – recent results of her darker thinking had yielded rather true results and although she greatly detested the man who had that day become her husband, she would not like to think that her idle thoughts caused his death. No-one would know that it had been her who had caused such a thing to occur other than her, although Thurstan and her mother may have their suspicions, but *she* would know and to have to live with it would be a burden upon her. She would not like to have to exist knowing that she was a murderer, despite her great distaste for the man.

She attempted to think of something else to clear her thoughts, but just as she was doing so

Brack *did* slump forward in his seat. She gasped as she realised that he had, in fact, passed out just as had been her thought. What happened next seemed to pass before her eyes in slow motion. She watched as he fell forward and saw the blade of the dagger gleaming in the candlelight for a brief moment before it disappeared further into his mouth as his head lowered. She held her breath and waited for the tear and sickening crunch of metal piercing flesh and hitting bone. If the angle was right, the blade could well pierce his brain. However, with luck or with some intervention from something higher, the blade entered at an angle and she watched devoid of any emotion as she saw the metal pierce through the flesh of his left cheek as his head hit the table with a thud. The blood stained blade winked in the light as drops of the sticky crimson liquid began to fall from the weapon onto his hand. A steady flow of blood oozed from around the point of exit and dribbled down his cheek on to the table. The mead that raced through his body had clearly exacted a powerful hold over him, for he remained still in the position into which he had slumped, not having felt anything and being totally oblivious to the painful predicament into which he had placed himself. She stood up and pushed back her chair with the back of her legs as she did so.

"My Lord Modig," she announced with no emotion in her voice. "It would appear that your son, my husband, has injured himself in a manner most fearful."

The conversation along the table ceased instantly and all eyes fell upon her, but neither Modig nor Oswald moved to the assistance of their kin. It was Aubreda who rose from her chair hurriedly and went to the aid of her youngest son, flapping her arms in panic and wailing when she saw the bloody state of Brack as he continued to sleep off his over-indulgence. "Husband, for heaven's sake show some concern for your son. Assist me!" she shouted. Modig's head rolled in his own mead-infused stupor as he placed his hands on the table and heaved himself into a swaying standing position. As he passed by Berowen he belched loudly and she moved backwards as the odour emitted from his mouth gushed forth in her direction. She watched passively as the two struggled to get Brack back into the seated position, where his head slumped backwards grotesquely with his mouth wide open and the weapon still embedded in his cheek. The movement caused the flow of blood to quicken and it ran from the blade and soon made a small dark puddle on the floor, which was slowly absorbed by the sparse coating of straw that covered the wooden boards. The smell of blood attracted one of the hounds that had hidden under the table from the sound of thunder crashes and it sniffed inquisitively at the growing stain, until Modig kicked it sharply in the ribs and it crept off slowly with its tail between its legs, and whining at the punishment its curiosity had attracted.

Further down the table Brack's dysfunctional family carried on with their own activities. Oswald showed his concern for his brother by raising another mazer of mead to his lips and downing it in one go, and his wife sat quietly rocking back and forth with Brack's offspring sitting beside her curled into her arms; one on each side, and as such both children had not witnessed their father's misfortune. Upon consideration, Berowen thought that it was probably prudent that the woman had detached herself from the events at the other end of the table, although she could not help wondering whether this action was out of concern for the children or purely out of extreme disinterest of Brack's calamitous incident.

Medical help was called for and a servant raced down the hall and out into the storm. As the doors were opened the wind took advantage of the opening and rushed into the hall, extinguishing several of the candles before finally reaching the end of its power. Whilst the incident had ensured that Berowen need not worry about her pre-conceived disgust as to the end of the evening, it did place her with a different dilemma. As Brack's wife, she would surely be expected to attend to his recuperation once the doctor had treated the wound, but so far she had been totally excluded from the attentions he was receiving since she had announced his accident. This position she was more than happy to relinquish to the loving attentions of his mother, but she did not wish to appear callous by doing nothing. Her careful upbringing had successfully managed to instil a certain amount of behaviour expected of her class and whilst she detested her new family greatly, she did not wish to embarrass her own kin by behaving less than she would be expected so to do.

If her family had not been present, she would probably have made her excuses for leaving the hall by stating that the sight of her new husband in such a condition was greatly upsetting to her. She may even have staged some kind of fainting episode to ensure her escape from the situation, but with the current state of affairs, she could not for they would know that she was evading her responsibilities by cunning, and would be deeply ashamed of her behaviour.

So she was caught and could only wait for whatever transpired.

This last occurrence was the last incident of the day with which Ethwen could cope and she made her hurried excuses to anyone who cared to hear that she felt quite ill and would have to leave to return to her chamber forthwith. She wished Aubreda and Modig a polite goodnight and voiced her hope that Brack made a full recovery, before she retreated to the back of the hall where the stairs would lead her away from the horrors of the day.

Eneas and Amleth took their mother's exit as a justification to leave also and rushed after her with the excuse of escorting her to her room and looking after her if necessary. No-one took any notice of their leaving other than Berowen and her father. He looked slightly lost as to what action to take; although his sons had pre-empted him somewhat in an easy withdrawal from the hall, he thought it his duty to remain behind as the figurehead of the family, and to support his daughter, the latter reason probably the most important at that particular time. He looked across at Berowen and was not too sure what he could see in her face. Her expression was almost blank as she stood and watched Aubreda fuss over her youngest son, him still being unaware of his physical state.

The doors opened and the servant came running back, followed a little further behind by the doctor. His ageing years meant that he could not run as fast as the young lad who had summoned him and by the time he reached the stricken Brack, he was panting considerably from the exertion.

Berowen felt suddenly stifled and slowly moved backwards towards where her father was standing. "I need some fresh air," she whispered. "I need to get out of here," and she made her way towards the great doors. Aelwulf followed her. Nobody took any notice of their leaving – Oswald's wife had dozed off with each of the children now resting their heads in her ample bosom, after Edywth had gone to her son's aid, and Oswald had collapsed from the mead and was slumped in his chair.

"I have need to speak with Thurstan, daughter," said Aelwulf as he caught up with her. "He has, apparently, something he needs to speak with me about."

Neither of them were quite prepared for the severity of the storm that raged outside. As they stepped across the threshold, they became soaked to the skin in minutes. Berowen looked skywards and blinked as the rain stung her eyes. The dark clouds were still circling the keep and lightning streaks followed the crashing thunder, the kind of which she had never witnessed before. She shivered. To the side of the steps there was a river of rainwater gushing down the hill. It took with it mud and anything it picked up in its grasp as it swept its way downwards.

"You should stay here, Berowen," shouted Aelwulf over the sound of the lashing rain. "You are already soaked and you are ill-prepared for such weather. I shall speak with Thurstan and return as soon as I can."

Berowen replied loudly, "At least I have an excuse now, father, for leaving the hall and retiring to my chamber." She wanted to give a laugh of relief, but felt better of it.

Aelwulf turned to look at her briefly and nodded. "It would seem so, Berowen. I am so sorry."

She held out her hand to her father and took his offered hand in return. "You have nothing over which to apologise, father. Give Thurstan my greetings, and request him to ask dear Kipp to pass on my thanks to the troupe if you see them. I hope to be able to bid my farewells to them on the morrow if they do not leave too early."

"If this weather keeps up, Berowen, they could be here for another day or so. The marshes must be almost impassable by now."

He disappeared into the storm, his way illuminated by the few braziers that were sheltered from the rain, and which spluttered and sizzled as drops fell against them, refusing to allow the water to extinguish their light. Berowen returned to the hall, shivering from the dampness of her gown. As she approached the table she could see that Brack had awoken; he was wriggling in his seat as the doctor stooped over his head. She could see the whiteness of his knuckles as he grabbed the doctor's elbow. As she came alongside them she could also see Brack's expression of fear and pain as the doctor tried to pull out the blade. He was having a great deal of trouble as his patient refused to stay still and no matter how much Aubreda and Modig tried to hold him down, Brack squirmed underneath their grip.

Much to her relief, although also to her irritation, Aubreda waved her away when she neared them. Under other circumstances she may well have challenged the gesture, but she was only too happy to leave her husband at the mercies of the doctor and she left without a word, making her way to her chamber as quickly as she could just in case Aubreda changed her mind.

Once in her room, Berowen could hear the rain beating down against her window. The gusts of the blustery weather blew it against the panes with such force that she feared they might break. She could see nothing out of them; the water ran down in sheets that completely obliterated her view. However, she remained standing, staring out into the rain-lashed darkness, but her mind was elsewhere – somewhere she did not know, although it did seem very familiar to her.

LXII

R ain and fairies do not mix well. It is not that they melt under its touch of course, but that they *do* become very sour-tempered and apt to argument and bickering if they get too wet. Quite simply, they do not like being cold and soggy. They are only small and those rain-filled muddy puddles that seem so inconsequential to ordinary sized people are like ponds to them. It should not be forgotten that they stand only one and a half feet high, perhaps a few inches more if you catch them standing on tip-toes which is not often, but can be witnessed on the more frivolous of occasions. The rain that fell over the treetops of the Forest of Whispers was not as ferocious as that which would soon fall over Grimfell but it was bad enough. Mog and Peg were more annoyed than the others in their kin for they had been foraging on the edge of the forest when the storm had broken without warning. They knew by instinct that it was not a storm borne from natural causes; the way in which the clouds had darkened and moved so swiftly over the forest was not normal. There had been such a gust of wind that it had blown both of them off their feet into the thickets, and they were far from amused at receiving the painful result of landing in the prickly branches. Then, to add insult to injury, the heavens opened as suddenly as the wind had arrived and within minutes they were both soaked to the skin.

Back under cover of the forest, they looked up and watched as the tops of the trees swayed in the wind's grip. It wailed as if a hundred banshees had been released from their confines after years of captivity. It was not a pleasant sound and they covered their ears from the noise. Something evil was afoot, but they knew not quite what it was. Whatever came on that wind was malicious and they hoped that it passed on its way without harm to those that dwelt within the trees. Without doubt, this winter in the forest was the strangest that they had ever experienced before; it was usually a quiet season within the shelter of the tall trees.

Thus as the storm made its way, unbeknown to Mog and Peg towards the fortress on the edge of the marshes, the two faeries spent an hour or two extracting thorns from each other's sore bottoms and backs. They bickered as they did so, and shouted at each other if one caused discomfort to the other in the extraction. The longer it took, the more bad-tempered they became until the cheeks on the wrinkled faces became as red with annoyance as the cheeks of their bottoms were red with soreness.

They cursed the weather and whatever, or whomever, was behind such a deluge of rain. They threatened the wind with appalling punishment if it repeated such a heinous crime upon them again. They raised their fists to the sky and growled as they shook them in defiance. Woe betides anything that crossed their angry little paths on that eve, no matter how big or small, and no matter whether friend or foe.

And that is exactly what Root and Knot discovered as they came across their two kin with bare bottoms beaming in the glow of the lanterns. The two youngsters guffawed loudly and jumped up and down with glee at such a sight, but soon realised their error when – without pulling on their breeches – the afflicted Mog and Peg chased after them screeching as if possessed. They cursed and shouted as they chased Root and Knot and their noise aroused many sleeping creatures within the forest as they went. Many a sleepy head popped from beneath the undergrowth to investigate the furore and whilst most just went back to sleep, some joined in the spectacle and followed the bare bottoms through the forest. It was not often that faeries presented themselves in such a state of undress and those that followed were intrigued as to the reason.

In truth, Mog and Peg would never have thought of showing such immodesty, and – in fact – their state of undress did not dawn on them until they had run after their younger kin for many minutes. It was when Peg looked at Mog's shape slightly ahead of her that the realisation hit upon her and she stopped dead in her tracks. She stopped so suddenly that the hare and mouse who had been trailing close behind could not stop themselves quickly enough and crashed into the back of her legs. She turned and hissed at them, but realised that her present physical state did not demand any respect of her admonishment, and she became rapidly embarrassed and self-conscious. She called out to Mog to stop, but her cry was stolen by the wind.

Unbeknown to Mog in her rage, she carried on her chase alone and was surprisingly sprightly for her aged years. However, as the chase progressed, Root and Knot were slowly gaining a substantial lead until at last they managed to shake her off and disappear into a dark hole in the ground, where they sat motionless, almost daring to breathe.

They knew that Mog had a temper, but they had never witnessed such a display of rage as they had on that evening. They would have to avoid contact with her for many days in the hope that their transgression faded within her mind.

Mog continued to run until she realised that she was chasing after shadows. Slightly out of breath, she sat down and, when her bare skin touched the damp forest floor, she realised her lack of breeches. She looked around for Peg and was horrified, and somewhat irritated to find that her friend was no longer with her. She was not completely alone though; as she looked around she noticed many pairs of eyes watching her intently and she became as self-conscious as Peg had a few minutes earlier. She waved her hands and shouted at the inquisitive creatures and the sound of a great scuttling of feet on twigs and undergrowth announced the departure back into the depths of the forest of those that had followed the events. And then with one hand holding her lantern aloft and the other across her buttocks, as if that action would hide her predicament, she made her return journey as fast as her tired legs would carry her.

The two booted legs that walked on to the path ahead of caused her to stop in her tracks. She did not notice them until it was almost too late as she was running with her head tilted downwards in order to make sure her feet landed safely to avoid the further embarrassment of tripping over. She dashed sideways off the track, flinging her lantern down beneath her, and crouched behind a tree trunk cursing under her breath as her bare flesh received yet another attack, this time from the low thicket she had failed to notice in her rush to escape from sight. The flora of the Forest of Whispers seemed determined to mete out some peculiar kind of punishment upon her wizened frame on this eve and she was becoming exceedingly irked by the incessant attacks upon her person by such things.

Satisfied that no crashing through the undergrowth signalled that she had gone unnoticed, she slowly peeped around the side of the trunk to investigate further what had interrupted her return homeward. It did not take her long to identify the two-legged that still stood on the track where he had walked out from the shadows of the forest. He was close enough for her to make out the bushy beard as he turned his head from side to side as if searching the darkness for something. She wagered that in the light of day, this beard would prove to be red. She shuddered. She did not like these red-beards at all – their presence within the forest was unnerving and she had not yet fathomed out their reason for being there. Moreover, his comrades could not be far and their presence this eve so near to her home was greatly disconcerting. And *why* was he just standing there in the middle of the track? This was most irritating as it would mean she would have to take a circuitous route through the thick undergrowth and in her current state of undress that option did not sit favourably with her.

She also did not relish the thought of having to remain where she was for much longer. The sounds of the forest at night were terrifying even for the most hardened faerie. The howling and screeching had begun to echo in the darkness; the calling of beasts she did not wish to meet in her wanderings.

The red-beard sniffed the air. Some strange scent had reached his nostrils and he was curious as to what it was so near to him that emitted such a strange aroma. Mog stiffened as she watched him take a step backwards and nearer to her hiding place. He, in turn, noticed a faint glow coming from the undergrowth and clumped noisily towards it to investigate. Mog realised that she was about to be discovered and instinctively moved to draw her tiny dagger from her boot and with a sunken heart remembered that she wore no boots. Thinking quickly she prepared to defend herself in the only way she knew how in the current circumstances. As the great hairy hand descended to part the undergrowth around her she launched herself at it and sank her teeth deep into its flesh. It withdrew sharply, throwing her off to the ground with a resounding thud. She jumped to her feet immediately and prepared herself for another attack. The hand came down again, this time followed by a leering face peering down at her in the darkness, the faint light of the lantern casting a hideous shadow across the repulsive face. She saw the mouth smile exposing a set of rotting teeth and she launched herself again -

this time at the ugly face. Again she sank her teeth into the flesh and this time with her fingernails also to gain some semblance of purchase upon the revolting skin.

To an animal of her size or smaller, both of these actions would have proved extremely painful, but to the red-beard they felt more like irritating pin-pricks and he roared with anger as his hands flailed around his head to try to remove her. This did not take long – one faerie against such a giant figure was no match – and soon Mog found herself dangling unceremoniously by her hair as the red-beard raised her to eye-level and scrutinised his attacker. He tapped her with his other hand so that she swayed in his grip. She wrinkled her face and snarled at him. He would be able to snap her body in half quite easily she knew, but she was determined that she would escape – she had to for if she died there and then, it would mean certain death to all her race for there would be no meeting with 'the one' and then 'the one' would destroy them all. She clawed and kicked the air with her hands and feet as she swung around by her hair.

The red-beard eyed her with amusement and poked her in the stomach with a podgy finger. She swayed back and forth from the effect of his jabbing. She eyed his fat juicy nose in the way she had once seen Scrimble eye a fat hare before leaping upon it.   If only she could swing closer and sink her teeth into its bulbous flesh.

The red-beard was enjoying himself playing with this tiny creature. The days on the road and camping out in the forest were becoming tedious and any chance to be vindictive was most welcome. He guffawed loudly as he continued to play with his prey much as a cat does when pouncing on a mouse. He would kill her once he had had his fill and became bored, but for now the helpless creature was of great amusement to him. He swung her around like a windmill and poor Mog became dizzy and nauseous, and her head began to hurt from having her hair pulled so tightly. She had never before come across a being that was quite as cruel as that which now held her captive so roughly.

As she dangled in front of her torturer she espied two faint lights coming up the track behind him. It must be Root and Knot returning under the impression that Mog had long since reached her home. Hope at last. Perhaps if they attacked the red-beard would release her, enabling her to escape into the depths of the forest. Root and Knot could then also make their own escape and all would be able to return home safely.

The two young faeries walked, arm in arm, down the track. They had indeed assumed that the bad-tempered Mog would have reached the sanctity of her home by then and were striding along laughing and giggling at their own quips merrily, the glow-worm lanterns swaying as they marched. They heard the sound of deep chuckling before they saw the great shape looming ahead of them out of the darkness. It put them on their guard instantly and they slowed to a creep, before jumping to the side of the track to search for cover as they did so. They looked at each other with wide eyes and made their way slowly towards the shape. Then they saw something dangling from a raised hand and soon, to their horror, realised that the swaying object was Mog.

Overhead the boughs of the trees swayed and creaked in the wind and, mixed with the usual eerie sounds of the forest at night, they became frightened. A wave of extreme alarm crushed their usual brash personalities, and they clung to each other for comfort and support. What were they to do? They needed to rescue Mog, but their tiny bows and arrows being their only weapons, it was clear that these would not cause much damage to the figure that held her captive. They would have to plan carefully any rescue attempt. They bolstered their lacklustre courage by whispering to each other that if they managed to save Mog, their exploits would be forever immortalised in song and word. They would be heroes of the faeries of the forest and would receive great accolades for their noble deed. They puffed out their tiny chests and, clasping their hands together, they shook them furiously to seal the pact.

Their bravado suitably raised, they crept further towards the figure. They needed to be in clear sight of their target. The most obvious target for their arrows would be his face, but for that they needed to circle around and approach from the opposite direction. They also needed light, and that would be almost impossible to achieve. They looked skyward to the gap in the canopy overhead. The sky was dark and unforgiving with angry clouds moving swiftly across its expanse, pushed along by the howling gusts. The pale globe of night was up there somewhere, but was obviously impotent against such an angry sky. Their only hope came in the spasmodic flashes of lightning that lit up the heavens briefly – but hopefully giving enough time to let their arrows fly accurately. Once they had the angle in their mind, a quick follow up may also hit the target.

They crept to their positions, one on either side of the track. Each placed an arrow in its respective nock and they waited. It was an interminable wait and their arms began to ache, but they remained in position, the thoughts of their undeniable heroism swelling their hearts with determination.

At last, the forest lit up with the startling light and two arrows cut through the air on their way to their mark. The red-beard was taken completely by surprise as one arrow embedded itself in his left cheek and the other glanced his right cheek before falling to the ground. He roared with surprise and his whole body twirled this way and that trying to locate the origins of the attack. It felt as if a tiny winged creature had stung him. Another two arrows hit him, this time with more potency as one found its way into the corner of the bottom of his left eyelid, the other his lip. As hoped, the surprise caused him to release his grip on Mog's hair and she fell unceremoniously to the ground with a thud. She wasted no time in getting to her feet and running off for the nearest cover.

Root and Knot saw her fall and disappear into the night and they both congratulated themselves at their success and canny trick. The arrows had not done much harm to the red-beard, but they had incensed him in their audacity at causing him so much discomfort and surprise. He plucked the tiny arrow from the corner of his eye and inspected it closely. It looked like a splinter of wood, until he realised there were tiny fletchings at one end. His mouth curled into a snarl as he realised that he had been duped by something that must be tiny to fire such a missile upon him. How could a creature that must stand no higher than the cuff of his boot outwit his prowess as a great warrior?

He growled with anger at being fooled in such a way, and trampled through the undergrowth with a great rage searching for his antagonists and he swept the branches away with his arm. There became a great confusion and Knot just managed to avoid a heavy boot coming down upon him as he scuttled out of the way and ran further into the forest. The red-beard lurched to the other side of the track and trampled on the undergrowth with great force, hoping to crush anything alive beneath its shelter. In a foreign tongue, he shouted and cursed in a deep growl. Root turned and ran as fast as he could away from the stamping feet. A great rumble of thunder echoed through the trees, followed shortly afterwards by a streak of white light that split the air with its crack. There was a sizzling noise and a great snapping sound as the lightning hit a tree and sliced its way through the trunk to the ground below. The stricken tree split in two and one half creaked and fell to the forest floor with a thump, the whole area vibrating with its contact with the earth. It laid there, its jagged burnt edges bare against the foliage, steam rising from the torn bark as the rain hit and cooled the mortal wound.

The sound of a moan filled the air. The red-beard was pinned to the ground under the weight of the fallen trunk. They both lay dying on the forest floor, the occasional flash of lightning revealing the agony upon the red-beard's bloody face as the weight of the wood slowly crushed him. His back was already broken and he would not last long in this world, but he would die in the agony that befits such an evil creature, and in the sacrificial death of the tree, Mother Nature had meted out her retribution for the crime against a child of the forest.

LXIII

As the cold light of foredawn spread across the sky, the woodwose stirred in his den grateful that the storm had at last passed. He had spent the night curled up in the farthest and darkest corner of his home covering his ears against the crashing sound of the thunder and burying his head as far into his chest as he could to avoid seeing the ghostly light of the thunder's companion. His muscles ached as he stretched himself out and he slowly crawled out into the coming daylight and stood to relieve his body from its cramped position from the night before. He smelt the air. The smell of the forest after rain was delightful and he took in a deep breath of the fresh scent. Everything around him seemed to be relaxing in the calm after the storm, and he listened to the awakening bird song and the faint dripping of the last remnants of rain as it fell to the ground, where it would be soaked up by the undergrowth.

He had occasionally heard many odd sounds during the night. Others that he did not know had accompanied the usual eerie callings of the creatures of the night. He knew not from what or whence they had come, and had paid little attention in his quest to deaden the sound of the rumbles overhead. As he exercised his legs by walking to the stream, he decided to take the easier route of the well-worn deer track, and it was in doing so that he came across the fallen slice of the tall tree, which lay across his way. He gazed with sorrow at the victim of the storm and did not notice, at first, the second victim as it lay beneath the weight of the tree's broken half. When at last he saw the two booted feet protruding at an odd angle from under its confines, he investigated further and found the body of the broken red-beard, the eyes in his scarred face staring emptily skywards. He scratched his head and seated himself on the trunk, where he remained for a few moments staring at the body. He brushed off the tiny splinter of wood that seemed to be stuck in its cheek and then noticed that it looked like a missile of some sort. This he could not understand, and he lifted it closer to his face and examined it. He had seen enough of these missiles before in hares that had made their way back into the wood before dying. He inspected the arrow more closely; the fletching was all but destroyed, but the hand-crafted wood and honed blade were definitely the work of some tiny hand. A faerie hand perhaps; one of those little folk who persisted in teasing him whenever they could. The odd sound that he had heard in the night must have come from some sort of battle here on this very track, so near to where he sat crouched in his den.

The glint of metal in the bushes nearby attracted his attention and he slowly stood up, his leg muscles still not quite ready to face the day. Bending down he drew out the sword from where it had come to rest and ran his hand over the blade. Sharp. This time he would keep it. He glanced again towards the boots as they protruded from under the tree and looked down at his dirty, bare feet; feet that were cold in the early morning air. Perhaps they would offer him some small comfort in the coming weeks. He pulled them off the body and gingerly placed a foot into one, then the other foot in the other. He laughed when they fitted perfectly and he jumped up and down in them happily chortling, completely forgetting the soreness in his limbs, like the children in the villages across the land jump in and out of puddles.

The wildman went on his way, with sword in one hand and his feet covered with boots for the first time in years, but he did not go far when he noticed a small quiver in his path. Its contents had spilled out and the tiny arrows were scattered on the ground. The tree had fallen at an angle and the top end had crashed into the undergrowth on the opposite side of the track. Further up, just before it disappeared into the forest, he noticed a broken bow peeking out from beneath it. He was beginning to feel uneasy – a scattered quiver and a broken bow. He began to search for anything else near the bow and slumped to the ground with a heavy sigh when he saw the tiny arm poking out. A feeling that he had not felt in a long time rose up from his stomach and he began to cry, not out of fear or madness, but out of real sorrow. He lay his big hand against the tiny one that lay palm up; it was icy cold.

After a while he began to dig with his hands around the body in the hope that he would be able extract the corpse from beneath the trunk. There was no way at all that he would be able to lift it and he could also not leave the tiny creature here. He needed to return it to its kin and the only way he could think of achieving this was to dig a hole beneath the body in the hope that he could pull it free from its confines.

He gently pulled out the body, where it was laying face down embedded in the earth below from the weight and force of the falling tree. Turning it over he wiped away the dirt from the face, which had not been damaged from the accident owing to it being received into the soft earth. The face he recognised as one of those little folk who had been playing in the tree when he had ended up lying on the ground dizzy from being whirled around in circles. He held no grudge against this faerie for that, but felt a deep sorrow at its passing. Its permanently beaming face within its wrinkly visage was rigidly set, and the eyelids were closed over the once sparkling eyes. The woodwose laid the body on the ground and left it to retrieve the broken bow which he placed beside it. Then he returned to where the arrows still lay scattered and bending down, picked each one up, replacing it in the quiver before returning to the body.

He decided to bury the sword and return for it later. And once he had done this further in the forest, and had marked its spot by a clever arrangement of twigs and cones, he returned to the faerie and picked up the bow and quiver with one hand and scooped the body up with the other into the crook of his arm. He slowly made his way back towards where he thought the faeries dwelt. He knew he would not see them unless they wished to be seen, but he presumed that the sight of him carrying one of their own would bring them out of their hiding places.

And this it certainly did. He reached the glade by the mossy-banked stream and stood still for a moment. Sure enough, from behind every rock and tree trunk, from beneath every large tuft of undergrowth and from under every large leaved shrub appeared one or more tiny wisened faces. He noticed a slow circle being formed around the perimeter of the faerie hideout by archers, their bows already loaded ready to fire their tiny arrows in his direction on the bidding of their leader. Mog herself had been awoken by Peg and had placed herself on the highest boulder in the stream. She signalled her tiny army to stand down and immediately all the archers lowered their bows and withdrew one or two paces back into the foliage.

Whilst certain that some of the others were undoubtedly suspicious of the circumstances of Root's demise, Mog knew that it would not have been the wildman who had caused it. She beckoned him closer and signalled for him to lay Root's body down on the ground. This he did, along with the bow and quiver before standing again and taking a step or two backwards. He began to gesticulate with his hands to try to explain where he had found Root. He pointed skywards and mimicked thunder and lightning, before running to a tree and miming something chopping it in half. He then made hand movements to describe the tree falling to the ground.

Mog pointed to the boots upon his feet and looked puzzled and somewhat concerned at their appearance before her. He stood as tall as he could and puffed himself out, making movements with his hand to show a big bushy beard, which was even bigger than the one that adorned his own chin. Mog put a hand up to halt his acting and disappeared for a few moments before reappearing holding a clump of red hair. She pointed at it and the wildman nodded his head furiously in recognition of the colouration of the hair.

Mog, of course, knew that he was miming the truth as she had been there herself and she knew that Root and Knot had both been present. She told the others the story of the night before and they were aghast at what she related. They raised their fists and stamped their feet – those with weapons brandished them aloft.

Knot had not been present when the woodwose had arrived – he had been out at first light to search for his friend now that daylight had dawned to make the way easier. He had been concerned when Root had not returned, but would never have thought that something dreadful would have happened to him. He thought that he had most likely sat down to rest somewhere and had fallen asleep – that would have been so like Root to do such a thing. Knot had gone as far as the spot where the fallen tree now barred the way. The appearance of this surprised and worried him at first, especially when he saw the body of the red-beard. For a fleeting moment he wondered whether his friend Root had suffered the same fate, but upon searching the area and not finding him, he returned back the way he had come to the faerie glade, satisfied that he would probably find him there waiting for him. Then they could have fun avoiding Mog for the rest of the day and plotting their next foray into mayhem.

When Knot reached the faerie glade he was confronted with a scene he had not witnessed before. There in the middle of the glade sat the infamous wildman of their wood; the same wildman who accompanied them every year on their seasonal trips over the moor. So why was he here now, amidst Knot's own kith and kin? It was a faerie rule laid down many ages ago that the faeries kept themselves to themselves unless circumstances dictated a union with another creature of the wood or forest. Thus Scrimble had been approached days before in the unfortunate episode with Mog's secret box. There must be a very good reason for the wildman to be here now, and Knot had a feeling that it was not a good one. All his kin seemed to watch every move he made as he approached the centre of the glade. Something had happened to Root, that must be it. He must have been injured in some way and the wildman had brought him back. He would have to thank the wildman for such an act.

But when Knot saw Root laying still, aside his quiver and broken bow, he knew that it was much worse. He sat cross-legged beside his friend's body and, without a sound - took a cold hand in his and gently stroked it. As with all faeries, he did not reveal any signs of outward emotion at the passing of his friend, but all that were present in that glade of sorrow would know exactly what he was feeling at that moment in time.

Funerals for faeries do not occur very often for they generally live to a venerable old age, and it would take at least four generations in terms of human lifetimes before such an event may be heard of.

This had been the first time that a funeral had been held in the winter months; there had been several in this kin during the late summer, and these had been graced by many flowers of all different shades and sizes. At this inhospitable time of year there were no flowers available to grace the mourners or the body, so acorns would be used instead. The faeries worked quickly and soon Root was wearing a delicately strung crafted headdress of acorns around his tiny head, with trails of ivy that hung down and twirled around his tiny body.

Other faeries produced little shovels from their back packs and were busy digging a hole near the stream at the base of a tall pine tree. In the summer, it would have been lined with petals but there were none to be had anywhere so Root's eternal sleeping place was lined with branches of pine covered thickly with soft green moss. The positioning of his resting place was significant as it represented the origins of his name and the tree would protect his grave from disturbance. Over time the roots of the tree would intertwine around the spot and his body would be forever embraced in their protective arms.

The woodwose sat and watched the faeries at their toil. He watched as Knot bathed his friend's face with the cold waters of the stream to clean away the mud of the earth where his face had lain. He observed the faeries delicately placing the acorn ring upon Root's head and watched them weave the ivy around his tiny body tightly so that he was encased in a wreath of green. They placed holly leaves upon his headdress so that they stuck up like the points of a crown; the bunches carefully harvested to include red berries which gleamed like jewels against the dark green and brown of the acorns.

This would be a hero's burial. His bow was mended with stems of the tough bindweed and his quiver lay beside him – its full complement of ten arrows was minus the two he had fired at the red-beard.

Once the preparations were finished six faeries, including Knot, stood around the body and waited for Mog to appear at their head. When she had placed herself correctly she signalled to them to raise Root on to their shoulders and two elder fairies solemnly picked up the bow and quiver and positioned themselves between Mog and the bearers.

Mog called over to Peg who then ran towards the wildman where he still sat on the boulder. She beckoned him to follow the ever-growing line of mourners who had lined up behind the bearers, before she ran off to take up her own position. He stood and waited for the last of the faeries to pass before joining in the procession.

It moved slowly towards the stream and made its way stoically and silently across the log bridge to where the dark hole awaited. The wildman noticed that the birdsong had fallen silent and only the sound of the slow rhythm of walking feet could faintly be heard as the funeral procession made its way across the forest floor.

Six faeries jumped into the hole and lifted their arms to guide the earth's charge into its final resting place. Once satisfied that Root rested comfortably, with his head to the east and his feet to the west to follow the rise and fall of the sun, the six were handed his bow and quiver. These they placed across his chest before the six were helped to clamber to the surface where they joined the others to silently stare into the chasm before them.

The woodwose stood a respectable distance away from the main gathering of Root's kind and what he witnessed next he would remember until the end of his own days upon this earth, which sometimes seemed so cruel, especially in the light of what had recently taken place. From somewhere deep within their tiny bodies the faeries found voice – a voice so loud that it seemed unreasonable to believe that it arose from them. As one they started a low hum which increased in level until it was so loud, the very earth beneath seemed to quake under its volume. From out of their mouths poured a song that was deeply solemn and yet, at the same time, melodious. It danced on the air and filled the glade with its sombre notes, and as it lingered on their lips, they became bathed in a silvery powder which encompassed each and every one of them. Abruptly it all ended and it seemed to the woodwose that all the faeries took a deep breath before they all blew silver dust into Root's grave.

The ceremony was over. And they all made their way back across the stream, save for three of them who set to work with their tiny shovels filling in the earth above their departed friend and Knot who stood silently. The woodwose remained where he was also, and watched them at their work. Once the earth had been replaced, heavy boulders were put on the fresh mound in order to keep any scavengers at bay while it settled.

Eventually the woodwose left Knot to his solitude and made his way back through the glade. There was no-one to be seen, all the faerie folk had returned to their hiding places, and he slowly ambled back to where he had buried the sword.

LXIV

Brack had suffered greatly at the hands of the doctor, who had pulled and tugged at the dagger until it eventually eased itself out of the stricken man's cheek. Brack had not helped the situation by refusing to sit still, so what could have been a straightforward extraction was hampered greatly by his fidgeting. Eventually his parents had managed to get him to his chamber and had left him to sleep off his mead, nursing a poultice on the wound, which had been secured untidily and hastily around his head by a bandage to keep it in position.

Berowen had heard the commotion as her husband was escorted to his room. She had decided that she would pretend to be asleep and would not open her door to investigate and enquire as to Brack's state of health. In truth, she cared nothing about his accident other than a modicum of bizarre guilt that she had perhaps caused the whole episode to occur by merely thinking about how it would serve him right for his repulsive behaviour.

She would arise early in the morning in order to ensure that she could bid her farewells to her friends – Kipp, the troupe and Thurstan had become familiar faces amongst Grimfell's strangers over the past days, and she would miss them all. She was impatient to learn of what Thurstan had talked to her father about during the ill-fated evening before. It must have been of some importance for the meeting to have taken place in such a clandestine manner, but she also knew that it must be a matter of which she was not to be party in, or her father would have told her. However, that only served to make her the more curious and she was determined to find out as soon as she could. She was also intrigued about the red-haired girl she had spotted amongst the dancers and wanted to find her again before they left.

She could not sleep despite feeling exhausted by the events of the day. She lay on her back staring at the canopy over her cot and listened to the sound of the storm outside. It had almost blown itself out and the period between claps of thunder and streaks of lightning were lengthening. She could still hear the wind though as it howled and whistled around the parapets atop the keep. The candle slowly melted away on the small table beside her and eventually the room was plunged into darkness, but still she stared upwards. The sounds of the keep at rest were eerie; there were faint footsteps to and fro along the corridor, presumably someone tending to Brack. Every so often she heard the creak of a door being opened and shut, and whilst open she could hear the faint moans of her husband issuing forth. Despite being under the heavy influence of mead, his wound was obviously keeping him awake. No doubt, his obstinacy in not letting the doctor tend him properly had aggravated the wound even more. She tried her best to feel remorse, but felt none and she could not but help possess an overwhelming sense of guilt at her complete emptiness.

She decided that it was futile trying to force herself into going to sleep. She rose from the bed and a little too hastily made her way to the door in order for her to light another candle from one of the braziers in the corridor. As she did so, she stubbed her bare foot against the leg of a wooden cabinet and hopped up and down on one leg in discomfort and annoyance. The pain made her feel nauseous and when she looked down at her foot she was horrified to notice that her little toe was sticking out at right angles to the rest of her foot. She put her weight on to the afflicted foot and winced at the pain. She could not believe that she had been so stupid and now she was left with what appeared to be a broken toe. Perhaps she was being punished in some way for her involuntary cause of Brack's dilemma and if so, then she could not really complain at any retribution dealt by those powers that float beyond consciousness.

However, she would not make a fuss. It was not her way. She hobbled to her door and slowly pulled it open. Gingerly she peeked her head out and was relieved when the way ahead was clear. Slowly and painfully she limped to the brazier and lifted the candle to the flames. Once her candle was lit, she returned to her room, closing the door behind with a degree of relief and satisfaction that she had not been discovered wandering the halls so late.

By the yellow light of the candle she dressed herself as quickly as she could. Whilst she was relieved to see that her little toe had all but returned to its natural position, she was shocked to see that her foot was already swelling and a dark bruise was forming on her little toe and the one next to it. It would be difficult to get her shoe on, but she gritted her teeth and pulled as gently as she could. The ache was excruciating, and she bit her lip to control her desire to cry out.

Extinguishing the candle, and limping even more now that her foot was confined in the, albeit soft, leather of her shoe, Berowen looked carefully into the corridor again. Just as she did so, the door to Brack's room opened and she withdrew sharply back into her room, easing the door slowly to a position where just a thin gap allowed her to peek through. The flickering light from a candle within his room lit up a small part of the hallway and she watched as his mother crept out and disappeared further down the corridor towards her own chamber, leaving Brack's door slightly ajar.

Berowen decided to look in and see exactly how her husband was faring. He was clearly delirious and moaned and thrashed about under his coverlet. The bandage around his head was red with the blood that had seeped through the poultice. In the candlelight she saw him turn his head towards her. "Away wench," he spluttered. "Leave me to my agony. You have poisoned me with your sorcery."

She flinched from the accusation. Did he really know that her idle thoughts had caused his suffering or was he under the grip of delirium to such an extent that some weird voices were talking in his head and trying to convince him of some witchcraft that he so dreaded? Would his family really think that she had cast some evil spell on their youngest son? If so then she was indeed in mortal danger. And so were her family. Or perhaps in his addled mind he was thinking of the visitor who had come upon them with his terrifying gust of wind. Now he truly must be a sorcerer.

Brack began to dribble and the sight of clots of blood mixed with his spit turned her stomach. In an act of kindness – from where she knew not – she picked up a piece of cloth and wiped away the liquid that oozed from his mouth. She was unprepared for the sudden movement of his right arm as his hand wrapped itself tightly around her wrist. With a strength she could not believe, he pulled her closer towards his face. "See what they have done to me," he spat causing more of the bloody mess to emanate from his mouth.

She pulled away from him as forcefully as she could and inwardly sighed with relief at his admission that it was not *she* specifically that he was blaming for striking him down with whatever had invaded his body. The exertion had exhausted him and his arm flopped down on to his coverlet. He remained still, his breathing erratic, and she backed off and left the room.

She made her way, as quickly as she could, down the steps and through the Hall. The hounds paid no attention to her but merely carried on snoring or chasing hares in their sleep. As she opened the great doors a strong gust of cold air forced itself through and her candle extinguished. It carried on its way through the Hall and blew out any source of light it met until it lost its strength and dissipated. As she stepped outside she could see the sky light up in the distance as the storm took hold and wreaked its havoc over somewhere on the far horizon. Eastward, dawn was slowly approaching and she made her way carefully down the slippery steps, the rushing water that had been so evident when she had stepped out the night before with her father, having eased off to a slow lazy trickle. Her foot ached interminably but she was determined in her path.

In the pale light of the encroaching dawn she observed a black mass making its way across the sky towards Grimfell. She stopped and looked, raising a hand to her forehead and squinting to try and make out what it was that approached. The sound of them arrived on the wind before they did, and soon Berowen realised it was the ravens returning to their noisy circling around the keep that flew across the cloudy skies. If one raven is supposed to predict death, then a roost such as this must cast an omen of much more.

Pulling her hood over her head to shield her from the biting wind, she reached the bottom of the steps and made her way towards the gatehouse.

The lights in the apothecary's hut were burning brightly through the window. Cynefrid and Wirt had obviously been up all night preparing potions for the stricken Brack. As Berowen passed, the door flew open and the young Wirt rushed forth, his eyes swollen from lack of sleep. In his hand he clutched several phials of odd-coloured potions that he was packing into his bag as he went. He had his head down concentrating on his task, and did not notice her at first, but stopped suddenly when he noticed the two feet in front of him.

Berowen saw Cynefrid standing in the doorway. "You should not let the boy go alone, kind apothecary," she warned lifting up her wrist to show the red mark left by Brack's grip. "Although his body seems poisoned his strength comes in waves of extreme power."

Cynefrid stepped forward and crossed the threshold into the pale light of the morning. He eyed her suspiciously, and took her raised hand in his and inspected her wrist closely. "You will need a soothing poultice for that bruise," he murmured. "But for your foot something slightly more potent."

"How did you know about my foot?" asked Berowen aghast. But Cynefrid did not answer as he re-entered the hut and disappeared for a few minutes, before returning with a bundle of herbs that he wrapped in a cloth as he walked back outside. Taking her arm again, he wrapped the damp, sweet-smelling package around her wrist and secured it with a knot. "Many strange things have occurred since your arrival here, my lady," he said. "And methinks they are not over yet," he continued as he looked skyward and watched the ravens as they resumed their noisy circling high above. He handed Berowen a small package. "For your foot, my lady." She thanked him and wondered again, upon how he had known of her injury.

"Grimfell was built on an ancient land, my lady," began Cynefrid. "The land was taken by force and those that were stripped of their life and their beliefs have long awaited the return of those who will help them take back what is theirs. In the past week there have been signs that those who will give their aid are making their way here – in fact several have already arrived. The barrens lands of the Eastward will soon be rich with life again methinks, and when that happens Grimfell will fall, mark my words."

Berowen listened to the old man's words with interest and an encroaching concern for those innocents that dwelt within the walls of the fortress. "Then why do you stay, Cynefrid?" she asked. "And why do you not warn others of the impending doom?"

"It is not for me to do such a thing," replied Cynefrid with a sigh. "The ancient ones will call to those who are innocent when the time comes. Be at ease, my lady, for those who are blameless shall be cared for I am sure."

Before Berowen could speak Cynefrid looked at Wirt, who had fallen asleep whilst leaning against the wall of the hut. "Boy, what are you doing still here?" Wirt awoke with a start and started to mumble incoherently.

"I beg of you not to send the boy," pleaded Berowen. "At least not alone as I have asked before."

Cynefrid raised an eyebrow under the hood of his cloak. "Very well," he answered in apprehension of disobeying the woman who stood before him. He closed the door of the hut, and with an arm around the shoulders of Wirt he urged him forward. "Come Wirt, let us put our dislike behind us and attend the injured Brack, although methinks such a gathering that flies around atop of us would seem to foretell it is a waste of our efforts."

They started the long climb to the keep and Cynefrid called back to Berowen, "Apply the poultice to your foot as soon as you can, my lady, for it will ease your discomfort greatly the moment it is applied."

Berowen replied that she would and when they had turned the bend in the steps and had disappeared out of sight, she continued on her way to the gatehouse. She left the guard muttering after her, as she ignored his demands for stating her purpose in passing.

The ground between the inner and outer walls had almost become a bog under the torrent from the skies above and the stream of water that had run down the steps from the keep. The small cottages had fallen victim to its deluge and the inhabitants were now sweeping out water from within with weary expressions upon their faces. Berowen smiled at them sympathetically, but they did not seem to notice her passing as they continued in their fruitless task. It would take many days for the inside of their homes to dry out, and with the coming season of ice and snow it would make for a very damp existence.

She found Kipp already packing up his cart. He had already retrieved Bessie from the stables and she was standing fetlock deep in the mire as he tacked her up to the cart. The wanderer was surprised to see Berowen and exclaimed, "Bless me be, what is you doing up and about at this hour, and in these conditions?"

She smiled at him. "I could not let you leave without wishing you a fond farewell and safe journeys, old friend," she replied.

He beamed at her in his usual jovial fashion, the rain from the night before not having outwardly dampened his spirits. "That be kind of you, m'lady, I'm sure," he replied.

"Where are you going?" Berowen asked to which Kipp laughed. "Oh I be goin' wherever Bessie 'ere says I be goin'. As usual," and he winked.

She laughed and continued, "Well take good care of yourself and Bessie, Kipp. Perhaps we shall meet again one day. I shall look forward to it."

Again Kipp laughed, "Ah well, if you 'appen to be goin' my way, we might. But you won't find me callin' back 'ere that's fer sure."

Although empathising completely Berowen could not help but look crestfallen at his honesty.

"No reflection on you though m'lady," Kipp quickly added. "But, you know, Grimfell 'ere is not exactly 'ospitable to travellers." He looked skyward and pointed at the ravens that still soared around the keep.

"I know, I know," she said softly. "I did not take it personally." And she hugged him. He was not used to such an act of affection and seemed slightly embarrassed. Berowen laughed again, "I shall miss you Kipp."

She patted Bessie on the neck and walked on to where the troupe were rising, and preparing for their journey. Upon seeing her, they all flocked around her and greeted her with pats on the shoulders and hugs and even a kiss or two on the cheek. She thanked them over and over again for their kindness and what appeared to be their good wishes on her marriage. She searched amongst them for the red-haired girl but she was nowhere to be seen. This was getting more puzzling. Her face would not have been missed because, although the other girls were all pretty, this girl had been the most beautiful she had ever seen. Surely she had not imagined her presence the day before?

A familiar voice spoke to her. It was Thurstan who had heard the commotion and, upon hearing Berowen's voice, had come to investigate. She smiled at him and welcomed his interruption as she was beginning to feel slightly claustrophobic amongst the throng. She edged away smiling and although she knew they would probably not understand a word she was saying, she thanked them once more and wished them well on their journey.

She walked with Thurstan to where his mare was already saddled and ready to move out. He had a rendezvous to attend with Felagin and could not be late for the man was unreasonable about tardiness. Berowen babbled out the events that had occurred after he had left and he listened intently. He could not quite believe Brack's accident and subsequent illness, and asked Berowen to repeat what she had told him. She asked him if Felagin could have been responsible in some way and he told her that whilst it was possible, it was extremely unlikely unless there was something about Brack of which they were unaware. She told Thurstan of her conversation with Cynefrid and of his tales of ancient ones and their bid to reclaim their lost lands. Thurstan recalled his own conversation with the apothecary and agreed that there may be some truth in what he had said. Perhaps then, Grimfell's downfall had begun with the impending death of Brack. The ravens must be persisting in their attention to Grimfell's keep for some reason and perhaps it was indeed a far greater and ominous motive than most would imagine.

Berowen asked Thurstan whether he had noticed a beautiful red-haired girl in the dance troupe but he had to admit that he had not. He had seen them return to their camp the previous evening, but had not noticed anyone different. This concerned Berowen and she voiced her misgivings. Thurstan could offer no solution and could only offer the suggestion that perhaps one of the girls usually wore a false head of hair to hide the redness of her locks for some reason. But upon Berowen's insistence that the face of the girl was nowhere to be seen he had no answer for her.

Thurstan took Berowen's hands in his and told her, "I must be leaving, Berowen, for I fear Felagin will be growing impatient."

Berowen sighed. "Indeed, Thurstan. I know you must leave. Do you think you will ever return to Grimfell?"

"I doubt that I shall, Berowen," he replied. "However, that does not mean that our paths will not cross again. I have a strong suspicion that we shall come across each other sometime in the future, for I believe that we are intertwined in something of great import."

"Then I shall look forward to that day, my friend," said Berowen. "I can only bid you a fond farewell and hope that you are safe upon the road that you are about to tread."

He raised her hands to his lips and kissed them softly. "And I wish you well, Berowen, until we meet again."

Thurstan raised himself aloft his mare and urged her to a walk towards the barbican, and disappeared into its shadows. Berowen heard the mournful screech as the drawbridge was lowered, and then raised again.

It was then that she remembered that she had not asked Thurstan why he had asked to speak to her father. She tutted to herself and became unreasonably angry at her lapse of memory. She would just have to quiz her father instead, although she knew it would be futile.

LXV

Mog had intended to wait until her audience with The One was over, but she realised that if she were to fail in appeasing The One's desire then there would be no chance in casting her retribution upon Oram, the stoat. As a result of the untimely death of Root, her desire for blood was paramount. And whilst she knew that she could not satisfy this blood lust by exacting revenge upon the red-beards, for they were too fearsome a group to be tackled by her kind even in large numbers, she did know that if a trap was planned well enough, Oram could be the well-deserved recipient of her desire for blood. So she set about forming her plan with relish.

Oram sniffed the air outside her den cautiously. She was uneasy and had been so ever since she had discovered the treachery of her son Cob. She had hunted him down and dealt out punishment of the most lethal kind. For his treason, his body had been wrenched limb from limb by her chosen assassins. Even a son does not escape the wrath of the great Oram should she so wish it. Hand-picked carefully, she had sent two of her other offspring plus two others of her kind – the most vicious she knew - to track him down. She would make certain that her sons knew that even they were not immune to her power and vindictiveness. She need not have been concerned. One day she would be succeeded by one of her sons, and they had no care whatsoever of dispatching one their siblings – after all it made the claim for power a lot easier if there was one less, and they went about their killing with great delight. However, she was also well aware that faeries are not to be crossed. Some may think them sweet in their tiny forms but she knew that a faerie angered was one to avoid. Ever since the treachery had been discovered she had surrounded herself with those she trusted most. She went nowhere on her own and slept with two at the entrance of her den.

Mog chose her assassins as equally well as had Oram when hunting Cob. Sap was renowned for his skills with the knife and Root's place beside Knot was taken by Bark, another archer of great aim as well as a tracker of notoriety. Acorn and Oakapple were experts at stealth, whilst the aged Leaf, Elm and Ash were unsurpassable in their skills with traps. The trio of female sword-wielding faeries – Birch, Berry, and Twig - were adept at their skill which they employed in a very unladylike manner. Indeed all the faeries of the Wood Clan were skilled in the art of ambush, and each had been named in honour of those that offered them shelter throughout the seasons. The other clan that dwelt under Mog's leadership was that of the plants that grew within the woods and forests. The Clan of the Thickets were proud of their skills. Prickle, Holly, Weed, Thistle, Burr and the omnipotent Thorn were skilled in the spear and those they carried now were of formidable sharpness.

Mog led the motley crew of weapon-laden faeries towards their target, with Peg following behind her carrying the well-honed skinning knife. The nineteen experts in their field were followed by thirty others who had brought with them their bows, swords, sticks, clubs and anything they could lay their hands on that would serve to cause as much physical damage as possible. All the Wood Clan had painted their wrinkly faces green by mashing up pine-leaves, the Thickets sported brown faces from the mud of the earth and the others had daubed themselves in any colour they could find amongst their surroundings. Most were red from the fleshy berries, but there were a few odd concoctions and some even had twigs sticking out of their hair, making them look quite foreboding in the gloaming.

The small army of faeries thus crept up to the clearing and watched as Oram surveyed her domain. Her long body eased its way across the undergrowth as she checked that her guards were in place before returning to her den for her slumber.

Mog signalled for the scouts, Acorn and Oakapple, to scour the area for guards or traps. They returned and reported their finds and Sap was dispatched to follow them and deal with the guards. Leaf, Elm and Ash were sent to disable the traps and lay some of their own to deal with as many escapees as possible from the battle that would soon take place. Time was of the essence and they needed to act before darkness fell completely upon the glade. As soon as Sap had returned, wiping his bloodied blade against his leggings, and the three had confirmed that traps had been set Mog raised her hands and silently asked the blessing of her forefathers before dispatching the members of her army to their respective places around the glade. A circular movement would slowly tighten around the glade, killing all that tried to break it or escape, until Oram would stand alone amidst the army of faeries. Her own escape route to the safety of her den would be made impassable by the careful positioning of club-bearing, berry-red-faced faeries.

As they all positioned themselves, Mog sent the reminder message to the faeries standing next to her that Oram's pelt – her victory prize - was to remain as untouched as possible and this instruction was repeated from one to the other until all had been reminded.

And thus the punishment of Oram's transgression began. The circle slowly closed and tooth and claw battled against arrow, sword and spear. The deadly snap of traps echoed as stoats were thwarted in their escape, followed by a squeal as a spear dealt its deadly thrust. It was important that the closing circle did not break, but here and there a faerie went to the aid of another before returning to their place in the circle. Thorn went about his lethal business with unstoppable precision, his spear flying through the air to pierce flesh with deadly accuracy. The ground around Oram became littered with dead and dying stoats. She squealed in defiance and anger and tried to return to the darkness of her underground den but was greeted by six anarchic grins upon six grotesquely reddened faces. She snarled at them but was met with a barrage of clubs upon her head and she soon retreated. She looked around for her sons but they had long escaped into the coming night and she cursed them under her breath for their cowardice, or was it perhaps a retreat of cunning in the hope that their mother would soon be relinquishing her claim to the title, albeit under unforeseen and quite fortuitous circumstances?

She knew at this point that she would die; she had been out-matched and out-witted but she was determined that she would take the leader of this well-trained army with her in her demise. She called out for Mog.

A silence befell the circle as Mog stepped forward into the glade. All were prepared for some sly trick from the defeated stoat and stood with weapons ready. They had all heard of the tricks stoats play on prospective victims and did not trust Oram one iota. Instinctively Oram rose to her back legs and began to dance a small jig. Mog laughed out loud. "You think you can catch me out with that?" she shouted. Several of the less experienced faeries began to sway as if hypnotised by the dance, but Mog was having none of it. She backed away slightly as she noticed Oram had cleverly moved slightly closer to her. This faerie was canny, but with nothing to lose Oram took a large step forward in preparation for a final lunge. At that moment the air was filled with flying arrows and spears as they sped towards her exposed breast and belly. They all found their mark perfectly and Oram fell to the ground, still twitching in her death throes. Mog grabbed Sap's knife, and ran forward and with sleight of hand cut the stoat's throat to make certain of Oram's death.

A great cheer arose from the circle of faeries as Peg handed Mog the skinning knife. As darkness finally enveloped the glade, the task was complete and Mog wrapped the skin around herself ignoring the fact that it still dripped with the warm blood of Oram. It trailed behind her as she proudly paraded around the circle and the cheers continued. There was a pool nearby which was obviously used by the stoats to drink from so she gave instructions for the carcass to be dropped into it. With satisfaction in her heart, this would surely ensure that they would have to move on to another part of the forest.

Upon the return to their own glade, the victorious army were welcomed with dancing and music. Mog sported Oram's bloody skin for the whole evening and reflected upon her victory with pride.

LXVI

As had been predicted, Brack died later that morning. The bell tolled his death and Grimfell fell silent. One by one, the ravens left and flew back across the marshes until only one remained which sat upon the tallest parapet and ruffled its feathers against the biting wind.

Brack's whole body had become twisted in a macabre pose and he uttered forth a loud moan as the last breath left his body. His mouth remained gaping upon his hideously deformed face as whatever flowed through him filled his veins to the point of them bursting through his skin. They were dark blue under his flesh and pulsated even after he had died. No-one wanted to go near him for they feared being infected by the pestilence that had raged through his body. Even his mother balked at touching her dead son, but her motherly instincts bade her see to her son's final preparations. No matter how she tried, she could not make his body return to a restful pose and she despaired at her failing efforts. She bathed his swollen face and closed his staring lifeless eyes gently and was about to close his mouth when she heard a gurgling sound coming from deep within his chest. Suddenly he sat up and issued forth a great sigh and as he did so, a dark grey mist flew from his mouth into the room. She jumped back in horror and watched the mist form a shape before her. It formed the head of a beast not unlike that which had appeared before them when the stranger had come forth upon them the afternoon before. Aubreda backed into the corner of the room and raised her hands above her head as the form flew towards her, with mouth open uttering forth a deep hissing sound. She screamed and the door flew open to admit the two servants who were waiting outside for their orders to enter and help her dress Brack for his final journey. Their faces became ashen when they saw the shape hovering over their mistress and they fled with arms held high in terror. They passed the priest on the steps and screamed of the devilment in Brack's chamber.

When the priest had been informed of Brack's passing he had become nervous. He did not wish to set foot back into the keep for some time after the unfortunate events of the day before, but his standing within the fortress deemed it necessary for him to attend the departed to give blessings on the body. The screaming servants and the sound of Aubreda screaming from within the chamber scared him. He faltered in his stride and was sorely tempted to run from whatever awaited him. However, the appearance of Modig by his side, who had also heard his wife's screaming and was on his way to investigate, gave the priest no choice but to continue on his way to Brack's bedside.

When they reached the doorway and saw the apparition tormenting Aubreda they both stopped dead in their tracks and were terrified. The priest saw the features and inwardly cringed at the familiarity to the thing that had caused him such distress the day before. Nothing would impel him to enter the room and he backed away sharply to the other side of the corridor. Modig, however, had been supping mead since he had arisen to the news that his youngest son had left the world. His body fuelled with this false bravado he entered into the room and challenged the spectre, which immediately turned its attentions to him and flew towards him with gaping maw. Modig watched as a ball of light rose from within the shape and exited the mouth, turning into a small ball of fire as it did so. He ducked as it flew passed him and hit the wall behind him, scattering into hundreds of tiny sparks that flew around the room. Then the apparition slowly disappeared and the room fell silent once more. Modig just stood there completely dumbfounded as to what had occurred and how close he had been to having his face burnt beyond recognition. Aubreda slowly rose from where she crouched in the corner and left the room as quickly as she could. She passed the priest who saw her face was as white as a sun-bleached piece of cloth.

He walked to the doorway and looked at Brack who was still sitting stiffly upright in his bed. As he gave him the required blessing, the priest decided at that moment that he would relinquish his post at Grimfell and leave at the first opportunity.

Brack's final resting place should have been amongst the others of his ancestors in the crypt beneath the small chapel, but under the strange circumstances surrounding his death and the accompanying demonic events, it was decided that his body would be burnt instead, and as soon as possible. The servants in the end, helped by Berowen who had no fear whatsoever of what had befallen him, prepared his corpse. Her lack of fear encouraged those selected to see to him to go about their sombre toil swiftly and neatly.

The bell continued to toll as the funeral procession made its way down the steps, through the gatehouse and barbican and out on to the marshes below Grimfell. It made its way to where Brack's body had been laid on the pyre; his body covered in a sheet so as not to display his contorted shape. As his widow, Berowen walked at the head of the procession followed by his parents and brother. The priest's final act as religious guide of Grimfell was to perform the service as quickly as possible. Berowen was handed a blazing torch and she moved slowly forward and touched the wood at the base of the pyre, which immediately burst into flames. She stepped back and watched as the flames consumed the thin cloth before they licked around Brack's deformed body. She could faintly see his skin begin to melt within the flames before she turned and made her way back to the barbican. She left his family to mourn for their departed kin, and with her own family she returned to the keep.

She had no idea where this left her. Now that her husband was dead was she to stay at Grimfell as his widow or would she be expected to leave? She approached Aelwulf and enquired of him his thoughts on the matter. He was not sure of course, but advised that as a widow she was not beholden to anyone to stay at Grimfell if she did not wish so to do. She could also return with them to Brundannon if that is what she wished. They were to be leaving on the morrow for the long trip home. This reminded Berowen about the conversation her father had had with Thurstan and she asked him for more detail.

"It is of no concern to you, daughter," was all that he would say.

This is what she had expected, but she persisted. However, Aelwulf would not tell her that Thurstan had warned him against taking his family back to Brundannon alone. He had listened with interest to Thurstan's theory about Modig perhaps wishing to dispatch the inhabitants of Brundannon in order for him to gain more land. But whilst Aelwulf had agreed with this possible outcome, there was no other choice but for them to return. They could not stay at Grimfell and there was nothing else that could be done. However, he knew his daughter well enough to know that she would not give up in her questioning until she had received an answer. He also could not lie to her. Carefully choosing his words, he explained that Thurstan had warned them that the road could be dangerous and that it may well be wise to send for an escort from Brundannon first. Berowen agreed immediately that Thurstan was right in recommending such an action. She was not pleased though, and frowned at her father, when Aelwulf continued by explaining that this was not an option as they had been away from Brundannon much too long already and to wait for a messenger to reach there and for an escort to return would take far too long.

"If you wish to travel with us Berowen, you are most welcome," said Aelwulf. "I am certain that your mother would welcome your return to Brundannon. We shall take to the road at first light."

"I am not happy with your leaving tomorrow without escort, father, but understand that you cannot dally too long away from home," she replied.

"But you will not be travelling with us," said Aelwulf with a resigned note to his voice.

"I cannot, father. I shall not remain here though. There is another path that I am destined to follow and I shall be taking that on the morrow also."

Aelwulf nodded. He knew that his daughter would follow Thurstan. There was a connection between the two that he had noticed growing whilst on the journey to Grimfell and although he knew it was not born out of love, he recognised an affinity between them both.

"As you wish daughter," he said. "I hope your road leads you safely to your destination, wherever that may be."

Berowen remained outside as her family disappeared into the great hall. Eventually the members of Brack's family passed her solemnly on their way to their own chambers.

Once certain that she was alone, Odi soared down from where he had watched the proceedings from his perch high up on the parapet. He cocked his head from side to side and uttered a deep sound from his throat in welcome. She stroked his head and smiled at him.

"It seems that you and I, dear Odi, are to embark upon a journey into the unknown," she said softly. He bobbed his head up and down and flapped his wings.

The woman and her raven gazed out upon the marshes below them.

LXVII

The wind finally faded with the sun and Berowen spent that evening preparing for her journey. She would leave at the same time as her family and would say her farewells once they were all outside the barbican. It would be hard to bid them goodbye, but it was a time that all knew would come.

She slept well that night; somehow a heavy burden had been lifted from her heart and she found herself looking forward to the days ahead. She would be travelling into the unknown but knew that with Thurstan and Odi with her that it would be filled with companionship.

She awoke just before dawn, her inner self gently rousing her from her slumber. For the first time in days she jumped eagerly from her bed and dressed herself in the icy cold room. Gathering the possessions she would take with her, she left her chamber for the last time and made her way down the corridor, through the great hall and out into the fresh cold morning air. She crept into the stables and saddled her horse as quietly as she could for she did not wish to awaken Mouse, whom she knew would be fast asleep somewhere amongst the piles of hay. She whispered goodbye to him just in case her voice would enter into his dreams and walked her horse slowly out of the stables and on downwards towards the gatehouse.

The sentry was dozing as she passed through, but he awoke with a start and challenged her. "Be quiet oaf, and go back to sleep," she said curtly. Then on towards the barbican where a similar event occurred only this time she demanded the guards to lower the drawbridge.

Once outside she mounted her horse and guided her down the path where, when at a safe distance by the signpost, she stopped and awaited the arrival of her family. A short while later the drawbridge lowered again and she watched as they rode down towards her.

The tears flowed as they said their farewells. She hugged and kissed them all goodbye and watched as they faded into the distance.

Then she turned her horse onwards and followed the path that she and Thurstan had taken days before. She instinctively knew that this was the route that Felagin and he would have taken. Once her family had disappeared from view, Odi reappeared and flew overhead and they made their way quietly along the road. After a short while the silence became overwhelming and Berowen started to hum to herself. It lifted her spirits and she spurred her horse into a canter. She had been riding for about two hours when she came across a bend in the road. There was a path to the left of her and to the right, and for a moment she was not sure which to take. Odi, however, seemed to know exactly where to go and took the left path.

They had not gone far before Berowen noticed two figures sitting astride their horses on the road. She became wary – it would be a strange thing indeed to find two strangers on this road at this time of the year. She reined her horse to a halt and observed the figures from a distance. Odi however continued on his way. She trusted the raven and spurred her horse forward again. As she became closer to the two travellers she recognised Thurstan's mare and sighed with relief. The other must be Felagin, although he did not look the same as when he had entered the hall two days before. This time his tall figure was shrouded in a grey cloak and cowl. He sat astride his horse with his arms tucked into opposite sleeves to keep them warm. Thurstan spoke first, "You have made good time Berowen. It is good to see you."

She was somewhat bemused but smiled in return. Once again he had been expecting her, although she had said nothing of her plan to him. She stared at Felagin. His face was different. He had dark bronze skin with close cut greying hair beneath his cowl. Upon his chin he had a short, stubbly, greying beard, but it was his eyes that startled her. They had stark white irises with a deep yellow pupil and they stared at her from within the shadow of the cowl. "What did you say?" he asked in a deep whisper.

Startled, she stuttered, "I did not say anything."

"Oh but you were thinking it. My dear, do you not understand that whatever you think can speak volumes to those that can hear such thoughts? You have to curb your thoughts for they can be dangerous." His tone changed from an almost menacing whisper to one of curt instruction.

She did not reply.

"You asked yourself whether I could help you."

In truth this is exactly what Berowen had briefly thought when she had seen Felagin. He was clearly a sorcerer of great supremacy and whilst she knew nothing of the exact details of his connection with Thurstan, he would seem to be someone who might be able to help her control whatever power seemed to be growing within her day by day. But, nevertheless, she was completely surprised with the ease and complete accuracy that he had displayed at reading her thoughts. She would have to exercise caution in her mind, for she would not wish to divulge anything that she wished to keep to herself.

"I cannot deny, sir, that you speak the truth, although it was but a fleeting thought. Forgive me, for I did not wish to offend." Her cheeks reddened as she spoke, and he was quick to notice her honest embarrassment.

He laughed loudly. As he did so, it seemed to evoke an even more sinister air to his appearance – those menacing looking eyes did not match well with mirth.

"I am not offended," he said calmly once his amusement had waned. "In fact I should look upon it as flattery that you would think that I may be able to help you, and methinks it should be I who should blush."

His mood all at once changed and Berowen noticed the corners of his mouth rise slightly in the corners. She was inwardly relieved that she had not offended the man before her. Still she did not know quite what to make of him.

Felagin suddenly called out to Odi in greeting, with a remarkable impression of the bird's own call. The large black bird flapped around his head and chattered with him enthusiastically. It brought to Berowen's mind the terrifying creature that had accompanied the tall man only one day before when he had entered uninvited into the hall to seek out Thurstan.

"And what of your travelling companion?" she tentatively asked of him. "Does he not travel with you today?" In some ways she dreaded the answer, for she did not really wish to see the ghastly apparition appear again.

"Beodin takes many forms – he shifts his shape to whatever I deem to be most appropriate for the occasion. However, there are those times when he takes it upon himself to transform in whatever way he chooses. The visit to the hall was one of those such occasions," replied Felagin with a wry smile upon his lips.

"Shifts his shape?" asked Berowen. She thought about it for a moment and the meeting with the strange fellow who had confused her with riddles a couple of days before came to mind. She glanced at Thurstan who raised his eyebrows and half-smiled at her.

"You are thinking again, Berowen," said Felagin. "Riddles? What riddles? Ah those riddles," he continued. "Does one at last make sense to you?"

"I..I think so," answered Berowen. "Odi....?"

"Come, come girl. I did not think you slow in mind," goaded Felagin. He tutted and sighed. He threw back his head and laughed, his cowl slipping to his shoulders as he did so. As suddenly as he had laughed, he stopped and stared at her, his eyes narrowing. "Did you honestly think that a creature such as a raven would – as if from nowhere – come upon you and give up of itself to be your pet?" He urged his horse forward and walked it around her as she sat upon her own mount. "A pet? A raven does not make itself a pet to anyone, girl. It is a creature of the skies, its intelligence and power much too great for someone as lowly as you."

Berowen softly spoke; she was uncomfortable with the wizard's closeness and his words. "I don't understand."

"Then you are not worthy of my time, child. Be off with you, back to your Brundannon and your soft, pampered world," Felagin sneered. "Thurstan, we go. We have wasted enough time here with people with whom we have no concern."

He pulled his cowl up around his head once more, and urged his mount forward. Thurstan, however, did not follow. "You defy me?" Felagin called back without turning or halting his horse.

"You should help her," Thurstan called back. "Do not do to her what you did to my mother."

Berowen looked up at Thurstan's words, the hot tears welling in her eyes at her abrupt dismissal. Felagin stopped his horse. "What do you mean?"

"You know what I mean, Felagin. Do not try to extricate yourself from the facts."

"I did nothing to your mother, boy, nothing."

"Exactly. That is my point, Felagin. You did nothing. She came to you for help and you dismissed her, just as you are dismissing Berowen."

"You do not know what you are talking about, Thurstan. You were only a few weeks old when your mother died. How could you possibly know anything of what may or may not have transpired between your mother and me? You have been listening to gossip I fear. And you know that gossip is the worst enemy of facts."

"It depends from whose mouth the gossip comes, Felagin."

Felagin turned his horse back towards Thurstan and coaxed it to a halt when beside his apprentice.

"And what did you learn from this gossip? Pray do tell," Felagin asked his apprentice.

"You turned her away, Felagin, when she came to you for guidance. She knew her power was growing within her and she needed tuition on how she could channel it safely. You were her brother's – the king's – magician, healer, seer. You should not have cast her out as you did. I was to be a warrior in my uncle's garrison. I trained hard with the sword. And here I am now, your apprentice. Why is that Felagin? Out of guilt on your part?"

"So that is what this is all about, eh? I took you away from your war games did I? And you are stamping your foot now, boy?" Felagin took a deep breath. Of course he wasn't stamping his foot. That was not fair. The boy had been trained to take his place at his uncle's side. But then it was realised that he had inherited his mother's power and his uncle could not lose him the way that he had lost his sister. Thurstan was given to Felagin to tutor and his days with the sword were over.

"No, I did not cast her out, Thurstan. She refused to listen to my guidance. She left of her own accord to chase her heart. It was her heart and not her head that cast her out. An affair of the heart, Thurstan. Your mother let that get in the way of her gift. Your father was her downfall, not me. And your uncle knew that and let her go."

Thurstan bristled from these words. "My uncle?"

"Your uncle saw a good marriage, Thurstan. He let her go to her union, knowing that her power was raw. I do not think he realised how powerful she was. I tried to warn him. You may think I do not tell the truth and that I am attempting to transfer blame. But it is true that I warned him many times as his confidante that it would ruin her. But he would not listen. When she returned she was turned. She was insane, out of her mind with voices in her head, she could not be rescued. I tried Thurstan. I really tried to help her then, to bring her back to this world, but she was gone. Lost. Her power had taken hold of her in the darkest way."

Thurstan raised his face to the skies and swallowed hard to stop the tears of anger, and hurt, from erupting from his eyes. "And what of my father?"

"He died when your mother was carrying you. Nobody would dare question her word when she said he died from an illness that saw him bedridden for weeks, out of sight of anyone. She would let no-one near him on his death-bed. It was only after he had gone did she allow any to go to him. They thought she was heartbroken at his illness and his leaving her, and let her be. Some say it was she who gave him poison, but this could not be proven."

"And what do you think, Felagin? Do you think as others do that my own mother murdered my father?"

Felagin balked at answering this question. He had known this conversation would raise itself at some point, but he had not reckoned on it being here, now in the middle of a road in a place far away from his own home. The accusations from his apprentice had angered him at first, but telling Thurstan about the real reason his mother had left his tutorage had touched a deeply hidden soft spot within him. He could see how it was destroying his apprentice, and he deserved an answer. So what would it be? Truth or a lie?

"I do not think your mother killed your father, Thurstan. But I think that the darkness within her that had overwhelmed her may have done."

Thurstan coaxed his horse into a walk and man and beast strode away a short distance.

Berowen watched Felagin slump slightly in his saddle; no longer did he look like a powerful wizard, but just a spent old man, and she suddenly felt sorry for him. Without a word to him as she passed, she walked her horse to where Thurstan had pulled up his own. She laid her left hand gently on his right arm and he in turn laid his left hand on hers and gently squeezed it. She looked at the scarred, tanned skin that lay against her pale hand and she felt as one with it; she was somehow part of him and she felt the pain that flowed through his heart as if it were her own.

After a few minutes he softly spoke. "We are cursed you know, you and I. We are cursed with something that can wreak havoc within us with not a speck of compassion. We have to learn to control it or it will take us where it wants to go regardless of our own feelings and our own rights. The fate of my parents has proven that."

"I am sorry about your mother and father, Thurstan."

"If it cannot have us then it will put an end to us, for the only love we are to be allowed is that of our parents and our siblings. It does not permit any other to intrude upon its rule over of us. Do you not miss that?"

"I do not, for I do not think I have ever known any other."

He turned towards her and his eyes looked into hers. "Then you are lucky, Berowen, and we shall speak no more of it. Come, let us rejoin Felagin for I have an apology to offer him."

Berowen assumed that her imminent departure from his company had caused the tear in her heart at his last words. "We shall not, my friend, because I am now to leave and it is doubtful that we shall meet again in this world. I bid you good fortune and safe travels, and give you my thanks again for your assistance on the recent journey."

She guided her horse back towards the road and walked her horse on towards Grimfell. As she passed Felagin she sat upright in her saddle and gave not one glance to him as she rode by. She held up her hand and Odi appeared over her. She smiled at the bird and then tears rolled down her cheeks at her parting with Thurstan.

Felagin had regained his composure by the time Thurstan returned to him.

"I offer you my apology, Felagin," said Thurstan with a slight nod of his head in his tutor's direction.

The wizard bowed his head and replied, "And I offer mine, Thurstan. I should have told you many years ago, but could not find the right time or the right words."

"We shall say no more about it. Let us continue on our journey. There is a task ahead that I would welcome completed as soon as possible," replied Thurstan and with one more glance at the departing Berowen, he urged his horse forward in the opposite direction.

"You are well aware of the unwritten and unspoken rules, Thurstan. What is it that you want from me?" asked Felagin.

"To teach. To guide. To help a friend, Felagin, that is all I had hoped," was the response.

"A friend? So be it. Let us continue on the teaching of shape shifters," Felagin said, a wry smile creasing the corner of his mouth. He shut his eyes and took a deep breath.

Berowen was thinking hard of what to do next. If she hurried she may well be able to catch up with her family on their way back to Brundannon, so she urged her mount into a canter to follow them. All was well until suddenly her horse cantered round in an arc and she found herself being carried back the way she had just came. She could not coax the horse into stopping, walking or anything she wanted. It continued on its mission until she finally arrived back at Felagin's side.

He bowed his head at her arrival, "The power of thought, Berowen. It is strong is it not?" he asked.

"You made my horse return?" she asked, knowing full well that that was indeed the case. "Why? Are you to berate me more?"

"Berate? No child. Ah, but it does seem as if you have a dim view of me."

"Is that not to be expected?"

"Come, Berowen. Let us start again shall we? Thurstan has scolded me for banishing you as I did and I have been reminded that you seek my aid. Hence we shall continue our lesson shape shifting."

"Odi is a shape shifter I assume."

"Ah yes, Berowen at last you understand," sighed Felagin.

"It was how, when and why that I do not understand, Felagin."

"And there is not an easy answer to give, only that you summoned it, or rather something inside you called it forth."

"The once dormant seed that is now growing within me like a child, but one that will not be born to the outside world to continue to flourish. Something that will grow to its adult form within me and control me more and more until it has me forever in its grip. And it tempts with toys like shape shifters does it? It aims to soothe the capture of my soul with them, is that it?"
"Hmmm, something like that if you wish to look at it in such a demonic way," responded Felagin.

"How can I not after the recent story you told?"

"Odi is not a pet and is not a toy, but is a companion, an ally and a protector. He can go places where you cannot, and he can use its own senses where you have none. He can guard you against harm and keep you company on many a long journey that you make on your own. He will fight with you, for you, and he will never desert you. He and is other forms will die only when you die."

"Other forms? Odi would not be a shape shifter if he didn't have at least one other form would he?" asked Felagin with an uncharacteristic wink.

"But how do they change forms? Do they do it on their own or do I have to ask them?"

"Odi is the main form in your case, as he was the first to show himself, and he will be the most powerful. He will have three other forms though." At this statement, Berowen wondered what Odi's three would be and was about to ask Felagin how to make them appear, but changed her mind. Felagin was beginning to fidget in his saddle and his words were being spoken in more of an irritated manner the more she asked him questions. Just one more and she would be quiet on the subject.

"But, if I may be so bold as to enquire, what is Beodin's original form?" As the question left her lips she realised that it could well be that the form that had already shown itself *was* the true one.

Felagin fiddled in the pouch that dangled from the belt around his waist and pulled out a tiny mouse.

"A mouse!?" she exclaimed. She didn't know whether to laugh or take it seriously.

"Not very foreboding a creature is he?" stated Felagin somewhat flatly. "But at least I always know of his whereabouts when he is but a mouse; it is when he shifts to something greater that he can sometimes become somewhat tiresome. He is ancient you see, and possesses as obstinate and cantankerous a nature as any should be allowed to own at such an age. And no matter to what extent it irritates, I have to show a reasonable amount of respect. However, I do have to admit that I am becoming nervous as to his possible behaviour when we reach our destination. He, and the person who is awaiting our visit..." Here Felagin broke off to ponder on his last statement. He was presuming that this person's awareness of such things remained as sensitive as it used to be, but there was always a chance that her foresight may have dwindled with age. This was something that he had not thought of previously and now that he had, he became a little unsettled. She was not one to catch unawares; her testiness was quite renowned. He was just going to have to hope that she was still powerful in that gift and was indeed expecting them.

Felagin glanced at Berowen, who sat astride her horse with a patient look upon her face waiting for him to finish his sentence. Felagin stroked his chin thoughtfully before continuing. "Hmmm where was I? Ah yes. I was explaining - they have a mutual animosity towards each other, and although such meetings have been few, the outcomes of all have been etched forever in my mind for their ferocity."

"Who is this person who holds such sway over Beodin? Surely they must be foolhardy to tackle such a being as he?" enquired Berowen.

"Foolhardy? Most definitely not that my lady," replied Felagin. "In fact I would wager that it is Beodin who could be accused of being that. We do, after all, speak of Mildthryth and she endures his impudence purely because he is part of me. And she would not dare cross one such as me for she knows that she would suffer such dire consequence."

"Mildthryth? That is her name, this woman we are on our way to meet? Who is she and for what purpose is our visit?"

"Hmm 'tis Thurstan's purpose, but although he made obvious his wish to fulfil this on his own I have sought him out in order to offer my aid, for I am certain that he shall need it."

Berowen looked across at Thurstan, who had remained silent since her arrival back to Felagin. He clearly possessed no wish to break this silence, for he sat quite still in his saddle and stared ahead as if in some deep contemplation.

Looking back towards Felagin it was clear that he was waiting for Thurstan to reply and sat tight-lipped with his strange gaze firmly fixed upon the other.

"Thurstan?" urged Berowen in search of her answer.

He took a deep breath and turned his head slowly to face her. In almost a whisper he uttered three words, "To kill her."

Her eyes widened in disbelief at this information and she looked from one man to the other in the hope that either would elaborate further on this stark statement. No further comment came. She felt uncomfortable of her position amongst them both. "So I am to become an assassin?"

"No-one asked you to come. And no-one is asking you to travel further in our company," snapped Thurstan.

Berowen felt a tear prickle the corner of her right eye at the curtness and coldness of his response. It was such a sudden and dramatic change since their private moment together only a short while before. And she had never seen him so cold before - it was so unlike him, and the sudden burst of anger that had so recently emanated from him shocked her so much that she felt that their friendship had suddenly turned to a betrayal. It was like the time she had been gently stroking a kitten many years before and it had suddenly turned on her with tooth and claw, its tiny sweet delicate face contorted with angry spitting and hissing. She had felt so hurt that it had scorned her tender affection that she had burst into tears. This was what she felt now – hurt.

"Assassin is perhaps not quite the right word to describe Thurstan's role, my lady," added Felagin. "Or yours even if you decide to stay with us and accompany us further. Think of it more as a disposal of something dangerous. Or even as a healer, if you will, curing a sickness perhaps, ridding this world of something that fills it with disease and evil. I do cringe at the word 'assassin' for it does give the impression of coin crossing the palm of a gloved hand while the other grasps a dagger held in stealth."

"But if she is that powerful will she not know that we are travelling toward her with ill-intent? Surely she will be prepared for such treachery?"

"This is true, my lady. You are indeed sharp as a blade in your observation," replied Felagin eyeing her slowly with a stare that made Berowen feel utterly wretched and uncomfortable. She turned her face away from his and pulled the hood of her cloak more closely to her head. "However," he continued, "Thurstan has made the necessary protection against such an observation of that kind. She will know we are coming, but she will think it on other business. She will be under the impression that we seek her help and that will flatter her ego greatly, for she does possess a great desire to be depended upon. It enriches her life to wallow in such reliance for some unaccountable reason."

Berowen flinched when she realised that her next thought would be heard by Felagin, and she awaited his caustic reply. She did not have to wait long and he responded with a loud guffaw. "Kindly little old lady, eh?" he spluttered. "You think that perhaps she could be just a kind old lady who likes to help those in need? You obviously have no knowledge of Mildthryth, and nor should you I must admit, if I am to be perfectly truthful."

"Then perhaps you would care to explain," responded Berowen, her body beginning to stiffen with irritation at the scorn showered down upon her from Felagin. "Instead of making fun of any comment I make in error of knowing the truth – as you would tell it."

"Aha, she bristles," Felagin declared before leaning forward in his saddle and grabbing the reins of her horse, pulling her closer towards him. "The truth – as I would tell it you say. Is that rather than the truth as it is? You are accusing me, Felagin, of distorting the truth now are you, my dear? Now, I do not imagine that it would be the best thing to do would it?"

"I cannot truthfully declare whether it would or would not be, sire. For – up until a short while ago, although I knew that you were somehow connected with Thurstan, I did not know in what way you were linked with him or why, for no-one had – until recently – had the courtesy to explain such to me. I know that you are practiced at deceit for you present yourself before me now in a much darker way than you did at the doors of the great hall when we first met. You surely must understand then, that my view of anything you may do or say will be influenced by this marked change in your demeanour."

"Hmmm so icy cool, I feel that if you touched me the blood in my veins would freeze," he replied. "I like you," he added as he tossed her reins from his grip and sat straight in his saddle again. He then addressed Thurstan, who was again staring into the middle distance, and quite loudly as if to snap the other out of his daydreaming, said, "Shall we move on?"

Berowen cleared her throat, still somewhat unnerved by the jumping from one mood to the other of Felagin, and said, "Excuse me, both, but I would still welcome an explanation of why this woman is to meet her end. And before I am told once again that it was my choice to be here," she continued before Thurstan had the chance to interject, "I shall remind you that I have no idea why I was drawn to arrive amongst you both, even though it is clearly evident that I was expected, nor why I was so rudely dismissed and then forcibly gathered back into your company."

"You are here because you requested help. You are here because they will be coming. Grimfell will burn, I have said as much before," replied Felagin sombrely.

With a glazed look in her eyes, Berowen recalled her dream of a few nights before, "I have dreamt of such. I awoke to the stench of fire and escaped as flames enveloped Grimfell, but it was just a dream and cannot mean that it will come true."

"Dreams not come true? They can and do to those who have the will," replied Felagin enigmatically. "I have spoken of it and you have seen it....they will come."

"Please do me the honour of not speaking in riddles, Felagin. I would have you tell me exactly what is occurring here, that is if Thurstan will not."

"When Modig's father died, Modig sought out Mildthryth to make a pact with her. If she kept the creatures at bay to enable Modig to make his expansion of property and land easier then she would be left alone to continue with her unsavoury practices."

"What creatures? And what practices? You are confusing me Felagin."

"Those that live within the cave system in the hills that border Grimfell on the edge of the marshes. You must have noticed those hills for they are imposing on the horizon."

"Yes but what creatures are they that you speak of?"

"I am sure you can guess about what creatures I am referring if you recall the name of the hills beneath which they were once known to dwell."

"You forget, Felagin, that I have no knowledge of these parts, or the names of any landmark around here other than those I have recently travelled near. So please do not play with words, for they are lost on me."

"DO NOT PLAY WITH WORDS?!" shouted Felagin. "Do not taunt me my lady." But after a pause he added more gently, "But what you say is no doubt to be taken in consideration. I do indeed forget that you are not a native to these parts and that you are not a seasoned traveller. It is only the likes of me and Thurstan here, and of course that Kipp fellow, that are apt to wander the land and widen our knowledge of other places."

"That sounds like an accusation Felagin," bristled Berowen. "Am I inferior because I have spent most of my life in one place, with no need to travel far from the safety and comfort of its walls?"

"Indeed no, my lady. I was not meaning to suggest that you are in some way lacking due to the accident of your birth. In truth, there are not many folks who do wander too far from the boundaries of their villages. But there are some whose life is mapped out before them and their destiny is to follow whatever path opens, to places they never knew existed, and would never have seen if that seed of adventure had not been sown within them whilst still in their mother's womb."

"You are rambling, my friend," interrupted Thurstan quietly, slowly waking from his daydreaming. "Berowen asks a very good question and it seems only fair that she is given an answer without any further ado or incessant ranting from you."

Felagin glared at his companion and grunted under his breath. "And you sir, are a trifle testy," he snapped.

"Under the circumstances Felagin, my dear friend, is that not surprising?" replied Thurstan. Turning to look at Berowen, he continued, "Berowen, Mildthryth is an old hag of the most undesirable sort. She has, for a long time, been the subject of many a story told of missing travellers and even villagers from around these parts. It is thought that she kills them and some say that she even eats them, but that is perhaps one of those gruesome additions that are added purely to dissuade folks from straying too far off the known path. However, it is well chronicled amongst those who know such things, that she did indeed make a pact with Modig to keep the large-wings at bay, just as Felagin described briefly earlier. The only way to break that pact and to release those that are held captive below the hills is to kill her."

"But what creatures?" exclaimed Berowen, her patience now gone on the wind.

"If you recall I mentioned to your father that we would travel through the forest and then down towards the Dragon Hills....."

"Dragons?" exclaimed Berowen. "Surely you are not telling me that dragons dwell under the hills near Grimfell?"

"I had doubted it myself, until the woman Lin told me something the other night about the land Eastward and how the crops were failing. Their position near the hills aroused my suspicions that perhaps there was some truth in the tales."

"But why release such beasts? They are surely best left where they are?"

"The dragons here lived in harmony with the people; they guarded the borders against marauders and evil-doers. It was Modig's desire for power that ceased that alliance between man and the great beasts. Modig will now pay for his greed and the land, here at least, shall return to normal. And not before time, see what has occurred since they have been gone. The red-beards for example are spreading across the land again, for what reason it is still to be told."

"But if what Felagin says is true, and my dream was indeed a forewarning of the fate of Grimfell, what of my 'Mouse', and Cynfrid and Wirt. And the other innocents? How are they to be warned? How will they survive? Surely they are not to perish? Why was it me alone that was drawn away? You cannot let them perish!" cried Berowen, a feeling of panic overwhelming her at the thought of those she spoke of being sacrificed in such a heartless way.

Felagin interrupted in a gruff tone, "Bah. You are too sensitive for others of your race. You will never progress if you are to think of your kind in such a sympathetic manner."

"Then perhaps, sir, I wish not to progress. Innocents should be protected not treated as mindless creatures that were in the wrong place at the wrong time. As far as I am aware, from my short stay at Grimfell, there are many more innocents than guilty residing there," stated Berowen. "You two should leave to go about your secretive business, but you shall journey without me for I am to return to Grimfell and counsel those who need to be warned."

"And warn those who are guilty also, my lady? I think not. Humans have loose tongues and the warning may well reach an ear of one who should remain deaf to such news."

"And so I am now to become a prisoner too?"

"Felagin, will you be quiet!" shouted Thurstan who then beckoned Berowen to follow him to an adequate distance away from Felagin's earshot. "He cannot hear us or read your mind from here," he said as he reined his horse to a halt. "It has always irritated him that his ability is not as strong as Mildthryth's in this matter. I have to apologise for the loss of any social skills he may have had many years ago. He is apt to now speak his mind regardless of what affect it may have on those to whom he speaks it. In short he is a man of many talents, but the intricacies of diplomacy have been lost to him."

"How *old* is he?"

"That is a question to which I have no answer. I am at a loss to his age and no-one I have asked knows the answer either. He has been a member of my family's household for generations, that I can tell you. He has spoken of events that have taken place in this world that have long drifted into epic tales. I have often known him to correct facts in a manner that reflects firsthand knowledge, so that I have been left in no doubt that he has spoken the truth, as he saw it, when he was present at the event in question."

"But what did he mean when he said that you could not do it alone?"

"As you heard, I was chosen as his apprentice when I was a young boy. Even one as he cannot dwell upon this earth forever, and he made it known to my uncle that he wished to train another. You know the story now of how I came to be here and that I had no wish to be. This is my test. This is to see if I have learnt well and am able to take over his role. However, Mildthryth is by all accounts very powerful and it would seem that Felagin does not have total trust in his teachings for he has searched me out – presumably to make certain that if I fail the task is carried out as is necessary. He has a certain amount of cause for concern, I must admit, after my error at the standing stones. I have no real wish to use my skills and would much rather have been allowed to make my own way in life."

"And if you fail? You will be free from the apprenticeship?"

Thurstan smirked. "Aye, Berowen. If I fail then I shall certainly be released from such an arrangement, but I shall have not a care, for it will mean that I shall be dead anyway."

Berowen winced at her own indelicacy and she inwardly kicked herself for her stupidity in asking such a question. She was embarrassed by her error and did not quite know what to say to remedy the indiscretion.

"It is of no matter, Berowen," offered Thurstan on seeing her discomfort. "It was a natural question to ask and you were not really to know the truth behind the answer. But we must make haste, for Arra will have carried out her instruction by now and the bewitchment will not linger for long."

"Arra?"

"My companion, Berowen. I am sure that it does not really surprise you to hear that I too have one?"

Berowen shook her head, "No, of course not. It would be clearly obvious that you should, although you have kept her existence well hidden. As, indeed, you have your whole identity."

"And you are angered by that?"

"Oh no, angered is not the word. I am sorry that your life has been planned for you as it has. In a way I suppose that I empathise with you, for my own path was chosen as you know, but yours holds a far greater danger than mine ever did. I am sorry, Thurstan, that your burden is so great, but know that I shall aid you in any way that I can in your task to ensure your life continues after your mission is completed."

Thurstan bowed his head in thanks but remained silent. Berowen knew that there was probably nothing whatsoever that she could do to help, but she was determined to show that she would try and that his friendship was too dear to her for her to allow it to cease in such a way. "So," she added cheerily. "What form has your companion taken to carry out its bewitchment?"

"A goose – Mildthryth is known to have a great fondness for fowl."

After being presented with the sight of Felagin's mouse, Berowen had half-expected to hear that Thurstan's companion would be taking the shape of a frog or some such creature, but a goose was the last thing she would have thought of. But she took the announcement in her stride and asked, "A fondness? Hopefully not as an ingredient for the pot – is that not a bit risky to send such a bird?"

Thurstan laughed, "You have a natural aptitude for raising my spirits Berowen. For the pot, indeed. Well I surely hope not for that would not do!   Arra would be most upset at such an occurrence and would not speak to me for days."

Berowen smiled uncertainly at the man before her – the man who may by the end of the day's events not be one of this world.

Totally misinterpreting the sadness on her face, Thurstan added, "You will have the opportunity to warn those you wish – the dragons have been asleep for many years and it will take them time to rouse themselves before emerging from their prison. I am sure that Odi can take Cynefrid a message, for he is the best person to alert in the first instance. He is one of the elders and I know that he can be trusted to do as you bid."

And waving at Felagin, he shouted, "Come we must begin our task."

They had travelled mostly in silence until Berowen had to ask the question that had been burning on her mind. "How do you train your companion to change its shape?"

Felagin spoke first. "I have been thinking on that since it first popped into your mind about an hour ago. Or rather I have been thinking on how to phrase the answer so as not to offend you."

Berowen shot him a glance with narrowed eyes.

"Oh, you damn me do you?" enquired Felagin in response to the thought that ran through her mind as she did so.

"Just answer her, Felagin and be done with it," implored Thurstan. "Pray do not begin to taunt her again."

"Well, if she wants me to help her, then she has to learn to think quietly," answered Felagin.

"Think quietly?   And how am I supposed to achieve such a nonsensical thing?" asked Berowen curtly.

"Bah. Too long to go into here and now, girl," replied the old man impatiently. "However, to answer your first question. What makes you think that it does not know how to already?"

"I have never witnessed such," replied Berowen suddenly feeling silly that Odi had perhaps been changing his shape behind her back ever since she had first come into contact with him and that she had not realised such a thing.

"You are so inept at this, child. You have never thought to ask him?"

Her hackles rising yet again at this old man's lack of pleasantries, Berowen replied, "Why would I ask such a thing? It was not until today that I learnt that such things occurred. I may be inept, but these things are new to me. Your insults are ill-founded, sir."

"You did not think that it odd that this bird of the day-sky flies in the dark? You did not think to question how such a thing could be? Bah, inept is only too well-founded a word. Ask him. Ask him now, to show you how he manages to fly in the dark without bumping into something and breaking his neck."

Deeply hurt and angry with herself that such an obvious thing had escaped her, Berowen silently called out to Odi. He appeared ahead of them, flying low to the ground as he approached before landing on the grass next to her. She asked him the question and in a shimmer of light a moth appeared where the raven had previously been. Forgetting her anger and embarrassment, a gasp of girlish delight came forth from her lips.

Thurstan explained, "All companions can change into three different creatures apart from their original form. Each companion has a selection of their own. It would be wise, Berowen, to learn Odi's for you may depend on one of them in the future for different instances you may find yourself in. But for now you should return Odi to his original form and keep the discovery of others for another time. They should not all be shared with others, not even friends. You know two of Felagin's and you know one of mine and it should be left at that."

Berowen nodded and requested Odi to return to his original form. Another shimmer of light and the black bird called and lifted into the air, before flying off ahead of the group once more.

LXVIII

Eventually they turned off the well-worn path and followed a track through a small copse. The atmosphere around them changed; it became close and, in a way, sickly sweet. The further they ventured, the sparser the trees became until eventually they came across a clearing with one solitary giant oak tree planted firmly in the centre of it. They were not yet close enough to see any real detail but the area around it was completely devoid of life; even the grass that was left was brown and dried as if choked of water and sunlight despite the lack of tree cover and complete access to the sky above. The only movement they could see from their position was the thick grey smoke that puffed its way upwards from mid-way up the trunk. Something was being cooked and Berowen cringed at the thought of what it may be.

As they approached the wide gnarled trunk Berowen thought that she could make out faces etched into the bark. They seemed to contort and stretch with expressions of sorrow, fear, and anger. Strung from the boughs were chimes that tinkled in the breeze, bones that cracked and clattered against each other, and trinkets that caught whatever sunlight they could and shone their sumptuous colours for all to see. The pathway along which they trod was lined either side with skulls that stared with empty eye sockets as they passed.

However, Thurstan was correct in his statement that whoever dwelt there was fond of geese. Ahead of them, in their path, was a gaggle of around twenty such birds, all squealing, barking and screaming at each other in their quest for space and food. If one of these birds was indeed Thurstan's companion, then it was well disguised amongst this gathering of pure white, big, aggressive and beautiful fowl.

Felagin chuckled as he led the way, which under the circumstances that surrounded their visit, Berowen felt was distinctly unwarranted. "If you think that Cynfrid possesses oddities in vials, you will be quite surprised at what lays ahead within the giant trunk of this old man of the forest. His roots are sunken deep into the ground and he has stood on this spot since the fruit of his mother brought forth his life where it fell many centuries ago. She has long passed, as have his brothers and sisters, all victims to the desire from humans that wanted their wood for warmth and shelter."

"No more is it so, but in the past many have made their home in the comfort of his shade or the shelter of his once leafy boughs. There was only one who dared make their home within his wisened frame and there she has remained since she opened his belly with a lightning bolt so strong that it burnt all around where it struck the earth and bore deep into the ground. Hence he stands alone now on this barren hillock adorned with her trinkets and those she has stolen from her hapless victims. His boughs no longer bear fruit and barely manage a few diseased leaves each year. But as long as she dwells within his body she keeps him alive."

"The bark seems to move with a life of its own," observed Berowen.

"With lives long lost you should really say. You are seeing the faces of those who lost their way and wandered – or were enticed – into the waiting arms of Mildthryth. Remember, Berowen that although not all can read the thoughts of others, Mildthryth can so if you must think of anything be sure that it is of nothing that will rouse her suspicions or give her warning. She may have had her senses dulled by Arra, but precaution is always a wise stance to take. Speak not unless you are spoken to and avert your eyes from her face unless invited to utter forth. She has no patience for prying eyes for she is sensitive to the punishment that the ravages of time have meted out upon her features. And please remember to take whatever she offers, no matter how distasteful it may seem, for she is easily offended."

"But what does that matter under the circumstances?" enquired Berowen with a slight tone of sarcasm.

"Lull the prey into a false sense of security, my dear, of course. To catch it off guard using the pretence of awe and respect, you know. Works every time in my experience," he answered slyly with a quick wink from his starkly cold left eye.

"But how do we pass her guardians? Those birds do not appear to be welcoming."

"No need to worry about them," answered Felagin with another wink, this time directed at Thurstan. "They will disperse soon enough methinks. They may make good guardians, but they still have their own self-preservation at heart. You are about to witness Thurstan's companion's second alias, my dear. That, if nothing else, makes us equal at two each, and fairness is, after all, a must for most."

Berowen did not really know what to expect, but she found herself watching the geese intently for that shimmer of light. She was not to be disappointed for it soon did appear, to be replaced by the powerful shape of aggression itself, a wolf. It instantly snapped at the flurry of feathers around it and ignored the defensive show of flapping wings, hisses and screams from angry beaks. As anticipated, once they had realised that to fight was fruitless the group of snow-white guardians scattered in all directions to save themselves from the grip of the hungry jaws, leaving the way clear for the visitors to go about their business.

The dilapidated wooden door flew open and a plump old woman screamed at them as she stood in the doorway. "There was no need to do that to my poor ladies. All you had to do was ask, Felagin, and I would have made your entry clear. But no, you have to get that Beodin to perform whatever malicious mischief he can don't you?"

Felagin did not reply, but merely stood and grinned at her misconception.

"You are earlier than expected or I must have dropped off to sleep. It is not convenient. Go away and come back later," she nagged. "And who are you?" she said to Berowen. "I do not know you and I was not expecting you. And you...." she pointed a bony finger in Thurstan's direction. "Do I know you? I sense something from you. Go away all of you."

It was then that Berowen noticed a small trail of, what looked very much like, smears of blood upon the rushes covering the woman's floor in the room behind her. She shivered at the tales Thurstan had told her earlier about this woman's supposed liking of human flesh. Remembering Felagin's instructions, she wiped the thought from her head as soon as it entered and began to think of something completely different and innocent. Mildthryth threw her a look of mistrust at the same moment and Berowen froze in her saddle.

"We shall not go away, Mildthryth. We were expected, and we have arrived," announced Felagin firmly, yet politely – his tone surprising Berowen. "If we have interrupted something then that cannot be helped, but we request that we are allowed to enter as arranged. Or do you have something to hide?"

Slightly ruffled by the last question, the old woman wrapped her shawl tightly around her shoulders and replied, "And what makes you think that I should have something to hide?"

"Only your reticence to allow us entry, Mildthryth. And the smell of meat cooking – it is such an enticing aroma that seeps through your door. Perhaps you are making your evening meal and have no wish to share it with visitors?" responded Felagin slyly. "Come to think of it, I am very hungry and I am sure my travelling companions are also, for not a morsel of food has passed our lips all day. Thurstan? Berowen? Does that smell not entice your stomach juices?"

"It does indeed," replied Thurstan immediately. "What say you Berowen?"

"It certainly does remind me of my hunger," responded Berowen quickly. "It does smell unusual however." She saw Felagin tense slightly in his saddle and rapidly continued, "You must have added some unusual herbs and spices to the pot? Yes that must be it."

Felagin relaxed and laughed. "Ah it takes another woman to recognise such alchemy when cooking is concerned. I thought it was hare, plain and simple, but then what would I know, being a mere male."

The three visitors waited for Mildthryth's response. Had they managed to fool her in their intentions or had she seen through the idle chatter?

The old woman stood in her doorway, the flickering light of the candle inside casting eerie shadows on the right side of her wrinkled face. Berowen took only brief glances in her direction remembering what Felagin had told her, but the glances were enough to make out the small, hunched frame and the long nose that protruded hook-like from the sucken, baggy old face, the skin of which hung in large creases around her cheeks and chin. A large black cat appeared beside her and wrapped itself around her legs, weaving in and out while making very loud purring noises.

Always ready to grasp on to any small chance of insulting Felagin the old crone at last replied, "You are indeed a mere male, Felagin, and one that has plagued me for many years with your inflated view of your powers and your sex. You have always thought yourself more superior to me just because you *are* a mere male. For what is your purpose here today anyway?"

"We shall discuss our purpose once in the comfort of your warm kitchen, Mildthryth," answered Felagin. "Once that warm, delicious food has reached our bellies, I am sure our conversation will be most convivial."

"Hah, you use the excuse of food too often. You must think me a fool indeed if you think I shall give you entrance into my humble kitchen."

"If I may...," interrupted Berowen, beginning to feel ill at ease and sense that the conversation was getting them nowhere. "I am certain that Felagin is sincere in his compliments regarding your food. He has spoken of your prowess with the pot more than once on our journey together. I know not of the reasoning behind his and Thurstan's visit, as I met them on the road recently, and they agreed to give me safe passage once their visit to you was over. However, his talk of your skills has on more than one occasion made my mouth water with anticipation."

She hated lying but she saw it as the only way to try to get the situation moving once again. The old woman eyed her up and down slowly and carefully with a suspicious look in her dark sunken eyes. She scratched her thinning grey hair as she thought. Although she was slightly apprehensive, for reasons she knew not for she was still under the effect of the bewitchment of Arra, the flattery was most welcome.

"Tut. Wait out here. I need to clear up first." And she slammed the door shut.

The three visitors looked at each other in turn. Each knew that by clearing up she meant hiding the evidence of some heinous and sordid action, and although no-one spoke a word they all knew that whatever was cooking in the pot was certainly not hare.

There had been only one small window cut out of the great oak's trunk and through this they watched the silhouette of the woman as she bustled around inside hiding whatever evidence she had to secrete from the eyes of those who waited outside for entry.

After a short while, the door flew open again and the old crone stood smoothing down her grubby skirts before beckoning them all to follow her inside. Dismounting and leaving their horses tethered loosely to a low hanging branch, they stepped over the threshold one by one.

It was certainly cramped inside this hollowed out trunk; there was just enough room for them all to stand inside without brushing against each other or knocking over an item of rickety furniture. Berowen gazed quickly around the room. At one corner there was a badly made bed, currently being used by another cat for its scratching antics. At the opposite side was the fire, a large black pot steaming and bubbling gently over the flames. The wisps of smoke disappearing into the hole above on its way upwards and outwards into the cooling air outside.

All along the walls were rows and rows of shelves, filled with vials, bottles and pots brimming over with dried flowers, herbs, parts of animals and whole creatures that were suspended within their confines in some peculiar coloured humour. They stared out at the visitors with blank expressions and Berowen shivered under their lifeless gaze. Thick cobwebs clung to the corners of the room; so thick that they seemed to be holding up the structure from within. Each of the shelves seemed also to be the home to some spider as long strands of gossamer threads interwined around each shelf and seemed to drip over the sides, hanging like strands of thin, greying hair and wafting in the breeze created by any movement near them.

But it was Mildthryth's sudden movement near the fire that attracted everyone's attention at the same time. No matter how hard she may have tried, her quick shuffling of feet on the tattered rush mat beneath her was not unnoticed. They all saw the dull metal ring that was just poking in sight before she managed to manoeuvre the mat over it. Clearly there was some kind of storage place beneath their feet, deep within the roots of the tree.

"I see you are indeed prepared for visitors," stated Felagin. "The last time I visited there were only two stools and today there are exactly four around the fire. You are indeed caring of your guests."

Mildthryth' mouth shaped a lop-sided open smile, exposing a severe lack of teeth, "Of course. If nothing else I am hospitable. However, I am afraid to impart that the food will not be ready to eat for another hour."

"Oh dear, really?" enquired Felagin. "That is a shame, but no matter. I am sure our stomachs can wait for that period of time to elapse at the thought of them being satiated with such a delicious concoction."

Looking at Berowen, the old woman frowned. "But you, my dear, look as if you are to pass out with hunger. Perhaps you should try some of my shrew butter. It is my own recipe, and, even though I say so myself, it is very satisfying on the tongue."

Berowen shot a glance at Felagin, but received no look of assistance. She remembered his advice from earlier and bravely smiled at her host. "That is most kind of you. I am sure it will be delicious."

Mildthryth picked up the large knife that sat on the small table beside them and sliced off a piece of dusty, stale looking bread. From the pot next to it she scraped out a portion of odd, brown coloured paste and spread it on the slice before handing it to Berowen.

"I swear by it," she said gleefully. "It takes a long time to gather enough of the little creatures to make one pot you know. My precious cats are good at hunting and they usually catch me at least one each a day, but it takes a good week or two to get enough."

Berowen raised the slice to her lips and just as she was about to take the smallest bite possible, the old woman continued, "Skinning the little beasts is nigh on impossible you know. It does no good whatsoever to get one piece of fur in the mixture, for it ruins the whole pot. Bones don't matter; by the time they are ground down you would not know they were there. Then add a pinch of powdered acorn and a splash of curdled milk from old Pen over there.." Berowen turned to follow the woman's pointed finger and saw – in the shadows of the corner – a cat nursing four kittens as black as the night. She shuddered. "Old Nib is a randy old sod, always getting Pen in kitten, but what is good for the goose is good for the gander you know. My shrew butter benefits from the milk as Old Nib benefits from Pen." And she cackled.

Felagin noticed as time wore on Mildthryth's mood and manner were changing. She was beginning to lose the slightly benign demeanour of the old woman of the oak tree, and was returning to the natural old hag of uncertain pleasures and hobbies. It was time to act before she regained all her natural malice and power.

"Where are all the cats?" asked Mildthryth with an evil look in her eye. Berowen shot a look at Felagin and Thurstan. It was evident that the woman was now reading thoughts again. "I have not got room for a constant supply of Old Nib's ill-gotten offspring and meat is a rare thing round here you know. Some do escape though....."

"Enough!" shouted Berowen standing, her stool toppling over with the momentum.

Mildthryth took one step back and laughed, her laugh turning into a malicious cackle and she threw back her head and uttered forth a demonic screech.

"I know now why you are here!" she bellowed. "You bewitched me, Felagin, and you shall now feel the wrath of Mildthryth for your insolence."

The cat that had continued to rub itself around the woman's legs stopped and hissed at Felagin, its face screwed up with piercing blue eyes wide and threatening.

"Enough of your spitting, ill-humoured creature," he bellowed and stared at the hissing mass of black fur. Immediately it cringed and shrank behind its mistress, growling deeply and slithering away slowly across the floor towards the darkest corner it could find.

Thurstan sat motionless staring into the fire. There was a deep look of concentration etched upon his face and Berowen could see his lips faintly moving as if in silent speech. Mildthryth screeched again and flung her hands over each of her ears. Her head was filled with the noisy chattering of each of her visitor's thoughts; they came all at once. "Don't try to confuse me with all your thoughts!" she bellowed. She settled on Berowen as the weakest of those around her and the latter felt as if her head would burst. Her eyeballs felt they would pop out of her skull at any moment, they ached and pulsated so much from the old woman's stare. Felagin jumped from his stool and stood in front of Berowen as if to break the connection between the tormented and the tormenter. It worked briefly and Berowen had to take a step backwards when released from Mildthryth's powerful gaze.

The door burst open and Thurstan's wolf leapt inside and placed itself beside the woman. It growled, saliva dripping from its jaws. "A wolf eh?" cackled the crone. "Aha a good match indeed, but not good enough methinks for Ursa." She snapped her fingers and the cat on the bed disappeared in a flash of light to be replaced by a large bear that jumped towards Arra. Thurstan's task had begun and it was now up to him to prove his worth in front of his mentor. Arra was the most powerful of his companion's aliases and she tore into the bear with such ferociousness that fur literally flew across the room. There was no room and the great beast thrashed around, knocking everything off the shelves in its wake. The two animals bumped into the humans who continued their own onslaught upon the woman. Thurstan turned and Berowen saw that his eyes were now like Felagin's; gone were the soft features of his face, replaced with one of anger, power and hardness. She backed into the corner where the nursing cat remained feeding her offspring. It took no notice of her but continued to purr softly as her kittens palpated her stomach as they suckled.

The two battling animals continued their fight, which soon carried them out through the open door, but their weight and size took it off its flimsy hinges as they went, sending it crashing on to the ground outside. Berowen could feel the great tree heaving as the battle raged on inside and outside of its gnarled trunk. Everytime Arra or Ursa was thrashed against the bark Berowen could hear the trinkets shaking furiously, the sound of their weird music echoing around the glade.

"Your treacherous pact with Modig is now over, Mildthryth. And you shall no longer continue your evil practices upon those who wander into your grasp," rasped Thurstan. He winced as the woman muttered something under her breath and gestured with her hand. Whatever she had done had caused him great pain in his left side and it was all that he could do to stand upright as the seering pain gripped him from his hip to his shoulder. Felagin did not interject and remained standing in front of Berowen, who peeped over his shoulder with desperation as her friend appeared to be irrevocably under the old woman's powerful grip. Thurstan stepped back and flailed out a hand to prevent himself falling, this hand landing on the red hot hook from which the cooking pot dangled over the fire. He removed it instantly, the pain of his burning flesh bringing him to his senses. But as he did so the hook loosened its own grip on the pot and it fell into the fire with a great thud, before slowly rolling over to spill its contents on the floor. The flames flickered, and finally lost their battle against the liquid and the fire went out with a long, loud hiss.

Berowen stared in horror as the wrinkled hand and arm sat motionless upon the hearth, the thick liquid in which they had been boiling slowly oozing into the rushes around Thurstan's feet. He took no notice, after all it was as they had all expected the contents of the pot to be, and although she had thought this herself, Berowen could still not help but heave at the sight.

"Methinks Odi may be of some help to Arra," whispered Felagin over his shoulder to Berowen. "I had not bargained for such a creature from Mildthryth, it is a new one to me. And I cannot get involved, as you know. Unless...." and he went no further, but he had no need to for Berowen knew exactly what he meant.

Berowen nodded and thought hard, willing her raven to come to the aid of the wolf and it was not long before they heard the familiar calling of the large black bird outside.

Odi flew down at the bear, using his strong hard beak to good use. He pecked and clawed with his sharp claws at the head of the beast, trying to find the soft, warm eyes while Arra continued her attempts at finding a grip on its neck. But the bear was huge and was not going to surrender that easily. The ground outside was littered with the fallen bones, trinkets and chimes that had been shaken loose from their places amongst the boughs with each knock against the tree from one or the other.

Frantically trying to recall the things he had learnt from Felagin, Thurstan faltered slightly. The old woman saw this and cackled again before waving a hand as if tossing something invisible towards him. This time it hit him in the chest and he gasped and struggled to take a breath. He had always known that this battle would be a matter of life or death for him and although he had been well aware that he would have to find something deep within him to win and survive, this task was much harder than he had thought possible. Perhaps he was not destined to take over where Felagin left off after all; perhaps it had all been a mistake in the first place on the part of the old man and his father. But however much he disliked his father for pushing him into this path he was on, a basic morality remained within him. He would not let his father's name be shamed by his failure, and he would definitely not show weakness to his mentor.

He searched within himself for that which he had been taught over the long years. He shut out all other thoughts from his mind and concentrated hard. He let himself listen to the secret voices in his head as they gabbled their instructions back into the front of his memory. He saw hundreds of pieces of parchment turning over and over, he saw the mathematical symbols and strange writing, he watched as his own hands made potions in his mind's eye and most importantly he heard the whispers that spoke in that part of his mind that could release the magick that dwelt there. It was like a candle flaring into life and his whole body came alive with an energy so great that he had to find a way to release it. And he knew that it was this action alone that would help him succeed in his task. He raised his hands above his head and opened his palms skyward. His body started to shake and a myriad of tiny dust-like particles arose from his palms and arced above his body like a rainbow of shimmering light. He clapped his hands together above his head and drew them down sharply to his sides.

Mildthryth seemed alarmed at first by Thurstan's actions but then began to laugh again. "Ah, I see it now. This is your apprentice Felagin and this is to be his initiation. It is always so touching to witness such a ceremony. They are always so entertaining when a student suddenly unleashes all their power for the first time. Let us hope that this apprentice is well-versed on keeping it under control or it may backfire on him as it so often does under these circumstances. A pile of burnt bones sizzling and spitting at one's feet is so inconvenient don't you think? And such a waste too."

Felagin remained silent. He understood completely to what the old woman was intimating. He could only hope that Thurstan could keep control of his power for he knew only too well that such dire consequences as she had mentioned were not that uncommon amongst newly-weaned apprentices. The wording of any incantation had to be spoken succinctly and plainly or confusion could arise that would turn everything back on the caster. This was continually and all too plainly explained to students, but sometimes, in the heat of the moment, they would forget or let the general excitement of the moment overtake them. He could only hope that Thurstan's usually sensible and serious demeanour would not cause the latter unwise emotion.

The old crone had worked out the situation well and Felagin knew then that she would use all in her power to try to trick Thurstan into confusion in his naivety. He would have to keep his wits about him, and Felagin would have to scrutinise every move of both of them closely. It could soon be the time that, if necessary, he may have to step in.

Thurstan, however, took quick advantage of Mildthryth's brief lack of concentration as she spoke to Felagin, and threw her a stealthy blow on the air that hit her between the eyes with such force that she then found herself being thrown backwards. She steadied herself on the table behind her and Berowen saw her fingers wrap themselves around the handle of the knife where it lay beside the mouldy loaf of bread. Quick as a flash of lightning the knife flew through the air towards Thurstan, but he was too quick for her and with a look from his eyes he stopped it mid-flight and it crashed to the ground with a dull thud on the rushes. "Bah," she cried. "The young are always so much quicker in their reactions, but at least I now know that that is not your weakness."

"Perhaps then, she is," announced the hag as she turned her attention once more at Berowen who was still hiding behind Felagin. She began to itch and was horrified to watch as hundreds of ants climbed over her feet, rapidly running up her clothing on to her arms, each one biting her skin as they climbed towards her neck. She danced up and down, screaming, and trying to brush off the tiny red assailants.

"She is a friend, but not a weakness, old woman," stated Thurstan, no emotion at Berowen's distress evident in his expression. Instead, he returned the favour towards Berowen's attacker and Mildthryth squirmed as a snake weaved its way up her leg under her skirts flicking its tongue as it went, her attention of the petrified girl waning, with the ants dissipating into thin air. It was now the old woman's turn to dance on the spot in an attempt to loosen the tightening grip on the reptile as it made its way to the darkest, dampest spot available to it.

Felagin chuckled under his breath. "No-one been there for a while eh Mildthryth? Although I am sure a promise or two have been offered to ensnare such that filled your pot today."

"Jealous are we, old man?" retorted the crone as she at last managed to deflect the wandering snake from climbing any further. It fell to the floor and disappeared, leaving only a slimy green stain on the rushes.

Felagin threw back his head and laughed. "Jealous? Of what? A dry old hole as loose as a whore's tongue?" Berowen balked at the repugnant suggestion.

"There was once a time when you did not say that, Felagin," she said sarcastically. But before she could continue Felagin interrupted with a wave of his hand, a stamp of his foot and a hiss from his lips, "Whisht" he said. "What occurred when you were slightly pleasing on the eye has no relevance here." Berowen stared at the back of his head. Did he really once have some relationship with this horrific woman?

"Stop toying with the boy, and Thurstan cease your delicacy in the matter. She may be a woman but a woman with a bite much worse than her rasping bark," boomed Felagin, but she was sure that the slight blush that Berowen observed that was not hidden by his cowl, was not one borne from the anger in his tone, but from the embarrassment of some very distant past liaison.

Without taking her stare from Felagin, Mildthryth, shot out her right arm and Thurstan was lifted from his feet to crash against the side of the oak's hard shell. He slithered to the ground and shook his head from the sudden attack. "Let us begin, boy," she said. "Enough of this idle play as Felagin would have it."

As he tried to stand up, a vial full of a strange looking liquid flew through the air towards his head, but he ducked at the last minute and it crashed to the wooden wall behind him, splintering and showering its contents across the floor. The aroma from the liquid was putrid and once again, Berowen found herself gagging.

Unphased by the latest onslaught Thurstan stood and responded, sending a cascade of bottles, which had managed to sit unharmed from the crashing around of Arra and Ursa, raining down upon the old woman. She stood perfectly still and each one of them missed her by inches, all falling and smashing on to the floor. It was as if she had somehow enveloped herself in an invisible shield for they seemed to bounce in the air as they approached her.

Not waiting for a response Thurstan then turned the wooden wall to Mildthryth's right into a mirror and with every inch of his power he made her turn to face it. She resisted as hard as she could and it took a while for him to achieve it. She saw her reflection and wailed in frustration and anger at having to see herself as she was now. She tried to shut her eyes against the vision, but Thurstan ensured that he commanded every part of her body; every muscle and nerve was his to be under his control. She could but stand and stare at her own reflection and wallow in its ugliness.

"Excellent," whispered Felagin. "The student has found a weakness. Outstanding. But can he maintain his hold I wonder."

The answer to this did not take long to manifest itself. Be it a lapse of only a second, his concentration waivered and Mildthryth saw her chance. She lunged out at the mirror and smashed it with her fists before turning enraged upon Thurstan. She was dribbling with anger and her eyes flashed with wickedness as she slowly hobbled towards him. As she did so, his body moved as if being hit with invisible punches. His head swayed from side to side and blood soon dribbled from his mouth, his ears and even his eyes. Berowen saw Felagin's shoulder tense in front of her, as if in readiness for a sudden intervention of the situation that was unfolding.

Her vainness insulted, the old woman continued with her vicious barrage upon the hapless Thurstan. He may have found her weakness, but he had also unleashed her full anger upon him and this power took no quarter. She was relentless in her attack and before long Thurstan lay curled on the floor in an attempt to protect himself from the onslaught. The bare flesh of his hands was being ripped to shreds by some unknown force, and invisible blades tore at the clothes on his back, penetrating through to his skin and ripping it apart as a knife rips through butter.

Berowen could not help herself. She flew past Felagin, pushing the old man out of the way and screamed at Mildthryth. "Leave him alone, you ugly bitch!" She saw the knife where it lay on the floor and tried to will it to rise and plunge itself deep into her heart. Nothing happened. She gritted her teeth and gave it all of her attention, but still it lay prone where it had fallen. The old woman looked at her and spat at her, sending the foul-smelling globule on to her left cheek. Berowen took a step forward, wiping the spit off her face, and grabbed the hag's right arm, bending it backwards as far as she could, with as much viciousness in her grip as she could find within herself. Mildthryth snapped it away and snarled, but was stunned when the girl slapped her around the face with such force that felt as if she had been hit with a rock.

The unexpected intervention from Berowen gave Thurstan his chance and where Berowen had failed, he succeeded in raising the knife from its place on the floor. It turned itself with the blade pointing at its target and flew through the air with such speed and force that no-one saw it happening. It submerged itself into the flesh of the old woman and pierced her black heart, the sticky lifeblood oozing from the wound and seeping into the material of her tattered dress. She look completely shocked and tried to pull out the weapon, but Thurstan had already scrambled to his feet and was pressing it further into her body. He wrenched it upwards and downwards making sure that her heart was torn to shreds within her body.

"You dare..." she gasped.

"It was your idea, Mildthryth," he panted between painful breaths. "If my youth gives me quick reactions then it seems obvious that one so old as yourself would not possess ones as sharp. It is your mistake in stating such that has proved your downfall in the end. Although it was your conceit that was always your weakness, it was your loose tongue that failed you."

"What makes you think you have killed me? What makes you think I shall not return?" she coughed.

"Your trap door hides the remains of those you have killed does it not? I am certain that my assumption will prove true when we open it and toss your decrepit carcass into it, before setting the whole horde alight. After we have disembodied you limb from limb of course."

Mildthryth gurgled and uttered no more.

"But the tree?" cried Berowen.

Felagin took hold of Berowen's shoulders and said softly, "The great oak is dying now that its inhabitant is dead. There is nothing we can do for it now, but we have given it its release from the evil being that took its own heart many years ago. I suggest you leave Berowen for I do not think you wish to witness the final carving up of this old hag."

She shuddered and left through gap where the door had once been. Outside all was quiet – Arra sat licking her wounds and Odi was busy pecking an eyeball that he held down with one foot. There was no sign of the bear, presumably it had disappeared when its mistress had died.

She looked at the great oak tree as it stood dying before her. The faces that were etched into its bark were fading by the minute as if the spirits of those killed by Mildthryth were now at peace and had moved on, knowing that their murderer had met her well-deserved demise. Berowen ran a hand across the gnarled bark as it groaned and creaked and she found herself apologising to it for the way it had been abused. It seemed to sigh and she said farewell.

After a short while Thurstan came through the doorway and slumped into a sitting position some distance away from the tree. From inside came the aroma of burning flesh and Berowen knew the task had been completed. She too moved away from the tree to avoid the stench from within.

Felagin emerged holding the nursing cat and her kittens in his arms. The other cat had long-since disappeared, presumably it had escaped unnoticed. "Not sure what we are going to do with these poor creatures," he announced. "Nowhere to take them, but I am sure they will do well enough on their own. I assume that living with Mildthryth must have taught this mother a certain amount of self-reliance." He deposited the mother on the ground, followed by the kittens and watched as she disappeared into the undergrowth at the far side of the glade, to return shortly afterwards. They watched as she collected her offspring one by one before trotting off gently holding each one in her teeth before disappearing for the last time with the third.

The great oak finally toppled over with a resounding creak and died, just before the flames enveloped it from within.

Felagin checked Thurstan over and declared after examining him from head to foot, "You'll live." And then to Berowen he sternly said, "Now is the time to send that message, for they will be coming soon and...."

"Yes, Grimfell will burn," she interrupted. "I know."

She searched in her pack for some parchment and her quill and ink, thanking her forethought for packing such things when she left. She scribbled out a note for Cynefrid and, rolling it into a scroll, gave it to Odi, silently giving him precise instructions as to whom he should deliver it. "Make haste, winged one," she declared as he rose to the skies and disappeared over the treetops that circled the glade.

"Where to now?" she asked of Felagin and Thurstan once Odi had gone out of sight.

"To the monastery methinks for Thurstan to recover and then on to Bole," responded the elder of her companions.

"Monastery? Bole?" she enquired. But she knew that she would not get a straight answer and had already resigned herself to another journey into the unknown.

LXIX

Aedre was on her way home, coaxing her family's cow across the all but dead fields that lay on the outskirts of her village. The animal had wandered off in search of palatable pastures, and it had been Aedre's task to find her and return her home before darkness fell over the land. She had cursed under her breath at the request of her father to search for the errant bovine; it was always wandering off and it was nearly always her task to locate and return it.

And so it was that she found herself just at the edge of the barren field when the earth around her began to shake beneath her feet. After being given an encouraging pat on the rump, her charge was already slowly meandering her own way back over the grassy knoll that bordered the field, towards the small building that Aedre called home. Aedre ran off the well-ploughed sod and on to the knoll. Turning, she watched in horror and disbelief as the whole field that now lay in front of her – where she had only just been walking - began to vibrate; great clumps of earth being tossed into the air as if thrown from some invisible force. It seemed to Aedre that the land before her - this meagre piece of land that her family had tended for so many years - was being sucked into itself. An island of earth rose at one end as all around was swallowed into the chasm that was developing around it. In dismay she saw what was left of her family's livelihood disappear and as the 'island' rose higher she could see a large, grotesque, and scaly head begin to appear before her that was bigger than any beast she had ever seen before. Its nostrils flared and its golden eyes seemed to squint from the daylight as if it had been a long time in darkness. She had never seen such before, but had heard the tales from her parents and other elders in the village. These great creatures had disappeared from the land a few years before she had been born; they had existed in reality once, but for all of her life they had existed merely on the tongues of those to whom she had listened. But now, as she stood face to face with this great creature, she realised that what she had been told was far truer than she could ever have imagined.

Slowly the head emerged and as it breached the surface of the broken ground it brought with it an odour so strong and foul that she nearly vomited. Clumps of sod tumbled from its large cranium as its head eventually cleared the earth. It opened its great maw and a forked tongue flicked out through giant teeth. Then from the earth, followed a long neck that seemed to rise endlessly skywards, before it was eventually followed by two short stout legs with three toed feet that ended in huge sharp claws that hooked around into a deathly curve. It hauled itself out of the world below and eventually its two back legs appeared, scrabbling to gain purchase on the crumbling surface.

The beast towered over her. All the tales that spoke of these creatures living in harmony with the people of the village raced in her head, but the truth seemed hard to believe at the sight of such a formidable being. It continued to slowly walk across the field, to her relief in the opposite direction, trailing its long scaly tail behind it. A tail that sported a vicious-looking spike at the end of it; a tail that she could imagine would break every bone in your body if it was swung against you. But it was the huge leathery wings that suddenly unfurled that made her scream in terror. All the fear that she had bottled up inside her when the earth first began to move came rushing to its peak with this final emerging act of the creature.

As she stared and watched the dragon, Aedre became aware that she was no longer alone on the knoll. Whether it had been her scream or whether they had come to investigate the earth's movement she was not sure, but looking around her she saw the rest of her village all grouped together, their eyes fixed upon the creature from the depths. There were gasps and mutterings from the older folk and Aedre could hear the soft sobbing from the younger inhabitants.

They watched for more to emerge and did not have to wait long before another, slightly smaller, creature emerged from the hole that was once the field. It too blinked in the fading light and stretched its massive wings as it followed the other towards the shape of Grimfell that loomed beyond in the light of the setting sun.

"Modig beware," uttered one villager, this utterance followed by others. "Oswald will suffer for his avarice," and "They will burn in this world and the thereafter."

After the fifth had emerged there was a long pause and daylight turned into gloaming. Some of the villagers had brought burning torches with them and now these sent shadows across the land and flickered in the faint night breeze. The earth shook once more and all eyes reverted to the chasm to see the largest of all emerge from the darkness below. "'Tis the female," someone whispered behind Aedre's ear. The scales of the she-dragon glistened in the torchlight as she hauled herself to the surface. The horns on her head were larger than those of the males that had come before her and the beard that hung from her chin was long and curly. As she shook herself from the cramped position she had been confined in for so long she opened her gigantic mouth and uttered forth a low bellow so loud that all covered their ears from the sound.

"That will scare the shit out of them," said one of the villagers. "I'll wager they heard that alright."

The she-dragon coughed and opened her mouth and a small flicker of flame came forth. She shook her head and tried again but nothing emerged. "Hmm she needs food before that flame will come," said someone. The children whimpered at the thought and the women sushed them quiet. "No need to fear little ones," announced one of the elders with a voice of authority. "Them beasts don't harm us. They will be searching the fields for some tasty deer or they may even fly to the great waters and have themself a feast of those large fish that I heard of. Great beasts they are. They lumber the seas roundabouts."

"Look!" shouted another. "Look, they take flight!"

And indeed they were doing so. Their dark forms against the light of the waxing moon were flapping their giant bat-like wings; wings that had been unused for so many years that they must have been difficult to unfurl and painful, yet exhilarating, to open and use again. Slowly, one by one, the first five of the dragons took a slow, ponderous flight from the earth and all were eventually airborne, beating their great wings slowly and methodically to gain height. They soared overhead, the moon being totally obliterated by their size, as they waited for the female to join them.

She unfurled her great wings and beat them slowly up and down, the draught from their action nearly blowing some of the youngsters who stood watching on the knoll off their feet. Aedre's hair blew with the breeze and she somehow felt joyous by the sight. One, two, three and on the fourth great beat, the beast was aloft. She soared directly upwards and circled with the others. They played together in the air and seemed overjoyed at their freedom. They divebombed the onlookers, only pulling themselves upwards at the very last minute, but not before most who were watching had ducked to the ground in anticipation of either being taken and eaten on the wing, or being knocked unconscious.

Then they were gone. The sky was empty once more, save for the moon and the scattering of stars that twinkled and winked overhead. To where they had gone no-one knew, but it was certain that they had gone in hunt for the food that would not only feed their hungry stomachs, but would also feed their ability to breathe fire. The fire they all felt certain would destroy Grimfell and the person dwelling inside who was responsible for the beasts' incarceration for the long years before this day of their resurrection.

One by one, the villagers returned to their humble homes. Mothers carried their tired children and fathers chatted amongst themselves of the retribution that was sure to follow. Aedre waited until the last of the torch-wielders returned before following their light.

Inside the great hall of Grimfell, the bellow had indeed been heard, but most had dismissed it as just another sound of the approaching night. "A pack of wolves probably," announced Oswald as he supped his mead and pinched the bottom of the young kitchen girl who had brought the new jug of potent brew to replenish their mazers. Modig, however, was not so sure. He sensed something far worse than a distant pack of wolves, but decided to ignore this feeling and continued to drink down the mead, whilst pondering on his next plan of assault upon the lands that bordered his own.

In the small house at the foot of the high steps, Cynefrid re-read the message that had been delivered to him by the raven, which sat on the table in front of him preening himself quietly. Berowen had instructed him to remain in case he could be of some help to Cynefrid.

The timing of the instructions would be of the most importance – too soon, and the alarm would be raised amongst those who were undeserved; too late and those who were to be saved would be lost. He had already instructed Wirt to gather certain supplies from the well-stocked shelves and pack them carefully. He was loathe to leave his books, for they were old and well-stocked with information, but he resigned himself to a selective few of the ancient ones. Col sat on the stool by the fire, wide-eyed at the industry within the small building. Wirt had been sent to find him immediately Cynefrid had first read the note and the small boy had been secreted out of the stables and into the house. He had been fed and watered and now sat very still, watching every move that Wirt made with complete non-understanding of what was going on around him.

There would be no warning when the beasts would attack, which made Cynefrid's task even more difficult, but he had decided that the best place to watch would be at the top of the high steps. He had scoured the writings within the great volume of such historical events as this and had learned that beasts such as these usually attacked from out of the sun and would first lay fire to the ground around their target. Then they would go in the attack, cutting off any escape from those at the top of tall structures. Wirt had been instructed to keep Col close to him and alert those in the small habitation at the base on a signal from his mentor. There would be no way to alert the servants who worked in Modig's household. To get to them he would have to pass Modig and then the desired surprise would be lost. He did not even know whether he would have time himself to reach the base of the steps before the attack began, but as long as he knew that Wirt, Col and his chosen tomes were safe he would be satisfied.

The volume had been filled with records entered by the hand of many a survivor of such attacks, and all had stated that the attack had occurred as the day's sun reached its zenith. Dragons *can* see in the dark, but their vision is much impaired and they prefer a surprise attack with the sun behind them. There was still plenty of time to finish loading the pack bags and to get Wirt into the stables, once the marshal had left for his nightly visit to the inn, to saddle up four horses, and load one of these with the bags in readiness. Wirt was also charged with adding a sleeping draught to the barrel of mead that the marshal supped on throughout the day. He was well known for having his first drink as soon as he arrived in the morning, so that would keep him from discovering the ride-ready mounts.

By midnight all seemed in place. Col and Wirt had both dozed off by the fire. Even Odi had tucked his head under his wing and was snoozing quietly with one leg tucked up beneath him, but Cynefrid was still deciding whether there was room for any more books or potions. Besides, he could not sleep. All was ready for an attack on the morrow, but what if that attack did not occur then? What if it was days before they came? .

LXX

The villagers had already staked their various individual claims upon their own spot on the knoll. In the distance they could see the tall keep of Grimfell rising to the sky and they would remain in their positions all day if necessary so as not to miss the fall of the imposing structure. Work could, and would, wait for this was a spectacle not to be missed. If they did not come today, then the villagers would repeat the process on the morrow. It would be fair to conjecture, no doubt, that if the dragons did not appear after a couple of days, then some of the villagers would give up the vigil and get back to their own business. Especially the women, indeed those with young children would be at pains to keep their youngsters amused and out of their hair for as long as possible, and children are not known for possessing the greatest patience. It would not be long before their interest on the knoll would wane.

A great fire had been lit to keep the cold at bay and the children ran around the legs of their parents chasing each other in a continual game of noisy tag. They shouted, giggled and screamed as they caught one another and many a time they ran into an adult's leg to be rewarded with verbal abuse or a cuff around the ear for their recklessness. They were all under strict orders not to stray too far from their parents, but children being the fearless creatures they are, they did not take too much notice of these instructions and there were constant calls and cries for errant youngsters to return to the bosom of the gathered crowd.

There had been a murky start to the morning, but it had gradually turned into a bright, winter's day. The sky was a cloudless blue, which belied the coldness that enveloped the earth below, and there was great anticipation among the watchers that the dragons would come to wreak their revenge for the years they had spent imprisoned underground.

The noonday sun shone down upon them as it peaked. It would soon begin its descent into the west and the villagers were all agog for what may occur at any time. In front of Aedre, two of the younger children hopped up and down with one leg in front of the other as they began the strange bladder dance, the steps of which only children seem to possess; their tiny hands clasped between their legs as if trying to hold in the inevitable flow. She was about to oversee their relief by taking them slightly out of the throng when they both looked up behind her and pointed, the amazement in their wide eyes alerting her to turn around and follow their stare. As she did so they stopped their dance and the predictable straw coloured liquid dribbled down their dirty legs, beneath their tattered leggings, and left a trail of pale flesh as it went.

The brightness of the sun was dimmed by the shapes of five great winged creatures as they slowly beat their giant wings in flight. By now all the villagers had been alerted and all craned their necks to watch as the dragons flew overhead, the draught from their wings scattering ash from the fire as they went.

The sixth beast, the great female, was at the back, as she followed the formation towards Grimfell. The closeness of the creatures was even too much for some of the most bold children, who ran to the bosoms of their mothers and buried their heads in the soft curves of comfort as the beasts flew on.

At the top of the steps of Grimfell, Cynefrid shielded his eyes against the glare of the sun. He had begun his vigil at dawn, after awakening Wirt and Col whom he had dispatched to stand guard at the doorway to wait for his signal should one be necessary.

And then he made out the dark shapes looming in the distance towards Grimfell from out of the sun, just had been written in the great volume. There would be much for his quill to record after today's events; this would be too good an opportunity to miss and the thought that he would have his name forever immortalised in ink after recounting the experience that unfurled before him, made him greatly excited. He would even sketch pictures of the spectacle for posterity's sake. He watched in awe of the oddly magnificent sight, and as the dark shapes slowly drew closer he called to Odi. The great black bird dived down towards where Wirt and Col stood, while Cynefrid made his tentative way down the steps. Being mostly in the shadow of the wall, most of the steps were still awash with the morning's dew and he descended slowly and carefully so as not to slip. That would not do - an opportunity of literary note lost due to carelessness and wrong footing would be the most ironic of accidents.

As Odi flapped and hovered in front of the young apothecary's assistant, Wirt knew that this was the warning he had been primed to expect, and he grabbed Col by the hand and raced towards the stables. Cautiously entering, he peeked his head around the stable door to see if the marshal had managed to resist the temptation of the barrel of mead. There was no reason to expect that he had, even at such a young age Wirt had already learnt that you cannot change the habits of a lifetime, but he still felt that it would be prudent to make sure before dashing headlong for the saddled horses.

His cautionary manner proved unnecessary, however, upon the sight of the marshal snoring quietly as he slumped on the stool next to the barrel, his right hand still half clutching a tankard. It was suspended at an angle as it dangled from his forefinger, and a puddle had formed beneath it where the un-drunken mead had spilt to the floor when he had fallen asleep. The potion had done its work and, signalling to Col, Wirt dragged the boy behind him towards the stalls. Col ran sideways, staring at his master as he was pulled along, his scrawny legs almost treading the air with the speed that Wirt propelled him. Wirt hoisted him into the saddle of one of the horses before grabbing the reins of all those standing ready. With a click of his tongue he encouraged them to move and follow him out of the stables. As they passed the slumbering marshal, Wirt tugged at his forelock mockingly and, upon seeing this act of insolence, Col joined in the game by flicking his front teeth with his thumb.

As they exited the stables, Wirt glanced at the steps to see if his master was in sight, but there was, as yet, no-one to be seen descending them. Col wobbled unsteadily in the saddle, his legs much too short to reach the stirrups, being only able to stay seated by grabbing the mane of the horse in his grubby fists and squeezing as hard as he could with his tiny legs to gain a grip.

The first hurdle was to pass the guard at the gatehouse. Indeed this had been thought of as the first hurdle during the planning the night before. However, the preparations had not accounted for the possibility of anything untoward occurring such as that which faced Wirt as they turned the corner just before the gatehouse. He was leading the horses and Col at a fair speed down the slope, mumbling the announcement that he would make to the guard under his breath as he went, when he was confronted with just such an awkward occurance.

As he turned the corner he walked straight into a figure that was ambling its way towards the inn. Before he knew what was happening he found himself in the sudden embrace of Pip, the serving wench which whom he had once had a rather sordid and rapid dalliance, and the flibbertigibbet to whom Cynefrid had referred only days before when Thurstan had first paid them a visit. Although the pairing of the two had been a drunken groping in the alley behind the inn many months before and much regretted by Wirt, unfortunately for him, Pip refused to accept that they were not a match made in heaven. She had beset Wirt with flirtatious winks, gropes and kisses every time they had met since that night and had often lay in wait outside the apothecary's house to waylay him on any errands that Cynefrid had bade him perform.

And now here she was, all bosom and sweaty flesh wrapping herself around his squirming body and giggling joyously at such physical contact. "Now where you be off to, me luverly?" she tittered.

He blushed and sighed inwardly. How was he to be rid of this awful young wench? Things were not going well – this delay could prove distrastrous, not to mention the impending display of wrath from Cynefrid should he come upon them in such a manner.

Wirt wriggled free of the groping embrace. How he could have thought this spotty young wench attractive he knew not, and for a fleeting second vowed silently that he would never sup mead to the extent that he should ever think so again. "Aw Wirty don't ya be so prudy. Hows about a quick 'un? Get rid of the boy and we can go an' 'av a quick go behind inn, like that night," and she winked at him as she wiggled her ample cleavage in front of him.

He balked at the idea and felt slightly nauseous at the thought. How could he have immersed himself in such a girl so wholeheartedly and without impunity?

"For gawd's sake let me be," implored Wirt, desperately trying not to curse her very existence. "I am on urgent business, and if I were you, you would turn around too and follow."

"Ooo Wirty, you tryin' to make away wi' me?"

"I can assure you that is the last thing on my mind," stated Wirt, his blushes now not from embarrassment but from an anger welling within him from this girl's foolish thoughts. "I am charged with warning all those beyond the gatehouse to make haste and leave Grimfell. You can leave or stay as you wish. If you choose the latter then be prepared to meet your maker, whomever or whatever that may be."

He clicked his tongue again and continued on his way to the gatehouse, leaving Pip slightly unsure as to whether he was joking in his last statement. Then Cynefrid turned the last corner in the steps and came rushing passed her as quickly as his sandled feet would carry him. "Be gone girl, and leave the lad alone you silly wench. If you value your life you will leave this place."

Just then the sky above turned dark. Looking up Pip saw a great winged beast soaring overhead. She screamed and turned, and ran back towards the gatehouse pleading with Cynefrid and Wirt to wait for her.

They were too busy to take any notice of her callings. They were alerting those who lived in the squalid huts to pack up what they needed and to leave Grimfell as soon as was possible. By now others had seen the figures in the sky above the tower and there was great confusion below. The woman, Llinos, grabbed Cynefrid and thrust her son towards him. "Take the boy. I cannot leave without me 'usband and Lord knows where 'e is – somewhere up in soldier's barracks." Cynefrid stared at her, while the boy wriggled in his mother's arms as she tried to loosen his grip upon her. "Take 'im, I begs yer. 'E's a good lad. 'E won't be no trouble. Me and me 'usband'll catch up wi' yer."

She ducked as a great shadow loomed overhead. Cynefrid stood his ground and did not flinch as the four smaller beasts circled the walls of their target. With a final shove, her son Eni was thrust into the arms of the apothecary and they both watched in horror as she disappeared towards the steps to find her husband. Eni wept loudly and tried to follow his mother, and it took Cynefrid's quick wits to manage to keep a hold of the squirming boy. Whilst feeling humbled at the actions of this woman in trying to find the boy's father, he felt anger at her for leaving him under his protection. He understood her motives but in following these he also thought her selfish. It was almost certain that she would meet her end, along with her husband, leaving the boy an orphan. If she had left her husband to his own devices, then at least the boy would still have his mother. But there was no time to dwell on his moral judgements, and he took hold of Eni's hand and swept him along towards the barbican. The drawbridge had already been lowered; the guards there were not about to hang around when escape was so easy, and a rushing crowd of people squeezed their way through the building and out across the drawbridge to the freedom and relative safety of the marshes.

Wirt was having trouble keeping a hold on the horses' reins. Amid the shouting and screaming of the townsfolk there had been several occasions when a hand had tried to grab one of the mounts away from him and he had had to use force to deter them. Several times he had kicked a prospective thief, and although he had no wish to cause any harm to anyone, his boot had found its way home on each occasion, leaving a bloody nose or two in his wake. In the confusion he had become separated from Cynefrid, but could only hope that his mentor had made it through the barbican safely and that they would meet up again eventually. His charge was hanging on for dear life in the saddle, and had even helped to deter any grabbing hands by biting them – a job at which he had found he was extremely adept.

Bolts of fire struck at the ground around the barbican entrance; the onslaught had commenced. Looking up Cynefrid took a mental note of the sight of the dragons spitting out their weapon of fire, diving down and then ascending sharply after releasing their grisly load. They would make timeless sketches in the history volume.

News of the attack had spread like wildfire throughout the garrison and soldiers were running everywhere, not really knowing what they were supposed to do, but knowing that they would be expected to do something other than run for their lives. In an unorganised frenzy the archers were ordered to let their arrows fly, but their attempts were futile. If an arrow did find its scaly target, it simply bounced off the beast's natural armour and toppled to the ground far below.

Eventually news of the attack reached Modig and he had rushed out of the great oaken doors to stand impotent upon the steps as he watched his assailants circling overhead. The family were being ushered through the great hall to their escape, but as they began to descend the steps the great shadow of the female loomed overhead. She circled once and then, with her mouth open and nostrils flared she breathed the flames of death towards the centre of the tower. Anything flammable – and that included those rushing for safety – was instantly aflame. The screams of agony echoed around Grimfell. After delivering the first volley the female lifted herself high above the tower once more, before diving towards the structure. She hit it sidelong with all her weight and the great stone keep wobbled under her strength. She retreated. And then she hit it again. She repeated this until large stones started to loosen and hurtle down, crushing whoever was in their way as they crashed below.

Modig remained where he was, his hands resting on the wall. His skin was ashen underneath the trails of blood that ran from the cuts on his head and face, as he watched the smoke and flames of death rise silently from the charred remains of his family.

He stood perfectly still, as if resigned to his departure from the world, although the exact manner in which this would occur was yet to be revealed. He heard a slow, heavy wing-beat not far from where he stood and out of the corner of his eye he saw the great shape come into view. The female dragon hovered at eye level, her great leathery wings heavily beating to keep her air-borne, her great skull dwarfing him in her shadow.

He looked into the great golden eye – its pupil dilating as it focused upon him. She snorted, sending trails of grey smoke upwards into the ever-cooling air. Modig waited for the jaws to open and send a trail of fire down upon him, but to his surprise, she gave one giant beat of her wings and flew away. He exhaled, his whole body shaking from fear, desperation and hopelessness. He could not escape; there was nowhere for him to go. The great hall was all but demolished behind and above him, and below him the steps were cracked and wavering beneath the onslaught. He could see Grimfell ablaze below him and he contemplated ending his own life by merely jumping into the flames. It would easy to do, there was nothing left for him here – his family lay in smouldering blobs of melting flesh and charring bones, and his home would soon be in ruins.

However, his thoughts were usurped by the actions of the she-dragon as she once again appeared in his sight. She flew down upon Grimfell at great speed, turning again at the last minute and with a mighty blow crashed into the side of the wall that circled the steps. They crumbled instantly, and Modig lost his balance and found himself falling. However, smashing his body on the ground below was not to be his final fate. The dragon intercepted his tumble and in a flash of her huge teeth and his blood he disappeared into her mouth, the only part of him to reach the ground being the sheared off remains of his left leg, which rolled to rest against the burning door of the stables. The flames that ate at the wooden stables found their new prey and it was soon enveloped in their hunger.

Over at Eastward a loud triumphant cry filled the air as the villagers watched the tower collapse and the flames leap ever higher into the sky. A thick plume of grey smoke drifted upwards and spread like a blanket over the marshes.

"That'll teach 'em", shouted one villager, waving his fist in the air.

"May they rot where they lay," added another.

Villagers started dancing with each other, the men locking arms with their womenfolk, and indeed other men's womenfolk, and danced around in circles until some collapsed with exhaustion and others with the effects of dizziness. The children joined in the festivities and soon all sported cheeks flushed with the redness of joviality as the village dogs barked and chased each other. Aedre found herself being dragged into a jig by Barmy the village simpleton. Barmy was less than agile on his feet and was prone to falling down or bumping into things. He was also very muscular and had no apparent awareness of his own strength.

Aedre had been quite distressed when Barmy had shown a more than passing interest in her many years before. She had become quite adept at avoiding him whenever possible, but on this occasion her guard had been let down and he had swooped upon her unsuspectingly. Now she found herself being almost thrown around in an energetic dance that she really had no wish in which to partake. More than once his heavy feet crashed upon her own delicate toes and she winced and cried out in pain, frustration and anger. To the other villagers it was great sport to see Barmy enjoying himself in such a vigorous manner. No one came to Aedre's aid, and even the imploring glances she threw at her father as she was whisked passed him proved unfruitful.

As suddenly as he had grabbed hold of her to join him in his lumbering 'dance', he stopped dead in his tracks. His crooked face with slightly withered right eye bent down towards hers and she placed one hand on each of his shoulders and pushed him away as much as she could in an attempt to escape his inept amorous advances. She winced as his drooling mouth puckered in a childish attempt at kissing her. She turned her head away and his sticky, wet lips landed heavily on her left cheek. He guffawed at his cleverness and slapped her behind, which made the villagers roar with laughter, and clap and cheer at his audacity and ineptitude. In the space of a few minutes the downfall of Grimfell seemed to have escaped their minds and had been replaced with the sport before them – the taming of Aedre by Barmy, the simpleton.

A low whisper was joined by another, and another, that became louder and louder until all present became as one voice. It was painfully clear to Aedre that the population of the whole village were trying to egg Barmy on in his amorous advances and she became scared of their apparent ignorance of her distress at the situation. The chant of 'kiss', 'kiss', 'again', 'again', became almost demonic. The assumed death of Modig and his kin had aroused some primal instincts within them all; their lust for blood and retribution had been replaced with those basic animal instincts that held no quarter, instincts that forgot the ideals of decorum. Even the innocence in the children seemed to have been replaced with wickedness as those of them who were old enough, joined in with the chanting.

Aedre became fearful for her virtue and even her life as Barmy responded to the attention he was attracting. In his simple mind he was doing no wrong. With the villagers' vocal support he was revelling in the interest he had attracted and, placing a hand on each of Aedre's hips he raised her into the air above him. She thought for a minute that he was going to toss her skywards, but just as he raised her he caught sight of the six winged beasts approaching. He stopped and stared before releasing the stricken girl and pointed in the dragons' direction. Aedre fell to the ground with a thump and lay prostrate for a few moments, gaining her breath. Silence fell upon the villagers as they all watched the victorious great winged beasts fly above them on their way back from whence they had arrived a few hours before.

Aedre breathed a great sigh of relief at their return, and immediately picked herself up and ran back to the safety of her home, leaving the rest of the village to stand in awe as the dragons slowly flew overhead.

LXXI

Felagin, Thurstan and Berowen left the copse and joined the track that took them away from the scene. It took them through dense scrub until the trail entered into a narrow path, bordered on both sides by high verges. Most of the bushes that clung to the verges had been picked bare of their heavy load of autumnal fruits and the skeletal branches protruded barrenly as if attempting to scratch anything that came too close to mete out a painful wrath at being laid bare. There were some, though, that were ripe with red berries and every so often a bird would flutter noisily from the camouflage of the shrubs to twitter angrily at being disturbed from its foraging by the travellers that passed through their feeding ground. Ivy trailed itself around any branches in its way, entombing the plants in its suffocating grip and crisp, yellowy brown ferns withered as they died, their life put on hold deep under the ground waiting for the hint of spring to unfurl themselves again in their bright green youthful tendrils.

All was peaceful down this path, apart from the heavy plodding of the horses, and the occasional rustle in the undergrowth of wildlife searching for food. The sun was low in the clear blue sky and its rays caught the golden brown hues of the leaves that still clung to their branches in defiance of their impending doom. Their stubbornness in falling to the ground to rot back into the earth would eventually be thwarted and within weeks this path would be cloaked in the white blanket of snow and a glittering covering of frost.

The path changed again and the three found themselves descending into a tree lined avenue. To one side a stream made its way slowly over mossy rocks, the fall of leaves choking it in its path. Great trees lined the banks precariously, their roots visible as they clung to the ever eroding earth. The scent of rotting vegetation was rife and the dampness was a haven for the moss and fungus that covered the rocks and sides of the banks. Great clumps of pale brown fungus clung to some of the tree trunks, giving the impression of steps leading up the outside of the tree.

On the other side the wood clung to the steep incline, here and there bare rock visible beneath the thinning earth where the rush of rainwater dislodged it a bit more whenever the skies emptied its dark clouds overhead. The track was littered with rocks of every shape and size that had lost their grip under the deluges and the moss had been quick to take advantage of their predicament, covering them in a carpet of deep green hues.

They came across a dilapidated building long deserted and left to the ravages of nature. Its wooden roof had collapsed and the stone walls had mostly fallen away, leaving a hollow shell, now filled with nettles, ivy and one or two tiny oak saplings. A crude wooden cross that stood at an angle in the ground next to the side of the building, marked the desolate final resting place of someone. The intersections of the cross had been bound with twine that had frayed over time. There was no clue as to whoever rested beneath the cross and Berowen looked upon it with sadness at its isolation.

Moving slowly on, the travellers found themselves rising slightly again and out on to grassland where their sudden emergence frightened a herd of deer that had been grazing quietly just out of cover of the wood.   The animals all raised their heads in unison, their mouths still chewing slowly, before bolting in every direction to escape the perceived danger from this sudden interruption of their solitude.

Once outside in the open, it became obvious that all was not well with Thurstan. As they continued their journey onwards, he became paler and his whole body slumped in his saddle. Despite Felagin's bold and somewhat confident assurances, it would seem that Thurstan may not mend quite as easily as he had said. Berowen was concerned for the health of her friend and implored Felagin to stop for a while in order for Thurstan's wounds to be investigated further, but the old man would hear none of it. "We are to stop but once on this journey, and that will be at our journey's end," was all that he would say.

"And where is this end to our travel?" she asked curtly.

"The monastery. The brothers will be able to see to his wounds."

Berowen felt her irritation with the old man rising again. "Yes, but how long is left of the journey? Are we to be out of our saddles soon or is there much more riding for Thurstan to endure?"

Felagin raised a hand in the air in despair at the questioning, and waved it around above his head. "Questions. Questions. Why do women always ask questions?" he growled, more to himself than to anyone else.

Berowen had heard enough and, leaning over to grab the reins from Thurstan's hands, pulled his and her horse to a halt. Felagin appeared not to notice and just carried on walking his horse forward. She watched his straight back as he sat majestically astride his mount, his shoulders perfectly square in his omnipotence. Then her eyes widened in puzzlement as he raised his other hand above his head also and then she watched as he made flapping movements with both arms; slowly up and down they rhythmically went. His bottom bounced in time with the movement of his arms. Was he about to take flight, she wondered to herself?

Such an odd occurrence would not surprise her one bit under the circumstances for he was certainly an odd, as well as infuriating, fellow.

But he remained firmly seated in his saddle; his horse plodding forward with no direction from a tug on the reins, which hung limply across its shoulders. A shout rang out. "On your head be it, my lady of concern, if he dies. Brother Fyn is the only one who can administer the antidote for the poison that rages through his body. The plants are only found in the monastery gardens, planted there and tended to lovingly by Brother Fyn himself. He has the gift you know. But he is an odd character to be sure and it is likely most beneficial that he has taken the cloth, for to have him loose on the world would be tantamount to chaos."

Berowen would not be fooled into moving a muscle until she had received a satisfactory answer to her question. "On the contrary, Felagin. Methinks it will be on your shoulders should he die, purely because you are too stubborn, or arrogant, to answer a simple question when asked."

"What a strange predicament. Thurstan's life for the answer to a question. It does not give the impression of a fair barter to my mind, my lady," responded Felagin.

His curt reply caught her unawares and guilt overcame her, for she knew deep down that this was true. In an attempt to conceal her mistake she retorted in a similar curt way, "Then if you shall not answer, I shall have no choice but to return to Grimfell and seek aid from Cynefrid."

At this Felagin let out a sinister laugh. "Grimfell is it? See that hill ahead of us aways? From there you shall be able to see Grimfell, or rather, methinks, what is left of it. I'll wager Thurstan would receive no help there today." And again he flapped his long, scrawny arms up and down.

Berowen shivered at the realisation of his peculiar playacting. "They came?"

"You will see. And do not fret too long, my dear, for beyond that hill is the valley in which the monastery dwells." Although the words were sympathetic, there was no softness in his voice, not that she would have expected any, and she urged her horse forward, trailing that of Thurstan behind her.

On the near horizon Berowen could indeed see the hill to which Felagin was referring. She was completely lost as to which direction they had travelled since leaving Grimfell and was not at all sure where they were in relation to the fortress. But the hill did not seem too far away and she led Thurstan's horse slowly after Felagin. Thurstan seemed to be in that world between consciousness and unconsciousness and barely coped with keeping himself seated. He wobbled this way and that and she decided to draw his mount alongside hers on a tighter rein in case she had to lend a hand in keeping him steady. The mentor's apparent disregard for his apprentice caused her some disquiet, but she dare not utter forth any further negative comments towards the latter. She had learnt that his mood was as changeable as the very weather, but felt it prudent to leave him to stew in his own sour temper for now.

Besides, his reminder regarding Grimfell weighed heavy on her mind. She had not realised that the death of Mildthryth would have resulted in such a rapid response and she began to fear for the safety of Odi. He had not yet returned to her and if, as Felagin had predicted, Grimfell had been attacked she would have expected the bird to find his way back to her by now. And what of Cynefrid, Wirt and little 'Mouse'?

Berowen became uneasy and the feeling in the pit of her stomach made her feel unwell. She willed the journey to become quicker so that the hill could be reached. Only then would she know whether, upon the death of Mildthryth, Grimfell - in truth - had fallen.

The hill grew slowly closer and it was not too long before they had reached its base. From a distance it had given the impression of being easily traversed, but once at its foot it revealed its rocky structure. Scree and rocks littered the surrounds and the horses found it difficult in places to maintain a solid grip. It was also higher and steeper than Berowen had imagined and she found herself having to tighten her grip on the reins of Thurstan's horse in order to ensure it did not fall behind. She began to panic as she watched the stricken man precariously waiver where he sat.

The climb was laborious for the horses and they snorted and grunted at the exertion, thin wisps of breath clouding the air as they plodded along the track. Eventually they reached the summit and Felagin raised his hand in instruction for Berowen and Thurstan to stop. He pointed and Berowen slowly followed his finger's direction. The sun had begun to set behind them and she could easily see the pall of dark smoke rising from the fortress of Grimfell and the glow of flames flickering in the fading light. There was no longer a turret rising to the sky, and no flags fluttered in the breeze. It had been destroyed and was destined to be a ruin on the landscape to meet the eyes of any who travelled that way in future.

Felagin grunted in affirmation of his earlier statement and Berowen could see the satisfied look in his eye at being proven correct. Although, in general terms, she was not unduly concerned at the fortress' demise, she voiced her concern at the health and whereabouts of Odi and her friends and with sadness in her eyes she looked to Felagin for assurance.

"We must make haste, for the sun will soon be gone," stated the old man. "If all is well and Odi carried out his instructions, the others shall meet us at the monastery. It is not far now, but we have this bloody hill to get off and to attempt that in the gloaming, never mind the dark, would be a fool's errand."

Felagin clicked his tongue and prompted his horse onwards to begin the descent. With one last look at Grimfell, Berowen followed still holding the reins of Thurstan's horse as well as her own. Felagin was correct in his curse of the way down, for it was as treacherous as the climb had been exhaustive. The loose ground was not ideal for horses, but rather than dismount and lead them, making the journey much longer than it would have been in the fading light, Felagin decided to continue on horseback, but slowly and carefully. They could see their destination nestling in the bottom of the valley and as twilight fell, a hundred or more candles slowly flickered to life within its confines. A plaintive rhythmic toll from the bell in the tiny chapel tower rang on the faint breeze to announce vespers and if the three had been closer at that moment they would have witnessed the shadowy figures of the monks slowly but purposefully making their way through the candlelit corridors towards the chapel.

Berowen could not answer for her companions but she had a hunger that was beginning to churn her insides. It was obvious that Thurstan had gone beyond the need of sustenance – his condition worsened with every hoofbeat. Her first concern would be to make sure that the Brother to whom Felagin had referred tended to his needs, and only then would she seek out a morsel to ease the gnawing in her belly. She then wondered whether there would be any food on offer for travellers; after all, monks were well known for their frugal lifestyle. The food for their table would have been grown themselves, just as the milk and cheese would have been from their own cows. The winter months would surely not yield much for the pot, and the supplies that had been stored away would have been well noted and accounted for if it were to last the long winter season. She resigned herself to the thought that she would probably be given a chunk of stale bread and perhaps a piece of home-churned cheese, but that would be most welcome, however paltry an amount.

The bell toll ceased and soon the air was filled with the faint sound of the glorious, soothing voices of monks chanting. The travellers passed through a sheltered field that was strewn with beehives, all now covered for the winter by straw hackles to keep their occupants warm. These jackets of straw stood silently and eerily in the fading light, standing like old armless scarecrows. The monks would check the condition of the hackles throughout the winter months to ensure that they stayed intact and were protecting the precious honey bees that supplied the wax for candles, and the honey for the mead that was brewed within the kitchens of the monastery. It was the monastery's only source of outside income and Grimfell had been the main source of this welcome monetary benefit. The monks would be the only casualty of the fall of the fortress, and it was yet to be seen how they would manage without the constant demand for the potent drink, specially brewed by Brother John to his own secret recipe.

By the time the trio came to the stonewalled boundary of the monastery grounds, vespers were over and the monks were returning to their evening duties. Berowen and Felagin dismounted and helped Thurstan out of his saddle. His legs buckled beneath him and he fell to his knees, whereupon Felagin rapped on the wooden gate with urgency in his movement. It was not long before the small partition in the top of the gate opened to reveal a hooded face, half in shadow and half lit by the candle lantern that was held aloft to scrutinise those who had knocked for attention and possible entry.

"Who knocks? And for what purpose?" came the quiet request.

"We are come to seek the aid of Brother Fyn. I am Felagin of the north and my friend is in need of the good Brother's special remedy. We both came upon Mildthryth, the hag of the Great Oak, and my friend's life is fading with every moment after he fell foul of her. Her temper was worse than we had been led to believe and her hospitality less than adequate. Methinks we should have listened and taken the longer route rather than try and pass through her wood."

"Ah, the great Felagin," came the response. "Your reputation precedes you. Brother Fyn has spoken often of your skill with the various fauna and flora that share the earth with us. I, though, have not heard of this Mildthryth woman, but she does not seem to be the most pleasing of characters by your words." And with a bang the partition was closed to be followed by a great clunking of various locks and keys, which precluded the great door being pulled open to allow them entry. "You and your companions are welcome, great Felagin of renown."

"My thanks, Brother," responded Felagin. "I am to take it that you have received no other visitors today?"

The hooded figure shook its head. "No-one else has knocked on our door today."

"Ah, well they shall most likely arrive on the morrow then. I am sure that you will allow them entry and afford them a welcome entry. Come, we need assistance good Brother, to get my companion inside."

The monk bowed his head and rushed down the path, to return a short while later with three other monks, two of whom assisted Thurstan while the third took charge of the horses. Berowen watched as the two helped Thurstan to his feet, and tried to go with them but was stopped by the gatekeeper who apprehended her with a gentle tap on the arm. "Forgive me, my lady, but you must remember that you are about to tread in a place that is inhabited by those who have taken certain vows and as such, there are places in this monastery that are not to be visited by those of the fairer sex. There are, however, quarters that have been set aside for travellers such as yourself, my lady, and you will be instructed as to what parts are restricted."

Suitably chastised, all Berowen could do was stand and watch as the monks disappeared with Thurstan through the main door of the monastery. With a wave of the hand, the monk who had allowed them entry beckoned them to follow him along the muddy path and through the same door, whereupon he bade the travellers wait while he searched out Brother Fyn.

LXXII

Berowen had spent one of the most uncomfortable nights she had ever experienced, partly due to her concern over the welfare of her friend and partly because the cot on which she had lain was less than well-made. The straw that filled the mattress poked through the many holes of the cloth that covered it and she was more than certain that it was full of irritating bed bugs for her skin had itched all night, making a restful sleep impossible.

The room in which she had been placed was spartan, containing only the cot and a small rickety wooden structure that she assumed was to pass as some sort of table on which her candlestick had stood. The small window was ill-fitting and she could feel the wintery breeze squeezing its way through the cracks on to her face. If this was to be her room for her stay at the monastery, many things would have to be changed and to while away the tortuous dark hours she made a mental list of her needs, although she knew at the back of her mind that most of them would not be met.

Her attempt at rest had not been aided either by the mournful toll of the bell in the early hours – the bell that called the monks to yet more prayer. Her quarters were situated in a dormitory not only out of bounds but also well separated to those that dwelt within the monastery, but she could still hear the soft sound of the melodious chanting as it passed her window on the night breeze. It was strangely soothing, and after a brief moment or two she found herself having trouble keeping her eyes open and began to drift off to sleep. But her respite was short-lived when she felt something scuttle across her hand as it rest upon the blanket that was sparsely draped across her. Immediately sitting up, with the aid of the flickering light from the candle, she just saw the tail of a mouse disappear down the tiny gap between the cot and the wall. She found herself briefly searching for the tiny creature in the vague possibility that it may well have been Felagin's companion rather than just an ordinary mouse. Perhaps it was carrying some tiny message for her from its master to inform her of Thurstan's health? However, she soon reached the conclusion that this action would have been highly unlikely for it had become apparent since their recent journey together that such a subtlety would be far removed from the sorcerer's mind.

She found herself once again musing on the high possibility that he had had some relationship with Mildthryth in their younger days and she grimaced at the thought of the old hag and him embarking on such a dubious affair. However, it really was none of her business, and however lurid it appeared to her, for she could not – try as she might – visualise a younger Mildthryth, she had no right to question such a dalliance. She tried to put the vision out of her mind by once again attempting to relax and tempt sleep to take her away for a few brief hours to a place that would hopefully be far more hospitable than that in which she now found herself.

LXXIII

After the confused exodus from the burning fortress of Grimfell, Wirt and Col had found Cynefrid - and his new charge Eni – and they had all followed Odi unquestioningly. Whether out of tenaciousness or sheer luck, they had managed to keep a hold of all the horses, although there had been at least one shaky moment when the pack horse had nearly been stolen by a more than determined guard who had decided that it was best to save his own hide rather than stay and try to defend Grimfell from the assault. He was not alone of course; many of the guards who had been able to escape had taken the opportunity to do so. It was only those soldiers who were unfortunate to have been caught in the barracks who had been given no such freedom of choice.

Cynefrid had been under no illusion that Eni would not see his mother again. It was also highly unlikely that the boy's father would have survived the attack, so the young lad was now under his care, and he felt obliged to see that the boy would at least be taken to a place that he deemed safe and of benefit to the orphan. And as much as he had no wish to adopt another waif and stray, if no such position could be found, then he would have to take him under his own wing.

Try as hard as he could, Wirt found it impossible to shake Pip from his presence. It seemed that everywhere he went that she would follow as if attached by an invisible piece of rope. He had even found himself silently vowing that he would never again get drunk so as to avoid the possibility of this harassment in the future. And, as young and relatively unwise as he was, this oath was made with such vehemence that if he had spoken rather than thought it, most who had heard it would have laughed out loud at such an unrealistic vow.

Pip was becoming more than a little irksome in her constant quest for attention. As they sat by the crackling fire, she buzzed around Wirt as does a fly around a rotting piece of meat in the hot summer months and if he could have swatted her he would have done so. Oh if only it was that easy to rid himself of her cloying attentions - a mere rapid slap of the hand and that would be the end of it. But unfortunately that was, of course, impossible and besides, he had a sneaking notion that if he did try to slap her that she would probably look upon it as an act of some weird variety of affection - such was the strangeness of the lass that seemed intent on smothering him in her ample bosom.

Cynefrid watched the 'passion' play unfold before him and smirked to himself in the shadows. The boy, Eni, had fallen asleep long before, and was currently leaning against Cynefrid with his head nestled under the apothecary's armpit. In the dancing light of the fire, Cynefrid watched his assistant's expression change constantly from tolerance to frustration; to embarrassment; and then to pure and unequivocal anger as the girl constantly pressed any piece of flesh against him that she could in her attempt to persuade him to let all his youthful lust run rampant under the scratchy irritating blankets that had been spread by the fire. Her repetitive ploy of tantalising him with the promise that any activity under those blankets would keep them warm against the cold night air fell on deaf ears, however, as he looked across the flames at his mentor. Cynefrid raised a hand to his mouth and pretended to cough in order to disguise the smile. Wirt's romantic interludes had always been entertaining, but none more so than this particular partnership and he was intrigued as to how the young, somewhat naive, romantic would deal with the maiden with the one-track mind and over-zealous lust for physical contact of the naked variety.

It was clear that Wirt was now looking for assistance from Cynefrid, but the apothecary was enjoying the spectacle far too much to intercede at this stage. Besides, it was time Wirt grew up a bit and learned a valuable lesson in the art of wooing a lass. Up to now, it appeared to the *old* man that the *young* man seemed to think that a quick sojourn down a dark alley with a willing female was all that was needed, and that the girls were only there for the gratification of basic sexual instincts. He did not seem to have any idea that there were girls that would think it completely unacceptable to undertake such a visit whilst being wooed as a prospective wife. Yes, it was time that young Wirt learned a modicum of responsibility and perhaps even thought about the prospect of settling down with a good, respectable young female. To this end, Cynefrid decided not to come to the lad's assistance at this stage and was content with sitting back and watching the drama unfold, as Eni slept soundly beside him.

It was Col who intervened, in his childish innocence, completely unaware of the superb timing of his nighttime wanderings. He had dozed off at around the same time as Eni had fallen asleep against Cynefrid, although the stableboy had simply lain down on the bedding that had been laid out for him rather than having the comfort of physical contact as he fell asleep. At his age, such a luxury would have made him feel so much better, but neither Wirt nor Pip seemed interested in affording him that small treat. The boy had awoken from his fitful sleep frightened by the nightmare that had tormented his thoughts almost as soon as his eyes had closed. He had sat up, and rubbing his eyes had started to whimper, but no-one paid him any attention. It would not have crossed Wirt's mind to offer sympathy and, although Pip's maternal instincts may well have prompted a tiny morsel of motherly comfort, this was vastly outweighed by the basic desires that surged through her veins whenever she was in Wirt's company and she found it easy to ignore the sound of Col's obvious discomfort. In truth it was the same when she found herself in close proximity with any young man of a certain year, for at her age and due to her lackadaisical upbringing, she was not particularly fussy with whom she shared her wares.

And so while Wirt was absorbed in the warding off of his tormentor and the latter was intent on getting her way in the end, Col wandered towards the centre of the drama as he made his way slowly and sleepily towards Cynefrid over on the opposite side of the fire. He had noticed Eni fast asleep in Cynefrid's embrace and yearned to have such comfort himself. It was bitterly cold and Col shivered as he walked slowly and uncertainly towards the old man, the blankets wrapped around him as tightly as possible to keep out the chill. And as much as he was enjoying the spectacle unfolding before him, and his apprentice's clear uneasiness and discomfiture, the sight of the stableboy touched Cynefrid's soft side and he called out to Wirt knowing full well that this intervention would cease the show for that evening.

"Your charge would seem to need some comforting, Wirt," he suggested. "And it is late and I suggest that all of us should take advantage of the heat from the fire and settle ourselves between our meagre blankets for the night in the hope that we may sleep swiftly and soundly until it is time to move on upon the morrow."

Wirt stood up instantly, nodded his head in agreement and some relief, and took hold of Col gently around the shoulders, guiding him back to his place of sleep, whereupon he lay down beside him and pulled up the blankets. Sharing their body heat would hopefully afford them enought warmth for the wishes of Cynefrid to come true and tucking his arms around Col, Wirt settled down to sleep.

"Well that is just fine!" exclaimed Pip from where she stood by the fire, with a hand on each hip, as she watched both Cynefrid and Wirt settle down with their respective young charges. "And what am I s'posed to do? Who is goin' to keep me warm this cold night?"

"I am sure the fire in your blood will keep you warm enough to fall asleep, my dear girl," responded Cynefrid with a grin on his old wrinkled face. "And not forgetting that you are at an advantage in that, unlike us four males who are all but skin and bone, you have more ...erm ... layers of ......um.....natural heating than us."

"And what is that s'posed to mean?" demanded Pip, her cheeks reddening with vexation as she thought more about the last statement and heard a low chortling sound from the direction of Wirt and Col's heap of blankets and bodies.

"Simple fact of nature my dear girl," continued Cynefrid in response, calmly and covering his amusement well. "Women have a softer and more comforting frame than us men. A body made for cuddling up to and ..."

"But ain't no-one cuddlin' up to me is there?" she demanded and Cynefrid could almost see her foot stamping on the ground in agitation and chagrin. "And I still think you bein' rude about me figure. And tryin' to cover it up by talkin' about cuddlin' and the like. You must think I were born yesterday or summat. I can tell yer that I've 'ad many a kind word said about me figure."

"I am sure that you have," answered Cynefrid wryly. "Now, young Pip, I really would urge you to settle yourself down," he continued. "The hour is getting later and the air is getting colder. You should wrap yourself up for sleep while you are still warm to conserve any body heat you already have."

"Under that extra layer of lard," muttered Wirt under his breath who then fretted that his words had been louder than he had thought. He froze in anticipation of the covers being ripped from his grip and a hand making contact with his head. Nothing of the sort occurred and he sighed with relief. Silence at last befell the small encampment and Odi ruffled out his feathers, tucked his head under his wing and at last closed one eye content in the knowledge that those whose safe passage was temporarily under his watchful gaze were at last asleep, at least for the moment.

LXXIV

Berowen woke up shivering beneath her flimsy blankets and felt utterly miserable at the situation in which she found herself. To be relegated to some cold damp cell had not been what she had expected when she had decided to journey with Thurstan and Felagin and she was both angry and despondent. The cold draught that had plagued her all night had not helped either, and that and her rash decision to travel thus far, ensured that her mood was as melancholic as it was.

She rose from her cot and wondered what she was supposed to do. Was she to wander around the corridors and try to find where they had taken Thurstan the night before? Or was she to wait for Felagin to come and inform her of his progress? The latter seemed highly unlikely in her mind, but she was very concerned regarding her friend's health.

And was she to wait in her cell for someone to collect and lead her to wherever the meal that would break her fast was to be served? Or was she to creep about the corridors and try and find her own way, perhaps it would be just a matter of following her nose? But then what would these monks eat for this first meal of the day? Would she actually smell anything anyway? However, if her sex were as abhorrent to those who dwelt here as she had been led to believe the night before, surely she would not be allowed to wander anywhere even in the company of a suitable escort, let alone on her own.

She flopped herself dejectedly back down on to her cot, which wobbled and squeaked under her weight. No-one could ever describe her build as heavy, but the cot was so rickety and badly made that the sudden extra weight upon it, no matter how small, caused it much distress. She sat with her hands clasped together in her lap and waited. And then she started shivering again. She watched her warm breath spiral into the cold air in front of her as she exhaled.

A heavy rap on the door interrupted her solitude, followed by the voice of Felagin asking her whether she was awake and whether he could speak with her. Berowen did not think it at all proper that he should enter her cell to speak, but she was not sure whether she would be allowed to stand in the corridor either. However, she leapt up from the cot and hastily pulled open the door. Before the old man had a chance to speak, she immediately asked: "What news of Thurstan? How fares he under the care of your friend?"

"He fares well enough, Berowen, but the process will take many days, even weeks, yet."

She felt miserable again and her gaze fell to the floor.

"I trust that you slept well last night after the tedious events of yesterday?"

"I think I can truthfully say that it was the worst night I have ever experienced," was her answer, followed by a quick description of the night's attempts at rest. When she mentioned about the mouse Felagin told her in future to ensure that all effort was made to catch such creatures – food was always scarce at this time of year and any morsel, no matter how tiny, was to be made of use and the brothers would have eagerly accepted it. She hesitated a second, not being too sure as to whether he was joking with her or not, before continuing with her tale of discomfort from the night before.

Felagin raised his hand in an attempt to cease her detailed description, which he really had neither time for, nor real interest in hearing. "If it please you my lady, I do have news to impart, in fact the reporting of such information was the real reason that I came to your door. I thought that it would please you to know that Odi has returned with his charges."

Berowen looked up and for the first time that morning felt a raise in her mood, although this was short-lived when Felagin continued his news. "Our hosts are more than hesitant in allowing admittance to Odi, his kind well known for being rather ominous in their motives for arrival. I have assured them of his innocence in such matters, but they are in need of more assurances."

Felagin paused and watched a look of anger and irritation cloud Berowen's face. "However," he continued. "They are happy to receive the apothecary and his apprentice, plus the others who are with them."

"There should be just one other – a young boy," snapped Berowen somewhat unfairly perhaps at the messenger, but she was deeply annoyed at the refusal of entry of Odi.

"It appears there are *two* young boys plus a young woman," continued Felagin. "The young lady has caused a certain amount of consternation amongst the inhabitants of the abbey. I think, in other words, that your presence is sorely needed in the courtyard."

"I know not of whom you speak. I know of no young woman travelling with them. But of course I shall make haste to the courtyard before more problems arise," Berowen said, brushing passed Felagin who, for some reason unbeknown to her, had decided to remain in the same position, thus half-blocking the way out of Berowen's cell. She knew him by now to be an awkward old man, but his lack of manners still infuriated her. Thus, as she squeezed passed him, she made sure to tread on one of his feet as she did so. Even more infuriatingly he just laughed and said in a monotone, "Predictable, my dear girl. You really should learn to resist such conventional retaliations."

Berowen ignored him. She thought it the best solution; the last thing she wanted to do right then was open up some dialogue with Felagin that would go round and round in circles, with no real winner and with her just getting more and more frustrated and angry at his superciliousness.

A monk was waiting for her at the end of the passage. When she approached, he bowed his head slightly and – with not a word spoken, nor a gesture of the hand, for they were both tucked inside the sleeves of his habit – he led her down the warren of corridors until they reached the door that opened out onto the courtyard.

Berowen instantly understood why the unknown woman's presence had caused so much disquiet as reported by Felagin. As she walked briskly across the courtyard she waved to Cynefrid and then beckoned for him to approach. With Eni's hand firmly clasping his, Cynefrid did as he had been bid. Berowen gave the boy a motherly smile and listened while the apothecary told her why the lad came to be standing next to him in the courtyard of the abbey. She nodded sympathetically and understood perfectly why the boy could not have been left behind. "Who is the young woman, Cynefrid? And what is her purpose of travelling with you?" she asked.

"Name is Pip, my lady. She is a friend of my apprentice. Well, I say friend. More of a past acquaintance really I should perhaps say. She has developed some sort of unhealthy attraction for him and will not cease from plaguing him with her affections. She attached herself to us when leaving Grimfell before it fell to fire, her appearance being quite coincidental on the day."

"Hmm," uttered Berowen. "News came to my ear that she had caused some upset by her appearance, and I can understand why. Presumably she had no time to pack suitable travelling clothes before she left by your description of how she came to be here."

"Not at all, my lady," replied Cynefrid. "It came as a complete surprise to her."

Col came running over and wrapped himself around Berowen. As she knelt down to welcome him, she looked up at Cynefrid and said, "Well we must do something about it. Perhaps the monks here have something to spare with which she can cover herself up. I am surprised she has not frozen to death on the way here, dressed so inadequately in such a scant manner. The semi-circular cloak she wears does nothing to preserve warmth at this time of year."

"Indeed, my lady," replied Cynefrid. He had been awoken that morning by Pip's whining about how cold she was and how uncomfortable she had been throughout the night, and would perhaps have raised an eyebrow if he had been aware that Berowen had done exactly the same thing to Felagin. However, her constant cries for sympathy and attention had roused him at first light, and had not ceased for the rest of the journey to the abbey.

When Col had run to Berowen, Wirt had followed him – his pace picking up when he realised that he was now unprotected against the attentions of Pip. It was a sorry state of affairs in which to find himself where he had such a young lad as protection against a young woman. However, thus it was and thus he made his way swiftly to where Berowen was talking to his mentor, Col and Eni. But as usual, where Wirt went Pip was sure to follow and soon the whole group were huddled around Berowen. She looked at Pip and beckoned her to one side.

She did not introduce the subject of her taking her aside with a few minutes of idle banter, but came straight to the point. It was very difficult not to let her eyes wander to the ample cleavage that was on show in front of her – it was not difficult to miss and drew you towards it no matter how disinterested you may be or how much you tried to simply ignore it. "You are amongst those who have taken vows and my serious suggestion is that you do not walk around in such clothing, Pip. Have you nothing else with you? Surely you must be nigh on freezing to death in such scant costume? Is this your usual daywear at this time of year?"

"I got now't else wi' me," squawked Pip indignantly.

Cynefrid had quietly approached Berowen and was standing just behind her – far enough away for Pip not to be able to hear him, but close enough for him to whisper in Berowen's right ear.

"I think you could say that she is no better than she should be, my lady."

Berowen nodded her head in silent agreement, knowing full well the meaning behind the comment.

"And how come you to be travelling with my acquaintances?" she continued toward Pip.

"Wirt saved me, my lady, and brought me away from Grimfell."

"She tagged along," whispered Cynefrid.

"Him and me are getting wed," gushed Pip

"I think that would be surprising news to Wirt," continued Cynefrid quietly behind Berowen's ear.

"Where did you find work in Grimfell?" Berowen asked Pip.

"I worked at the inn my lady," was the somewhat proud reply.

"A serving wench ..... in more ways than one," came the explanation in a whisper from Cynefrid.

"I see," said Berowen with one eyebrow raised. "And you came to know young Wirt from there I assume?" she continued to Pip.

"Oh yes, m'lady, him and me hit it off like nobody's business," continued Pip.

"Like a bee to a pot of honey," added Cynefrid. "But methinks the honey was slightly tainted by previous tastings. I am afraid she is a baggage; a strumpet my lady, through and through."

Berowen cleared her throat at Cynefrid's latest aside, the tone of his utterances appearing to be attaining a higher level of vindictiveness with each sentence that he spoke. She had to admit that she was more than a little shocked, not only at his blatant insults and the disparagement of the girl before them, but also for the fierceness in which he spoke of her. She had not seen this side of the apothecary before, and considering that she had only known him briefly that was no real surprise, but it was quite clear that he had no respect for the girl before them whatsoever. Berowen was undecided as to whether she should banish Pip from her sight for being such a girl of ill-repute or whether to feel mildly sorry for her, with fate having dealt her such a hand, resulting in the subsequent abysmally low opinions cast upon her character by all and sundry.

She turned to Cynefrid and in a low voice suggested that he should attempt to obtain an article of clothing that may be of some use as quickly as he could before the girl found herself unceremoniously tossed outside the monastery gates for fear of the possibility of her corrupting any of those who dwelt within its confines. The challenge of tempting an innocent man may well be one of Pip's favourite pastimes, but the Abbot would definitely not receive it at all well to hear of her possible affect on those living under his austere gaze.

Cynefrid did as he had been bid, and Berowen then turned her attention to the problem of Odi being allowed entrance. She had not actually seen any sight of him since she had arrived in the courtyard, nor had she heard his characteristic calling. She had presumed that he would change into a more monk-pleasing shape to gain entry, but he had yet to reveal such a form, or so she assumed. She looked round and scrutinised the area but could see no extra being in the vicinity. Berowen was not actually too sure as to what she was supposed to do in such circumstances. Would Odi know to change into something else to gain entry, or was she to instruct him so to do? Looking back to the door from which she had emerged into the winter sunlight, she searched for Felagin in the hope he would be within hailing distance. But he was not there.

Berowen did not take too much notice of the gate-keeper pulling open the heavy door onto the outside world. Not, that is, until she saw the dog trot through and heard the monk call out, "Does this cur belong to one of you travellers?"

However, before anyone could answer, the dog had reached Berowen and had circled her once before seating itself patiently beside her. "Odi, I presume?" muttered Berowen under her breath, and the dog's brown eyes glinted.

"Good Brother," shouted Berowen across to the gatekeeper. "My travelling companion, Felagin, informed me that you were somewhat suspicious of a black bird that had arrived at the same time as my friends?"

"It was as you speak, my lady," replied the monk, slightly taken aback at her loud questioning. "It was a bird of bad omen, my lady, a raven."

"Surely a bird is able to fly wherever it wishes to go? I have seen birds here, if only a few. How were you going to stop this bird of bad omen and prevent entry, may I ask?"

"They do not dare fly around these buildings. These stones are built and blessed with good my lady. No evil can penetrate these confines. If it were to try it would be struck down."

"Really?" asked Berowen sarcastically. "By what or by whom? I see not one sentry with longbow slung across a shoulder. Are you saying that there are monks here who are prepared at a moment's notice to arm themselves, and kill a creature of nature; its ominous infamy only endowed upon it by people such as they? Do they rush about in their dowdy habits and fire arrows of death into the skies?"

Berowen felt a slight, but nevertheless painful, dig in the small of her back by something blunt and heavy. Felagin spoke behind her and she realised the prod had emanated from his walking staff. "What the good monk means, Berowen, is that no bird of evil would be able to fly through the confines of the Abbey due to the invisible forces of good preventing it from doing so. It would not be able to penetrate such a strong energy."

"Then how were you allowed entrance, Felagin?" she demanded. "Surely a man of your.... standing.... should not be allowed to cross the threshold? How is it that you are allowed to roam freely around such a sacred place? This I do not understand."

Berowen saw him bristle and instantly regretted goading him. She stiffened and braced herself for the retort. She could have kicked herself for such an outburst. When would she learn to keep her thoughts to herself with respect to this man who managed to madden her so often and with such ease? And what had made her behave so rudely towards the monk? Something had triggered a rush of anger and feelings of injustice within her and she could not help herself from offering forth such an escape for them.

She bowed her head and Odi, sensing the animosity directed at his mistress from Felagin, curled his lips slightly to reveal pink gums and a perfect shiny set of deathly white teeth as he let a low growl emanate from deep within his throat. Felagin stared at the dog and with this action being unsuccessful in effecting a silence from the beast, he then tapped it slightly on the head with his stick. Odi snapped at the offending length of wood as the old man withdrew it.

"Your companion's loyalty is to be commended, even though it is slightly mismatched in its defiance of me."

Berowen raised a hand and smoothed the head of Odi, "Hush now, friend, mind your manners as I should mind mine."

"Is that said by way of an apology for your appalling insolence so recently displayed at me?" asked Felagin, smirking.

"It is an apology for bringing up such things in public, Felagin. But not an apology for wishing to know the answer at some future point when we are away from prying eyes and ears."

At this point Cynefrid returned from his mission to find some suitable warmer covering for Pip. He had a look of triumphant satisfaction upon his face as he held aloft in his hands a rather tatty looking habit and cloak. Wirt had to turn his head away to hide the fact that his face was beaming from ear to ear with a smile of complete pleasure at the loud protests that came forth from his unwanted admirer's mouth. He had a sneaking suspicion that there would be parts of her anatomy to be covered all day that had received no such attention for many years hence.

"But surely this belongs to some monk?" pleaded Pip as she took the rather smelly, ripped and dirty article of clothing between her forefinger and thumb.

"Oh it did," Cynefrid confirmed. "But he no longer needs it as he died. As you may have noticed it is rather ripped in places and there is a large hole of missing material in the front."

Pip grimaced as she inspected the reported hole. "What are these stains around the fraying threads? They look like dried blood! They are not dried blood are they?"

Cynefrid cleared his throat. Berowen and Felagin both turned their heads in an instant to await the answer. They were both completely taken in by the story unfolding before them. This monk had clearly not died in his cot.

"Stains? Oh dear, are there? Brother Alfred insisted the garment had been soaked to remove such evidence," Cynefrid continued, his voice dripping with obvious pleasure at Pip's growing discomfort before him.

The stricken girl tossed the garment to the ground. "I will not wear such a thing. I cannot be expected to wear an article of clothing that someone has not only died wearing, but has his bloodstains upon also."

Berowen interrupted. "What happened to the fated monk, Cynefrid? How came he to shed his blood in such a way?"

"No-one knows for sure, my lady," replied Cynefrid. "The monk went outside into the copse to find some berries to dye some cloth by all accounts. They found him a day or so later, dead as a pig on a spit. He was an aged, doddery old man I was told. They think that he must have just died as there were no wounds upon his body to speak of."

"But the bloodstains?" queried Felagin, his curiosity heightened by the omitted information and conflicting story. "If he died of natural causes, how was there a hole in the front of his habit and bloodstains? Stains that appear to have been so abundant and strong that soaking could not remove them all?"

"Ah those, yes. As to the manner in which he died they know not as I have said, but as his belly has been ripped open they assume a wild animal or two must have been scavenging and found his corpse. The smell of death would have attracted many a corpse eater in these parts. It is fair to say that one or more such creatures ripped his habit as they made their way to the rotting flesh beneath."

Pip screamed in horror. "Never! I shall not wear such a piece of clothing."

"Waste not want not as the good monk said to me," declared Cynefrid.

"I do not blame her, apothecary, in the circumstances," said Berowen in Pip's defence. "Did the cloak belong to the deceased monk also?"

"No," said Cynefrid. "There are several to be had that have been left here by departing occupants of the monastery."

"Departing?" asked Berowen in search of an explanation of the word. "Departing as in leaving the abbey by way of their own two feet, or departing as in breathing their last and being buried beneath the ground?"

Cynefrid laughed. "Ah, yes... I see what you mean - the former my lady."

"Then I see no reason why Pip cannot wear the cloak. As for the habit, I think you should return it to where you acquired it and perhaps suggest that it is either washed and repaired, or burnt. If it were for me to give an opinion on the choice, then I would choose the destruction thereof considering its somewhat tainted background."

Cynefrid, somewhat begrudgingly, Berowen thought, picked up the discarded habit and left to find the monk who had kindly given him the articles of clothing. Pip picked up the cloak and after inspecting it for anything undesirable through it around her shoulders and fastened the clasp at the neck. She would not admit it there and then, but the warmth it offered was much appreciated.

Upon his return, Cynefrid, plus Wirt and the two young boys were taken away by the gate-keeper to their respective quarters, while Berowen was left outside in the company of Pip, Odi, and Felagin, who was standing silently beside Berowen. She found herself, once again that morning, in a quandary. Was she supposed to find her own way back to her room and if so, what was she supposed to do with Pip? Surely, they were not expecting her to share her cot with the girl? That would be intolerable, although she had to admit that it would quite likely be a lot warmer at night. But then she tutted when she remembered the unstable state of the cot which seemed to sway at every turn she made, so with the possibility of two sleeping upon it, she could assume that there would be no hope that it would not collapse altogether. However, when she realised that her thoughts had taken her to the point of actually accepting Pip as a possible bed-mate, she instantly reverted to a state of frustration and brewing distate that such a thing would be expected of her. Surely they were used to travellers of both sexes stopping off at the abbey and in that light they were bound to have more than one available room for such eventualities – although she had to admit that it was far more likely to be men who would use the place as a stop off point.

As she thought to herself she continued to smooth Odi's head as he sat patiently by her side. Felagin grunted and nodded his head occasionally as her thoughts ran through her mind, but when she realised that once again she was thinking too loudly as he so often told her, she ignored the fact and continued so doing. If he wished to listen in on her private conversations that occurred in her mind on a regular basis, then he may well learn something that he would rather not have, especially where his own character was concerned.

"Where did that dog come from?" asked Pip quite suddenly and completely out of the blue as if the fact that she had not seen it before had only just popped into her head. "And where did that 'orrid bird go?"

"The dog is my companion on the long roads," answered Berowen satisfied that what she spoke was basically the truth. "He possesses an excellent nose and I had let Cynefrid use him to track my whereabouts as we were to travel along different paths."

"But I thought we was followin' the bird. That's what Wirt told me," queried the puzzled girl.

"Did he now," interrupted Felagin gruffly. "What nonsense girl. Why would anyone in their right mind follow a bird of ill-omen?"

"Wirt don't lie, and why would Cynefrid need the dog anyhows?" persisted Pip.

"You ask too many questions, girl. Hush your mouth until you can utter words of sense," growled Felagin glaring at her. And to Berowen he said, "Methinks your thoughts of sharing may be transforming into a truth."

"As I had feared," responded Berowen. "Perchance you could have a word with someone to find out where this young girl is to be put whilst she stays here? That is, of course, if you do not mind carrying out such a favour on my behalf. In the meantime, I shall return with her to my quarters and await some satisfactory resolution of the matter."

Felagin pondered for a moment. Here was his chance to afford retribution for Berowen's challenge earlier. There was no way that she could find the answer to her problem by herself, and for a fleeting moment he was tempted to refuse her request, or simply to agree and then accidentally forget. But as bad-tempered and sour-faced as he may have become, Felagin could not fail to do as Berowen bid. He had grown fond of her over the days they had travelled together. She may question his every motive, and doubt his every decision as well as challenge him on his own misdemeanours, but he admired her honesty and refusal to be overshadowed by his omnipotence.

"I shall do my best to resolve the problem, my lady," he said.

"My thanks, Felagin," replied Berowen, somewhat suspicious of the softness in his voice. "And, please, give my best wishes to Thurstan."

"I shall do so of course," agreed Felagin. "In fact, I am somewhat surprised that you did not find some way of keeping the habit that was flung in Pip's direction earlier. I am sure it would have given you excellent cover for sneaking about the place and coming into Thurstan's company yourself quite easily. Methinks you slipped up there Berowen, or am I to assume that its previous owner's fate sat uneasy with you also?"

Berowen laughed. "It did flash briefly across my mind, Felagin, as I am sure you are only too well aware. As for any hesitancy on my part, you should know by now that such matters do not affect my disposition so easily. No, I did not take it, but only for the very reason that it was offered to Pip in the first place."

Felagin cocked his head to one side and frowned. "You are not making yourself plain, Berowen."

She laughed again. "Aha, I have confused the great Felagin. Come Odi, and come Pip, let us depart for what passes as comfort in this place. My room is not far and I am sure Felagin can give us the necessary escort to ensure that we do not make good our perceived mission of immorality and rampage through the abbey in our wantoness as is obviously expected of us."

Pip looked even more confused, but followed behind Berowen quietly. Felagin, however, growled under his breath at Berowen's refusal to complete the explanation of her decision not to take the clothing. With a glint in her eye, Berowen turned to Felagin and said defiantly; "I shall continue my explanation after you have explained to me how you gained entry to such a place as this without question. And how one such as you is in acquaintance with one such as Brother Fyn." And she smiled demurely at the old man, who instantly threw back his head and let forth the loudest belly laugh that she had ever come across.

"So be it," he laughed. "So be it, Berowen. It seems that we have an accord, and a strange one at that."

Once back in her cell with Pip and Odi, Berowen sat on the cot and examined her four-legged companion more closely. He was black as night, save for a white chest and four white paws and a white tip to his tail, which seemed to wag from side to side constantly. His lips were pink, dappled with blotches of black and his lip seemed to have healed awkwardly at some time, presumably from an injury sustained during some previous incarnation, giving him the impression of having a lopsided grin, through which the tips of his white teeth glinted. She played with his soft ears and leant forward to whisper to him, "So Odi, you have chosen to be a handsome hound indeed I see and not just any ordinary cur of the back alleys." She bent down further to wrap her arms around his neck and buried her face into his fur. "My dear friend, I have missed you these past days. I am glad to have you back."

Pip sat herself on the bed with a heavy sigh and let out a loud gasp as the construction wobbled and groaned beneath her. She threw out both hands to steady herself, and looked wide-eyed at Berowen, who had turned her head slightly to glare at her new companion for being so clumsy. "Be careful," she warned. "If you and I *are* to be bed-fellows tonight then I think we would be much better served if our bed were not the cold stone floor. This cot is passed its best and requires much gentle handling."

"Bleedin' 'ell!" exclaimed Pip. "They don't go much on 'ospitality round 'ere do 'em? Just because they like to keep 'emselves as frugal as they can, don't mean they should do same for them that are visitin'." She picked up a corner of the blanket, "This is deemed enough to keep a body warm at night is it?" she asked sarcastically. And then she rambled on and on about the state of the room, and the scarcity of any useful furniture. Berowen blocked out her voice as much as she could, but when Pip began to complain about the draught that pushed itself through the cracks between window and wall, she really could not keep quiet any longer.

"Pip," she began. "I would consider it a great relief and favour if you could give your opinions a rest for now. I am fully aware of the draught, as well as the meagre bedding supplied. You seem to forget that I did sleep here last night and found it extremely unsatisfactory, a matter I shall pass on to those concerned as soon as I have found who they are and how I can get a message to them, considering that – as a woman – I am not allowed to wander the cloisters unaccompanied. I do not, however, expect to have any situation remedied at any time soon and I suggest that you – like me – resist any further temptation to speak of your grievances."

Pip stared at Berowen and opened her mouth in reply, but before she could utter forth anything further on the matter, the latter continued, "Beside, Pip, you can have no real cause for complaint. After all, it was really quite by choice that you find yourself within the confines of the walls of this monastery. It was, was it not, your decision to follow Wirt under whatever premise you had when Grimfell was attacked? You and I came here under our own will and we should, in reality, give thanks to the brothers for their generosity in letting us stay." The awareness of the truth in her last sentence caused Berowen a feeling of mild guilt at having mildly reprimanded Pip on her complaints when she had spent some of the morning doing exactly the same thing to Felagin.

There seemed to be a long silence between the two women until, at last, there was a light tap on the door and Berowen opened it eagerly to reveal a figure completely shrouded in a habit. The head was bowed so as not to reveal even the smallest morsel of the monk's face that hid beneath the hood, and the flesh of both hands were hidden, safely tucked in the garment's

sleeves, the arms crossed across the front of the loose fabric. A voice softly spoke from the shadows of the cowl, "I have come to escort you to your room. Please follow me."
Pip jumped off the bed and walked swiftly towards the door, "'Bout time too," she said.

"I have been sent by the Abbot to escort the Mistress Berowen only," was the hurried response. Pip stopped in her tracks with a horrified look of disbelief upon her face.

"Me?" asked Berowen. "The Abbot?"

"The Abbot had wished to welcome you to the Abbey my lady, but has been called away on urgent business elsewhere. He hopes that you will still be here upon his return so that he can meet with you, although he suspects that you would have left before his homecoming. However, he was horrified to learn that someone as gracious as yourself had been given such a cell in which to rest last night, and has ordered your removal to somewhere far more suitable for a lady of your standing."

"And what about me?" enquired Pip, hands on hips and pouting unattractively.

"I have received no instruction regarding your removal from here," came the soft, yet, firm reply.

Berowen again found herself feeling sorry for the poor girl. There was at least one thing that she could do to try to make Pip's stay a little more comfortable perhaps. "Brother..... may I ask if it were to be possible that some more blankets could be supplied to this cell. I found it to be bitterly cold last night, and was barely able to sleep and if it is to be as cold this eve, then I am afraid that the poor girl may freeze in here."

The cowl moved slightly up and down followed by a quiet, "Yes, mistress Berowen, I shall see what can be arranged of course."

Berowen hastily picked up her belongings, and clicking her tongue for Odi to follow, she left the room after the monk, leaving Pip standing in the darkening gloom of the room, the fury caused by her needs being ignored plainly displayed upon her tight-lipped grimace, her narrowing eyes and the deep frown etched into her forehead. As the rays of the setting sun streamed through the small, draughty window beside her, the bloom of rage on her plump cheeks was just visible.

LXXV

The cell that Berowen had been transferred to was a lot less draughty and slightly more habitable than that which had suddenly become Pip's living space. They had all been at the monastery for nigh on two weeks and in that time Berowen had managed to speak to Felagin only a few times to enquire into the health of Thurstan. She could not help but feel that his sickness and the cure thereof had become shrouded in an ever-deepening mystery and that she was only privy to the certain parts of it that Felagin chose to impart.

Cynefrid had decided to stay at the monastery until spring. This would give him time to record the experiences at Grimfell on parchment and to ensure that when he and Wirt did leave the relative comfort and safety, that they would be able to travel without the torment of freezing cold weather. Whether or not Eni would be staying at the monastery or travelling on with them had not yet been decided. It was equally uncertain as to what would happen to Col, but Cynefrid presumed that Berowen would be looking after him as it was she who had specifically wished him to be rescued. Wirt, of course, would stay with his master and help him in his writings. One of his daily tasks was to be dispatched daily out of the gates and into the valley beyond to forage for whatever medicinal plants and berries he could find. To Cynefrid's pleasure – and even Wirt's to a lesser degree – the monks were a fount of knowledge of such things and over the weeks both the inhabitants and the visitors had already gained much out of their conversations and discussions of such things.

Wirt was also pleased that he was able to keep a respectable distance between himself and Pip. Once the monks had been satisfied that their presence was in no way detrimental to the monastery, the two women were, in reality, only prohibited from entering the strictly male areas of the monastery so were not prevented from taking the air in the main courtyard, or even entering some areas such as the kitchen. They were not prisoners and were not treated as such, and as long as they respected the ways of the monks, Berowen and Pip were, on the whole, ignored. The travellers' prolonged presence, for visitors only usually stayed for days rather than weeks, had caused some concerns with the older, more committed members of the abbey, however, and there were constant rumblings of dissent amongst the brothers when grouped together for meals.

Wirt and Pip would meet up occasionally, however, and Wirt was courteous enough not to ignore the girl completely, but was able to maintain a certain amount of detachment from her, especially whilst in the company of others. For the first time since knowing Wirt, it dawned on Pip, during these weeks of almost enforced solitude, that her so-called relationship with the young man was perhaps not as much in the forefront of his mind as it was in hers. After all those months of throwing herself at him as soon as he came into her sight it became apparent - only now - that his mind was not fixed on only her and what her body had to offer him in the way of comfort or satisfaction of his youthful, almost insatiable lust. It was clear that he had other things to occupy his mind and she abruptly became aware that theirs was only a dalliance based on physical contact and not on anything else lasting or meaningful. The realisation hurt deeply and she felt a fool. It was blatantly apparent now why those around always appeared to not have one good word to say about her, or – indeed - to her face. The comments that she had refused to admit as having contained hidden insults since her body had changed from child to young woman, or even veiled doubts upon her breeding all now seemed to reveal their true meaning.

Perhaps her sudden awareness had been borne out of being confined amongst those of such extreme, seemingly unbreakable vows. Or perhaps she had just experienced an intuitive insight at last into the reality of her life. She was not sure what had taken place, but she knew that she would have to change or she would risk descending deeper into the realms of drunken exploitation until she reached such low depths that she would find it impossible to claw her way out again.

She had not known her father and there had always seemed to be a steady stream of soldiers from the garrison in and out of the house coming to visit her mother. At a young age she had been sent to the inn to fetch mead or ale and had become well-known to those that frequented the place. She would chat and laugh with them in her innocence as she went back and forth. When her mother decided that more money was needed in the household and – more importantly - that her daughter was becoming ever more in the way, or rather, was attracting too much complimentary attention from those that visited her, Pip's mother sent her daughter to work at the inn. There was always the hope that any perks of leftover food or perhaps, instead of wages, even the odd jug of mead would make their way homeward here and there at the end of the girl's long days.

Feeling utterly wretched after recalling how the innocence and naivety of her childhood suddenly ended and introduced her to a life of shame, she lay down on her rickety cot and wrapped her blankets around herself. She wished to see no-one, nor speak to anyone for the rest of the day. Her usual happy, outgoing demeanour had been flattened in an instant and all she wished to do was remain in her solitude, in the darkening room. Such was her distress that even if Wirt came knocking upon her door she would shout for him to go away.

And thus it was that Berowen found her, and that is exactly how her taps on the door were received. Berowen had wanted to see Pip to say goodbye as she was leaving at first light with Felagin to make the journey to the place known as Bole. Pip had forgotten that her only female company was leaving the next day, and when Berowen softly reminded her through the closed door she wailed with desperation. Berowen was unsure as to what to do but Pip insisted that she would be better soon and that there was no need for anyone to be concerned. She would not, however, open her door until the next morning at the earliest and even then it would be well into the morning before she so did. Such was her disposition and such it was that Berowen left her to her solitude.

It had been a few days after their verbal battle that Berowen finally managed to catch Felagin and challenge him on his part of the accord that they had swiftly agreed upon previously. She had not been unduly surprised that he would not keep his part of the agreement until she had explained to him her reasons for not taking the habit that Pip had been offered. Berowen told Felagin that the cloak was too infamous within the monastery, after all it had a hole in the front which allowed any other garment that was being worn underneath to be plainly seen. Hence, it would not have been a very good disguise for her to adopt if she wished to go unseen anywhere within the monastery confines. It would also be recognised for its grisly infamy. It all seemed rather obvious to her, and she could not imagine that the great wizard had not thought of it himself so she just assumed that he was being gracious in not saying that he had guessed it was so. But then again that would be definitely unlike him.

She waited for Felagin to keep his side of the agreement, but there was a long pause and she began to worry that he was going to renege on his part. This would not have surprised her – *nothing* surprised her about Felagin's actions.   She cleared her throat in an attempt to give the impression that she was waiting for him to say something. She sensed that Brother Fyn was not all that perhaps he should be, considering his standing in the monastery. He was supposedly a great healer, but she had the idea that his skills had not necessarily been learned by brains or experience, nor were they just attributed to a simple gift of nurturing fingers. How he came to know Felagin was an intriguing point in itself, let alone how her companion had managed to gain entry to the abbey so easily considering his 'occupation'. She waited for a response.

Suddenly, he pulled Berowen to one side and they both stood in a corner of the courtyard, well out the range of any passing ear. It would not do for anyone to overhear anything of Brother Fyn's past, for it undoubtedly would be the end of his life at the monastery. He had given up all and had intended to spend the end of his days within the walls of this place of quiet reflection, and it would be more than a personal catastrophe if he had to leave. However, Felagin had no intention, of course, in divulging all to Berowen, and merely spoke but a few words, but those that he did offer forth explained everything immediately: "As Thurstan is one now, I was also once an apprentice."

Berowen's eyes widened at the clear implication of Felagin's words. "So you introduced yourself to the gatekeeper as the one-time apprentice of Brother Fyn? But in what capacity? I am sure it could not have been as a wiz....."

"As a healer," Felagin interrupted quickly. Berowen wished to know more, particularly how Brother Fyn had managed to gain occupancy himself at the abbey – surely he had not lied to the Abbot of his background? This was intriguing and she could not let the matter end there. She grabbed Felagin's arm and they walked slowly out of the corner as if they were two friends on an afternoon stroll rather than two people with a secret to share. To her disappointment and frustration though, he could not be coerced into divulging any more information on the matter so she eventually decided to leave her questions for now, and changed the subject to that of her friend's progress.

It appeared that Brother Fyn's talents – and here Berowen was not sure what those talents were exactly - were slowly having a positive effect upon the injured Thurstan, but Felagin told Berowen that it would be many weeks before he would be back on his feet, and even then there would be much more recuperation required. Berowen had the feeling that there was something crucial that the venerable old wizard was not telling her but she decided that it would not be prudent to quiz him over it at that time. He had, she felt, probably said much more than he was comfortable in so doing already.

Felagin informed her that he thought it would be best for them both to leave Thurstan in Fyn's capable hands, and that they should make their way to Bole before the snows set in. Yule was only three weeks away, and the winds and rain that rolled in from the north were getting colder and more vicious by the day. If they were to go, then they would have to go before another week was out or they may find themselves caught out by weather that would have them frozen to their saddles.

And so it was arranged that they would leave for Bole in five days time. Berowen insisted that they took Col with them for she would not leave her 'Mouse' behind under the care of the monks, and Cynefrid already had Eni to look after. Felagin had grunted and grumbled under his beard when she had told him this, but try as he could to find some good reason for not taking him, he could find none. The boy was a rider of fair capability, she argued, although – as the wizard pointed out in response to Berowen's insistence - he ought to be considering he was once a stable lad. Berowen guaranteed that there was not much that Col did not know about horses, which was something that may even prove useful on the journey to come.

Berowen was quite happy to leave the monastery, although she was loathe to leave Thurstan behind. She did not like the uncertainty of not knowing the full extent of his recovery and could not even be sure that they would cross paths again. She had to presume that he would join Felagin and her in Bole when he was able to, but as to when, or indeed if, that would be, she could but wonder.

HOW TO START A PUBLISHING EMPIRE

Unlike most mainstream publishers, we have a non-commercial remit, and our mission statement claims that "we publish books because they deserve to be published, not because we think that we can make money out of them". Our motto is the Latin Tag *Pro bona causa facimus* (we do it for good reason), a slogan taken from a children's book *The Case of the Silver Egg* by the late Desmond Skirrow.

WIKIPEDIA: "The first book published was in 1988. *Take this Brother may it Serve you Well* was a guide to Beatles bootlegs by Jonathan Downes. It sold quite well, but was hampered by very poor production values, being photocopied, and held together by a plastic clip binder. In 1988 A5 clip binders were hard to get hold of, so the publishers took A4 binders and cut them in half with a hacksaw. It now reaches surprisingly high prices second hand.

The production quality improved slightly over the years, and after 1999 all the books produced were ringbound with laminated colour covers. In 2004, however, they signed an agreement with Lightning Source, and all books are now produced perfect bound, with full colour covers."

Until 2010 all our books, the majority of which are/were on the subject of mystery animals and allied disciplines, were published by `CFZ Press`, the publishing arm of the Centre for Fortean Zoology (CFZ), and we urged our readers and followers to draw a discreet veil over the books that we published that were completely off topic to the CFZ.

However, in 2010 we decided that enough was enough and launched a second imprint, `Fortean Words` which aims to cover a wide range of non animal-related esoteric subjects. Other imprints will be launched as and when we feel like it, however the basic ethos of the company remains the same: Our job is to publish books and magazines that we feel are worth publishing, whether or not they are going to sell. Money is, after all - as my dear old Mama once told me - a rather vulgar subject, and she would be rolling in her grave if she thought that her eldest son was somehow in `trade`.

Luckily, so far our tastes have turned out not to be that rarified after all, and we have sold far more books than anyone ever thought that we would, so there is a moral in there somewhere…

Jon Downes,
Woolsery, North Devon
July 2010

CFZ PRESS

Other Books in Print

Weird Waters – The Mystery Animals of Scandinavia: Lake and Sea Monsters by Lars Thomas
The Inhumanoids by Barton Nunnelly
Monstrum! A Wizard's Tale by Tony "Doc" Shiels
CFZ Yearbook 2011 edited by Jonathan Downes
Karl Shuker's Alien Zoo by Shuker, Dr Karl P.N
Tetrapod Zoology Book One by Naish, Dr Darren
The Mystery Animals of Ireland by Gary Cunningham and Ronan Coghlan
Monsters of Texas by Gerhard, Ken
The Great Yokai Encyclopaedia by Freeman, Richard
NEW HORIZONS: Animals & Men issues 16-20 Collected Editions Vol. 4
by Downes, Jonathan
A Daintree Diary -
Tales from Travels to the Daintree Rainforest in tropical north Queensland, Australia
by Portman, Carl
Strangely Strange but Oddly Normal by Roberts, Andy
Centre for Fortean Zoology Yearbook 2010 by Downes, Jonathan
Predator Deathmatch by Molloy, Nick
Star Steeds and other Dreams by Shuker, Karl
CHINA: A Yellow Peril? by Muirhead, Richard
Mystery Animals of the British Isles: The Western Isles by Vaudrey, Glen
Giant Snakes - Unravelling the coils of mystery by Newton, Michael
Mystery Animals of the British Isles: Kent by Arnold, Neil
Centre for Fortean Zoology Yearbook 2009 by Downes, Jonathan
CFZ EXPEDITION REPORT: Russia 2008 by Richard Freeman *et al*, Shuker, Karl (fwd)
Dinosaurs and other Prehistoric Animals on Stamps - A Worldwide catalogue
by Shuker, Karl P. N
Dr Shuker's Casebook by Shuker, Karl P.N
The Island of Paradise - chupacabra UFO crash retrievals,
and accelerated evolution on the island of Puerto Rico by Downes, Jonathan
The Mystery Animals of the British Isles: Northumberland and Tyneside by Hallowell, Michael J
Centre for Fortean Zoology Yearbook 1997 by Downes, Jonathan (Ed)
Centre for Fortean Zoology Yearbook 2002 by Downes, Jonathan (Ed)
Centre for Fortean Zoology Yearbook 2000/1 by Downes, Jonathan (Ed)

Centre for Fortean Zoology Yearbook 1998 by Downes, Jonathan (Ed)
Centre for Fortean Zoology Yearbook 2003 by Downes, Jonathan (Ed)
In the wake of Bernard Heuvelmans by Woodley, Michael A
CFZ EXPEDITION REPORT: Guyana 2007 by Richard Freeman *et al*, Shuker, Karl (fwd)
Centre for Fortean Zoology Yearbook 1999 by Downes, Jonathan (Ed)
Big Cats in Britain Yearbook 2008 by Fraser, Mark (Ed)
Centre for Fortean Zoology Yearbook 1996 by Downes, Jonathan (Ed)
THE CALL OF THE WILD - Animals & Men issues 11-15
Collected Editions Vol. 3 by Downes, Jonathan (ed)
Ethna's Journal by Downes, C N
Centre for Fortean Zoology Yearbook 2008 by Downes, J   (Ed)
DARK DORSET -Calendar Custome by Newland, Robert J
Extraordinary Animals Revisited by Shuker, Karl
MAN-MONKEY - In Search of the British Bigfoot by Redfern, Nick
Dark Dorset Tales of Mystery, Wonder and Terror by Newland, Robert J and Mark North
Big Cats Loose in Britain by Matthews, Marcus
MONSTER! - The A-Z of Zooform Phenomena by Arnold, Neil
The Centre for Fortean Zoology 2004 Yearbook by Downes, Jonathan (Ed)
The Centre for Fortean Zoology 2007 Yearbook by Downes, Jonathan (Ed)
CAT FLAPS! Northern Mystery Cats by Roberts, Andy
Big Cats in Britain Yearbook 2007 by Fraser, Mark (Ed)
BIG BIRD! - Modern sightings of Flying Monsters by Gerhard, Ken
THE NUMBER OF THE BEAST - Animals & Men issues 6-10
Collected Editions Vol. 1 by Downes, Jonathan (Ed)
IN THE BEGINNING - Animals & Men issues 1-5 Collected Editions Vol. 1 by Downes, Jonathan
STRENGTH THROUGH KOI - They saved Hitler's Koi and other stories by Downes, Jonathan
The Smaller Mystery Carnivores of the Westcountry by Downes, Jonathan
CFZ EXPEDITION REPORT: Gambia 2006 by Richard Freeman *et al*, Shuker, Karl (fwd)
The Owlman and Others by Jonathan Downes
The Blackdown Mystery by Downes, Jonathan
Big Cats in Britain Yearbook 2006 by Fraser, Mark (Ed)
Fragrant Harbours - Distant Rivers by Downes, John T
Only Fools and Goatsuckers by Downes, Jonathan
Monster of the Mere by Jonathan Downes
Dragons:More than a Myth by Freeman, Richard Alan
Granfer's Bible Stories by Downes, John Tweddell
Monster Hunter by Downes, Jonathan

Fortean Words

The Centre for Fortean Zoology has for several years led the field in Fortean publishing. CFZ Press is the only publishing company specialising in books on monsters and mystery animals. CFZ Press has published more books on this subject than any other company in history and has attracted such well known authors as Andy Roberts, Nick Redfern, Michael Newton, Dr Karl Shuker, Neil Arnold, Dr Darren Naish, Jon Downes, Ken Gerhard and Richard Freeman.

Now CFZ Press are launching a new imprint. Fortean Words is a new line of books dealing with Fortean subjects other than cryptozoology, which is - after all - the subject the CFZ are best known for. Fortean Words is being launched with a spectacular multi-volume series called *Haunted Skies* which covers British UFO sightings between 1940 and 2010. Former policeman John Hanson and his long-suffering partner Dawn Holloway have compiled a peerless library of sighting reports, many that have not been made public before.

Other books include a look at the Berwyn Mountains UFO case by renowned Fortean Andy Roberts and a series of forthcoming books by transatlantic researcher Nick Redfern. CFZ Press are dedicated to maintaining the fine quality of their works with Fortean Words. New authors tackling new subjects will always be encouraged, and we hope that our books will continue to be as ground-breaking and popular as ever.

Haunted Skies Volume One 1940-1959 by John Hanson and Dawn Holloway
Haunted Skies Volume Two 1960-1965 by John Hanson and Dawn Holloway
Space Girl Dead on Spaghetti Junction - an anthology by Nick Redfern
I Fort the Lore - an anthology by Paul Screeton
UFO Down - the Berwyn Mountains UFO Crash by Andy Roberts

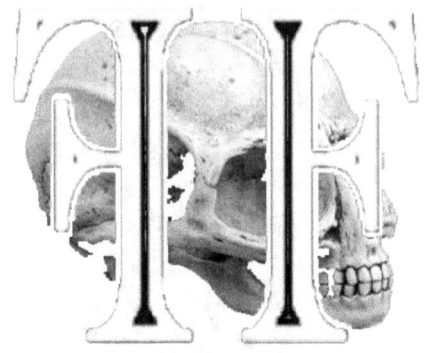

Fortean Fiction

J ust before Christmas 2011, we launched our third imprint, this time dedicated to - let's see if you guessed it from the title - fictional books with a Fortean or cryptozoological theme. We have published a few fictional books in the past, but now think that because of our rising reputation as publishers of quality Forteana, that a dedicated fiction imprint was the order of the day.

We launched with four titles:

Green Unpleasant Land by Richard Freeman
Left Behind by Harriet Wadham
Dark Ness by Tabitca Cope
Snap! By Steven Bredice
Death on Dartmoor by Di Francis
Dark Wear by Tabitca Cope
Hyakymonogatari Book 1 by Richard Freeman

CFZ Classics is a new venture for us. There are many seminal works that are either unavailable today, or not available with the production values which we would like to see. So, following the old adage that if you want to get something done do it yourself, this is exactly what we have done.

Desiderius Erasmus Roterodamus (b. October 18th 1466, d. July 2nd 1536) said: "When I have a little money, I buy books; and if I have any left, I buy food and clothes," and we are much the same. Only, we are in the lucky position of being able to share our books with the wider world. CFZ Classics is a conduit through which we cannot just re-issue titles which we feel still have much to offer the cryptozoological and Fortean research communities of the 21st Century, but we are adding footnotes, supplementary essays, and other material where we deem it appropriate.

Headhunters of The Amazon by Fritz W Up de Graff (1902)